The
NIGHT
AWAY

BOOKS BY JESS RYDER

Lie to Me
The Good Sister
The Ex-Wife
The Dream House
The Girl You Gave Away

The
NIGHT
AWAY

JESS RYDER

bookouture

Published by Bookouture in 2020

An imprint of Storyfire Ltd.
Carmelite House
50 Victoria Embankment
London EC4Y 0DZ

www.bookouture.com

ISBN: 978-1-83888-936-4
eBook ISBN: 978-1-83888-935-7

For my father

CHAPTER ONE

A few weeks before

I come to Lilac Park every day to look at babies. They are every-where, as numerous as the squirrels. Two women are standing by the entrance gate, idly pushing their prams back and forth as they chat. A few metres away, a toddler is running circles around a tree. A young mother is walking towards me, pushing a bright red buggy and smiling into the late-afternoon sunshine. My stomach flutters in anticipation. I feel dizzy, as if somebody is spinning me around. Turning away, I pretend to watch the ducks in the pond, but my heart races as she trundles past, the buggy wheels squeaking cheerfully.

There's plenty to see and do here: tennis courts; a children's play area; a rose garden and ornamental pond; a bowling green; two football pitches where matches are played on Sunday mornings. And there's the park café, of course. On weekdays mums flock there like pigeons, clogging up the space with their expensive buggies, fighting over the few available high chairs. They cluster around the tables in large groups, breastfeeding and chatting and sipping their organic chai lattes. Sometimes I sit at the counter and listen to them discussing sleeping problems and sore nipples, debating the convenience of disposable nappies against the need to save the planet. I hear their little ones crying for attention. I want to pick them up and give them a cuddle, but of course I don't. Daren't.

Nobody ever notices me. Why would they? I am a single person. Unattached, unburdened by baby equipment. They might have acknowledged me in the past, but now I'm of no interest. How could I possibly understand what it's like to be a parent? How could I have any idea of what they've been through or what their life is like now? They assume I have no horrific birth stories or funny anecdotes to share, no tiny prodigy to boast about. I've been to the café countless times, but they never see me. I am invisible.

It's not just the mums who ignore me, it's the dads too, although not many use the park during the week. Dads tend to prefer papooses to pushchairs. I suppose they think it looks more manly and also more caring to carry their babies rather than push them about. They like to have them pressed close, sniffling and dribbling onto their jackets. They wear the stains of fatherhood with pride.

At the weekend the park is heaving with young families – mums, dads, babies, toddlers, school-age children – often with grandparents in tow. They gather around the edge of the play area, talking in gender-segregated groups, with one eye vaguely on their charges. Sometimes I sit on the wall by the sandpit and watch the children digging holes or making castles. There are arguments over plastic spades and attempted thefts of unattended scooters. I want to mediate, to explain about sharing. I want to help the toddlers climb the slide and catch them at the bottom, or lift them onto the see-saw and sit on the other end, but interacting with other people's children is only allowed if you have one of your own.

Hanging around the park is torture, but I have to come here to check on Mabel. She lives with her mummy and daddy in the house opposite the main gates. Number 74. It's a purpose-built Edwardian maisonette with its own front door and lots of original features – the sort of place that's very popular with hipster types retreating from Hackney. The primary schools have better ratings here and there's less pollution. Being further from the city centre, house prices are lower.

Amber and George's flat is on the first and second floors. They have a loft conversion. I only know this because there are windows in the roof. On the ground floor, there's a narrow entrance hall where there's just enough room to keep the buggy. I've seen Amber struggling to get past with her shopping, running up and down the stairs with the bags, trying to get it all into the kitchen before Mabel wakes up. She has no idea that I'm in the park opposite, hiding in plain sight amongst the joggers and dog-walkers, the pram-pushers and duck-feeders. Watching.

Amber is clearly not enjoying motherhood. There's no smug glow about her like the mums in the park café. Her expression is vacant but tinged with sadness, as if she's grieving for someone, or something. A previous lifestyle, I'm guessing, although she must have known what she was letting herself in for. It's obvious to anyone that she's not coping. She can't be bothered to brush her hair or put on make-up, and she wears the same grey joggers and purple fleece every single day. As my grandmother would have put it, she's letting herself go. I wonder what George makes of that …

Her orbit is small, consisting of trips to the tiny supermarket at the end of the road, the pharmacy and the health centre. She always takes the same route, cutting across the park. Off she sets with the buggy, head down, eyes fixed on the path. Other mothers talk on their phones while they're walking, or bump into other parents they know, or sit on a bench and take their babies out to play, but not Amber. She avoids making human contact with anyone. For her, leaving the house is a necessity not a pleasure. It's as if she's been ordered to have fresh air, but doesn't want to breathe it in.

I've never seen her at weekends, not once. I think she must spend them in bed. She and George don't go out together; you'd never know they were a couple. They share the childcare and there are no overlaps, no doubling up. George seems to like being a dad a lot more than Amber likes being a mum. He loves the park; he can't get enough of it. He puts Mabel in a baby carrier, which he wears on his back, reminding him of his trekking days, perhaps, when he used to go travelling to far-flung places. Occasionally he takes her to the family-friendly pub on the high street, presumably to meet his mates and watch football. I don't follow him inside, because that would be too risky. Too obvious.

I stare at number 74, willing the front door to open and Amber to emerge. I haven't seen her for a few days. It's worrying, not to say annoying. Soon the park gates will be shut. Time to make my way home, I decide.

It's a short bus ride to my flat, which is in a less fashionable and therefore cheaper area than Lilac Park. I hate the place, but I needed somewhere to live at short notice and it was all I could afford by myself. The living space looks onto a brick wall and there's black mould in the bathroom that I can't get rid of, no matter how hard I try. The staircase is shared with other tenants, most of whom I've never seen, and nobody bothers to clean the common parts – least of all me.

I let myself in and climb the filthy stairs to the top floor. The door to my flat has a dent at the bottom where somebody has tried to kick it in. There's one bedroom and an open-plan kitchen/diner/living room. The furniture is all cheap beech laminate, badly assembled, and the sofa is hard and uncomfortable.

I haven't had the motivation to make the place more homely. There have been no jolly dinner parties, no weekend guests – no visitors at all, in fact. It has been my secret hideaway, my self-imposed prison. I don't see old friends any more and have little desire to make new ones. I came off social media and got rid of my smartphone. I'm virtually off the grid; it's easier that way.

Nobody can ask how I'm feeling or what my plans for the future are. Nobody can track me down.

Hanging my coat on the peg, I walk into the living area and stare at my dismal surroundings. The coffee table is stained with mug rings. Boxes of books and ornaments are still stacked against the wall and my pictures remain in bubble wrap. When I moved in, I couldn't be bothered to unpack, and now the boxes have become makeshift furniture, surfaces for dirty plates and junk mail or to rest my feet on.

Taking a bottle of wine from the fridge, I pour myself a large glass. I can't go on like this; the situation is killing me. I've become a ghost of myself, haunting a life that never was and can never be. If I had any sense, I'd leave London altogether and start afresh. I even have somewhere to go to.

I should leave Mabel behind too. The trouble is, I'm not sure I can.

CHAPTER TWO

The weekend before

Amber has never been a morning person. Seven months ago, she'd have only countenanced waking at 5 a.m. for a holiday – and even then, she would've slept on the way to the airport. But these days it feels horribly normal to be up and about two hours before the sun comes up, doing the all-too-familiar daily chores: sterilising bottles, wiping down the changing unit, hanging countless little sleepsuits over the radiators. She's already had breakfast; by ten o'clock she'll be ready for lunch. No wonder she can't shift the baby fat, she thinks as she takes off her dressing gown and briefly catches sight of her body in the mirror.

On the subject of which, what on earth is she going to wear this evening? She can hardly turn up in her usual sloppy jogging bottoms and baggy T-shirt stained with baby vomit. None of her old dresses fit, and she's refused to buy a bigger wardrobe on the grounds that it would be accepting defeat. But she feels defeated anyway, so what difference does it make?

She sighs as she gets dressed. It's all right for George, who's already got out his best suit and a cool designer shirt and laid them on the bed. He'll look as gorgeous as ever. Fatherhood has taken no visible toll on him – he doesn't even have bags under his eyes.

Weirdly, he seems to like getting up before dawn. She can hear him now, singing to Mabel as he baths her. The walls in these maisonettes are paper-thin; he really should keep his voice down so early in the morning. It's not Mabel's usual bath time, but she woke up with a full nappy, the contents of which had mysteriously spread up her back, and it was the easiest way to clean her up. Judging by the protests coming from the bathroom, her daughter isn't a morning person either.

She puts her fingers in her ears as she walks into the kitchen. *Please, George, make her stop!* Mabel's cries cut right through her; sometimes they're so piercing they make her want to jump out of the window.

'We've got to do something,' her sister Ruby announced a few weeks ago, when she turned up to find Amber sobbing her eyes out while Mabel screamed blue murder in her cot. 'You need a holiday, just the two of you. A week somewhere exotic. I'll babysit.'

'I can't leave Mabel for that long,' Amber replied instantly, despite her heart leaping at the idea.

'Five days, then.'

'No. She'd miss me too much … And I'd miss her,' she added, although she wasn't entirely sure she meant it.

Ruby wasn't giving up. 'Okay. How about a long weekend?'

In the end, they settled on just one night away.

One night. It feels simultaneously too long and too short a time. Amber knows that one night without Mabel will not be enough to fix things between her and George, but she's grateful to her sister all the same. She badly needs a break. But with only a few hours to go before they're due to leave, she feels nervous and wretched with guilt.

She surveys the table littered with dirty plates and foil trays from last night's takeaway. There's so much to do and she doesn't have the energy even to start.

Mum doesn't approve of their going away. 'She's too young to be without her mummy for so long,' she declared. Or her daddy, Amber thought, but she didn't challenge it.

'The royal family leave their babies behind all the time,' she argued instead. 'Nobody accuses *them* of child neglect.'

Her mother rolled her eyes. 'That's because they have full-time nannies who look after them from birth, so they already know them well.'

'Mabel knows Ruby well – she always smiles when she sees her. They get on brilliantly.'

'With all due respect,' her mother replied, showing no respect at all, 'Ruby knows nothing about babies. And you know what a scatterbrain she is, always with her head in the clouds. She'll forget to feed her or change her nappy.'

'Mabel will make sure she doesn't,' Amber retorted, irritated by her mother's lack of faith in Ruby. Why hadn't *she* offered to babysit, if she was so concerned for her granddaughter's well-being?

'Well it's not how it was done in my day,' Mum continued, seemingly oblivious that she was massively guilt-tripping Amber. 'I never left you to go on romantic weekends. When you and Ruby were tiny, I had no life outside the home, but it didn't bother me. You were my world. I was so happy to have you.'

Yes, that's the elephant in the room, reflects Amber as she gathers up the plates and loads the dishwasher. She's not happy. It makes no sense to her mother, who sees everything only from her own perspective and is consequently not a very sympathetic woman. In her view, there's nothing wrong with her daughter's life – quite the contrary. Amber is extremely lucky. She has a decent husband who earns enough for her not to have to hurry back to work, she lives in a nice flat in a just about acceptable part of London, and she's been blessed with an 'easy' baby. It's annoying how Mabel always behaves so beautifully in front of her grandma.

Although to be fair, she *is* easy, some of the time. She only cries when she's uncomfortable or hungry or over-tired or being bathed. It's *me* that's difficult, Amber concludes as she fills the dishwasher with salt. She so longed to have a baby – in fact, she was completely desperate, more than either her mother, sister or even her husband know. She sailed joyfully through her pregnancy, loving every second of it, even her labour, which was an awe-inspiring experience. Then Miracle Mabel, as she secretly called her, popped out, and within days, Amber had never felt more miserable or hopeless in her entire life.

Only Ruby, six years younger and with no experience of motherhood, seems to understand. If she knew the full story, though, she might think differently. Sometimes Ruby's support makes Amber feel worse, because she's never kept secrets from her sister in the past, and now there's this invisible barrier between them that only she knows is there.

Ruby keeps urging her to go to the doctor, or to confide in her health visitor, and Amber has promised to seek help but has done nothing about it. The truth is, she doesn't feel she deserves to get better. She views her depression as punishment for wanting Mabel too much.

Nevertheless, she knows she has to do *something*. This night away her mother so disapproves of isn't a selfish, frivolous act. It is, as Ruby puts it, a lifesaver. Amber and George, who've been together since they were teenagers, are in danger. Their relationship has been lost under a pile of dirty nappies. They haven't been out together as a couple once since Mabel was born, and they never do anything together as a family. The moment George comes home from work, Amber plonks the baby in his arms and goes to lie down, complaining that she's shattered. They never see their friends. They hardly even kiss any more, let alone have sex. Most concerning of all, in a way, is that they're both behaving as if this is the new normal. They never talk about it. Not properly.

Amber tucks a strand of hair behind her ear. It feels thin and greasy, reminding her that she hasn't washed it for several days and probably won't have time this morning. Sadly, her old beauty routine for nails, skin and hair – both the wanted and unwanted variety – is a thing of the past.

She hopes George isn't expecting them to make love tonight. The signs are worrying. He's booked a luxury suite at a boutique hotel in the middle of nowhere with its own Michelin-starred restaurant. If the website photos are to be believed, their room has an enormous four-poster bed and a deep free-standing bath surrounded by furry white rugs. It's too flashy for her taste and the bath looks especially provocative, daring guests to splash about together having wild, passionate sex.

Their last attempt at lovemaking was months ago and ended in failure. Amber insisted on turning the lights off and burrowed under the duvet like a shy animal, her confidence completely deserting her. She still can't bear to look at herself naked, let alone parade in front of George – not with those silvery-white stretch marks on her thighs and the folds of papery flesh around her stomach. She felt so beautiful when she was pregnant, her bump as firm and shiny as a conker, but since giving birth, everything has collapsed. George is being very patient, but as her mother says, men have needs. If she isn't careful, he'll leave her for somebody else. There are plenty of attractive girls at the gym where he works who'd be delighted to take him off her hands – staff *and* clients. Amber loves George and doesn't want to lose him, but right now it's the thought of being a single parent that frightens her most. She saw her mother struggle after Dad died when Ruby was a baby. She knows she won't be able to cope with Mabel on her own.

Yes, she thinks as she wipes down the kitchen surfaces, George will be hopeful of some sex tonight, and in theory, she wants to please him. It's important at least to try. If she gets drunk, perhaps she'll feel less inhibited and might even enjoy it. She can drink alcohol now that she's given up breastfeeding – another failure to add to the list.

'That bath wore her out,' says George, entering the kitchen and interrupting the latest round of self-deprecating thoughts. 'She fell asleep before she was even dry. Made it a lot easier to get her dressed, though.'

Amber grimaces. 'You shouldn't have let her sleep; she hasn't had her morning feed yet. Now she'll be all out of sync for Ruby.'

'She'll catch up.' He goes over to the window and winds up the blind.

'Don't do that, it's still dark outside.'

'We can watch the sunrise together,' he says. 'It's coming up over the rooftops.' She looks at him blankly. 'Or do you want to go back to bed?'

'Can't, can I? Got to get ready for this stupid trip.' Amber can feel the panic rising. 'The place is a tip. I need to hoover the stairs, make up the bottles, change the sheets so that Ruby can have our bed, put some more washing on and write out some instructions or she won't have a clue.'

'It's okay, babe, we'll sort it,' he soothes. 'Rubes won't care if it's a mess. It's not like it's your mum babysitting …'

'Why did you have to choose such a posh hotel?' she continues, her voice laced with anxiety. 'I've nothing suitable to wear, nothing that fits anyway. I'm so fat. And don't say go out and buy something, because there isn't TIME!' The last sentence explodes in tears, and she covers her face with her hands.

George sighs heavily. 'What are you saying? That you don't want to go?'

'Of course I want to go,' she replies from behind her fingers. 'But I haven't had a chance to prepare – I'm not ready, not in a fit state …'

'I don't care how you look or what you wear.' He tries to put his arms around her, but she backs off, unable to bear his touch. 'You can have dinner in your pyjamas for all I care. We'll order room service.'

'No, I *want* to go to the restaurant. We haven't eaten out in ages.'

'Great, we'll do that then.'

'But I don't want to let you down. I look so hideous.'

'You never look hideous. You're beautiful.'

'No I'm not. My hair needs cutting and I'm fat!'

'You're not fat, and even if you were, it wouldn't stop me loving you.' He moves forward again and this time she allows him to hold her lightly. 'I'll tidy up and make some notes for Ruby. You concentrate on getting yourself ready.'

'Okay … thanks. I'm sorry.'

'You need this weekend. We both do. We're going to have a wonderful time, I promise.'

'Yes, yes,' she murmurs. 'I do want to go – I've been looking forward to it. And Mabel will be all right without us, won't she? She loves her Auntie Ruby.'

'Mabel will be absolutely fine,' he assures her. 'In any case, it's only one night away.'

CHAPTER THREE

The weekend before

Ruby wheels her bike off the train and onto the platform. She intended to cycle the whole way but overslept and ran out of time. Lifting it onto her shoulder, she walks slowly down the steps, then swipes through the ticket barrier. It's downhill all the way to Amber's house – the ride won't take more than five minutes.

Fastening the strap of her helmet, she pushes off down the high street, making sure to keep to the cycle lane wherever possible. There's a lot of traffic about, as always, and she needs to stay alert for jaywalkers. She relaxes her leg muscles as the bike gathers pace. The weather's cold but the sun is starting to break through the clouds. Luckily, it's not raining. She'll take Mabel to the park this afternoon to feed the ducks.

She feels both excited and nervous about looking after Mabel on her own overnight. At least it isn't for a whole week, as she originally offered, rather rashly. She's surprised that Amber and George have agreed to go away at all. Until now, she hasn't been trusted to babysit for more than about half an hour while Amber pops to the shops or has a bath. She tried several times to persuade her to leave Mabel for longer, to meet up with the girls from the antenatal class or have a drink with friends from work, go for a swim or watch a film – *anything* – but until now she always refused. It's as if taking a break is a mark of failure, and Amber doesn't do failure.

Her sister is a high achiever, always has been, ever since she was a little girl – probably since the day she was born. Naturally, Amber assumed she would be as brilliant at motherhood as she was at everything else. All it required was research and preparation. As soon as she became pregnant, she embarked on a programme of self-directed study, reading numerous books and online articles until she was an expert in current parenting theories. But none of them can account for the mighty force of nature that is Mabel Rosebud Walker.

Ruby loves her only niece, admiring her feisty spirit and determination to get her own way. If Mabel isn't happy, she'll sure as hell let you know about it. Perhaps she'll be more contented now she's being bottle-fed, thinks Ruby as she waits to cross the main road. Poor Amber, she tried so hard, but Mabel was a hungry bunny and Amber couldn't seem to produce enough milk. Ruby suspects the problem was stress-related. She's no expert, but it's clear that her sister is suffering from postnatal depression. Amber, usually the first to google symptoms and pronounce a diagnosis, is in denial. Or rather, she knows full well what the matter is but doesn't want to do anything about it.

Mum doesn't help. She can't believe that her top-of-the-class daughter could possibly be failing, whereas if it was Ruby who'd gone to pieces, she wouldn't bat an eyelid, because it's Ruby's role in the family to mess up.

After years of resentment, she's come to accept this label and even turn it to her advantage. Her mother's expectations of her are so low it gives her full rein to explore and experiment. Since leaving university, she's tried her hand at documentary film-making, selling jewellery made from recycled drinks cans and starting a vegan ice-cream business. When her brave plans fail – as they usually do – her mother just rolls her eyes in that told-you-so way.

Now Ruby is working odd shifts at an escape room in Shoreditch, a job she would like to escape from herself.

She chains her bike and helmet against the park railings opposite and, after ringing the bell twice to no effect, knocks loudly with her fist. Eventually she hears the sound of footsteps coming down the stairs, and George opens the door. A gust of wind instantly blows dry leaves into the hallway.

'Sorry,' he says. 'I was making up feeds; I thought Amber was getting it.'

'No worries.' She follows him back up the stairs and shrugs off her coat, hanging it over the top banister. Mabel is in the kitchen, strapped into her high chair. She looks up as Ruby enters and gives her a big smile.

'Hello, gorgeous!' Ruby bends down. 'Is that another tooth I can see?'

'Yes,' answers George on Mabel's behalf. 'She was very grumpy while it was coming through, but the last couple of nights she's slept for five hours straight.'

'Clever girl! Please do the same tonight for Auntie Ruby.' She plants a kiss on the top of Mabel's head. Her wispy hair – as red as her mother's – smells of mashed banana.

'I've written it all down,' George says, nodding towards a piece of paper on the table. 'Don't feel you have to stick to the times; it's just a guide. She hasn't had any fresh air yet today, so if you want to take her for a spin around the park …'

'I'd already thought of that.' Ruby goes to the window and looks out. 'It's a beautiful day.'

'But only seven degrees,' Amber points out, entering the room. 'Wrap her up properly. Hat and mittens, no arguments.'

'Lovely to see you too,' says Ruby, unable to resist the dig.

'You know what you're like. You'll forget.'

'I won't.'

Amber shrugs, picking up the list of instructions and scrutinising it for omissions and mistakes. Unable to find any, she puts it back on the table.

'I'll follow it faithfully. Promise.' Ruby offers a pacifying smile. 'Please don't worry. Just forget about us and have fun.'

'Thanks, we really appreciate this, don't we?' George looks at Amber. She nods, but Ruby can tell that her sister is putting on an act. At least she's made a bit of an effort to spruce herself up. Her shoulder-length hair looks as if it's been attacked by a hairdryer, and she's wearing make-up for the first time in months. Amber has classic Celtic looks – bright auburn hair, pale skin that turns pink at the merest exposure to sun, freckles sprinkled across her face like a dusting of demerara sugar. Ruby has the same pale skin, but she's dark-haired, with not a freckle in sight. Amber has their father's height, while Ruby is short like their mother. They couldn't look more unlike each other and are consequently never taken for sisters.

'You look great,' says Ruby.

'Do I? Really? You're not just saying that?'

'No! I like that eyeshadow. Suits you.'

'I'd almost forgotten how to put it on.' Amber looks down at herself critically. 'Does this skirt look okay with these boots?'

'Perfect.'

'It needs an iron.'

'Nah, it's fine. You'll be sitting in the car for ages, so there's no point.'

Amber bends down to Mabel. She puts the back of her hand against her forehead and frowns. 'George … she feels a bit hot.'

'She's fine, just excited because Auntie Ruby has come to play.'

'Did you leave the thermometer out, like I asked?'

'You didn't ask, but I'll do it now.'

'I *did* ask.'

'I don't think so.'

'No, I definitely remember mentioning it.'

George bangs the bottle of formula down and walks out of the room. Amber closes her eyes, as if enduring real pain.

'I'm sure I won't need it,' says Ruby.

'That's not the point.'

George returns with the thermometer, which is shaped like a dragon, and puts it on the table next to the spare key. 'Shall we get going? I was hoping we'd be there in time for lunch, but that's not going to happen now. We'll have to find somewhere to stop on the way.'

Amber huffs. 'I can't get ready any quicker. I'm so tired, I feel like a zombie.' She turns to her sister. 'We've been up since five.'

Ruby grins. 'I only had four hours' sleep myself, if that makes you feel any better.'

'But you were out clubbing, I expect. We had no choice.'

'I know, I was just—'

'Will Lewis be joining you later?' asks George, trying to change the subject.

'No,' says Ruby. 'He woke up with a sore throat and didn't want to pass any germs on to Mabel.'

'Very considerate,' says Amber approvingly. Ruby nods, remembering the cross words she and Lewis exchanged that morning. She doesn't believe the sore throat story; there's always some excuse. Lewis hasn't seen Mabel for months, and Ruby's starting to wonder if he's sending out a subtle message to the effect that he doesn't want children. Not that they've ever discussed having a baby – they're too young for a start, and have only been together two years. She loves being Auntie Ruby, but Lewis reacted quite negatively to being called Uncle. Maybe he doesn't feel entitled because they aren't married. He can be old-fashioned like that.

Amber's voice cuts into her thoughts. 'Don't forget to turn on the baby monitor. Don't let her sleep in the bed. If she wakes up, just go into the nursery and talk to her calmly. You can lay a hand on her tummy but don't pick her up. If she gets really hysterical, let her have some water from her beaker. Filtered only, from the jug in the fridge, but don't give it to her freezing cold. Use the dummy only as a last resort. With a bit of luck, she'll sleep from about midnight to five.'

'Yes thanks, got it,' Ruby replies, not really listening. 'Honestly, we'll be fine.'

It's another twenty minutes before they're ready to leave. Amber gives her daughter a last cuddle and starts to cry, but Mabel doesn't seem to care. She's too busy playing peekaboo with Auntie Ruby and a tea towel.

Ruby hears the front door slam and immediately breathes out. 'Right, Mabel Rosebud,' she says. 'I don't care what it says in the instructions. We're going to see the ducks.'

She puts a thick jumper over Mabel's sleepsuit, then stuffs her into her waterproof all-in-one. The poor child looks like a sumo wrestler. Ruby lifts her up and carries her downstairs to the narrow hallway, where the buggy's waiting.

Mabel does not want to wear her hat or mittens, nor does she appreciate being made to lie flat. Ruby wins with the hat but loses with the mittens. She fiddles with the levers until the seat swings into a more upright position. Strapping her niece in carefully, she then leaps back upstairs to get her coat and bag. She's halfway down before she remembers the door key and has to go back again.

'How does your mummy manage it?' she says, pulling a bobble hat from her pocket. 'I'm worn out already.' She has to drag the buggy away from the door, then squeeze past so that she can open it. Cursing at the sheer awkwardness of it all, she finally manages to exit the house.

The sun is still shining – just about – but wintry grey clouds are gathering and it feels colder than before. They've missed the best of the weather, but Ruby is undaunted. She *has* to get outside, regardless of Mabel's schedule. The flat, perfect for a working couple, is too small for a family. You can't move without tripping over some item of baby equipment, the windows are constantly steamed up from the wet washing draped over the radiators, and it's full of dubious smells. It's a far cry from the cool, glassy office where Amber used to work as a management consultant. Is it any wonder she's not coping?

She crosses the road and heads into Lilac Park. It's lunchtime, and the place is heaving with families. Feeling a sudden pang of hunger, she steers the buggy towards the so-called farmers' market by the far entrance. It's no more than a few stalls selling incredibly overpriced bread and gluten-free cakes, craft cheeses, pasties filled with exotic ingredients and some rather limp-looking vegetables. She buys a spicy Moroccan wrap and a vegan chocolate brownie, then finds a bench. She puts the brake on the buggy and sits down.

Mabel is awake and alert. Her bright-eyed gaze follows the parade of pushchairs, scooters, bikes and marauding toddlers. There are lots of people about – joggers, couples, family groups, grandparents. Everyone seems in a good weekend mood and several people smile at her as they walk past.

Mabel suddenly gets excited when a pigeon tries to eat the crumbs from Ruby's lunch, flapping her arms until it flies away.

'Nasty things, pigeons,' advises Ruby. She's not sure whether Mabel is allowed chocolate – probably not – but she can't resist popping a teeny-tiny morsel of brownie into her mouth. Her eyes widen as her tongue explores the taste, making Ruby think this is probably her first time.

'You loved that, didn't you?' she says. 'Sorry, but I daren't give you any more.' She wraps up the remaining brownie and puts it in its paper bag.

They go to find the ducks, although Ruby has forgotten to bring any bread to feed them with. Not that it matters, because when they reach the pond, there's a sign saying that the ducks should only be fed with special food available at the park café. She looks at the long queue snaking out of the door and decides she can't be bothered to join it. Besides, Mabel has lost interest in the ducks and is starting to squirm uncomfortably in her seat. Either she's tired or she's done a poo. A quick sniff confirms it's the latter.

'Oh Mabel! That's a real stinker,' Ruby says, laughing. 'And in public too!' She spins the buggy around and pushes it in the direction of the house.

She rummages in her bag for the key and eventually finds it in the back pocket of her jeans. She turns it in the lock and the front door judders open. A fresh batch of dried leaves shuffles into the hallway along with the buggy, and at the same moment Ruby's mobile rings. She fishes it out and sees that it's Lewis calling.

'Hi,' she says, shoving the door shut with her bottom. 'What's up?'

'Nothing,' he says. 'Just wondered how you were getting on.'

'Why don't you come over, then you can judge for yourself.' Mabel starts to grizzle. Ruby tucks the handset under her chin while she undoes the buggy straps.

'I told you, I've got a cold coming. I don't want to infect her,' he replies.

'Hmm … Look, I can't talk now. Mabel's just done a whopping enormous poo. I'll call you back when she's having her nap.'

'Okay,' he says, clearly disappointed. 'Do you think you'll be home in time for lunch tomorrow? I could cook.'

'No idea.' She heaves Mabel out of the buggy and sets her on her hip. 'If it goes well, they'll hang around at the hotel; if it's a disaster, they'll head back straight after breakfast. Sorry, gotta go. This stinky baby is about to scream.'

CHAPTER FOUR

The weekend before

I had no idea when I woke up this morning that things would turn out this way. It felt like an ordinary Saturday. I was following my normal routine, arriving at Lilac Park just before 10.30 a.m. There's no point getting there earlier. Everybody's timetable shifts at the weekends: breakfast becomes brunch, lunch is forgotten or collides with dinner. People are more relaxed, less on their guard. And it's more crowded, which makes it easier to hide.

I popped into the park café, where I ordered a latte and sipped it perched on a high stool overlooking the play area. The place was as chaotic as ever, the tables crowded with inattentive parents who seemed to think it was fine to linger over their smoked salmon and smashed avocado while their bored children played hide-and-seek under other customers' tables and raided the ice-cream freezer. Not that I had any interest in them. I was only looking out for George.

He usually pops into the café at around 10.45 with Mabel bobbing about in the backpack carrier. He orders a double-shot cappuccino and has it poured into his own insulated beaker, then he strolls around the park drinking it. But he didn't turn up today. I was disappointed. And curious.

I left the café and took the path that leads to the main gate, virtually opposite number 74. Staying safely on the park side of the road, I strolled up and down for a bit, taking sneaky glances at the house. Amber and George's car – a white hatchback – was parked outside. The upstairs bathroom window was open. All the signs indicated that they were still at home.

Just delayed, then, I thought. I went back into the park and sat on a bench near the duck pond. If you sit at an angle, you can just about see number 74's front door from there. I don't know why, but I started to feel anxious. I hadn't had sight of them for days and was worrying that Mabel might be poorly.

After about ten minutes the front door opened and Amber and George came out. Amber looked very different. She was wearing a skirt, for a start, with high black leather boots and a dark green coat. The colour made a perfect contrast with her auburn hair, which was all fluffy and bouncy. George was looking smart too, and he was carrying two small suitcases, the kind you can take as hand luggage on a plane. It looked like they were going somewhere special and possibly staying overnight.

George put the cases in the boot of the car then opened the door for Amber to get in. She took a lingering look at the upstairs windows, then climbed into the passenger seat. A few seconds later the car drove away, disappearing around the corner.

I was rooted to the spot, amazed by what I'd just witnessed. Where was Mabel? Had they forgotten to put her in the car? I started to panic, then checked myself. There was no way even dopey depressed Amber would do that. Somebody must be looking after my little precious. Grandma and Grandad, perhaps. A friend? My thoughts went into free fall for a few seconds and I had to pull them back.

A few minutes later, the front door opened again and a girl pushed the buggy out. She was wearing a blue woolly hat with a huge orange bobble on the top. Wisps of black hair were escaping from under it, falling over her eyes and hugging the sides of her face. She had a baggy woollen jacket on, and equally baggy trousers, which tapered at the ankle and were stuffed into big laced boots. She looked like an art student. Underneath all those clothes, I guessed she was quite slim. I wondered whether I'd seen her before. Something about her was familiar, but I couldn't be sure. She looked very young. Too young for such an important job.

She crossed the road and entered the park. We were no more than a few metres from each other, but she was focused on her destination and didn't even glance in my direction. Even so, I deliberately walked away, knowing I could re-enter the park by the small gate that opened onto the rose garden and catch up with her without her realising. She was easy to spot in that silly hat, the orange bobble flashing like a beacon. Perfect for me. I could keep a good distance and merge into the crowd while still keeping an eye on her.

I followed her to the market stalls, where she spent ages debating what pastry to buy, then had to occupy myself while she sat down and ate it. To be fair, she was engaging with Mabel, talking to her and making sure she kept her hat on, which is more than Amber ever does. After what I guessed was lunch, she took her to the duck pond, but that didn't seem to last very long and soon she was pushing the pram in the direction of home.

The fun was over; there was no point in my hanging around. Anyway, I needed some lunch myself and the cold was pinching me. I was about to head off in the other direction when something prompted me to follow them all the way to their front door. Just for the hell of it. I was only a few metres behind her when she went through the gates. There's a newsagent across the way and I pretended to read the notices in the window, all the while watching her out of the corner of my eye.

She pushed the buggy into the front garden, then stopped to rummage around in her bag. She took a key out of her pocket and I saw her put it in the lock and push the door open as wide as it would go in order to steer the buggy into the small hallway.

Halfway through, her mobile rang and she answered it, shutting the door behind her.

I stared open-mouthed at the green-painted door. The key was still in the lock! What a careless, stupid thing to do, I thought. In London, of all places, where people are always on the lookout for opportunities to commit crimes: an unzipped handbag, a phone sticking out of a back pocket, an unpadlocked bike. A key in the front door. A baby inside being looked after by a fool.

Usually I would never have dared to get so close, but this was an emergency. I crossed over and stood at the front gate, which the babysitter had left open. Taking a deep breath, I stepped over the threshold, and instantly it was as if I'd entered a force field. Enemy territory.

I advanced across the small paved area shared with the ground-floor flat, carefully avoiding the sightline of anyone looking out of the downstairs window. After a few paces, I reached the front doors, which stand side by side under a small porch.

My vision zoomed in on the key. Shiny and silver.

I knew what a normal person would do in this situation. A normal person would ring the bell, and when the babysitter thundered down the stairs and opened the door, they'd say, 'Excuse me, did you mean to leave your key in the lock?' And the silly girl would gasp and put her hand over her mouth and thank the kind passer-by profusely as she yanked it out of the lock and put it in her pocket for safe keeping.

But you see, I'm *not* a normal person. I used to be, but not any more. I've lost too much to be generous towards others. Nevertheless, I wanted to do the right thing, for Mabel's sake. My finger hovered over the doorbell, but I couldn't push it, couldn't make that familiar ding-dong sound.

I stared at the key, wondering what to do next. I considered playing Knock Down Ginger – the game I used to play when I was a kid. My friends and I would pick on some poor old lady, bang on her door, then run away laughing while she opened it to find that nobody was there. It was a mean thing to do, but at the time we were just amusing ourselves. Should I knock loudly, then scoot off around the corner? No. That would be pathetic.

Instead, I decided that the simplest and least risky thing would be to post the key through the letter box. Reaching forward, I wriggled it out of the lock. With my other hand I gently lifted the flap of the letter box, revealing a narrow slit. I imagined pushing the key through the gap, releasing my fingers and letting it fall onto the tiled hallway with a gentle tinkle. It would eventually be found and the girl in the bobble hat would silently thank the kind stranger who had saved the day. But I'm not kind. Not any more. And I'm not a stranger either.

I gently released the flap without making a sound and walked calmly, but quickly away.

Now my treasure lies safely in my hand, fingers closed over it, forming a tight fist. It feels electrically charged, its jagged shape burning into my flesh. This little piece of metal gives me power. But I have to act quickly, or it will fade to nothing and I'll be back where I started – a bystander with no part to play.

CHAPTER FIVE

The weekend before

Amber feels a fresh rush of anxiety as George unlocks the door with a swipe card and they enter the hotel bedroom.

The setting is sumptuous, but also intimidating. George marches in with their overnight bags, setting them on the luggage rack, but Amber looks about her, absorbing the scene and all that it implies. The centrepiece is a super-king-size four-poster bed, its sides draped in soft muslin. The bed itself is covered with satin cushions in various tones of dull silver and plum and faces a large, extravagantly framed mirror strategically positioned on the opposite wall. The furniture is painted pale grey and is vaguely French in style – bowed legs on the dressing table, crystal knobs on the wardrobe doors and drawers. The silvery grey carpet has a velvety sheen on it and is so thick you could almost trip over the pile. But the most disturbing thing in the room is the polished pewter bathtub that sits brazenly on a platform in the bay overlooking the gardens. It's not as if the glass in the windows is frosted. Surely nobody actually takes a bath in full view of the other guests? Amber briefly plants herself into the scene, her dressing gown slipping off her shoulders to reveal her flabby naked body. She shudders visibly.

'You okay?' George asks. She nods and sits down on the bed. 'Stunning, eh?'

'Yes,' she fibs. She takes her phone from her bag and starts composing a text to Ruby. It's been less than an hour since they last exchanged messages, but it feels like days. The last she heard, Mabel had done a messy poo (the second today – a little worrying), and had just gone down for her afternoon nap. She was only forty-five minutes behind schedule, which considering Ruby was in charge wasn't bad at all. Amber's fingers fly across the screen.

Arrived. Hotel like something out of TOWIE. How are things? Send me a photo! xxx

'Amber,' George says warningly. 'I thought we'd agreed not to keep texting.' She stares at her handset, willing an image of Mabel to pop onto the screen. 'Please, babe. Turn the thing off and put it away.'

'How can I?' she responds crossly. 'What if there's a problem? What if Ruby needs to get in touch urgently?'

'She won't. She's fine.' He sits down and puts his arm around her. 'Oh dear, you're so tense.' He starts to knead the solid flesh between her shoulders. Her body wants to yield to his touch, but her mind won't let her. 'What shall we do first?' he murmurs. 'Go for a swim? Use the spa?'

Amber shakes her head. She would love a swim but can't bear the thought of wearing a swimsuit in public, which is why she deliberately didn't pack one. He digs his thumbs into her resistant muscles, then reaches around her and starts to undo the buttons of her shirt.

'George … please don't. The curtains aren't drawn. People can see in.'

'Only if they're up a tree – we're on the second floor! Anyway, I don't care.'

'Well I do.' She wriggles free and jumps off the bed. 'It's too early. I'm not – not ready.'

His face falls. 'I'm just trying to make the most of our time together.'

'Yes, I know. I'm sorry.' She goes to the window and looks out at the bare trees, blowing in the sharp February wind.

George is clearly not about to give up. 'We could order afternoon tea,' he says. 'In bed. Home-made finger sandwiches and little cakes.'

'You know I'm trying to cut down on sugar.'

'But this is our holiday, we're allowed treats.'

'*I'm* not.' She feels herself welling up. 'Ruby hasn't replied.'

'Give her a chance. I expect she's playing with Mabel, or making her afternoon snack.'

'It's too early for her afternoon snack. Something must be wrong.' She starts composing another text, but he walks over and snatches the phone out of her hands.

'You've got to stop this.'

'Hey! Give it back!' She cannot allow him to look at her phone.

'No. I'm putting it in the safe.'

'You can't! Give it to me. Please … It's *my* phone. I *need* it.' She stretches out her hand, demanding its return.

'If you're going to spend the whole time checking on Ruby, we might as well go home now.'

'Suits me,' she replies, her palm still facing upwards.

'You don't mean that.'

'Yes I do.'

'You were the one who wanted to go away for the weekend; it was your idea.'

'Actually, it was Ruby's. Give me the phone. Now!'

There are a few seconds of silent stand-off, then he angrily tosses it onto the bed. Amber grabs it immediately and unlocks the screen.

'Have you any idea how much this is costing?' he says. 'I really pushed the boat out. I was trying to please you; I thought it was what you wanted.'

She finishes the text. *Still waiting for my pic. Everything okay?*

It's his turn to stare out of the window now, his chest heaving as he breathes out his anger. Amber takes off her boots and puts her feet on the silky bedcover. Shoving aside some cushions, she lays her head on the crisp white pillow, clutching the phone to her chest like a comfort blanket, only there's not a shred of comfort in the cold, unresponsive metal.

'I'm sorry,' she says limply. 'I know I'm being hopeless and difficult. I'm trying, but it's so hard.'

He turns around to face her. 'What's wrong, Amber? Please. Throw me a bone.' He waits for her to respond, but she has nothing to give him. 'We've known each other since we were kids; we've always been so close, but you're treating me like a stranger. I was really hoping this weekend would bring us back together.'

'It's not an instant fix,' she says. 'I can't suddenly switch back to how it was when it was just the two of us. Things have changed. *I've* changed.'

'I told you, I still find you attractive—'

'I mean *inside*, George. I've changed inside. I'm not the same person I was before Mabel was born.'

He frowns at her, trying to understand. Her heart goes out to him. How can he understand when he doesn't know the truth? But this is not the time to confess.

'Would you like to go back to work?' he says after a long pause. 'I know we decided you'd take the full year off, but if you'd rather … We could get a nanny, or send Mabel to nursery.'

She shakes her head wearily. 'I realised months ago I wouldn't be able to go back. Remember those long hours I used to do? All that tedious entertaining – sometimes I didn't get home until three in the morning and then I'd have to be up in time for a breakfast meeting at eight. It was stressful enough then, without having a child to look after. Impossible now.'

'Why didn't you say, if that's what's been worrying you?' A flash of hope crosses his face. He comes towards her and sits on the edge of the bed. 'Maybe you should start looking for a different job.

Something part-time, more local. It could be really exciting – a whole change of career.'

Amber sighs. 'Just the thought of applying for things right now makes me feel exhausted.'

'When you feel up to it … There's no rush.' He pats her shoulder. 'It's worth thinking about. It could be the answer.'

There is no answer, she says to herself. No answer, no solution. It's just how it is. She made this bed and now she must lie in it, no matter how uncomfortable the mattress or how troublesome the night's sleep.

'Yeah, it's an idea,' she replies, leaving it at that.

He takes her hand and squeezes it. 'It's going to be okay, Amber, I know it. When we found out you were pregnant, it was the best moment of our lives – that and our wedding day. Remember how amazing it felt?'

She closes her eyes. Of course she remembers. Sitting on the loo clutching the test, staring at the two pink lines while the emotions she'd been holding down for all those months broke free and rose suddenly to the surface. A heady mix of intense joy and sobering responsibility. Of all her achievements, this was the one of which she was most proud. She'd done it. Finally gone and done it.

George kisses her, breaking the spell. 'I can't imagine being without either of you now. I know you love Mabel as much as I do, and you take really good care of her, there's no doubt about that; you're a fantastic mother.' He hesitates.

Her eyes open and she blinks at him. 'But …? But what, George?'

'You seem so unhappy,' he says, his voice breaking. 'I can't bear it and I don't know how to put it right.'

'I'm tired, that's all, just tired. I'm going to take a nap now, if that's okay?' He casts his eyes down. 'So that I can enjoy the evening. I don't want to fall asleep in my Michelin-starred starter.' She attempts a feeble laugh.

'Whatever you want, it's fine. We'll just chill,' he says accepting defeat – for now at least, she thinks. He unzips his overnight case and takes out his shirt, flapping out the creases before putting it on a hanger. Then he takes his toilet bag into the shower room and closes the door behind him.

Amber waits until she hears the shower going, then sits up and makes a call on her phone.

'Hi,' says Seth. 'Where are you?'

'In the hotel room,' she whispers. 'He's taking a shower – I haven't got long.'

'How's it going?'

'Really badly. I don't think I can do this.'

'Yes you can. Try to relax. Enjoy the break.'

'But it feels so false. All this lying and pretending, I hate it, it's sending me mad.'

'I'm so sorry, darling. I wish I could help.'

'You *do* help. All the time. If I couldn't speak to you, I don't know what I'd do.' The sound of the shower stops and she glances anxiously at the door. 'He got cross with me for texting Ruby, tried to take my phone off me. I was terrified he'd find our texts.'

'You should delete them.'

'I know, but sometimes I forget … Oh, this is awful. He's being so sweet and understanding, you wouldn't believe it. I know it's only because he wants sex, but it makes me feel so guilty.'

There's a short pause. 'Surely he'll respect you if you say no.'

'Yes, of course, he won't *force* me … it's not that.'

'What is it, then?'

The door of the en suite opens and George emerges, naked but for a towel around his waist. Amber quickly switches tone. 'Yeah, thanks for calling. Sorry, got to go now. Stay in touch.' She puts down the phone, turns to her husband and heaves a theatrical sigh. 'Huh! So much for my nap – couldn't get rid of her.'

'Who was it?' he asks, removing the towel and drying himself all over.

'Oh, just Polly. Wanting to know why I haven't been to any mums' meet-ups recently.'

He stands naked before her, his skin glistening, smelling of expensive products. She senses a tingling deep within her, in a place she can't reach, a feeling so unfamiliar she no longer recognises it as desire.

'And?' he says.

'And what?'

'Why haven't you been? To the meet-ups.'

Amber feels her cheeks turning pink. 'It's boring,' she says as he approaches. 'All they ever talk about is babies.'

'Even so … better than being on your own all day.'

'I guess.' She brightens her face. 'Shall we go downstairs and have afternoon tea? I suppose I could manage a little bit of cake.'

CHAPTER SIX

The weekend before

Ruby is worn out, even though she's only been looking after Mabel for seven hours and the little darling was asleep for two of them. They've done tummy time (which Mabel hated) and sitting-up practice. They've lain on their backs on the play mat and fully explored the Sea World Activity Gym – rattling the octopus's tentacles, squeezing the squeaky puffer fish and tinkling the tails of the seahorses. She's sung 'Baa Baa Black Sheep' – altering 'little boy' to 'little girl' for the sake of gender equality – a million times over and made up scurrilous new verses to 'Wheels on the Bus'. She's pulled funny faces and made silly noises until her head aches, and yet still Mabel seems dissatisfied. She wants more attention, more giggles, more entertainment, more FUN. When Ruby puts her in her bouncing chair while she opens a much-needed bottle of beer, Mabel snarls and kicks her fat little legs in protest.

'Jesus, kid, give me a break.' She leans against the kitchen counter as she swigs back the cool lager. Is this what it's like all the time? If so, no wonder Amber's at breaking point. Feeling sympathetic towards her sister – rather than slightly envious – is an unfamiliar sensation.

The six-year age gap between them has always made it difficult for them to connect. Growing up, they were at very different – and sometimes incompatible – stages of their lives. To begin with, Amber was keen to mother baby Ruby, but eventually grew tired of that game and wished she could go back to being an only child. In contrast, Ruby adored her big sister. She followed her around like a faithful puppy, copying her every move, trying to be part of the gang. Amber and her mates soon realised that a little squirt like Ruby could have her uses. She hunted for lost balls, brought cans from the fridge, raided the biscuit tin and ran whatever other errands they could think of. Whenever she got in trouble for losing or breaking things – which was often – Amber never spoke up for her and always took their mother's side in arguments.

Ruby strokes Mabel's wispy auburn curls and thinks back to when Amber started going out with Gorgeous George, as he was known. Half the sixth form had a crush on him, girls *and* boys. He was a sports jock: captain of the football and cricket teams, county-level javelin thrower, the fastest swimmer in the school. He was the brawn and Amber the brains. They became the school power couple – attractive, bright, destined for glittering success.

George always came round to their house after school. Mum worked late, so between four o'clock and seven, Amber was in charge. She resented having to babysit so felt it only fair that Ruby slaved for her and George in return. She commandeered the lounge, switching off Ruby's favourite TV programmes so she and George could play video games. Ruby was made to bring them drinks and snacks before being banished to her room, leaving them to snog and grope on the sofa.

When they left school, Amber with a clutch of A grades and George with more modest results, their relationship grew deeper and stronger, despite them going to different universities a hundred miles away from each other. Amber studied English while George did sports science. They spent all their free time together. Amber hardly ever came home in the holidays and the connection between the sisters, fragile as it was, fractured completely. She wasn't around to support Ruby through boyfriend crises, exam stress or various struggles with identity and self-confidence, though by then Ruby had long given up expecting it.

It was only in the last few years – finding themselves living a few miles apart by accident – that they'd really got to know each other. They had entirely different personalities but discovered they had more in common than they realised – dealing with the same difficult mother being one of them. Ruby was thrilled when she learned she was going to be an auntie. They went shopping together for baby clothes and nursery furniture.

But after Mabel's birth, the dynamic between them changed yet again. Now, for the first time in their sisterly history, Ruby is in control and Amber is the weak and needy one.

'What went wrong, Mabel?' Ruby asks, pulling the child onto her lap. 'Are you going to tell me, or am I going to have find out all by myself?'

It's half-six, not even dawn, when Ruby wakes, dragged out of a rather delicious dream by a noise she can't place. A kind of high-pitched wailing. A fox, perhaps, or a seagull? It sounds animal-like. Nor can she immediately work out where she is. She rubs her eyes and her lids slowly unstick. Lifting her head, she looks blearily around her. Oh yes … of course. She's at Amber's flat, sleeping in the marital bed on the top floor. Babysitting while Amber and George—

Oh God, *that's* what the noise is!

She leaps clumsily out of bed and pulls a jumper on over her pyjamas. *Shit … shit …* She pounds downstairs and bursts into what Amber calls the nursery. Mabel is lying on her back, screaming hysterically. Rushing over to the cot, Ruby picks her up and holds her tightly, stroking her hair and kissing her sweaty red cheeks.

'I'm sorry, my little one, so so sorry,' she soothes, rocking her from side to side. 'You poor little darling. How long have you been crying? Bad Auntie Ruby for not hearing you.'

Mabel seems momentarily comforted, then picks up from where she left off, her shrieks penetrating Ruby's eardrums and no doubt the bedroom walls.

'No, no, please don't cry, you'll wake the neighbours. I know you're cross, but it's okay now, I'm here. Forgive me! I was upstairs in Mummy and Daddy's room and I couldn't hear you.'

She suddenly remembers the baby monitor and is dismayed to see that the light isn't on. She feels sick with guilt.

'Oh God, I'm sorry, I'm a despicable person.' Mabel continues to cry and Ruby rubs her back soothingly. 'Except I'm sure I switched it on last night … In fact I *know* I did.' She picks up the monitor with her free hand and studies it critically. 'Perhaps it's broken. Or run out of juice.' She presses the button and the green light comes on immediately. 'Nope. Oh shit. How did I forget? That's so bad. Don't tell Mummy, Mabel, or she'll kill me.'

Her niece has reached the sobbing stage now, taking deep gulps of air that make her tiny ribcage vibrate with effort. Then she starts to hiccup. Ruby carries her into the kitchen and sets about warming a bottle of formula milk – not easy to do with a distraught baby perched on her hip.

'I must be going mad,' she says to Mabel. 'I could have sworn there were two bottles left, but there's only one.' She glances over to the sink, where a clean bottle and teat are drying on the draining rack. 'Isn't that weird? I've no memory of giving you that. God, I know I was tired last night and had a couple of beers, but …' She pulls a face, ashamed of herself.

Putting Mabel to bed hadn't been easy. Ruby had stupidly overexcited her and then been unable to calm her down. She'd not enjoyed her bath and had refused to lie in her cot. All the instructions about being kind but firm and not cuddling had to be abandoned. Maybe that was when Ruby had relented and given her an extra feed. She remembers feeling at her wits' end, finally lifting Mabel up and taking her into the sitting room. She lay with her on the sofa and watched a film until Mabel eventually fell asleep, splayed out starfish-like across her chest. She tries to remember the final moments of the evening – returning Mabel to her cot, placing her in the correct position and turning on the night light so that she wouldn't be alarmed if she woke. She was sure she turned the monitor on too.

Feeling annoyed with herself for always being so scatty, she sits down at the dining table and moves Mabel onto her lap. At first the baby sucks eagerly, but after a minute or so she spits the teat out.

'Not hungry? That's a first. Maybe you're uncomfortable. Shall we change your nappy?'

She takes her back to the nursery and lays her down on the changing mat, which Mabel doesn't like one bit. She kicks and squeals as Ruby removes her from the sleeping pod and takes off her nappy.

'No wonder you were unhappy, you were all wet ...' She cleans Mabel's bottom according to instructions, and fastens on a new nappy. 'There you go, that's better.'

She yawns. It's not even 7 a.m. yet – this could be a long day, she thinks. She dresses Mabel in a clean sleepsuit and carries her up to the loft room, wedging her between pillows in the middle of the bed while she has a quick wash in the en suite shower room. She puts yesterday's clothes on, then picks up her phone, expecting to see a stream of anxious messages from Amber. But to her surprise, there are only two, and neither of them is particularly anxious. The last one was sent at 11.45 p.m.

'Must be having a good time,' says Ruby. 'I expect Daddy got her pissed.' Mabel laughs, as if she understands. Ruby lies next to her on the mattress and together they look up through the window of the sloping roof, staring at the sunrise – streaks of pink and mauve fading to grey-blue. How can it not even be properly light yet?

The morning passes slowly. After breakfast, Ruby makes up a new batch of feeds and puts them in the fridge. She still can't remember giving one to Mabel last night, nor washing the bottle, and it really bothers her.

She knows she's a scatterbrain – it's what her mother calls her. The trouble is, she finds the minutiae of life boring and prefers to think about other, more interesting, more important things. Like what career she's going to have, or whether she and Lewis are going to stay together, or the effects of climate change. Although it's true that she constantly forgets, misplaces or completely loses things (travel pass, purse, gloves, umbrellas, people's birthdays, dental appointments, even her precious bike), she always realises it at some point. She's spent half her life retracing her steps. But she's never lost a chunk of memory entirely, not even when she's been really drunk. It's very, very weird. Almost like her brain malfunctioned last night.

She won't mention it to Amber, or to her mother, and she probably won't tell Lewis either. She can hear his voice right now: 'Oh Rubes, what are you like?' There's no point reinforcing the stereotyped view they all have of her.

Maybe she needs to go to the doctor … Can you get early-onset Alzheimer's in your twenties?

Just need to get organised, she tells herself as she tidies Mabel's extensive collection of toys, hoovers the sitting room and even mops the kitchen floor. She gathers up the clean, dry washing and makes a pile of ironing – actually *doing* the ironing would be too out of character and would arouse suspicion, so she stops there.

For most of this time Mabel bounces happily in her chair, although she's frightened by the sound of the vacuum cleaner.

By the time Ruby's given her a mid-morning snack and changed two nappies in quick succession following an untimely poo, it's too late to go to the park. Besides, the sky has clouded over and it looks miserable out there.

'Let's do some reading instead,' Ruby says, reaching for a baby board book called *On the Farm*. She sits on the carpet with Mabel in her lap and makes animal noises and silly gestures, most of which Mabel finds very entertaining. Gratifyingly, she is giggling her little head off when Amber and George walk in.

'Aww, look at her!' says Amber, rushing forward and scooping Mabel up in her arms. 'I've so missed you. Have you had a lovely time with Auntie Ruby? Have you been a good girl?'

'She's been perfect,' says Ruby, lying more for her own sake than Mabel's. 'Don't take this the wrong way, but she didn't seem to miss you at all. Maybe when she first woke up, but other than that …'

'What time did she sleep until?'

'Six o'clock.' It's a guess, but Ruby tries to make it sound definite.

'Wow! She must have had a bad night.'

'No, not really.'

'What time did she go to bed? It must have been very late,' says Amber suspiciously. 'When was her last bottle? You didn't feed her after midnight, did you? I said only water—'

George intervenes. 'What she's trying to say is thank you so much for looking after her and doing such a brilliant job, eh, Amber?' He shakes his head in despair. 'Sorry, Ruby.'

Ruby shrugs, knowing Amber too well to take offence. 'Nothing to apologise for.'

'I just need to know where she is in her routine, that's all,' Amber says. 'It wasn't a criticism.'

Ruby smiles. 'It's fine. Tell me about your night away. How was dinner? Did it live up to its Michelin star?'

'Yes, it did actually,' Amber says, smiling slyly at George. 'Thanks, Rubes, it really helped to have some time away from the grind.'

'Any time.' Ruby stands up. 'If you don't mind, I'll get going. Lewis is cooking lunch – allegedly.'

'How is he? We haven't seen him for ages,' says George.

'He's fine.' Ruby puts on her jacket. She could add that he seems to have an aversion to babies, but decides that wouldn't be very tactful. 'Busy at work.' She casts around for her bobble hat and, finding it, pulls it over her head. 'Right. I'm off. Just hope my bike hasn't been nicked.'

'Oh, can I have the door key?' Amber asks. 'It's our only spare. I keep meaning to get more cut, but you know how it is …'

'Yeah, sure.' Ruby feels in her pockets, then looks in her bag, emptying it onto the carpet. 'Um … not sure where I put it … In the kitchen, probably. Or maybe by the changing unit.' She searches both places, but the key's nowhere to be seen. 'Sorry. I can't remember what I did with it.'

Amber groans. 'Oh Ruby, what's the matter with you?'

'When did you last use it?' asks George.

'Yesterday. We went to the park, then came home. Haven't been out at all today.'

He turns to Amber, who is now irritably opening and shutting drawers, picking up objects even though it's obvious the key couldn't possibly be lying underneath and slamming them down again.

'Relax, hon. It has to be in the flat, otherwise Ruby wouldn't have been able to get back in, would she? Don't worry, it'll turn up.'

'You don't understand, George, I've had a lifetime of this. Ever since she was little. She can't be trusted with a thing.' Amber kneels down and feels under the sofa. 'Think, Ruby. Think!'

'Maybe I tidied it up with the toys.' In truth, Ruby can't remember what she did with the bloody key, but as George said, it's obviously in the flat somewhere, so why is Amber making such a monumental fuss? She wasn't mugged, she didn't drop it in the street. It's not lost forever. Nothing bad has happened. Everything's fine.

CHAPTER SEVEN

Six days before

Amber marvels at the strangeness of the weekend as she tidies the bedroom. On the surface, it was a success – even Ruby seemed to notice the glow around them when she and George came home. But emotionally it was utterly exhausting, and when she woke up, she felt very confused.

George went off to work this morning with a spring in his step, despite Mabel keeping them awake half the night. The little terror is having an unscheduled nap now and Amber is going to let her sleep as long as she likes. She needs some time alone to process what happened, to replay the scenes in sequence and understand the twists and turns of the plot.

She hangs up her dress – it will bear another wearing – and puts her underwear in the laundry basket. George has already emptied his overnight bag and typically left his dirty washing in a pile on the floor. She picks up the shirt he wore on Saturday evening – tiny purple and maroon flowers with flashes of ochre – and holds it for a moment, closing her eyes as she remembers.

Their night away got off to a bad start – her fault, not his. She was nervous to the point of fear. George assumed it was because she was worrying about Mabel, but that wasn't really the case. She knew Ruby would cope; she only kept texting because she couldn't bear the stress of being alone with George.

She drops the shirt into the laundry basket. She feels ashamed that she called Seth while George was in the shower, but she didn't know who else to turn to – it was either that or running away. Seth calmed her down, as he always does, while subtly reminding her that her choices are stark. Either she makes herself comfortable with the lies or she confesses and risks losing everything she holds most dear. There are no half-measures or easy alternatives.

After their call, she tried her hardest to behave as normally as possible. She and George had afternoon tea in the conservatory, then took a stroll around the grounds before heading back into the warm. She remembers being reluctant to return to their room, suggesting instead that they go to the guest lounge, where there was a roaring fire. They found a couple of vacant armchairs and sat there for a while, wondering what to say to each other. Most of the other guests were retired couples, content to pore over a crossword or read a book. Amber envied their seeming ease in each other's company. If they had children, they must be long grown up and off their hands. She wondered whether she and George would still be together when they reached their sixties. It didn't seem likely, and that made her sad, because when all was said and done, she did still love him.

'I want to know the football scores,' said George, rising. 'Coming?'

She nodded and followed him back to their room. While he watched television, she prepared for their dinner date. Her dress – an emerald-green silky wraparound that showed off her cleavage – was creased and her stockings had a small ladder in them. For some reason, the heels she'd worn every day at work felt too tight, and she wobbled in them like a newborn lamb. She did her evening make-up but was dissatisfied with the result. No amount of concealer could hide the grey circles beneath her eyes.

By the time she'd finished, she was tired out, like she'd done a day's hard labour.

'You look stunning,' he said kindly, but she didn't believe him. He switched the TV off. 'Shall we go to the bar?'

Amber puts her make-up bag back on the dressing table and shoves her wheelie suitcase to the back of the wardrobe. The memories will not be so safely stowed away. Everything that happened earlier in the day was entirely predictable. It was when they went for dinner that things veered off in an unexpected direction.

In their pre-Mabel life, they'd had dozens, probably hundreds of such evenings together, choosing restaurants that had unusual menus and great online reviews. Fine dining wasn't necessarily a precursor to great sex, but it had often worked out that way: playing footsie under the table; exchanging glances full of erotic meaning; using sexual language to describe the food. Later, emboldened by alcohol and impatient to devour each other, they would sneak down an alley and snog like teenagers. They never went as far as having sex in the street, but a couple of times they got dangerously close.

She smiles to herself as she shakes the pillows and pulls the duvet over their bed. Oh my, those were the days …

Saturday night was different in every way. The air was laced with tension, but it wasn't in the least bit sexual. They found the menu bewildering and had to ask for help. The food was served as a series of tiny sharing plates, like tapas but without the charm. The chef dictated the order in which their chosen plates should be eaten, and they had to finish each one before the next was brought. It wasn't a meal – it was a military operation.

Amber felt increasingly anxious. She found herself over-complimenting every mouthful, prattling about the decor and the service. George kept quiet. She sensed his gaze penetrating her mask of false jollity, his ears filtering out her evasive burble.

It was embarrassing. She was behaving as if they were on a first date and he'd already decided she was not for him.

But as the plates of pretentious deliciousness came and went, something inside her started to shift. Thinking about it now on a grey Monday morning, there was no mystery to it: cocktails in the bar, a bottle of champagne with dinner, a glass of heady dessert wine and a fierce grappa digestif. Amber hadn't drunk any alcohol since she first found out she was pregnant, and it went straight to her head, loosening her muscles and opening places she'd kept padlocked for so long she'd forgotten where she'd put the key.

And suddenly there he was, Gorgeous George, sitting opposite her in his fancy floral shirt, brown eyes twinkling in the candle-light. Her teenage sweetheart, adoring husband. The man, believe it or not, whom she loves more than anyone else in the world. For a few moments she forgot that she'd betrayed him. They locked gazes and held hands across the table. She kicked off her shoes and stroked his shin with her stockinged foot. Before she knew it, they were back in the room, tearing at each other's clothes.

She continues tidying, blushing as she replays the details in her head. Even in his wildest fantasies, George wouldn't have expected *that*. They'd behaved like different people – strangers to each other and themselves. Where had this other Amber come from? What had fuelled her desire? Was it simply the alcohol, or was it something darker and more complex? Her secret-self taking over. She's half impressed, half disgusted by this new person. Since Saturday night, she hasn't been able to look at herself in the mirror.

Overcome, she sinks onto the bed. What is going on? For a few hours that night, she laid aside the burden of guilt she normally carries around with her and felt incredibly free. But on Sunday morning, when it was time to leave, she had to pick up the burden again, along with her toilet bag and wheelie suitcase. Back in the real world of cooking, cleaning, washing and caring for Mabel, the guilt seems to weigh even heavier than before.

Her mobile phone is sitting on the bedside table. She wants to call Seth but knows she mustn't interrupt him at work. All she needs is a few words of reassurance.

You can do this. It's okay. I'm rooting for you every step of the way.

She can't be honest with Ruby, it's impossible. Her friends from university are now also George's, so she can't confide in any of them. She has some good female friends from work, but she's hardly communicated with them since her baby shower, the week before she went on maternity leave. They wouldn't understand her predicament anyway. They are all career-obsessed, clocking up insane hours to gain promotion, delaying motherhood until the last possible minute before their eggs run out. When they do come out to play, they play hard – booze, drugs and other risky behaviour. She never felt comfortable in that environment, and now that she's a mum … well, it's out of the question.

She stands up and tries to shake herself free of her mood. This will not do. Maybe it's not a confidante she needs; maybe it's just a bit of adult company. The mums from her antenatal class are meeting up this Thursday for lunch. Maybe she'll go along – if she feels up to it and Mabel is behaving herself. It would please George and might even make her feel better too.

CHAPTER EIGHT

Three days before

I can't stop thinking about Mabel, even though five days have passed since I held her in my arms. The key to her home is on a piece of string around my neck, resting against my heart. I haven't taken my necklace off once, not to wash or shower or sleep. At night, I lie in the darkness running my finger along its sharp, serrated edge. I know every nick and turn of the cut. If I were a locksmith, I could make a perfect copy from memory.

It was about three in the morning, the dead of night, when I let myself into number 74, tiptoeing up the stairs in the darkness, feeling my way to the nursery. First I turned off the baby monitor. Mabel's eyes opened as I lifted her out of her cot, but she was still half asleep and didn't cry out as I carried her into the kitchen. Finding a feed already made up in the fridge, I warmed the bottle under the tap, then sat in the chair with her on my lap. She seemed hungry and I let her drink her fill. When she'd finished, I laid her against my shoulder and rubbed her back until she let out a tiny ladylike burp.

She was so tired and full of milk she hardly moved or made a sound as I walked around with her, trying not to make the floorboards creak, whispering words of love in her ear. I felt her growing heavier and heavier with sleep. She was as good as gold for me, the little darling, didn't so much as whimper when I laid her back in the cot. I can still smell her baby scent, still feel her soft rose-petal skin, still taste the sweetness when I kissed her on her forehead and wished her sweet dreams. How I long to do all that again.

But I'm worried. Amber and George must know by now that the key has gone missing. Maybe the babysitter remembered that she stupidly left it in the door and, finding it gone, raised the alarm. Assuming she confessed her mistake, the locks could have been changed by now, rendering my treasure utterly useless; crumbling my plans to dust.

I *have* to know if my key still works. I've been busy these past few days but there's still so much to do: preparations to complete, equipment to buy, false trails to lay, tracks to be covered. I don't want all the effort and expense to be wasted because I can't get into the house. Nor could I bear the disappointment of being so close to the finish line and falling at the final hurdle.

I should probably wait until the middle of the night to visit, but now I've decided to take the risk, I feel impatient to get going. It's Thursday morning. I don't know what Amber's plan is for the day; most mornings she makes a short trip out, but sometimes she stays in, hunkering down on her unhappiness. I could have a long wait in the cold, but that's fine – better than fretting in the warmth of home.

Dressing in my most anonymous clothes – jeans, hoodie, a dark scarf around my face to keep out the winter chill – I catch the bus to Lilac Park. I take a seat on the top deck and stare out of the window, not making eye contact with my fellow passengers. My nerves are as jagged as the key; I have to stuff my hands in my pockets to stop myself fiddling with the string necklace.

I get off at the stop before the park and walk up William Morris Terrace. My heart is beating as fast as it did last Saturday. Number 74 is at the end, just before the corner. I cross over to walk on the other side of the road, glancing up as I pass the house. Amber and

George's car is parked outside. The small window at the front is open. Everything suggests that someone is in.

I enter the park by the gates and do a brisk circuit of the paths to see if Amber is taking Mabel for a stroll in the buggy. There's no sign of her, so I buy a coffee from the café and take it to the bench by the duck pond. It's covered in bird shit, but in the perfect position. From here I have a distant but clear view of the front door.

I press the key against my chest through the layers of coat, jumper and T-shirt, breathing in the memory of Saturday night, the flood of adrenaline that coursed through my veins. I want to go inside but I have to resist the urge. I'm here to test the key, that's all.

The minutes tick by slowly. I'm like a cat standing guard at a mouse hole, waiting for my prey to emerge. I'm so fixated by the door of number 74 that I forget to drink my coffee. It's cold today; the pond is shivering in the wind and even the ducks are sheltering in the reeds. Nobody else is sitting on a bench. I won't be able to stay here much longer without drawing attention to myself.

Come on, Amber, my little mouse, out you come …

Fifteen minutes later, my prayers are answered. The door miraculously opens and Amber pushes the buggy onto the front path. She's not in her usual scruffy jeans and fleece, but is wearing that green woollen coat again, this time with slim black trousers. Her hair looks nice and I think she's even got some lipstick on. She's made an effort, which suggests she's going somewhere special. This is good news. It means she will be out for a while.

She pulls down the rain hood of the buggy and sets off along William Morris Terrace, heading away from the park. I watch her disappear, then stand up and pour my cold coffee into the flower bed before chucking the cup in the recycle bin. I'm itching to run over there and put the key in the lock, but I have to hold back and wait. If I'm seen entering the house only moments after

Amber leaves, that will look suspicious. There's also a chance that she might forget something and come hurrying back. Timing is everything.

I stand up and lean over the railing of the little bridge, pretending to watch the mallards and the squawking Canada geese. I feel for the string necklace and pull it over my head, transferring the key to my pocket. Okay, I've waited long enough … It's now or never.

In case anyone is watching, I pretend to check the time on my non-existent watch and do a little reaction, as if I'm late for something. This motivates me to walk briskly, but not too briskly, towards the park exit. I'm trying to look relaxed yet purposeful, as if I have an unquestionable right to enter the house. I could be a cleaner, for example, or a relative – somebody who comes and goes all the time.

I don't stop or pause, but cross the road immediately and walk through the front gate and straight up to the door. Got to be quick, in case the downstairs or next-door neighbour look out of their windows. My fingers tremble as I slide the key in, then ease it round until it bites and turns. I exhale with relief.

Now what? I promised myself I would only try the door, but now that I'm here, it's so tempting to go inside. I've no reason to – Mabel isn't there. It would be an incredibly risky thing to do in broad daylight, especially when I don't know when Amber will be back …

But I can't resist.

I push the door open. It shudders as its bottom edge scrapes over the tiles. I quickly enter and close it behind me, being careful not to slam it in case it alerts the neighbour. Pausing for a moment, I absorb the empty silence of the flat. I walk up the stairs – noting the treads that creak – and enter Mabel's bedroom.

Everything looks different in the daylight. Shabbier. The wall frieze isn't as pretty as I thought, the paintwork on the cot is a little chipped, the animal mobile hasn't been hung straight. There is condensation on the window, which can't be healthy for tiny lungs.

'Not good enough,' I grunt to myself.

When Mabel's with me, she'll have a bedroom fit for a princess, all pink and glittery, with a mural of rainbows and unicorns on the wall. I'll stick stars on the ceiling that glow in the dark and hang a silver moon for her to gaze at as she drifts gently off to sleep.

I pull open the drawer of her changing unit. It's full of sleep-suits, socks and little vests, all stuffed in together like a jumble of rags. I choose a couple of things at random and hold them against my cheek, inhaling deeply. The cotton feels rough and there's no scent of fabric conditioner. When I'm in charge of Mabel, I'll dress her in the softest, prettiest baby clothes that smell of lavender and roses.

Something's bleeping … An alarm? The sound is coming from the kitchen. I put the clothes down and go to investigate.

To my relief, it's only the washing machine, announcing the end of its cycle. Bending down, I open the door and take out a few items, rejecting anything that belongs to either Amber or George and removing a few of Mabel's clothes. I want to hang them on the airer, iron out the creases before the fabric dries stiff and hard. But I can't, of course. Not until I'm in my own place.

I check the time – nine minutes have passed. It would be foolish to risk staying here much longer. I stuff all the washing back into the machine and close the door. Just one more thing to do before I go …

I untie my string necklace and remove the door key. Where shall I put it? It can't be anywhere too obvious or Amber will smell a rat. However, it needs to be left somewhere it will be easily found – just in case she was planning to call a locksmith. I have to stay in control of the situation, have to make her believe her world is safe. Looking around, I eventually choose a place. I wipe off any fingerprints and place the key in the saucer of a plant pot containing a spiky cactus.

Time to go. I walk carefully down the stairs so as not to alert the neighbours beneath, then, taking a deep breath, open the door and march confidently out of the house.

I have made a copy of the key, of course.

CHAPTER NINE

Three days before

Amber pulls open the heavy front doors of the Queen's Head, holding them with her back as she manoeuvres the buggy inside. It's a family-friendly pub, one of several in 'the village' that compete to provide the healthiest children's menus, cleanest high chairs and most positive attitude towards breastfeeding. This is where the mums from her antenatal class meet for lunch every other Thursday.

Polly, Kendra, Hanima, Cora and Louisa. They were randomly brought together about nine months ago when they attended the same weekly evening sessions at the local community centre. Some women turned up once or twice and were never seen again, but the six of them stuck it through to the end.

Amber was the first to go into labour. As soon as Mabel was born, the women were texting and calling, demanding the inside track on the experience: did the breathing exercises work? Did she have to resort to pain relief? Did she use the birthing pool? Were the midwives supportive of her birth plan? Did she have stitches and did they hurt? Were there any shortcomings at the maternity unit they would need to look out for? But her elevated status only lasted a few days, because then Polly gave birth.

Polly works in quality assurance, heading a large department in one of London's universities – she went on maternity leave only days before her due date and is taking her full year. Within minutes of popping Belinda out with no pain relief whatsoever (or so she claimed), she knew everything there was to know about childbirth and soon had motherhood down to a fine art. Or was that a dark art? It was her suggestion to carry on meeting so that they could support each other, but Amber suspects she just misses bossing people about. She has lots of uncharitable thoughts about Polly.

At first, their conversations *were* supportive. Everyone (apart from you-know-who) openly admitted how tired they were feeling, how they didn't know what day of the week it was, how they'd forgotten to get dressed and spent the whole day in their pyjamas. But recently the conversations have become less about making each other feel better and more about scoring points. Whose child sleeps the longest at night, whose little darling is already sitting up, or waving, or possibly even saying what sounds like 'Mama'?

The mums are all here, grouped around a large table in the corner of the restaurant. Waiting for her. She's putting their carefully organised schedule in jeopardy. Amber pulls a face of apology as she approaches – first to give birth, last to arrive, she thinks. Another black mark against her.

'We were starting to wonder.' Polly stands up and starts guiding her into a space for the buggy in the way a man might help a woman to park a car. 'Not that way, go around the chairs and then back up next to Kendra's,' she instructs above the cool contemporary jazz music.

Amber smiles through gritted teeth, her progress halted as she lassoes a chair with the strap of the changing bag.

'Let me help!' Polly lunges forward and attempts to snatch the buggy out of Amber's hands.

'It's okay, I can do it,' she snaps, releasing her bag and parking up. She takes the spare chair between Cora and Hanima and sits down with a sigh. 'Sorry I'm so late.'

Everybody is anxious to order their food before the babies wake up, although Louisa's little boy is on a different timetable and finishing off a feed.

'I'll have a pepperoni pizza and a large glass of house white,' Amber tells the waiter. The others raise their eyebrows like a team of synchronised swimmers. She knows exactly what they're thinking – spicy food and alcohol can only mean one thing.

'Oh dear,' says Polly. 'You've given up breastfeeding. What happened?'

'Not enough milk.'

'You probably weren't drinking enough water,' says Cora.

'I drank gallons of the stuff.'

Hanima gives her a sympathetic smile. 'Maybe it was stress.'

'Possibly.'

'You should try a lactation consultant,' declares Polly. 'Luckily, I didn't need one because Belinda latched on immediately, but I've heard they can be very good. I'll ask around, find you a recommendation.' She leans across and pats Amber's arm. 'Please don't give up, for Mabel's sake.'

Amber clenches her jaw. 'I didn't want to give up, I tried and tried, but it just wasn't working. Anyway, I feel so much better now, and Mabel's happier too.'

Polly frowns, clearly thinking this can't possibly be the case. But Amber knows it's true. Mabel used to fret at the breast, either falling asleep with all the effort of sucking or biting her in frustration. Now she sucks contentedly on her bottle, secure in the knowledge that she won't be going to bed hungry.

Food orders placed and glasses of non-alcoholic drinks clinked in a toast to motherhood, Polly commands the undivided attention of the group, announcing that she has some important and highly sensitive information to impart, otherwise known as a bit of juicy gossip.

'It's about Sonya,' she says.

A heavy silence immediately descends on the group, punctuated only by the clatter of cutlery as the waiter lays their places. Amber looks towards Mabel, still asleep in her buggy, her stomach clenching empathetically as she remembers what happened last summer.

Sonya wasn't like the other mums-to-be. She didn't seem anxious or excited and wasn't really interested in learning about labour or childcare. Nobody knew much about her, other than she used to work out at George's gym, although being the manager, with only a few personal clients, he didn't remember her. She wasn't at all forthcoming, despite Polly's probing. It was as if she didn't really want to be at the class, but had been forced to attend.

For one thing, she refused to remove her shoes for the yoga-inspired exercises, despite all entreaties. 'My feet smell,' she said finally, going very red in the face. Her bump was small, considering how far gone she was, although this made more sense after Cora saw her smoking at the bus stop. She was a mystery.

She only turned up to two – maybe three – classes, then stopped. The rest of them agreed that she hadn't really fitted in; they even made jokes about smelly feet. Then the news filtered through that her baby had died in the womb and she'd had to deliver her. Everyone was very shocked and upset, full of pity for Sonya and fear for the precious parcels they themselves were carrying around. They felt guilty about not having liked her much and didn't know how to respond. Should they ignore the tragedy, or send messages of sympathy, even flowers?

Hanima heard via some other channel that Sonya wasn't with the father of the child, and Kendra had a theory that he was a married man. Without any evidence, they concluded that she was alone, unsupported and in need of sisterly help. Polly decided they should visit her en masse but Amber argued that would be extremely insensitive, given that they were all so visibly pregnant, and refused to take part.

As far as Amber knew, only Polly from the group had kept in touch. Occasionally Sonya's name came up at their meetings and everyone paused to feel sad for her, then quickly reverted to happier subjects.

'So? What have you heard?' asks Louisa, removing little Noah from the breast and doing up her bra.

Polly leans forward. 'Well, according to another friend who knows her from Zumba ...' silent drum roll, 'she's gone completely off the radar.'

'What do you mean?' says Cora, eyes widening.

'She's stopped answering her phone and come off all social media – Facebook, Twitter, Instagram, Snapchat, WhatsApp, the lot.'

'That's weird,' says Kendra. 'Why has she done that?'

'Doesn't sound good,' Hanima agrees.

'I'm really worried about her.' Polly takes a sip of her cranberry and soda. 'Ever since she lost the baby, I've been reaching out, about once a week, you know, just checking in to see how she's doing, then a couple of weeks ago, she blocked me!'

'That's rude,' says Louisa. 'I don't care how depressed you, you don't block friends who are trying to help.'

Amber is listening to all this with mild disgust. What was Polly thinking, as a new mum, pestering another woman who'd just lost her baby? She's not surprised Sonya blocked her; she'd have done the same.

'Well, I was quite hurt,' admits Polly. 'But then a few days later, I realised she'd disappeared.'

There's a collective gasp and slapping of hands across mouths. 'Oh my God,' says Cora. 'That's awful!'

Polly frowns. 'I don't mean *actually* disappeared, I mean virtually.'

'That's almost as bad,' says Kendra. 'I know she was in a bad way after, you know, it happened, but do you think … I mean, could she be, you know …?'

'Poor Sonya,' murmurs Cora.

'Well, that's what it looks like to me,' says Polly. 'Losing her baby like that, so late on, and all on her own … I'd be suicidal, wouldn't you?' Amber groans inwardly. Trust Polly to voice the word that others daren't let pass their lips.

'Have you tried going round to see her?' asks Hanima, whose daughter has been whimpering for the last few minutes. She lifts her out of the buggy and rests her on her lap.

'No, not yet,' Polly replies. 'I want to, but I've been really busy – haven't had a chance. To be honest, I'm frightened of what I might find.'

'Oh my God, you mean you think she might be …?' Louisa says.

Polly nods. 'It's really frightening, isn't it? I don't know what to do.'

The others consider the problem silently for a few seconds, while Amber prickles with irritation. Why is it suddenly up to Polly to put Sonya's world to rights?

'Perhaps you could talk to her friends,' suggests Kendra.

'Hmm … To be honest, I think Sonya's a bit of a loner. I've a feeling she already had mental health issues before the miscarriage.'

'Then I fear for her, I really do,' says Hanima. 'And without a husband or family—'

'Look, none of us really know anything about her, do we?' Amber interjects. 'We've no idea whether she's suicidal or not. Maybe she got fed up with everyone being sorry for her loss and needed some time away from social media.'

'But she's on her own,' protests Polly. 'Mad with grief.'

'You don't know that, you're just assuming. She may be coping okay with it.'

Polly rounds on her. 'How can you say that? You don't understand what it's like to lose a child.'

Nor do you, Amber says silently. Why are they being so ghoulish? It's really unsavoury. She withdraws from the conversation, but it carries on, gathering momentum.

The others start debating whether the NHS let Sonya down by not offering enough grief counselling, whether she's already dead, and even what method she might have used to kill herself. Amber starts to feel physically sick. They pause when the food arrives. She picks at her pizza while the rest of them tuck into healthier options, the discussion moving on from Sonya's supposed suicide to how lucky they are not to be suffering from postnatal depression themselves.

Amber drifts away mentally from the group. Have they not noticed how much she is struggling? Has she hidden it *that* well? Or are they just a load of smug, self-obsessed gossip-mongers? As she drinks her wine, she decides this is her last mums' meet-up. There's no need to fall out with them; she just won't turn up and eventually they'll get the message. Not that they'll care. It's not like any of them are real friends …

Unable to face giving Mabel a bottle under their disapproving gaze, Amber makes her excuses and leaves the pub. No doubt they'll be talking about *her* now, she thinks as she pushes the buggy back up the hill. Well, let them. Having been desperate to go out, all she wants now is to be at home where nobody can judge her.

'Hey, shush, it's okay, we're nearly there.' She leans over the buggy and peers at Mabel through the transparent hood, spattered with drops of rainwater. As she manoeuvres around the tree roots bulging through the pavement, she feels an alcohol headache coming on. She really shouldn't drink at lunchtime. The weather isn't helping either – the rain is furrowing her forehead, knotting the muscles in her neck.

She unlocks the door and enters the house, parking the buggy in the hallway and shutting the door with a backward kick of her heel. Mabel is crying properly now. Amber removes the plastic hood and wrestles her daughter out of the straps.

'Whatever possessed us to buy a first-floor flat?' she thinks aloud, tramping up to the nursery and dumping Mabel in her cot. Not grasping that this is only a temporary measure, Mabel starts to scream, but Amber blocks it out as she takes off her coat and shoes. Rubbing her wet hair roughly with a towel, she rescues her daughter and takes her into the kitchen, balancing her on one hip while she runs the water cold and searches for the paracetamol. Mabel wriggles and protests, so Amber puts her in the baby bouncer instead and shoves a rice cake into her hand.

The washing machine has finished its cycle, but to her surprise it's not bleeping at her in that annoying way it usually does. Nor is its light flashing. She bends down to pick up a stray sock of George's that's lying on the floor. To her surprise, it's soaking wet. She sniffs it – that's odd, it smells clean too. How could this be?

She replays her actions this morning before she left the flat. Mabel woke just before six and she got up to change her and give her breakfast. She entertained her and tried to keep her quiet so that George could sleep a little longer. He got up at seven, usual time. After he left for work at around eight, she gave Mabel a bath and dressed her, then put her on the activity mat, leaving her to play while she gathered up the dirty washing and put a load of coloureds on. Then she got ready for the mums' meet-up, changed Mabel again and put her outdoor suit on. She thought the washing machine was still going when they left the house. At least that's how she remembers it.

But she must be wrong. She must have put the washing on much earlier, and when it bleeped to tell her that it had finished, she must have opened the door to look inside for some reason, and at that point the sock must have fallen out. But why didn't she remove the clean clothes and hang them up? There's a simple answer to that: she was distracted by Mabel and then it slipped her mind. Except she has no memory whatsoever of any of this happening. A chunk of time has been completely wiped from her brain. She stares at George's wet black sock sitting in her hand. My God, she thinks, I'm going mad.

CHAPTER TEN

Three days before

Amber only wants to talk to one person right now – Seth – but he probably won't pick up. His lunch break is over and he'll be back at his desk or in a meeting. Predictably, the phone rings out, then click into voicemail. She doesn't leave a message because he often doesn't get back to her. Instead, she rattles off a text.

Can you talk?

He replies instantly.

Sorry, not right now. Everything okay?

Amber groans. *No. Freaking out here.*

Why?

Too hard to explain. Need to talk to you.

I'll call you later.

Soon as you can, please. G will be home around 7.

I know. Will do my best. Try to stay calm. Love you xx

You too xx

Then he sends his usual reminder.

PS Don't forget to delete.

When he finally rings at ten to seven, she's in the middle of bathing Mabel and can't answer. He leaves a message apologising for not being able to call earlier and suggests she phone him when she can. Amber feels irritated. He has no idea how difficult all this is. There's no way she can call him back tonight. There's Mabel to see to, the dinner to cook, not to mention the obvious fact that George will walk through the door at any moment.

She lifts Mabel out of the bath and wraps her in her fluffy hooded penguin towel. 'Oh, you're so cute,' she says, rubbing her dry. She starts to fantasise about going around to Seth's place. It would be so good to talk to him face to face, and he'd love to see Mabel. They haven't spent any time together for ages. It's not really possible for her to get away at weekends – a weekday would be better. Maybe Seth would be able to work from home one day next week, or even take a day off. Would he be prepared to do that for her? Perhaps, if he was seriously worried about her mental health. Then again, maybe she should just see a bloody doctor.

She hears the front door opening downstairs. 'Hi!' George calls up, shutting it behind him.

Amber does a quick change of gear. 'Daddy's home,' she says to Mabel, picking her up.

He climbs the stairs and pokes his head around the door. 'How are my two favourite girls?'

'We're fine, thanks. Can you finish off here while I get the supper ready? Sorry, I'm a bit behind.'

He pauses to contain his annoyance. 'Okay. Just let me get my coat off.'

She carries on drying and dressing Mabel until George takes over, then hurries into the kitchen. It's a quick-assembly meal tonight. Amber's never been an ambitious chef, but since becoming a mum, she's reverted to her old student menu of stir fries, pasta, oven chips and takeaways. Easy but boring. As she chops an onion, she thinks of their Michelin-starred dinner last Saturday and the incredible passion that followed. It feels like a lifetime away. Or rather, some other woman's life that she borrowed for a short time but had to return.

'I've got some bad news, I'm afraid,' George says as he puts Mabel – who clearly has no intention of going to bed yet – in her baby rocker and sits down to eat.

Amber's face falls. 'What do you mean? What bad news?'

'It's okay, no need to panic. I've got to go to a conference this weekend, that's all. The company's announcing plans for expansion. I wanted to send one of my assistants, but head office says all managers have to attend.'

'How long for? Where? Will you have to stay over?'

'It's two nights in Manchester, so yes.'

She stares into her bowl of tuna pasta, tears pricking behind her eyes. 'No. You can't. Please don't leave me on my own.'

George carries on eating. 'Sorry, love. I'd much rather be at home with you and Mabel, but I can't refuse. It's not like she's a newborn any more. I can't use her as an excuse.'

'But … but I need my weekends. I really, really need them. By the time Friday comes around, I'm dead beat. If I can't lie in on Saturday morn—'

He puts down his fork. 'You've only just had a break. Surely you can manage. It's just a weekend, for God's sake.'

'But you know I'm struggling.'

He sighs. 'Yes, yes, I do … I do my best, Amber, but if I gave up work, where would we be then?'

'They can't make you work weekends, it's not fair.'

'If you need support, ask your mum to come over.'

'No way, she just makes me feel even more inadequate.'

'Ruby, then.'

'I can't ask her two weekends running. Anyway, she's probably already got plans.' Amber looks at him imploringly. 'Please don't go. I need you here.' She pauses. 'Something's wrong …'

'What?'

'Something weird happened this morning ...' She searches for the rest of the sentence, but the words scurry away.

'What do you mean, weird?' His tone is ever so slightly impatient.

'I, er ... had a memory lapse.'

'What?'

She tells him about the washing machine and the wet sock, but he screws his face up, unimpressed.

'Everyone has moments like that,' he says dismissively. 'Like walking into a room and forgetting what you came in for. Or arriving home and not being able to remember the journey. You were distracted by Mabel, I expect. Nothing to worry about. If you're looking for a reason for me not to go to the conference, you'll have to do better than that.'

There are many things Amber could say in reply, but she decides to keep them to herself. She cannot, *will* not spend the weekend on her own with Mabel. The mere thought of it makes her insides roll over in waves of panic.

After dinner, while George is in the nursery getting Mabel ready for bed, she manages to exchange a few frantic texts with Seth, then makes a call to her sister.

'Rubes, are you doing anything at the weekend?'

'Hmm ... not sure ... possibly,' she replies. 'I'm not working, so Lewis and I were thinking of going to Bristol to see some friends.'

'Oh.' It only takes one small word to convey Amber's enormous disappointment.

'Why? What's up?'

'George has to go to a conference in Manchester, for two whole nights, and—'

'You want me to come over and keep you company?'

Amber lowers her voice. 'Well, what I really wanted to ask was if you could possibly look after Mabel by yourself, like last time.'

There's the tiniest of pauses. 'Oh, so you want to go with him? Another romantic night away, eh?' Ruby sounds pleased.

'No, no.' Amber cups her hand over the receiver. 'There's this yoga retreat I want to go on in Somerset. Gaia Hall. Usually they're booked out, but they've had a cancellation. It would really help me if—'

'Why are you whispering?'

'I'm not.'

'You are.'

'I was talking too loudly before, that's all,' she bluffs. 'George is trying to get Mabel down.'

Ruby doesn't respond immediately. Amber can tell she's weighing up the situation, trying to work out why her sister is lying.

'Okay,' she says finally. 'Can I bring Lewis?'

'Of course. If he wants to come.'

'See you Friday then. And make sure you've got some beers in.'

It's nearly eleven before Mabel finally accepts defeat and George manages to get her to sleep. Amber has already gone to bed but is sitting up tapping away on her laptop. She quickly shuts the lid as George enters.

'Look what I've just found,' he says, holding up a key.

She peers at it across the room. 'Is that the spare to the front door?'

'Yes!' He puts it on the chest of drawers.

'Where was it?'

'In the saucer of that cactus, you know, the one you bought me for my birthday about five years ago. God knows why Ruby put it there. She's such an airhead.'

'I know, she's impossible,' agrees Amber. 'Still, she's been incredibly good to us. I spoke to her earlier; she's coming to stay for the weekend.'

'Great.' He starts to undress.

Amber knows she ought to tell him that Ruby will be looking after Mabel by herself, but she holds back. He should like the idea of her going on a yoga retreat, but what if he objects and tells her to cancel?

'Odd about the key,' he continues. 'I'm surprised you didn't find it earlier.'

'I'm surprised *you* didn't,' she retorts.

'Yeah, but surely you would have seen it when you were watering the plants.'

'You're not supposed to water cacti during the winter – hardly ever, anyway. Besides, it's *your* cactus.'

'Yes, but you're at home all day.'

She tightens her jaw. 'So? What are you implying?'

'I just find it weird that you claimed you'd searched high and low when clearly you hadn't—'

'George! Stop being such an arse. You found the key, okay? Congratulations! There's no need to weaponise it.'

He pulls back his side of the duvet and climbs in next to her. 'I'm not. I'm just saying it's odd, that's all, when the thing was there all the time, staring you in the face.'

'*Us*,' she snaps, turning out the light without warning. 'It was staring *us* in the face.'

But later, as she lies there in the darkness, her irritation gives way to a fresh anxiety. She *did* search high and low. That cactus sits on the sideboard in the corner of the kitchen-diner. She gives it a few drops of water once a week, moves the pot whenever she dusts. She must catch sight of it several times a day, whenever she opens the cupboard or uses the drawers. So why didn't she see the key before?

CHAPTER ELEVEN

Two days before

Ruby pulls a face. 'Please, Lewis! Don't make me look after Mabel all on my own. One night was hard enough, but *two* …'

'Sorry, but I need to work this weekend.'

She stares at him suspiciously. 'Really? The last I heard, we were going to Bristol.'

'Things have changed. I forgot to mention it, sorry.'

She groans at him. 'Can't you swap shifts?'

'No. We're short-staffed, there's nobody else available. Why did you say yes if you didn't want to do it?'

'I don't know … She sounded desperate – I felt like I couldn't refuse. And I hoped you'd be joining me. It'll be so much easier with two of us. It's such a responsibility, you know, looking after somebody else's child.'

'I'll try to pop over on Sunday, how about that?'

'Okay,' she says, her voice sounding small. He moves forward and hugs her until she softens in his arms. 'The thing is … something else is bothering me.'

'What?'

'I think Amber and George are having problems.'

He instantly pulls away. 'What do you mean?'

'Amber's lying, I'm sure of it. She told me she was going on a yoga retreat this weekend – it's so not her kind of thing. Something smells bad. I don't want to be part of it.'

Lewis shrugs. 'If you feel uncomfortable, just say no.'

'I can't let her down now.' She sighs. 'But I'm going to have to have a proper talk with her on Friday, find out what's going on.'

'I thought everything was okay after their romantic night away.'

'So did I.'

'But a yoga retreat, that's good, isn't it? Sounds like she's finally doing something about the depression.'

Ruby shakes her head. 'Two days of saluting the sun isn't going to make the dark clouds disappear. It's a long-term thing. She has to start by being honest – with George, me, Mum, everyone. But most of all, with herself.'

On Friday afternoon, Ruby takes the Overground to Waltham Green, having decided it wouldn't be safe to leave her bike chained to the park railings for two days. She's still worried about what's going on behind the doors of number 74, but has decided not to confront Amber until she returns on Sunday, hopefully refreshed and relaxed.

She walks down the street, her small overnight bag bouncing against her back. The weather forecast is good – mild, dry and bright – ideal for long walks with Mabel. It's a shame that Lewis can't make it; she was looking forward to playing mummies and daddies with him, trying the idea on for size. Maybe he sensed that, she thinks as she approaches the house, and the sudden need to work is an excuse. Lewis can be so closed off. It's hard to know what he's thinking most of the time. And as for Amber and George, well, God knows what's really going on there. Why do all the people in her life behave so obliquely? She's heartily sick of it.

'You're late!' says Amber, throwing open the front door.

'No I'm not. You said two-ish.'

'Yes, and it's nearly three.'

Amber thumps up the stairs and Ruby follows, murmuring, 'Thanks for coming, sis' under her breath.

Amber gives her a torrent of instructions as she puts her coat on and zips up a small suitcase.

'The spare key's here,' she says, pointing to the kitchen counter. 'Put it back there, please, not in the flower pot.'

'I didn't—' Ruby starts to protest, but her sister talks over her.

'Mabel went down twenty minutes ago; don't let her sleep for more than an hour or you'll have problems later. If the landline rings, don't answer, let it go to voicemail. Don't contact George unless it's an emergency and you can't get hold of me first. I'll have my phone on silent – I don't think you're allowed them on retreat, but hey. Text is probably better.'

Ruby folds her arms and gives Amber an exacting stare. 'This is all sounding a bit cloak-and-dagger. George *does* know you're leaving Mabel with me, right?'

'I'll be back Sunday afternoon. George won't be back till the evening,' Amber replies, sidestepping the question. 'Gotta go. I'm supposed to be there in time for vegan supper, God help us,' she scoffs, forgetting that Ruby is a vegan herself. 'And thanks, I owe you big-time.'

'Are you okay, Amber?' Ruby searches her sister's face for clues. 'Only I'm worried about you, I feel like you're—'

'I'm fine!' Amber snaps. 'I can't stay and chat – I'm going to hit the Friday traffic as it is.'

'Okay. Drive safely.'

She tuts. 'I always do.' She picks up the case and thunders down the stairs.

Ruby waits until she hears the front door slam shut, then breathes out. So, she was right. George doesn't know about the yoga retreat. But why the secrecy? What's all this about?

*

Mabel sleeps beyond her allotted hour, but Ruby can't bear to wake her. She looks so contented and peaceful, lying in her pod like a plant sprouting out of a grow bag. Ruby pulls up a chair and pokes her arm through the bars of the cot. She lightly strokes Mabel's soft pink cheek, marvelling at her long eyelashes and her rosebud mouth, the wisps of auburn hair curling around her tiny ears. The connection between them feels unbreakably strong. It's not just the knowledge that they share ancestors and genes, it's more instinctive than that. She loves this baby more than she could ever have imagined. What might she feel if one day she has a child of her own?

It's easy to feel full of unconditional love when a child is asleep, she reflects a few hours later, as she battles to comfort a screaming Mabel. She's been fed, changed, bathed, played with, jiggled about to music, told stories, sung lullabies, allowed to watch TV … all to no avail.

'Oh dear, you're missing your mummy, aren't you?' Ruby says, holding her niece up and trying to interest her in the moon and stars mobile.

To her surprise, Amber hasn't been in touch once. The last time Ruby babysat overnight, she was constantly texting and asking for updates, but there's been silence for hours. Maybe there's no reception in darkest Somerset, or maybe her phone was confiscated on arrival.

George hasn't rung the landline either, although Ruby is less surprised by that. She prays he really is at a conference and not shagging one of his many exclusive clients. He's always boasting about the women who hit on him at the gym, particularly the older divorcees. Does Amber suspect anything? she wonders. She hasn't said, but that doesn't surprise Ruby. If there's one thing her sister has in spades, it's pride. Hopefully he'll be in the hotel bar, getting pissed with colleagues and having a laugh. Ruby doesn't begrudge him a couple of nights of freedom, as long as he behaves himself.

'Oh dear, oh dear, don't cry like that, you'll make yourself sick.' She walks up and down the room with Mabel, rocking her until her arms hurt, then transferring her onto her shoulder and rubbing her back. Her little face is sticky with hot tears, and every so often her body shudders with the effort of sobbing. She seems inconsolable and Ruby doesn't know what else to do.

Should she let her sleep in the bed with her tonight? She knows it's very much against the rules, but Mabel's not going to rat on her and it will probably do the trick. But it will also set a precedent, and if she starts refusing to go in her cot, Amber will twig and Ruby will be in big trouble.

She takes Mabel out of the nursery and back to the sitting room, lying down on the sofa with her sprawled across her chest. She squirms around like a giant slug, biting at Ruby's jumper and leaving a trail of wet slobbery stains. But Ruby gently strokes the back of her head and murmurs in soothing tones until Mabel flops against her chest, worn out by the fight.

Clasping the baby tightly, Ruby eases herself upright and stands. She slowly carries her back to the nursery and lays her down in her cot.

'Mustn't forget to turn your monitor on this time,' she whispers, pressing the button so that the light flashes. Then she tiptoes out of the room, leaving the door slightly ajar.

It's late. She climbs the stairs to Amber and George's room. It feels odd to be sleeping in somebody else's private space. There's a framed photo above the bed, taken on their wedding day. Amber looks so beautiful in her simple white dress, auburn hair falling over her shoulders, freckles dancing across her nose, a neat diamanté tiara sparkling in the sunlight. Gorgeous George looks even more gorgeous than usual in his impeccable grey suit and silky cravat. The perfect couple.

Three years on, and now look at them ... It's not good. As she gets ready for bed, Ruby thinks – in a vague kind of way – about how she and Lewis compare. They seem like a couple of kids playing at adult life. Sometimes she feels frustrated by his unwillingness to commit, but maybe he's got the right approach. At least they know how to have fun together and she doesn't have any worries about him being unfaithful. Before she settles down, she sends him a text.

Mabel finally asleep. Worn out! Wish you were here. Love you xxx
His reply arrives seconds later. *Well done. Love you too x*

She settles down in the bed and closes her eyes. Within minutes she feels herself falling into blackness and succumbs to it willingly.

The night passes in a series of vivid dreams. Mabel crawls around her head in a manic game of tag. Ruby chases after her, but every time she gets within grabbing distance, Mabel speeds up or turns a corner or even disappears. Another time, she hears crying but can't work out where the sound is coming from, outside the dream or within it. She wants to follow the noise, but her legs refuse to move. 'Where are you, Mabel?' she mouths, but the dream won't let her speak. Then the crying stops and she has the sensation of letting go of something, of falling backwards and sinking into the bottomless well of sleep.

CHAPTER TWELVE

The day

I've just seen the babysitter leave the house with the buggy and head into the park, off for their Saturday-morning stroll, by the look of it. Same baggy trousers, same silly bobble hat on her head. She passed within a few feet of me and a shiver of expectation ran through my body.

They trundle past the play area, then disappear behind the café building. As tempting as it is to follow them, I decide to leave the park immediately and go home. There's so much to prepare, so many plans to put into action. On my way out, I walk along William Morris Terrace, scanning the street for Amber and George's car. As I guessed, it's not there. Impossible to know how long they're going to be away, but surely they wouldn't leave Mabel for more than a couple of days? They may even return this evening. But if they don't … if the babysitter is on her own with Mabel tonight …

The rest of the day passes slowly, even though I'm fully occupied. I'm trembling with excitement as I go around the flat, packing and making final arrangements. By 5 p.m., everything is ready. I have nappies, clothes, formula, baby food, a travel cot, a car seat, a high chair and a lightweight foldable buggy that fits neatly into the boot of my car. I have enough food to last me several weeks, and only need to take the minimum amount of clothes. I won't be going out, apart from to take Mabel for walks in the forest. Must take my wellies too – it rains a lot down there. I dig them out of the cupboard and put them by the door, along with everything else. Can't pack the car until it gets dark.

I'm feeling too nervous to eat. I clean the fridge and wipe down the kitchen surfaces, more to give me something to do than because I want to leave the flat in good order. I'll have to keep paying the rent because I'm leaving lots of stuff here. Who knows when I'll be able to come back to collect it? Not that it matters; I don't need any of that stuff. It's all extraneous and unnecessary. I'm even leaving behind the presents I was given. Like an idiot, I was clinging onto them as some kind of feeble substitute, but I don't need them any more. Soon I'm going to have the only present I ever wanted.

Big changes are ahead. I feel dizzy with expectation. After months of living in the shadows, I'm walking into the light. I'm starting my life again; I'm going to be reborn.

3 a.m. Fully loaded, I drive the car to a quiet side street several hundred metres from William Morris Terrace and park in a dark spot, away from CCTV cameras and street lamps. The roads are so quiet; not a single car passes me as I walk towards the house. My heart thumps with every step, racing to keep up with me. The copied key swings on its string necklace and I press it beneath the layers of clothing. My hood is up; I'm wearing a scarf over my face and black leather gloves. Dark, anonymous clothes. Unremarkable footwear. Fortunately, it's cold, so I don't look out of place. There's nobody about, but I keep my head down in case any houses have security cameras.

The park looms ahead of me, grey blobs of trees rustling eerily in the night breeze. The gates are closed to all but the night creatures. I stop for a few seconds to listen to the wildlife going about its business. A distant fox is screaming; birds are singing in a desperate pre-dawn chorus. I'm the only human being around.

I turn onto William Morris Terrace and quickly assess the situation. To my relief, there's no sign of Amber and George's car. A quick shimmy through the open gate takes me to the front door of number 74.

Pulling the necklace over my head, I insert the key. It turns sweetly in the lock. Now to open the door without making a noise. Gently does it …

I'm in.

I push the door to, but don't shut it. Checking that all is quiet above, I start to tiptoe up the stairs, stepping over the third and seventh treads to avoid the creaks. The landing light has been left on and the door to Mabel's room is ajar. Holding my breath, I push it open ever so slowly, willing the hinges not to squeak.

The night light glows pink and purple, illuminating the room enough for me to see my way to the cot. Mabel is lying on her back, her beautiful face still in repose. I lean over the bars and study her for a few moments, allowing my pupils to dilate. She is breathing lightly, her eyelids flickering as she dreams. I lean across and turn off the baby monitor.

This is going to be the trickiest part. I have to pick her up in a single action and carry her downstairs without waking her. Quick but not hasty, quiet but not cautious. Even if the babysitter hears something, it will take her a while to realise what's going on. I can do this.

I unzip my jacket, revealing the baby sling I put on earlier. Then, tucking my hands beneath Mabel's body, I lift her and lay her against my chest. She shifts and murmurs, so I don't attempt to put her into the sling, but wrap my arms around her instead and leave the room. I descend the stairs, one hand on the rail, the other under Mabel's bottom. Reaching the hallway, I squeeze past the buggy and open the door, dead leaves crackling beneath my feet as I step out. I pull the door shut and the letter box clangs. My heart stops beating for a second – was it loud enough to wake the babysitter? I can't hang around to find out.

I look about furtively, but there's still nobody to see me. Pulling my jacket over Mabel, I walk briskly away, turning the corner and heading towards the side street where I left the car. I can hardly catch my breath. Mabel, who was so still at first, starts to fidget. I think she's waking up.

'It's okay, my darling,' I whisper. 'Sorry if it's a little bit cold out here, but you'll soon be inside where it's safe and cosy.' She makes a small snuffling sound. 'Shush, little one.' I rub her back soothingly. 'Keep quiet a few minutes longer. You can scream all you like once we're on the road.'

I quicken my pace. She becomes heavier with every step and my arms ache. I feel so buzzy and excited, I could drop her, but I won't, of course. She'll come to no harm with me. I'll look after her better than Amber, better than any babysitter. I'll hold onto her with my dying breath.

We reach the car. I open the rear passenger door and place Mabel in her special seat. She squirms and growls as I fiddle about with the straps. Can't afford to stay here too long. Got to get moving.

I've already worked out my route using a cycling app that takes back roads as much as possible to avoid dangerous traffic. It's the cameras *I* want to avoid. I whack the car heater up and it seems to lull Mabel back to sleep. We have approximately two hours until sunrise, when the light will expose us.

Progress is slow. There are speed bumps and mini roundabouts to navigate. As we journey west across London, more cars start to appear: workers coming home from the night shift, early starters, delivery vans. Soon joggers and dog-walkers will spill out of their houses and it'll no longer be safe to be in the back streets.

I glance at the milometer. I've only gone a few miles. I need to speed up and put as much distance as possible between us and Waltham Green. I should be far enough away to start using A roads now, but I'm going to steer well clear of the motorway. I don't want to stop at a service station. The car is full of petrol; I've a bottle of water and a packet of sweets if I need a sugar rush. As long as Mabel stays asleep, we'll be okay. Once we hit the countryside, I can pull over in a lay-by if necessary – change her nappy, give her a feed.

I feel amazing. I can't remember the last time I felt so alive and in control. I look into the rear mirror and smile at my darling baby girl, safely strapped into her car seat, dreaming the miles away. My Mabel.

CHAPTER THIRTEEN

Day one without Mabel

Ruby emerges from a long sleep, groggy and heavy-limbed. The bedside clock tells her it's after 9 a.m. This is normal for her, but Mabel never sleeps this late. Is she okay? Ruby listens. There are no sounds of gurgling or whimpering or even breathing coming via the baby monitor – just dead silence. That's not right. A horrible sick feeling floods her stomach.

In an instant, brain and feet connect. She leaps out of bed and runs down the stairs, calling, 'Mabel! Mabel!' as she rushes into the nursery.

The cot is empty.

'Nooo … no …' Her pulse starts to race uncontrollably. This cannot be. It *cannot be.* She stares and stares at the empty mattress as if by looking harder Mabel will magically appear. Her brain can't compute what her eyes are seeing. She's a baby. She can't get out of the cot by herself. Somebody must have picked her up.

Amber. Of course. She must have come home early. Maybe the yoga retreat didn't work out.

'Amber? Amber!' Ruby leaves the nursery and goes into the sitting room, expecting to find her sister lying on the sofa, dozing with Mabel in her arms. But they're not there. 'Amber? Where are you?' She runs out and walks down the corridor to the kitchen-diner at the back of the flat. It's empty. The air is stale and chilly. She looks for signs of Amber's presence – her coat, bag, car keys, a cereal bowl or coffee mug – but everything's exactly the same as she left it last night. Her dirty supper plate is still soaking in the sink. The kettle feels stone cold.

Troubled and slightly irritated, she turns around and retraces her steps towards the only place left to try. Her ears strain for bath-time giggles or nappy-changing protests, but there's nothing to hear. Hoping against hope, she opens the bathroom door. The emptiness stares back at her.

Amber must have taken Mabel out for a walk. Yes, that's it. She came back very early, fed and changed her, then took her out for some fresh air. That's fine, she has a perfect right to do that, but why the hell didn't she leave a note? Didn't she realise it would make Ruby panic to find Mabel gone?

She runs back upstairs to the top floor and grabs her phone from the bedside table. The call immediately goes to voicemail. She tries to soften her tone as she leaves a message. 'Hi, Rubes here. Where are you? Call as soon as you can, eh?'

What is Amber playing at? She starts to feel angry with her for being so inconsiderate. She's tried so hard to help her, and this isn't fair.

They must be in the park, watching the ducks or having a coffee in the café. Ruby swings open the roof window, standing on tiptoe to peer out, but all she can see are the tops of trees swaying in the wind. Dressing hurriedly, she runs back to the first floor and looks out of the sitting room window instead. There's no sign of Amber's car, which surprises her. Maybe she couldn't find a space and had to park around the corner?

Okay, she thinks, if Amber hasn't got the decency to call her back, she'll have to go and find her. Give her a piece of her mind. She throws on her coat and puts on her boots, not bothering to tie the laces. She picks up the door key from the kitchen counter and is on her way down to the ground floor when she halts, suddenly caught off balance by the sight of Mabel's buggy in the hallway.

Amber *always* takes the buggy. She hates wearing that backpack thing George uses, claiming it's too uncomfortable. What's going on?

Ruby squeezes past the empty buggy and opens the front door. Crossing the road without even looking, she enters by the gates and starts running down the path, her temper rising as she scans the park for a woman with long auburn hair. A few families are already out and about and the café is opening up, but there's no sign of Amber. She runs around the bare rose garden, but all the benches are empty, then scampers over to the playing field, where a group of men are preparing to play a football match. There's nobody who looks even vaguely like Amber standing on the sidelines.

Ruby bends over, hands on her knees as she tries to catch her breath. There must be a simple explanation for this. Maybe Amber's phone has run out of juice so she couldn't get in touch. Maybe she'll turn up soon with Mabel and a bag of croissants and tell Ruby off for making such a fuss. Maybe they're already back at the flat. But maybes are not good enough; she needs certainties.

She turns around and makes her way back across the park in the direction of home. Her brain starts to churn, spitting out horrible thoughts. What if the explanation *isn't* simple? What if Amber took Mabel without telling her for a reason? What if she's deliberately not calling her back? Her sister isn't well. She's got postnatal depression, even if she won't admit it. People with mental health issues can't think straight, they do stupid things to try to solve their problems. They put themselves and others in danger. Her mouth dries as she dares to imagine the worst. If Amber *is* feeling … she hates even thinking of the word, but it's there in her brain with a blue flashing light on top … if she is feeling suicidal …

No. She wouldn't do something like that. She would never harm Mabel.

Unless she's closer to the edge than Ruby realised. After all, she lied to George about going on the yoga retreat, and she didn't get in touch once yesterday to ask how Mabel was, which was really odd.

If only she would just bloody well call and put Ruby's mind at rest.

But what if Amber *hasn't* got Mabel? What if it's George who came home early and took her? Ruby considers this idea for a few seconds before dismissing it. He would have come into the bedroom and woken her up, demanding to know where Amber was and why Ruby was on her own. No, it *has* to be Amber who has Mabel. There is no other explanation.

She goes back to the flat and paces from room to room. Waves of panic are rising inside her, but she takes deep breaths and tries to swim through them. George needs to know there's a problem, she thinks; he must come straight away. But she doesn't have his mobile number and the only person she can think of who might have it is her mother. Alerting Mum is a high-risk strategy. It will set things in motion that will be hard to stop. She'll probably freak out and call the police, and if it turns out to be a silly misunderstanding, Ruby will get the blame, like she always does.

She'll give Amber another ten minutes, then she'll call the police herself and damn the consequences. Hopefully they can send a couple of cars out to find them. It's about time the family took her sister's mental health problems seriously. When this scary episode is over, they can make a plan to get her the help she so obviously needs.

Ruby stares at her phone, feeling more and more sick as the seconds tick by. Just as she's about to give up, the handset vibrates and rings. Amber's name and photo appear on her screen.

'Where the hell are you?' Ruby shouts.

'Hey, excuse me!'

'Why didn't you wake me up? I've been going crazy here.'

'What are you talking about?' Amber says irritably. 'I told you it would be difficult to call.'

'Where are you?'

'At Gaia Hall, of course. I'm not supposed to have my phone on. If I'm caught, they'll take it off me.' Amber pauses. 'Hello? Are you there?'

Ruby feels as if somebody has just plunged a dagger into her chest. Her heart heaves and cracks. She can't breathe. Amber isn't making sense. She can't still be in Somerset, it's impossible.

'Ruby? What's the matter? *Ruby!* Talk to me!'

'But … M-M-Mabel,' she stutters, feeling herself swaying.

'What about her? Is she ill? Has she had an accident?'

How can she tell her? How can she find the words?

'Ruby, what's wrong? You're scaring me.'

'I don't … don't understand. How …'

'How what?'

'I woke up and … and I thought … I was sure … I thought *you* had her.'

'What do you mean?'

'Mabel's not … she's not in her cot. She's gone.' Ruby hears a sharp intake of breath, followed by a scream. 'I have to go, have to call the police.'

'Ruby—'

'Come home, Amber. Come home now!'

This can't be happening, Ruby thinks, it simply can't be happening. There's been a misunderstanding, a stupid, terrible mistake. Her finger stabs at the handset, her heart racing wildly as she waits for the operator to answer.

'Police,' she says, her voice shaky. 'A missing child. She's missing, somebody's taken her. Please send somebody, please, I need somebody now.'

The operator asks her for her name and then keeps calling her by it, forcing her back into focus.

'So, Ruby, the little girl who seems to have gone missing, do you have her full—'

'Mabel Rosebud Walker. Please, I need help!'

'How old is Mabel?'

'Seven months. I told you, somebody's taken her.'

'Taken her from where?'

'From her cot, from her home!'

A slight pause. 'Are you Mabel's mother?'

'No, no, I'm her aunt. Her mother is Amber, my sister.'

'And Mabel's father?'

'George. George Walker.'

'Does he live with the family?'

'Yes!' Ruby snaps. 'But he's at a conference and my sister's away. I'm babysitting.'

'Is there anyone else who might have taken her? A grandparent? Friend? Neighbour?'

'No! They wouldn't do that. I put her in her cot last night and now she's gone.'

'Is there any sign of forced entry?'

Ruby hesitates – she didn't think to look. 'I don't know.'

'Any open windows or unlocked doors?'

'I'm not sure. Don't think so. Look, I'm not imagining it. She's gone. Somebody's taken her.'

'Okay. Don't move and don't touch anything. Tell me your address and we'll send a response team over straight away.'

The call ends. Ruby stands in the sitting room, frozen in a pose of despair. She *can't* move; if she tried, her legs would give way. Her heart is flapping against her ribcage, its wild beat reverberating through her body. Time has stopped. All she can think about is Mabel. She conjures up a vision of her, as if by concentrating hard enough she can use it as a tracking device. She has to find her before it's too late, before the trail runs cold. If Mabel never comes back, if – God have mercy – *if* the worst happens, Amber will never forgive her. Nobody will, and rightly so. She'll never forgive herself. The child was stolen while she was supposed to be looking after her, keeping her safe.

She hears the sound of police sirens approaching the house. Somehow, she needs to get downstairs to open the front door. Her legs are like jelly and her head is spinning, but she drags herself towards the doorway and along the corridor, leaning on the banister.

Don't touch anything. That was what the operator said. She takes her hand away and wobbles. The bell rings, followed by a loud knock.

'Coming,' she tries to shout, but her voice is hoarse. She descends the stairs slowly and opens the door.

'Ruby?' She nods. 'Come outside, please.' She shuffles towards the policeman, falling into his arms. He props her up and leads her slowly away. Out of the corner of her eye she sees three white ghosts walk briskly past her, carrying small metal cases.

'Just sit in the car for the moment,' says the officer, leading her to his vehicle. 'My boss is on his way to talk to you. Are you okay? Can I get you a drink of water?' She shakes her head. 'Stay there. I'll be back in a sec.' He shuts the car door, locking her in.

She stares out of the window at the intense activity going on all around her. It's unreal, like watching a crew arriving on a film set, trucking in scenery, putting props in place. Plastic tape, traffic cones, flashing blue lights. People in police costumes are talking into their radios. And she's an actress, playing the role of a young woman whose niece has mysteriously disappeared. It's all false, all fake.

Police cars have blocked off the road at either end of the terrace. An officer is closing the park gates and another is guarding the door of the corner shop, stopping people entering. Within seconds, rubberneckers gather on the other side of the railings, like birds flocking to a scattering of crumbs. Some of them hold up their phones and start to film.

She knows what they're thinking. Something terrible has happened behind the doors of number 74. A stabbing or shooting, an incident of domestic violence. Someone is dead and that woman in the car has been arrested for murder. Soon it will be all over the internet. She sees a man pointing at her and slides down in the seat, out of sight.

But this isn't an episode from a lurid TV drama, this is real. A baby has been abducted. There, she's said it – the word she's seen so many times on screen or heard on TV, the word she never thought in a million years would ever be part of her life. Her own sweet, darling Mabel has been taken from her bed, like poor Madeleine McCann. Who did it? How did they swipe her from under her nose? What do they want with her? Why do something so evil and cruel? Why, why, why? Questions pour out of her in sobs. Mabel has been abducted and the only thing she knows for certain is that it's all her fault.

CHAPTER FOURTEEN

Day one without Mabel

Amber sticks to the nearside lane of the motorway, driving well below the speed limit and refusing to overtake, no matter how slow the vehicle in front of her is travelling. It's like being a learner all over again – both hands gripping the steering wheel, brow furrowed in concentration, jaw tensed, eyes flicking between rear and wing mirrors. She listens to the sat nav like it's the voice of God, obeying every instruction, even though she knows the way like the back of her hand. I can do this, she tells herself. Then she catches sight of Mabel's empty car seat in the back, and her heart lurches violently, making the car veer suddenly to one side, as if to avoid an obstacle in the road.

Minutes after the call with Ruby, a detective inspector rang her mobile. He chose his words carefully and his gentle tone reminded her of her late father. He offered to send someone to collect her from Gaia Hall, but she refused, saying she needed to have her car and would manage.

The detective – his name escapes her – told her not to go back to William Morris Terrace, although she can't work out why. Surely that's where they should go to wait for their daughter's return. But no, she has to go to her mother's house instead, where a family liaison officer will be waiting for her. It's happening. Once these things start, they can't be stopped. There must be a protocol for missing children, systems that can quickly be put in place. She has no choice in the matter. Her role is to follow instructions and do as she's told. It's better this way. If she lets her thoughts have free rein, they'll drag her into the abyss.

Keep your eyes on the road, don't have a crash. You have to stay in one piece.

She's driving through familiar territory now. Mum still lives in the same house where she and Ruby grew up. These road junctions, zebra crossings, bus stops, this parade of shops, this library, railway station, hairdresser, chip shop and Chinese takeaway are part of her DNA. She passes the primary school she used to attend and the bank that's now a wine bar, then takes the third turning on the left: Faversham Road.

Coming here is like going back in time, becoming a child again. As she approaches the house, the strings that are holding her heart in place start to loosen. She has to make it to the front door, that's all. Then Mum will take over.

'Darling! Thank God you made it safely,' Mum says, standing on the front step. Amber shuts the car door and stumbles into the house. She falls into her mother's arms and they start to cry simultaneously. 'They'll find her,' Vicky says, her voice choked with tears. 'I know they're going to find her. She'll turn up, I promise, we have to have faith.'

'Is George here?'

'Not yet. He's on his way back from Manchester. Coming straight here.'

'Oh. Okay.' A tiny ripple of relief passes through her, but it's only temporary. She hasn't spoken to George yet. Somebody must have contacted him, because she's had about a dozen missed calls and voicemail messages on her mobile. She couldn't answer the phone while she was driving. Couldn't bear to speak to him at all.

'I've made up the bed in your old room,' Mum says. 'Do you want to go and lie down?'

'What? No! How can I lie down at a time like this? I should be out there looking for her.'

Vicky shakes her head. 'Leave it to the police. They've got it all under control, doing everything they can. Whoever's taken her won't get very far.'

'I should be doing *something*.'

A blonde woman in her forties emerges from the kitchen. 'Hi, I'm Sergeant Sally Morrison, your FLO – family liaison officer.' She holds out her hand and Amber shakes it limply. 'I can only imagine how awful this must be for you. I want you to know that I'll be here supporting you the whole way through.' Her round face and blue eyes ooze sympathy. 'How are you feeling?'

'She's utterly distraught,' Mum snaps on Amber's behalf. 'What do you expect?'

Sally doesn't react, turning instead to Amber. 'Shall we talk in the conservatory? It's nice and private in there.' The code is obvious.

'I'll make some tea,' her mother says, walking briskly into the kitchen.

Sally, who already seems to know her way around, leads Amber into what Vicky calls the sun lounge. There is no sun today, though, just a blanket of grey cloud.

'Please sit down,' she says, as if Amber is her guest.

'It feels wrong, being here.' Amber sinks awkwardly into a wicker armchair. 'I should be out searching for her. Or at least I should be at home, ready for when she comes back.'

Sally sits in the chair on the other side of the glass coffee table. 'I'm afraid that won't be possible right now,' she says gently. 'Your flat is a crime scene, you see. SOCOs are there now taking prints and DNA samples, looking for signs of entry, recovering evidence. Officers are making house-to-house enquiries, appealing for witnesses, tracking down CCTV footage. Your mother gave us a photo of Mabel. We've issued it to our search teams and they're scouring everywhere. It's been declared a major incident, Gold Command – that's as serious as it gets.' Her words are both reassuring and terrifying.

'How did they manage to take her?' Amber asks, her voice trembling.

'We don't know yet. We're trying to piece that together at the moment.' Sally stares into her eyes, demanding her full attention. 'Everything we do is evidence- and intelligence-based. We are trained not to have preconceived ideas about what might have happened. We explore every possible scenario and keep our minds constantly open.'

Amber's mouth dries. 'Yes, but what do you *think* happened?'

Sally holds out her hands. 'Like I said, we're not going to jump to conclusions. We're still assembling evidence. And you can help us with that.'

Amber looks at her blankly. 'How can I help? I wasn't there, was I?'

'These circumstances are extremely unusual. It's possible that the person who took Mabel planned the abduction. They may have known that she lived in the flat; they may even have known that you and your husband were going away for the weekend, leaving her with your sister. They may have had a key, or known where the spare was kept, or known how to get in. In other words, they may be somebody you know.'

Amber shudders. 'No, no, that's horrible.'

'You may not know them very well, or they may be somebody you used to know in the past. Somebody you fell out with. I want you to think really, really hard.'

'Nobody we know would ever do something like that. It's evil.'

Sally pauses, nodding. 'I know it's shocking, but often the answer is closer to home than we realise. So it's really important that you tell us the truth.'

Amber flinches. The truth is a bullet she's been dodging for some time now. 'Why wouldn't I tell you the truth? My daughter is missing!'

'I've worked in Child Protection for many years,' Sally says steadily. 'Most child abductions are committed by parents, often fathers who've been denied access by court orders.'

'Well not in this case, obviously,' Amber says, feeling herself prickling all over. 'You're barking up the wrong tree there.'

But Sally will not be dissuaded. 'As I understand it, you and your husband are together. You're not going through a separation or divorce? You both live with Mabel full-time and parent her jointly?'

'Yes, of course! What are you implying?'

Sally shifts uncomfortably on the padded cushions. 'I'm just trying to build up an accurate picture of Mabel's home life, that's all. You both went away for the weekend, separately, leaving her with your sister. That's quite an unusual thing to do, if you don't mind my saying, with a baby so young. Was there some particular reason for doing it?'

'You're asking a lot of intrusive questions,' says Amber defensively. 'You're judging me!'

'Not at all, I'm sorry if you—'

'You should be concentrating on Mabel, not me. She's out there somewhere, somebody's got her! We've got to find her before … before …' She doesn't complete the sentence.

Sally nods. 'It's true, time is not on our side; we have to work quickly, which means we can't always be as sensitive as we'd like to be.' She leans forward. 'Can you think of *anyone* – family, friends, acquaintances – who might think Mabel belongs to them?'

Amber stares at her. 'No! How could anyone possibly think that? They'd have to be mad.'

Sally remains undeterred. 'I'm really sorry to have to ask you this, Amber, but it's important, if only to rule it out … Is there anybody else who might have reason to believe he is Mabel's father?'

Amber's temper flares. 'How dare you even ask me that?'

'I'm sorry if I offended you, but please understand, we have to explore every possible line of enquiry. Our overwhelming priority is Mabel's safety; that's all we care about here.'

'You think *I* don't care? I'm her mother! She's my baby and she's gone! I can't take any more of this. This is a waste of time.'

Sally stands up. 'My gaffer, DI John Benedict, is on his way. I believe you spoke to him on the phone earlier. He'll want to talk to you again as soon as George arrives. I'm afraid he'll probably ask you all the same questions. I'm sure you understand we have to be thorough.' Amber glares at her. 'I'll … er … let you rest now.' She makes a tactical retreat.

Amber can't contain her emotions a second longer. A tsunami of anger, guilt and fear – dark, icy fear – rises in her throat and bursts forth in loud, ugly sobs.

'Now, now, this won't help.' Vicky enters with a cup of tea. She puts it down and tussles with her daughter, pinning her arms against her sides and holding her tightly. 'You must stay calm for Mabel,' she says. 'You're no good to her in this state.'

'I've lost her!' Amber wails. 'It's all my fault. I should never have left her with Ruby. She's *my* baby, mine! I wanted her so much, too much, and now she's gone, she's probably already dead! I'm a terrible mother, a wicked, terrible mother, and this is my punishment, this is my fault.'

'Stop this now! Listen to me.' Vicky shakes her by the shoulders. 'This is *not* your fault. There's a simple explanation for all this, it's going to be all right. Mabel is alive, I'm sure of it. She's safe and well, I can feel it in my bones.'

*

Amber is lying down in her childhood bedroom, pretending to have a headache, although a genuine pain is building behind her eyes. It's safer here, away from the wretched family liaison officer, who seems to scoop up her every word and gesture, popping it into an invisible evidence bag for later analysis.

She wants to call Seth, but daren't. Are the police able to recover deleted texts? One look at her mobile bill would betray her. They haven't asked to see her phone yet, or checked her alibi. Why would they? She's not a suspect. If only she could summon Seth before her, like a genie from a lamp. She conjures his voice in her head. 'Try not to panic,' he'd say. 'Stay calm. Mabel is safe. Everything is going to be all right.'

She tries to imagine where Mabel is right now and what she's doing. Is she missing her? She hopes she's not upset, that whoever has got her is looking after her properly. It's hard to picture her daughter when she doesn't know what she's wearing. One of her sleepsuits, presumably. Ruby will know – she must ask her. Except she doesn't want to speak to her sister.

The bell has rung again. Who is it this time? There have been numerous comings and goings this past hour – the front door opening and closing, unfamiliar voices in the hallway, heavy footsteps on the parquet flooring. Usually, this is a strictly take-your-shoes off house, but not today. Her mother hates visitors because they leave traces that she then has to eradicate – a toilet seat left up, a badly folded towel, stray hairs, human smells … Will she cast these neuroses aside in the light of the current crisis, or will she cling to them more tightly than ever?

The doorbell rings again. Amber holds her breath as she listens. Yes, that's George's voice. She is instantly filled with dread. He has stepped into the hallway and Sally is introducing herself. There's another voice, a man. He and George have a brief exchange. She can't make out what they're saying.

'Where's Amber?' George's tone is demanding. Footsteps bound up the stairs. She dives for cover, head under the pillow, holding it tightly against her ears as she waits for the explosion. The door opens and he bursts in.

'Why didn't you ring? Why didn't you pick up my calls?' he says accusingly. 'I've been going out of my mind!' He pulls the pillow off her and throws it on the bed.

She starts to sit up. 'I couldn't, I was driving.'

'Driving? You mean you were out looking for Mabel?'

'No. Driving home.'

He screws up his face, unable to comprehend. 'Driving home from where?'

She braces herself. 'I was on a yoga retreat.'

'A yoga retreat?'

'Please don't keep repeating what I've said.'

'But I don't understand. What do you mean, you went to an early-morning class or something?'

'No, it was a weekend – in Somerset.'

He stares at her as the words gradually gather meaning. 'Oh my God,' he gasps. 'You mean she was with Ruby when …'

'Yes. I'm sorry. I couldn't face looking after her on my own. I had to get away.'

'Why didn't you tell me?' he says, rushing forward and shaking her by the shoulders. 'Why? If I'd known you were that bad, I would have stayed. I would never have let Ruby look after her the whole weekend.'

'But nothing happened the last time; she did a good job. I wasn't to know …'

He releases her and stands back, breathing heavily through his nose. 'What happened? How did the bastard get in? Did she leave the front door open or something?'

'We don't know. The police are trying to work it out. Ruby's helping.'

'If anything's happened to Mabel, I'll kill her. And as for you …'

'I'm so, so sorry,' Amber says again, but she knows he can't hear her.

'We can't stay here talking and doing nothing,' he says, pacing about. 'We need to be on the streets. I'll get a search party together, friends, neighbours, guys from the gym. We have to get the word out on social media.'

'I think the police are doing everything—'

'She's *my* daughter – it's my job to find her!'

'Don't shout, please don't shout.'

There's a knock on the bedroom door. George and Amber exchange a glance.

'DI Benedict here,' a gruff male voice says. 'May I come in?'

George marches across the room and opens the door. The detective stands on the threshold. He is unusually tall, with blue eyes, olive skin and thick black hair peppered with grey. Why is he standing there? Does he have news?

'Well?' says George. 'Have you found her?'

He shakes his head. 'I'm afraid not, not yet, but we're putting all our resources into it. Hundreds of officers are—'

'I want to join the search party,' George interrupts.

'Of course, but right now, you're of more use here.'

George looks askance. 'Here? How?'

'For a start, we need to take DNA samples from you both. For elimination purposes. We've taken samples from Mabel's cot and changing unit. I need a list of everyone who's visited the house recently, their contact details and so on. And I want to talk to you about friends, neighbours, acquaintances, anyone you've fallen out with, anything out of the ordinary that's happened these last few weeks, anyone you've seen hanging around, suspicious phone calls, notes through the door, that kind of thing.'

'I've already spoken to Sally,' says Amber. She can't bear the thought of DI Benedict asking her the same excruciating questions all over again, especially not in front of George.

'Yes, I know, and she's debriefed me. I'd like to talk to you together first, and then separately. We can do it at the police station if you need more privacy.'

'You're making it sound like we're suspects,' says George icily.

'No, you're witnesses,' DI Benedict replies. 'Extremely important ones. You may not realise it, but you may already have the information that will lead us to Mabel.'

George gives him a grudging nod. 'Okay, let's do it here, quick as we can. Then I want to get out on the streets.'

CHAPTER FIFTEEN

Day one without Mabel

Ruby frowns as DS Ali Smart hammers away with her questions.

'Can you just take me through that again? You say all the doors and windows were definitely locked?'

'Yes.'

'At what time did you make your final checks?'

'What do you mean?'

'Last night, before you went to bed, you went around locking up, yes?'

Ruby hesitates. The idea of patrolling the flat like a security guard is completely alien to her. She's not even very good at turning off the lights at night, much to Lewis's irritation.

'No, not as such,' she replies finally. 'There was nothing to do. It was too cold to have windows open and I knew the front door was already locked so I didn't bother going downstairs to check.'

'I see …' The detective leans forward, elbows on the table, chin resting on her clasped hands. 'When you say "already locked", what do you mean by that? Precisely?'

'Um … well, I mean it was locked, like normal, with a Yale key, you know, the sort that locks automatically when you close the door.'

'You didn't use the five-lever deadlock or the bolts?'

'No. I wasn't given the deadlock key and I had no idea there were bolts.'

DS Smart looks mildly disbelieving. 'There are two, apparently, top and bottom.'

'Oh, right. Sorry, I hadn't noticed. It's not my flat ... and Amber didn't mention them.'

'No?'

'No.'

'Did she specifically ask you *not* to use the deadlock or bolts?'

'No. She gave me a load of other instructions about Mabel, but nothing like that. I guess she just assumed ...' Ruby tails off as she sees the detective freeze. She instantly knows what's troubling her, and now it's troubling her too. Why would Amber, who's so anal about protecting Mabel, be so relaxed about home security? Particularly when she knows Ruby is casual about such things to the point of negligence.

'What about your brother-in-law, George?' the detective continues. 'Before he left for his conference, did he remind you to lock up properly?'

'No.'

'Like Amber, he just assumed you'd remember to do it.'

'He didn't know I was looking after Mabel by myself. He thought, um ...' Ruby pauses, aware of the implications of what she's about to say. 'He thought Amber was going to be there too.'

'Oh, so he didn't know about the ... what was it?' She flicks through her notes. 'Yes, the yoga weekend. Why was it a secret?'

'Look, it's nothing to do with me. You'll have to ask Amber about it.'

'Yes, of course.'

DS Smart writes a note, then pushes the pad across the table to show her colleague. He nods, rises and leaves the room. Ruby feels sick. That's two suspicious marks against Amber. She didn't mean to dump her in it, but she couldn't help it; she has to tell the truth. Come to think of it, why *did* Amber lie to George?

'How are you feeling?' DS Smart says, after a pause. 'Can I get you another drink? Tea, coffee, glass of water?'

'No thanks.'

'I'm sorry to have to ask you all these questions, but they're extremely important.'

'I understand. I'll do anything to help find Mabel.'

The detective sits back in her chair, adjusting the front of her crisp blue shirt. 'Okay, so given that there were no doors or windows left open, no signs of forced entry, how do you think the abductor managed to get inside the flat?'

'I've no idea,' Ruby says. 'It's really bugging me.'

'Was your sister or brother-in-law in the habit of leaving a spare key somewhere – under the doormat, in a flowerpot?'

She almost laughs. 'No. They'd never do that. Not in a million years.'

'Anyone lost a key recently?'

'Not that I know of; you'll have to ask them.'

'What about you? Have you ever lost your key?'

'I'm not allowed my own key – I always borrow the spare.' She briefly remembers last weekend, when she couldn't find the key to give back to Amber. But it turned up later so that doesn't count. 'I've never lost it,' she adds.

The detective smacks her lips together. 'Okay, let's put aside the method of entry for now. All we know at this stage is that someone, somehow managed to enter the flat ... so the next thing that puzzles me is this, Ruby. How did the abductor manage to take a seven-month-old baby out of her cot and carry her downstairs without you hearing a peep?'

Ruby shrugs. 'I was on the floor above, fast asleep. Whoever it was switched off the baby monitor.'

'You didn't hear footsteps or creaks on the stairs, the front door opening and closing?'

'No. Nothing.'

'Surely Mabel must have woken up at some point? I'm really surprised you didn't hear any crying.'

'So am I, but I sleep very deeply – always have done. I often don't hear the alarm in the morning. My boyfriend has to wake me up.'

'Really?'

Yes, really, she thinks. Lewis says she could sleep for England, although now Mabel has been taken, she doubts she'll ever be able to sleep again.

Ruby walks out of the police station in a daze. She has spent the last two hours going over everything again and again in minute detail, and now she's exhausted. The more she talked, the less clear and more unreal it seemed. There were moments when it felt like she was making the entire thing up, recounting somebody else's tragedy about an abducted baby called Mabel and a negligent babysitter by the name of Ruby. Part of her brain still believes this kind of thing doesn't happen to people like her.

A taxi is waiting to take her home. She climbs onto the back seat and confirms her address. The car pulls away, leaving the police station car park and joining the sluggish Sunday traffic. Switching her phone back on, Ruby texts Lewis to tell him she's on her way. They only managed a brief conversation earlier. He sounded utterly grief-stricken, which surprised her. Not because Lewis is an uncaring person – quite the opposite – but she hadn't expected him to be able to process the news so quickly, or to respond with such emotion. She still feels outside of herself, not properly in touch with how she must surely feel within.

She cannot, *will* not, imagine the worst. Mabel will be returned, like a parcel that's gone astray. Very little post is actually lost forever. It may be delivered to the wrong address or not have enough stamps for its weight; it may sit on a sideboard for a few weeks before someone bothers to put it back in the postbox. But it always turns up eventually – maybe a little bent and creased, but safe nonetheless. Things don't vanish into thin air, as her mother used to say in an exasperated tone every time Ruby lost something. It's the same with people. They are always somewhere, waiting to be found. You just have to keep on looking.

The journey passes without her being aware of it, and suddenly the driver is drawing up on the double yellow line outside their block. She pays him then gets out and stumbles towards the large metal gate. Suddenly unable to remember the entry code, she has to press the bell. The gate clicks open immediately and Lewis comes out to meet her on the path.

'Oh Ruby,' he says.

She lets herself be enveloped in his embrace, and they stand locked together for a few moments, not saying anything, just listening to each other breathing. 'Come on, let's go inside.' He guides her gently into their flat.

As soon as he shuts the door behind them, Ruby lets out a long howl, like an animal caught in a trap.

'It's all my fault,' she wails.

'That's it, let it all out,' he says, helping her into the lounge and lowering her onto the sofa. He lifts her legs up and puts a cushion behind her head.

'Mabel's gone and it's all my fault!'

'That's not true, you can't say that. It could have happened to anyone.'

'A stranger took her and I didn't hear a bloody thing.'

'You were fast asleep.'

She picks up a cushion and hugs it to her as the tears run down her face. 'I should have stayed awake all night, I should have had her in the bed with me, I should never, never have left her downstairs on her own.'

'Amber and George do it.'

'That's not the point – I was looking after her and she wasn't safe.'

'You weren't to know …'

She throws the cushion to the floor. 'And this morning, I completely messed up! When someone goes missing, the first hour is the most important – the golden hour, they call it. I should have rung the police straight away, but I spent time looking for Amber. I thought she'd taken Mabel without telling me. I didn't think, it didn't occur to me that …'

'No, of course it didn't,' he soothes. 'I'd have made the same mistake.' She cries out in pain, and he quickly corrects himself. 'I mean, I would have done exactly the same thing.'

She looks up at him with liquid eyes. 'Really? You mean that?'

'Yes.'

'Oh. Thank you,' she whispers.

'Do you want a glass of wine? I know I need one.' She nods. He fetches a bottle of red and pours two large glasses. 'Here, get that down you. You're in shock.'

Ruby takes the glass and starts to drink. The wine makes its way to her head, and she immediately feels woozy. Lewis sits on the edge of the sofa and strokes her legs.

'I begged you to come with me, but you wouldn't,' she says.

'I had to work.'

She wipes her cheeks with the sleeve of her jumper. 'If you'd been there, they wouldn't have dared.'

'How on earth did they get in?'

She shrugs. 'The police are still trying to work it out. The detective who interviewed me seemed to think they might have had a key.'

Lewis's eyebrows rise. 'Really? Well, that narrows it down a bit. Who has keys? Cleaners … neighbours … builders?' He tips his glass, thinking. 'Hang on, the flat used to be a rental, didn't it? Did Amber and George change the locks when they moved in?'

'Probably, knowing them.'

'If they didn't, it could be a previous tenant. There could be dozens of spares knocking around.'

Ruby jolts. 'I hadn't thought of that. Should I mention it to the police?'

'Not now.' He pats her. 'You've been through enough for one day. They're bound to ask Amber and George about it.'

'My chest is so tight, Lew, there's this hard lump right here. It's like a piece of my heart has broken off and got stuck. It really hurts.'

'Just try to relax.'

'How can I, when she's out there somewhere, all on her own?' She sniffs up more tears. 'Have you spoken to Amber?'

'No. Nothing from George, either, but your mother left a message on the answerphone.'

'Oh?' She makes a move towards the machine, but he raises his hand.

'Don't listen to it. She was very upset; I'm sure she didn't mean some of the things she said, but I would steer clear of her place for now.'

'I knew she'd blame me.' Ruby drains her glass, then holds it out for a refill.

'Amber and George are staying with her tonight because they can't go back to the flat.'

'No, it's a crime scene.' Ruby watches the red liquid glug out of the bottle. 'They took my DNA. I've never had that done before. It made me feel so guilty.'

'You didn't do anything wrong.'

'Amber will never forgive me, not even if Mabel's found safe and well. Nor will Mum. The family's broken forever. I'm an outcast.'

Lewis shakes his head. 'How many more times, it wasn't your fault, just bad luck. If the guy had a key …'

'We don't know it's a guy.'

'Well, paedos are usually male.'

She rounds on him. 'We don't know it's a paedo! Please don't say that, I can't bear it. This is Mabel we're talking about – our Mabel!' Her eyes flash angrily.

'We have to face facts,' he says, standing up and walking restlessly across the room. 'That's what usually happens in these cases. Either the child just vanishes and is never seen again, or they're found d—'

'Please, Lewis, just stop!'

He holds up his hands in surrender and returns to the sofa.

They sit in silence for a few moments, each fighting off their own dark thoughts.

'We've got to be positive,' she continues. 'We don't have any facts, not yet. Anyone could have her. They might be looking after her really well.'

'Let's hope so,' he says, but she can tell he doesn't believe it. 'The police must have suspicions about who might have taken her. They have lists.'

She takes a sip and swills the wine thoughtfully around her mouth. 'They seem to think I've got something to do with it.'

'What do you mean?'

'I don't know, I just got the impression they thought I was lying. Covering up.'

'That's insane. Why would you do that?'

'They can smell a rat, I'm sure of it. Mabel wasn't taken from a hospital, or lured into a car, or stolen from a caravan or a camp-site – she was in her own home, with all the doors and windows closed and no sign of anyone forcing their way in. Whoever took her knew exactly where and when to find her. And what's more, she didn't wake up. Which makes me think maybe she was taken by someone she knew.'

'What are you trying to say, Rubes?' he asks slowly.

She wrestles the idea reluctantly out of its hiding place. 'I don't know exactly. But Amber's been acting really strangely lately, completely out of character. I put it down to postnatal depression, but I think it's more than that – or maybe she's not depressed at all. She's definitely been lying to George, and probably to me too. I get the feeling she's up to something.'

'What do you mean?'

She sits up straight. 'What if it wasn't a coincidence that I was looking after Mabel on my own last night? What if it was all part of the plan?'

CHAPTER SIXTEEN

Day two without Mabel

Amber refuses to go to bed, even though it's well past midnight. Eating, sleeping, washing and dressing are of no interest to her right now. She doesn't care if she stinks to high heaven; she'll wear the same clothes until Mabel is found.

'At least go and lie down,' her mother says. 'You need to rest. Keep your strength up.'

'She's right,' adds George. 'We've done all we can for today.'

'But I haven't done anything!'

'You've been helping the police.'

She sighs heavily. 'Not really. Not like you.'

After their interviews with DI Benedict, George insisted on driving to Waltham Green to look for Mabel. He wanted her to go with him, but she said she didn't have the strength. Besides, she knew it would be a waste of time. He was gone for hours, and when he returned, frazzled and defeated, he looked as if he'd aged ten years.

'Shall I make some hot chocolate?' her mother asks. They both shake their heads.

'Just go to bed, Mum. Please.'

'There's no point, I won't sleep.' Vicky rises from the armchair. 'It's getting chilly. If we're going to stay up all night, I'd better put the heating back on.' She leaves the room. Amber hears the whoosh of the boiler reigniting, the chink of crockery, the hum of the kettle – the sounds of her mother's heart breaking. Mum adores Mabel, although she hasn't been as active a grandmother as Amber expected. Maybe she regrets that now, Amber thinks, blaming herself for letting Ruby babysit when it should have been her job. Or maybe she's relieved that it wasn't her in charge.

George and Amber sit in uneasy silence for a few minutes. There's everything and nothing to say. They haven't been on their own together since George first arrived and lost his temper. The calm between them now is born of exhaustion, nothing more. Tomorrow, the blame game will doubtless be resumed. Amber has never felt so lonely. She's standing on an island, surrounded by a treacherous sea of secrets. Nobody can reach her. Only Seth, but she's afraid to contact him.

She yawns. Her legs ache with tiredness and she feels faintly sick. Hugging herself against the cold, she closes her eyes for a few moments and finds herself back in the interview with DI Benedict. All those questions … It was supposed to be a witness statement, but it felt more like an interrogation. She stepped carefully over his conversational tripwires, and stopped herself filling his deliberate pauses with nervous incriminating chatter. Despite that, she knows he knows she's lying – although probably not what about. Not yet, anyway.

She doesn't trust the family liaison officer either. She's meant to be supporting them, but Amber senses she's been put in the house to spy and eavesdrop on their conversations. Thankfully, she has gone home now, but she'll be back first thing in the morning. They need to be careful what they say in front of her; they need to present a united front.

Her mother comes back in carrying a mug of hot chocolate and a small plate of custard creams. She's done nothing all day but make drinks and arrange biscuits.

'Are you sure I can't get you anything?' she asks for the ump-teenth time.

'No!' retorts Amber.

'No thanks,' says George.

Vicky sits down and cradles her mug in her hands. 'I expect they've packed in the search for the night,' she says, thinking aloud.

Amber makes an agreeing noise. Part of her wants her mother to shut up and go to bed, but another part is grateful that she's acting as a buffer zone between her and George.

'Did the police ask you about people who'd visited the flat recently?' George says. Amber nods.

'I can't think why they needed to interview you together and then all over again separately,' her mother chips in.

'It's in case there's something we don't want to say in front of each other,' explains Amber. Her mother pulls a face to say she understands but still thinks it's wrong.

'I felt bad giving names of family and friends,' says George.

Amber shrugs. 'They want to test their DNA, that's all. For elimination—'

'Yes, I know … Still embarrassing. I don't want them to think we suspect them.'

'They'll understand.'

She's surprised by how small the number of regular and/or recent visitors to the flat is. Yet more evidence, if it were needed, of how much her social life has shrunk. They were always inviting friends over before Mabel was born, but hardly anyone comes by now. More often than not, her weekdays are spent alone. DI Benedict asked her about her mental health in a way that made her think somebody had told him she was depressed. George, she guessed, or possibly Ruby? She denied it, of course.

'Well, I might as well wash up those mugs,' says Vicky, rising the instant she finishes her drink. Amber can't stand her restlessness – it's making her feel tense. 'Then maybe I'll lie down for a bit. I won't be asleep. If you need me, just shout.'

'Okay,' Amber says.

'I've been thinking,' says George, as soon as Vicky leaves the room, 'I really hate even mentioning it, but I think I should put it out there …' He pauses.

'What?'

'It's just a theory, but the more I think about it, the more it makes sense.'

'What?!'

He takes a deep breath. 'Ruby.'

'What about Ruby?'

'I think she's lying about Mabel being taken from the cot.'

Amber's face puckers into a frown. 'Sorry, I don't … I mean, why would she? She's devastated. She wants the police to find Mabel as much as we do.'

'Hmm …' His lips purse together. 'We only have her word for what happened.'

'That's because she's the only witness. So far anyway.'

George clears his throat. 'What if – I know this is going to sound dreadful, but hear me out – what if there was an accident?'

Amber's blood chills. 'What do you mean? What sort of accident?'

'You know what Ruby's like; she doesn't concentrate, she forgets things … What if there was an accident and – well – Mabel got hurt. Badly. Like she suffocated or fell and hit her head. I'm not saying it was deliberate, but what if Ruby accidentally—'

'No … no … don't. Stop it, I won't hear it.'

He grasps her hands and takes them away from her ears. 'She could have hidden Mabel somewhere and then pretended she'd been abducted.'

Amber swallows hard. 'That's a disgusting thing to say. Why on earth would she do that?'

'Easy. She was afraid to admit what had happened because she knew we'd never forgive her.'

'No … that's … that's not what happened.'

'You said yourself she was always breaking things and lied to cover it up.'

'When she was a kid, yes, but not now.' A memory flashes before her – Mum in tears because her cut-glass vase, an anniversary present from their father, had mysteriously disappeared. She called the girls downstairs, demanding explanations, although she knew full well that Amber wasn't involved. Ruby hotly denied she'd broken the vase. She claimed she'd seen a burglar climbing out of the window with it under his arm – she was so convincing, Mum nearly called the police. But Amber knew her sister had been practising acrobatics in the sitting room earlier. She searched Ruby's bedroom and found the broken pieces of glass wrapped in newspaper hidden under the bed.

'Do you think I should mention it to the police?' George says.

'I expect they've already thought of it.' Amber looks down at her fingers, twisting in her lap. 'Sally said they consider every possibility, no matter how unlikely. And they will definitely have interviewed Ruby by now.'

'Yeah, but they don't know what she's like.'

Amber bristles. 'She's not a murderer, George. She's just a bit … ditzy.'

'I said it was an accident. She panicked, didn't know what to do. Mabel was—'

'Don't talk about her as if she's dead.'

'I'm not, I'm just trying to work it out. The police aren't stupid; they know Ruby's story doesn't add up.'

'I still can't believe my own sister would do something so appalling just to save her own skin.'

'Wouldn't she?' presses George. 'You don't know that for sure. You've no idea what she'd do when pushed to extremes … I'm going to tell DI Benedict tomorrow. He needs to know.'

When she wakes, Amber is lying fully clothed on top of the bed. She has no memory of climbing the stairs and going into the bedroom. How long was she asleep? Minutes? Hours? She should have fought back the yawns, propped her eyes open with matchsticks. She promised she would stay awake until there was news, and she's fallen at the first hurdle.

Mabel is missing. *Still* missing. The realisation jolts through her like an electric shock. She will never get used to this. Every morning, she'll feel her guts tearing apart again. Every evening, the day's hope will be flushed away in fresh tears. This is why she mustn't sleep – the agony of waking and experiencing it all again, day after day, will be too much to bear.

Turning over, she sees George lying next to her. He's on his back, eyes wide open, staring at the ceiling.

'You're awake too,' he says.

The room is dressed in greys. It feels like neither night nor morning. 'What time is it?'

He picks up his phone and checks. 'Half five.'

A lump rises in her throat. That's the time Mabel usually wakes. She chokes as she remembers how she used to moan about those early mornings, being dragged from deepest sleep by the gurgling baby monitor. How sometimes she would bury her head beneath the pillow and wait until the sounds grew louder and more insistent before going downstairs to Mabel. It was a terrible mistake to have the nursery on the floor below, to put so much faith in a baby monitor. If – when – Mabel comes back, she'll let her sleep in their bed every night, snuggled safely between them.

Tears drip down her face. Is there no end to the constant stream of guilt she's pouring over herself? She will drown in it.

A new day is dawning. Monday, day two of life without Mabel. The second of how many? she wonders. She imagines time stretching before her, days becoming weeks, months, then years. The relentless pain of not knowing whether her daughter is alive or dead. No news is good news, that's what her mother keeps saying, but she can't find any comfort in the tired old adage.

Maybe George is right and there was an accident. She should talk to Ruby, have it out face to face. If she looks her straight in the eyes, she'll know whether she's lying. Or her mother will – she knows Ruby best.

George sits up and swings his legs over the side of the bed. He rubs his eyes and runs his fingers roughly through his hair. It takes a great effort for him to stand, and when he gets to his feet, he sways for a few seconds before finding his balance. He's broken, she thinks, watching as he puts on the previous day's socks, shirt and smart trousers. All he has with him are work clothes. Sally said they could give her a list of what they wanted from the flat and somebody would bring it over. But Amber couldn't think of anything. Mabel. That's all she wants. Mabel.

'Tea?' he asks.

'Yeah, if you like.' She sits up. 'Don't bring it up. I'll come down with you, see what's happening.'

'Nothing's happening,' he says. 'Everyone else is asleep.'

The doorbell rings at 7 a.m. sharp. George goes to answer it, with Amber close behind. He opens the door to find Sally standing on the step. 'Have they found her?' he says anxiously.

Sally gives him an encouraging smile. 'Not yet. The searches resumed at dawn. First forensic results should be back later today.' She enters, shutting the door behind her. 'How are you both?'

George shrugs. 'What do you think?'

Amber's mum comes down the stairs, also still wearing yesterday's clothes. 'Well? Any news?' Her voice cracks with hope. They all shake their heads.

'Any chance of a cup of tea, Mrs Evans?' Sally asks, taking off her coat and hanging it in the coat cupboard, like she knows where everything goes.

'Call me Vicky,' Mum replies. 'Toast and marmalade all round?'

'Lovely.'

'Yeah, thanks,' says George.

'How can you even think of eating at a time like this?' Amber looks at them accusingly.

'It's just a bit of toast, babe. You should try and eat too.'

Mum nods. 'Keep your strength up.'

'If you say that again, I'm going to scream!'

There's an awkward pause. Mum disappears into the kitchen. Sally suggests that the three of them have a chat, and leads them into the lounge. Amber curses herself as she sits on the sofa. She shouldn't have snapped like that.

'Sorry,' she says. 'It's just – you know – the stress.'

'All perfectly normal,' Sally replies. 'Now … to update you. I'm afraid the whole thing has exploded on social media. There are some awful stories circulating on Twitter, some very, um … harsh comments. I'm sorry, there's nothing we can do to stop it. It happens every time there's a case like this.'

George clasps Amber's hand. 'What are they saying?'

'Just the usual nasty stuff. Really, you don't want to know. I'd strongly advise you not to go online, and *definitely* not to respond.' She shudders. 'Some people are disgusting. My boss wanted to wait until we had a clearer picture before doing a press conference, but there's no choice now. We need to take control of the media flow before it gets out of hand.'

'Surely the sooner people know Mabel's missing, the better,' says George. 'Witnesses might come forward. Somebody might know where she is, they might have seen her. It can't be easy to hide a baby.'

'It depends on the circumstances. Every situation is different and requires a different approach. This case is …' Sally struggles for the word, 'unusual. We have to tread very carefully so as not to panic the person who has your daughter. Getting Mabel back safe and well is the number one priority. It dictates everything we do.'

'So you think she's alive?' says Amber.

'So far, we've no reason to think otherwise. Our hope is that whoever has got her is looking after her, caring for her. We don't want to do anything that might jeopardise that. At the same time, we're keeping our minds open. Following every lead, no matter how small.'

Amber nods. 'I understand.'

'What about Ruby?' says George. 'She's been questioned, presumably.'

Sally swings her head round to look at him. 'Yes, we've been talking a lot to Ruby,' she replies evenly. 'She was the last person to see Mabel, which makes her a significant witness.'

George huffs. 'Too right. So what did you guys think? Is she telling the truth?'

There's a pause. Amber can almost hear Sally's antennae buzzing. It's scaring her.

'Why do you ask that?' Sally says, training her gaze on them. 'Is there some reason you think she might be lying?'

Amber doesn't know what to think. Has her sister changed, or can she still not be trusted? She closes her eyes and sees pieces of shattered glass.

CHAPTER SEVENTEEN

Day two with Mabel

I lean over the side of the cot and gently stroke Mabel's cheek. She has fallen asleep at last, poor darling. No wonder she's fretful. She's in strange surroundings with only my unfamiliar self to care for her, but I'll give her lots of care and in time she'll settle down and learn to love me. She'll be far happier here in the country. I hated her being cooped up in that tiny flat, with no garden and all that London pollution. The air is fresh here and the landscape is far prettier than Lilac Park.

'We're safe here, my darling,' I whisper. 'Nobody will find us.'

The afternoon sun is streaming through the window and shining on her face. I walk over to the window and draw the heavy floral curtains, then tiptoe from the room. There's no need for a baby monitor here. Everything is on the one level and my bedroom is right next door. She will never be more than a few feet from my side.

I feel drained, fatigued by the frantic planning as much as the execution. I found it hard to drop off last night; my brain was buzzing and I had backache from the long drive. My sleep was fitful and light – one ear always listening out for Mabel in case she woke. But miraculously she slept through until 6 a.m.

We had a lovely morning pottering around, getting to know our new home. I showed her all the rooms and took her briefly into the garden, although we didn't stay there long because it was so chilly. The back lawn is very overgrown, the grass tufted with dandelions. In a few weeks they will turn to seed fairies and we can have fun blowing them apart.

I let out a yawn and rub my eyes. I would love a nap, but I can't afford it. I must use the time when Mabel sleeps productively, because when she's awake, she must have my undivided attention.

My first job is to clean the kitchen units properly. The surfaces are dusty and the insides of the cabinets are greasy and smell stale. Don't want nasty germs in the house, giving Mabel an upset tummy. Bending down, I open the cupboard beneath the sink. There is a bottle of bleach, some old-fashioned scouring powder, plenty of cloths and a pair of yellow rubber gloves. As I run a bucket of hot water, I send a heavenly thank you to Great-Aunt Dolly, who lived here on her own until she died eighteen months ago.

Dolly, or Dorothy to give her proper name, was a primary school teacher, wedded to her vocation rather than to any man. I only knew her by reputation – according to my grandmother, she was opinionated and cared little for her appearance. I think I met her at a family wedding once when I was a child, but that was it. She led a solitary life. Not having any family of her own, she left the house to me in her will, with the rest of her estate going to an educational charity for girls in Africa. Frankly, I was surprised she knew I existed.

When I was told that I'd inherited Midsummer Cottage, I pictured a thatched roof, oak beams and roses around the door. Excited and intrigued, I hurried down to Dorset immediately. I was greeted by a single-storey rectangular building rendered in grubby white concrete. The outer walls were streaked with green mildew and the window frames had rotted. It looked more like a scout hut than somebody's home.

Inside, the decor was more cottage-like: dark wooden furniture, heavy brocade curtains, patterned carpets (different in every room), tapestry cushions (probably stitched by Dolly's own hand), cheap china ornaments on the heavy sideboard, and on the walls a collection of horse brasses and several paintings of dogs. It had a certain fusty charm, but none of it was to my taste. It was what an estate agent would call 'a project'.

I started to fantasise about refurbishing the place from top to bottom, or even pulling the bungalow down and rebuilding from scratch. It was all part of my fairy-tale vision of the future. Midsummer Cottage would make a wonderful holiday home for the family I was planning. Our children would run wild and free, we'd teach them the names of birds and flowers and trees, we'd take them fishing in the stream and build campfires in the garden. *Then* we'd be happy.

At that time, we were still together and the relationship, whilst up and down, was going through a good patch. We stole a weekend away to inspect the place. Rather than book into some boutique hotel, as was our usual habit, we decided to camp out in the cottage, just for the fun of it. We would embrace the hideous decor, dingy lighting, dodgy boiler, rattling windows and broken oven; even the toilet that took about ten minutes to refill. Everything was uncomfortable and inconvenient, but it was fun, and a relief not to have internet access, a landline or even a reliable mobile signal. Nobody could hassle us or pin down our location. It was the perfect romantic hiding place.

I can see us now, standing in the poky lounge that first evening, opening a bottle of champagne and filling two of Dolly's sherry glasses to the brim. We couldn't find more suitable glasses and had to constantly top up. I arranged a platter of antipasti bought from the luxury deli in London – sourdough bread, farmer's pâté, sweet roasted peppers, Serrano ham, giant green olives, fresh anchovies sprinkled with garlic. We covered the horrendous carpet with an Indian throw and picnicked by candlelight.

Later, we decamped drunkenly to the bedroom and snuggled beneath Dolly's satin eiderdown, which smelt of mothballs and lavender water. We bounced around on the creaky springs and made sweet, sweet love, while the rain splashed over the broken guttering and the wind whistled down the chimney.

When everything went so horribly wrong, I lost interest in Midsummer Cottage. I almost lost interest in living at all. Submerged in grief, I forgot the place existed – or pretended to forget. There were delays with probate, but I stopped chasing the solicitor. I couldn't bear to visit the place because the memories were too painful. Let it rot, I thought, just as my life is rotting. But now I see that it was all meant to be. Dolly's gift is far more important than I or she could have imagined.

I dry the inside of the cupboards with paper towels, then put the shopping away. When the food runs out, I will buy fruit and veg from roadside stalls, paying in cash, using honesty boxes when I can. Longer-term, I will dig up the garden and grow my own. The days will become longer and warmer, the earth will soften. All I need is a few seeds. When Mabel learns to walk, she can help me with the weeding. I'll plant sunflowers and she can watch them grow up the side of the house.

She's stirring. I can hear her kicking her legs against the mattress and cooing to herself. Time for her afternoon feed. I put a pan of water on the hob to heat her bottle, then go into her room.

'Hello, my lovely,' I say, picking her up. She throws her head back and gives me a strange look. She doesn't recognise me yet, but she will.

'Did you have a nice sleep in your new travel cot? I'll buy you a proper one eventually, don't worry. Now, let's go into the kitchen and get your bottle, eh? And if you're a good girl, you can have something yummy to eat.'

I put her in the high chair, propping her up with one of Great-Aunt Dolly's smaller tapestry cushions. She drinks her milk enthusiastically. Then I open a jar of organic apple puree and spoon it into her mouth. She grimaces and pokes out her tongue to expel it. I try an oatcake next, which she eats with relish. So hard to know her likes and dislikes, but I'll learn.

After she's eaten, I clean her up and take her into the sitting room. The throw I used for our romantic picnic is still here, draped over the end of the sofa. I shake it out and lay it on the carpet, just like before, then sit cross-legged with Mabel tucked into the well of my lap.

'Your pretty face is probably all over the internet by now,' I say to her. 'You're going to be famous.' She makes a few jawing noises, as if she's trying to reply. 'You might even be on the news. Shall we see?' I switch on Great-Aunt Dolly's television. It's about a quarter of the size of the one I used to have and by the look of it doesn't even have Freeview. It's too early for the news, so I turn it straight off again.

Mabel does some sitting-up practice – I'm surprised she's not completely supporting herself by now – and then I roll her onto her tummy. She doesn't like it one bit and arches her back defiantly.

'I'm sorry, sweetie, but if you won't lie on your front, you'll never learn to crawl.' She gives me a very straight look, as if to say, *What do you know?* Laughing, I pick her up and give her a cuddle, tickling her until she breaks out in giggles. Her fat cheeks turn rosy pink and she dribbles spittle down her chin.

Outside, the skies are darkening. I draw the brocade curtains and turn the ancient boiler up, praying that Great-Aunt Dolly had it regularly serviced. If it conks out on us, we'll be lost.

Eager to know what's happening, I turn the television back on. Mabel and I watch a dreary game show for a while, then the six o'clock news begins. Annoyingly, the lead story is about the Queen, but we're next up. I wonder whether they will show Amber and George, whether Mabel will recognise them on screen.

A reporter is standing by the park gates. Behind him, I can just about make out number 74, taped off and guarded by police. He tells us that, in the early hours of Sunday morning, a little girl called Mabel was taken from her cot in the Lilac Park area of Waltham Green. Her parents had gone away for the weekend, leaving their seven-month-old baby in the care of a babysitter. Hmm, I detect a strong whiff of disapproval here. I'd love to know how Twitter is reacting.

The camera pans across the line of trees that face William Morris Terrace. Lilac ribbons are tied around the trunks and a small group of mothers are standing there with home-made posters featuring a fuzzy photo and the words *Mabel is Missing*. There's already a campaign with its own colour branding and a catchphrase. God, it makes me sick.

Now we're at the press conference, which apparently happened earlier today. Amber and George are shown into a room crowded with flashing cameras and hungry journalists. They sit behind a long, low table, flanked by a rather good-looking male detective and a plump middle-aged woman. Amber is pale and tearful; George is grim-faced, trying not to show his emotions. They look suitably distraught and bereft. The detective reads out a short statement, giving the bare facts, then adding the usual plea.

'If you were in the vicinity during that time and noticed any-thing unusual or saw anyone acting suspiciously, please contact us immediately on the number at the bottom of your screens now. Or call Crimestoppers on …'

Click, click, flash, flash, questions from the floor, short replies giving nothing away.

Now it's time for the main attraction – the parents. Amber will do the talking, rather than George. The mother is always more convincing, more sympathetic. This is an important moment in the investigation. The parents' performance is crucial to securing public support. Will people judge Amber and George for leaving their baby and find them guilty? Of course, they will. They'll feed them to the social media lions.

The detective passes Amber the microphone and she holds it shakily. Her eyes are red and she's cried all her make-up off. When she starts to speak, her voice sounds weak and reedy, as if the words are being pushed through water.

Now she's addressing me personally. I hug Mabel tightly and listen.

'Please, please, I beg you, bring our little girl back safe and well. We miss her so much and she'll be missing us too. You've torn our lives apart, our whole family's broken. Just do the right thing. Please. Bring her back.'

'But we *are* doing the right thing!' I say to Mabel, spinning her round and lifting her up. 'Do you know what? I think Mummy's secretly pleased that you're with somebody who really loves you, somebody who wants to look after you all the time.' I kiss her on the nose. 'All this weeping and wailing is just for show.'

CHAPTER EIGHTEEN

Day two without Mabel

Ruby and Lewis sit on the sofa crying and holding hands as they watch the press conference on the evening news.

'I can't believe it,' she says. 'I just can't believe it. How can this be happening to us?'

'I know,' he replies, squeezing her fingers. 'It's a nightmare.'

The item ends with a final plea for witnesses to come forward, then the newscaster moves on to the next story. Ruby reaches for a tissue and blows her nose. 'They didn't mention me by name,' she says. 'That's odd.'

Lewis turns the TV off. 'The police try to keep some details close to their chest. It helps sort out the cranks.'

'Suppose so.' She grimaces at the thought of anyone wanting to hamper the investigation. 'Mabel's been missing for …' she counts back in her head, 'over thirty-five hours. That's a long time. They should have found her by now.'

'The police are taking it really seriously, Rubes, they're pulling out all the stops.'

'The longer it goes on, the less chance there is of her being …' She doesn't finish the sentence. 'Remember that case a few years ago when a teenager went missing? It was the uncle that killed her. The mother knew she was dead but she made this great big fuss, immediately printing off T-shirts, trying to fundraise. The police knew she was behaving suspiciously. They suss these things out straight away.'

'No one could say Amber and George were behaving strangely in that media conference,' says Lewis. 'They both looked devastated.'

'Yes, they did,' she admits. 'But did you see all those ribbons around the trees? Lilac for Lilac Park, I guess. And the posters saying *Mabel is Missing*? I'm surprised at Amber – she normally hates that kind of public show.'

'She might not have had anything to do with it. It looked like a bunch of locals trying to help.'

'Trying to get in on the action, more like.' She sighs heavily.

Lewis gets up and goes into the kitchen. She hugs a cushion in his absence. Since she returned from the police station yesterday afternoon, she has barely left the sofa. Her head is throbbing and her body aches all over, as if she's suffering from the flu. Lewis took today off to be with her, but he has to return to work tomorrow. She's terrified of being left alone.

He comes back with two bottles of beer and a packet of crisps tucked under his arm. He sets them down and bursts open the packet, spreading the crisps out on the foil. 'It's the last one,' he says. 'We'll have to share.'

'Thanks.' She pops a solitary crisp into her mouth, then puts the cold bottle to her lips and takes a large swig. The gassy liquid combines with the well of tears in her throat, making her splutter.

'I feel so sorry for you,' he says, rubbing her back. 'I wish I could make it better.'

'I wish Amber would call.'

'So you keep saying, but she's not going to. Not until she's ready.'

'She doesn't want to talk because she knows I know she's lying.'

'Everyone must know by now that she wasn't at the flat.' Lewis wipes a moustache of foam from his top lip.

'No, I mean she's lying about *other* things.'

'Like what?'

'The yoga retreat, for example.' She takes another crisp and it scratches as she swallows. 'As far as I know, Amber's never done a yoga class in her life. She hates exercise, and she despises alternative medicine and spiritual healing. Remember how she took the piss out of me when I started that Reiki training?'

'She was trying something different. For her depression.'

'No, it was a cover. She was spending the weekend with someone, I'm sure of it.'

Lewis puts his hand gently on her thigh. 'Look, I know you're really upset – of course you are – but concocting some conspiracy theory isn't going to make you feel any better.'

Ruby wants to tell him he's being naïve, not to say unsupportive, but she bites down on her reply. She knows her sister and she's up to something, simple as.

There's an uneasy pause. 'Better start cooking,' Lewis says, picking up his half-empty bottle. 'Mushroom risotto okay?'

'Sorry, I don't really feel like eating – not a proper meal.'

'I'll make a small portion.' He goes back to the kitchen and turns some music on.

Ruby drains the bottle of beer and puts it back on the table. Easing herself off the sofa, she stands and stretches her aching limbs. An idea has entered her head, and she feels suddenly compelled to act upon it. She creeps from the room and goes into the bedroom, shutting the door behind her.

A quick Google search for Gaia Hall brings her to an impressive website full of pictures of waterfalls and people in yoga poses with rolling landscapes behind them. First she checks their programme of retreats. It seems that one did in fact take place last weekend – a beginner's course offering guided yoga sessions and an introduction to mindfulness. 'So not Amber's style,' she mutters under her breath. It was the kind of course Ruby herself would love to do but could never afford.

She clicks on *Contact Us* and finds the phone number she was looking for. Dare she make the call? They're unlikely to tell her whether Amber attended – everyone is so cautious about giving out personal details these days. She'll have to ask in a roundabout way.

She follows the onscreen link and the line starts to ring.

'Good evening, Gaia Hall,' says a very posh female voice.

'Oh, hello, could I speak to the manager, please?'

'Speaking.'

'Good. It's ... er ... Amber Walker's sister here. Amber is Mabel Walker's mother, you know? The baby that's gone missing, you'll have seen it on the news. I gather she was staying at Gaia Hall on Saturday night.'

'Who is this?' The manager's tone is icy cold.

'Like I said, I'm Amber's sister.'

'Are you a journalist?'

'No, honestly!'

'You disgusting people. Why don't you just crawl back into the hole you came from?' The line goes dead. Ruby throws her phone down on the bed. What a horrible woman; she didn't even give her a chance to explain.

She paces about, feeling so angry and frustrated she could punch the walls. She has to know if Amber really went to Gaia Hall; a lot depends on it. Because she's not going to be the fall guy in this tragedy. Nor is she going to slot neatly into their mother's pigeonholes. Perfect, clever, goody-goody Amber and clumsy, stupid, walking-disaster-area Ruby. Mabel is missing and only the truth will find her.

She opens the wardrobe and takes out a thick jumper. She pulls it over her head, then goes quietly into the hallway and puts her boots on. Lewis is still cooking. His geeky classical music is wafting in from the kitchen. It feels bad, walking out on him while he's making dinner, but if she tells him where she's going, he'll try and stop her. She picks up her helmet, slips on her high-vis waistcoat and creeps out of the flat.

Unlocking the padlock, she wheels her bike down the path and presses the button to open the outer gates. It's dark, colder than she was expecting. She fastens on her helmet and pushes onto the road. Normally she'd never cycle all the way to Mum's, but tonight it feels like the only way to go. The intense concentration required to navigate the busy London traffic will make it an almost meditative experience, releasing her brain from thinking about Mabel for every fraction of every second.

As she sets off, sticking to the cycle lanes wherever possible, she senses her phone throbbing in the back pocket of her jeans. That will be Lewis, wondering where the hell she is. But she can't stop to argue with him now; she has to keep going.

The journey takes over an hour, and by the time she turns into the all-too-familiar Faversham Road, she's sweating. Only her fingertips remain cold from gripping the handlebars. She changes down a gear to tackle the steady incline.

Usually the road is quiet at night, but ahead she can see several vehicles double-parked, their headlights beaming across the tarmac. People are milling about too, some of them with large cameras and fluffy sticks.

It's the media, camped outside her mother's front door. They must have followed them back from the press conference. Or maybe the police tipped them off. Why are they still here at this time of night?

She stops a hundred metres away, resting her foot on the kerb while she considers the problem. There's no way of entering the house from the rear. To reach the front door she's going to have to run the gauntlet of reporters. Will they know who she is and what part she had to play? What if they ambush her? She doesn't want her photo splashed all over the tabloids tomorrow. She imagines the headlines: *Babysitter Barges In ... Babysitter Begs for Forgiveness ... Babysitter Was to Blame.*

But it's either face them or turn around and cycle straight home. She doesn't want to do that. She wants to speak to Amber privately, without George being in the room or their bloody mother earwigging. And if she won't answer the damn phone, that leaves her with no choice ...

She pushes off again and climbs the rest of the hill. When she's about twenty metres away, she jumps off the bike and rests it against a wall. Then she starts to walk briskly along the pavement, making a beeline for the driveway. She seems to have caught everyone unawares, but then she hears voices crying out.

'Who are you, love?'

'Are you part of the family?'

'What's your name?'

'Are you the sister?'

There's a surge towards her. It only takes a few seconds for the cameras to start flashing. She shields her face with her hand as she marches up to the front door and rings the bell three times.

The curtain of the lounge window is pulled back and an unfamiliar face peers out, then disappears. Ruby rings again. 'It's me!' she shouts. 'Ruby! For God's sake, open the door.'

She can hear talking in the hallway, some debate going on, no doubt, about whether to let her in. The reporters crowd around.

'Ruby! Talk to us! Any news about Mabel?'

'How are you feeling, Ruby?'

'Is she still alive?'

'Do the family blame you, Ruby?'

'Tell us your side of the story.'

'What happened, Ruby? Ruby?'

There's a click, and the door opens on the chain. The woman who was at the window is standing in the gap.

'I'm Amber's sister. Please let me in!'

She shuts the door to remove the chain, then immediately opens it again, just wide enough to let Ruby slip through.

'Oh my God, that was hell,' Ruby says, breathing heavily.

'You should have rung first.'

'I tried, but nobody answered.' She undoes her helmet and takes it off. 'Who are you?'

'The family liaison officer – Sally Morrison.'

'I'm Ruby,' she says, shaking out her thick dark hair. 'I've come to see Amber.'

'She's resting.'

'Oh. Where's my mother?'

'In the kitchen, I think.'

Ruby walks through and finds her in the middle of washing up. 'Mum?'

'Didn't you get my message? I told you not to come.' Vicky bangs a dripping plate onto the drainer.

'I know, but I had to. It's not fair to treat me like this. I'm hurting too, you know. I'm in a terrible state. I love Mabel as much as—'

'Go away, Ruby. We don't want to see you.'

'Please …'

'You've done enough damage. Now leave us alone!'

Ruby lets out an exasperated groan and goes back into the hallway, where Sally is hovering. 'Excuse me,' she says gruffly, almost shoving the officer to one side to get to the stairs. She walks up and knocks on the door of Amber's old bedroom.

'Amber, it's me. Let me in. We need to talk.'

Silence. Then whispering.

'Please. It's important.' Ruby grits her teeth as she waits. The door finally opens. Her sister is white-faced, eyes puffy with crying. George stands behind her, glaring over her shoulder.

'What do you want?'

'Can we talk? Please. Just the two of us?'

'Be my guest,' says George sarcastically, pushing past her as he leaves the room. He thumps down the stairs in a temper.

Amber nods for Ruby to enter, then shuts the door. 'You shouldn't have come,' she says. 'It's really difficult for me to see you right now.'

'I know.'

'I want to kill you. We all want to kill you.'

'I can see that, and I do feel really, really bad, but … but honestly, Amber, I don't think I did anything wrong.'

Amber looks at her, bewildered. 'You let some bastard steal my daughter and you don't think you did anything wrong?'

'The police think whoever took her had a key.'

'The only person who had a key was you.'

'What's going on, Amber?' Ruby says. 'What's *really* going on? Why did you lie to George about going away for the weekend?'

Amber pinks. 'That's not relevant.'

'Did you really go on a yoga retreat? I mean, it's not your thing, is it? All that touchy-feely, harmony-with-the-universe stuff.'

'Piss off.'

'The police will check, you know. They probably have already.'

'Ruby …'

'If you're having an affair, they *will* find out.'

Amber's eyes widen. 'How dare you talk to me like that? My baby is missing! She's gone, vanished!' Her voice cracks down the middle. 'Nobody knows who's got her or even if she's still alive.

She was taken while *you* were looking after her, and you won't even say sorry.'

'You know I'm sorry, I'll always be sorry, Amber, for as long as I live, but I didn't do it deliberately; it could have happened to any of us!'

'But it happened to you,' Amber retorts. 'Just you. Because you're an airhead. No, you're worse than an airhead; you're a fuck-up, you're not safe.' She advances towards her. 'Do you know what George thinks?'

Ruby has never seen such hatred in her sister's eyes. She backs away.

'He thinks you killed Mabel and buried her somewhere, then pretended she'd been abducted.'

'What?!' Ruby gasps. 'That's … that's obscene! I would *never* … You can't believe that, you can't. I love Mabel, I'd never do anything to hurt her.'

'The police will check,' Amber replies, throwing Ruby's words back with added venom. 'If you killed her, they *will* find out.'

CHAPTER NINETEEN

Day two without Mabel

Amber sits on the edge of the bed and sobs. It was very wrong to accuse Ruby – her sister's shocked and horrified expression will be forever printed on her memory. Worse than that, she spoke about Mabel as if she were dead. It's wicked even to contemplate the possibility that she's not alive. Wicked and unforgivable. Even if Mabel doesn't come home, Amber must never get to the stage of thinking about her in the past tense.

It was a horrible encounter, exactly what she was trying to avoid. She's deeply angry with Ruby, but despite what George thinks, she knows her sister would never hurt Mabel. It's true that she got into a lot of trouble as a child and tried to wriggle her way out of it, but as she grew up, she settled down. She's remained careless and chaotic, always picking up new projects and never finishing them, but there's no harm in her. She's her own worst enemy, not other people's.

Amber swallows down her guilt. She shouldn't have lashed out like that. It was only because she's under so much strain and Ruby accused her of lying about Gaia Hall. Attack has always been Amber's first line of defence.

But Ruby knows she has secrets, and that's very worrying. She doesn't know what they are exactly, just that they exist. If she keeps digging around, if she tells George … well, it could send him over the edge. Aren't they all suffering enough?

She dries her eyes with a tissue and throws it in the direction of the bin. It's bad tactics to make an enemy of Ruby. Unfortunately, it's too late to call her back and apologise. She fled the house immediately, straight into the pack of media hyenas prowling around the driveway. They will have sniffed that she was horribly upset. Amber hopes she didn't talk to them.

Amber and George have been warned about the tabloids. To begin with, Sally said, the media will be on their side in the search for Mabel, full of sympathy for their plight. But one false step and they'll turn against them. Amber remembers what happened to the parents of Madeleine McCann, how they were vilified for leaving their children unsupervised, even accused of killing Madeleine themselves. Apparently the press is already making comparisons with the case – the girls' names starting with the same letter doesn't help. One of tomorrow's headlines is apparently *First Maddy, Now Mabel*. Amber shudders. It's too much, way too much – arguing with Ruby, being besieged by the press; all it does is distract everyone from finding the real culprit.

They've been advised not to read any papers, not even the respectable ones, and Amber is going to take that advice. The thought that strangers will be talking about her over the breakfast table or by the office water cooler is incredibly upsetting. Particularly because it's something she's done herself in the past – judging others as a way of making conversation. She'll never do that again. When Mabel's found, she's going to change completely, become a better mother.

She puts her hands together and promises the God she's never believed in that she'll never complain again about the sleepless nights, the drudgery of washing and making up bottles and changing nappies, the lack of adult company, the boredom, the awful aching loneliness. If Mabel is returned safely, she will never once moan when George has to work late; or argue about whose turn it is to give her a bath. The sound of her daughter waking at dawn will bring her joy, not irritation. She will push the buggy around the park with a smile on her face and a song in her heart.

There's a knock on the door.

'Who is it?'

'Sally. Can you talk?'

'Er – yes. I'll come down.' Amber stands up and goes to the mirror, frowning at her haggard looks. No doubt Sally wants to know what went on between her and Ruby – it could be awkward. As she descends the stairs, she tries to work out something believable to say.

But the family liaison officer isn't interested in what just happened in the bedroom. There's been a small development, she says.

'What kind of development? Good or bad?' Amber feels her pulse rate quicken.

Sally doesn't reply, but leads her into the lounge, where her husband and mother are already seated. Their faces are twitching with anxiety. Amber sits next to George on the sofa. He reaches out and grasps her hand.

'You okay?' he whispers. She nods, although she isn't okay. Not a bit of it.

Sally takes the other armchair. 'First of all, DI Benedict wants me to tell you that he thought the press conference went extremely well. You were both amazing, thank you, I know how hard it must have been. The good news is, we've had a huge response from the general public and officers are analysing the data right now. I'm afraid these cases often generate a lot of irrelevant, even mischievous responses, so everything needs carefully sifting through. But one particular thing has come to light.'

'Has a witness come forward?' asks Vicky, unable to contain herself a second longer.

'Not exactly. It's more a piece of intelligence.'

'What do you mean?'

Sally takes a breath. 'We've been given a name.'

Amber's stomach flips. 'What name? Who?'

'Just tell us,' says George impatiently.

Sally glances down at her notes. 'Does Sonya Garrick mean anything to you?'

'Hmm … There's only one Sonya I can think of,' says Amber. 'She came to the antenatal class a few times.'

'Yes, that's Sonya Garrick. A friend of yours, Polly McQueen, told us about her.'

Amber wrinkles her nose. She wouldn't exactly call Polly a friend …

Sally looks at her searchingly. 'How well do you know Sonya?'

Amber huffs. 'Hardly at all. George knows her from the gym where he works.'

'Used to,' he replies quickly. 'She stopped going when she got pregnant. I only knew her slightly – she wasn't a client.'

Sally makes a quick note. 'Has she ever visited you at William Morris Terrace?'

'No,' says Amber. 'Never. I'd be surprised if she knows where I live. I only met her a couple of times, months ago. I probably wouldn't recognise her any more.' The cogs in her brain start to turn. 'Why did Polly … I mean, do you think Sonya might have something to do with … with Mabel's disappearance?'

'Apparently she lost a baby last year, quite late on in her pregnancy,' Sally explains. 'Your friend says she took it extremely badly, and after that started behaving strangely. Do you know about this?'

Amber pulls a face. 'Yes, sort of. I mean, I know she had a miscarriage, but as for behaving strangely … I wouldn't necessarily trust …' She pauses, not sure how to explain. 'Polly has a tendency to hijack other people's dramas. She over-empathises, makes it all about her.'

Sally nods. 'Okay, that's useful to know. She's the one behind the lilac ribbons, by the way.'

George releases Amber's hand and leans right forward. 'Sod the bloody ribbons. Can I get this straight? The police think Sonya took Mabel?'

'No, no, there's no evidence for that yet; it's just one of many avenues we're exploring. My boss wants to know if Sonya has ever visited you, or babysat Mabel, or – importantly – if you've ever had any problems with her.'

'No,' says Amber definitely.

'Okay. Thanks.' Sally makes another note.

Amber is surprised to find that the possibility that Sonya is the abductor is making her feel better, rather than worse. She knows that women who've lost babies can sometimes go a bit mad and steal other people's, usually from maternity hospitals but also from outside shops and other public spaces. Why not from their own home? She's read true-life accounts in tacky magazines at the hairdresser's. The stories are heartbreaking but they always have happy endings.

'Sonya … Sonya,' she repeats. 'I didn't make the connection before, but yes, it makes sense.'

'You've got to find her. Like now.' George jabs with his finger. 'We shouldn't be sitting here talking about it; you should be getting a warrant for her arrest, putting out an all-ports alert, splashing her face all over the internet.'

'We're not saying Sonya has definitely got Mabel,' Sally replies coolly. 'It's only a possibility at this stage. If she *has* got her, the last thing we want to do is let her know we're looking for her. We don't want her to panic and harm her. Which means it's really important – for Mabel's sake – that you don't tell anyone about this. And I mean anyone.'

'Okay, okay,' agrees George. 'As long as you get on with finding her. We've lost enough time as it is.'

'We're already working on tracing her. As soon as there's any news, you'll be the first to know.' Sally gets up and pops her notebook into her bag. 'Right. I'm going to the station now to give the boss an update. I'll be back in the morning. In the meantime, try to rest.'

'Thanks.' George looks abashed. 'Sorry to shout, I just—'

'It's fine. See you tomorrow.' She gives them a sympathetic smile and leaves the room.

As soon as she's gone, George covers his face with his hands. 'Sonya. Bloody Sonya. Why didn't we think of her before? It was staring us in the face. That headcase.'

'Sounds like you know her better than I do,' says Amber, looking at his slumped figure. A chill starts to creep up her back.

He shakes his head. 'Not really.'

'Why did you call her a headcase?'

'She had a bit of a reputation at the gym, that's all.'

'What for?'

He thinks about it. 'For being weird.'

'Weird? In what way?'

'You know, hitting on guys, including some of the married ones. She was a menace, if you must know.'

He's hiding something, she can see it in his body language. 'Did she hit on you?'

'A bit.'

She stiffens. 'You never told me that before.'

'There was nothing to tell. I could see she was trouble from the off – I gave her a wide berth.' He removes his hands and sits up straighter. 'To be honest, I think it was a baby she was after more than a relationship.'

Amber's mind skips back briefly, remembering how emotionally painful it was trying to conceive. The money she spent on pointless tests when her period wasn't even late. How oversensitive she was to signs of possible pregnancy – fatigue, tender breasts, a strange taste in the mouth – and how disappointed she was when they turned out to be figments of her imagination. Then, just as she was about to give up, the overwhelming sense of achievement when she finally got a positive result, as if she'd just climbed Everest in her bare feet and was standing on top of the world. Poor Sonya …

'No wonder she was devastated when she lost it,' she says.

'I guess so.'

'Do you know who the father was?'

'No, but several of the guys were shitting themselves … She never let on, not that I know of.'

'Well I hope it *is* Sonya who's got Mabel,' Amber says.

George turns to her, visibly shocked. 'Why? The woman's deranged!'

'Because she wants to be a mum. She'll be looking after her, loving her, treating like she's her own baby.'

'She'd better be,' George says bitterly. 'Or I'll wring her bloody neck.'

CHAPTER TWENTY

Day three without Mabel

Amber feels too alive, too much in the moment; the seconds stab at her, even during the few hours she manages to sleep. What wouldn't she give to rewind to last Friday afternoon and reset the clock? She lies in bed, remembering how it felt to drive away from number 74, leaving Mabel in Ruby's charge. It was as if she'd been at the bottom of the sea, weighted down with rocks of responsibility. Suddenly the weights were lifted and she felt herself rising to the surface, bobbing above the water and gulping in breaths of air. Now guilt is pushing her down again, the pressure heavier than before. There's a hard lump in her chest where her heart should be.

'George?' She shakes him awake. 'George …'

His eyes open, widening with hope. 'Wh … wha … What is it? Have they found her?'

'No … I mean, I don't know. I need to talk to you.'

'Okay …' He leans across to look at the time on his phone. 'God, Amber, it's the middle of the night.' His head hits the pillow again.

'I don't know how you can sleep at all,' she says ruefully. 'I've been awake for hours.'

'Couldn't help it; my body just gave in … Sorry.' He tries to rouse himself. 'You okay?'

She huffs. 'Of course not. My brain's on high alert. I'm constantly listening out for her, as if she's napping in the next room.

Then I realise she's not there and … What if we never hear her little voice again?'

'Don't say that.'

'I can't stop thinking about her, every single second; it's driving me crazy. But the thing is, I don't want to stop.'

He feels around under the covers for her hand and squeezes it tightly. 'I understand, I'm the same.'

'It sounds weird, but I actually hope Sonya's got her.'

'Hmm,' he says, unconvinced. 'The police will track her down, they always do. Nobody can hide for long these days. Eventually, she'll have to use her phone or buy something and—'

Amber releases his hand and sits up. 'George! I've just remembered. Polly said Sonya had gone off the radar; you know, shut down all her social media accounts, stopped answering the phone. The girls thought she was having a breakdown, but … Oh God, do you think she might have been planning the abduction for weeks?'

'I, er … I don't know.' He wrinkles his nose. 'Possibly.'

'I think the baby she lost was a little girl, but Polly and Hanima also had girls. So why pick me?'

'Did you fall out with her?'

'No. Not at all, I didn't really know her. After the miscarriage, everyone else in our group went round to "support her".' She makes quotation marks in the air. 'They took cakes and flowers and stuff. I thought it was grief-bombing, so I didn't go.'

He considers. 'Maybe she resented you for that.'

'I can't think why. I was trying to be sensitive. I didn't want to turn up there with my enormous tummy sticking out.'

'You never know how other people are going to react. Maybe she thought you didn't care. Maybe she wanted to take revenge to show you how it felt.'

Polly's words at the last meet-up suddenly crash into her head. *You don't understand what it's like to lose a child.* Could it be true that

Sonya was angry with her? Was *that* her motivation for taking Mabel?
And if so, does it mean that she, Amber, is once again to blame?

It's not even 8 a.m., but the media are already milling around
outside. Vicky, who is peering through a gap in the bedroom
curtains, announces that there are more of them today. She
recognises one of the journalists from the telly and comments on
his attractiveness. Amber nearly hits her when she says this, but
George lays a restraining hand on her arm and suggests they get
dressed and go downstairs.

'Try to eat,' he says, guiding her into the kitchen. He puts the
kettle on and rummages in the bread bin. 'Toast?'

'I hate them,' she says. 'They're disgusting, the lowest of the
low. They don't care about us or what we're going through; they
don't even care about Mabel. All they want is a juicy story.'

He puts two slices on and pops some tea bags into the pot.
'Ignore them, forget they're there.'

'How can I? It's like there's a party going on outside. I've a
good mind to—'

'If you open the door and give them a mouthful, it'll be all over
the front pages. Sally said there was already a load of negative stuff
about us on social media; don't make it worse.'

She puts her hands around the side of her head and pulls at
her hair until it hurts. 'I don't care what they say about us,' she
cries. 'All I want is Mabel back.'

The doorbell rings. 'It's okay, it's only Sally,' Vicky calls out.
'I'll get it.'

There's a burst of noise as she opens the front door. Amber
and George wait until Sally is safely inside before going into the
hallway to meet her.

'God, they drive me insane,' Sally says, catching her breath.

George steps forward. 'Any news?'

'Yes and no.' She removes her coat, giving it to Vicky to hang up. 'Shall we go in the conservatory, where it's quiet?'

'Okay,' says Amber.

Sally turns to Vicky. 'I didn't manage a cup of tea this morning – I'm gasping. Would you mind?'

A flash of disappointment crosses Vicky's face as she realises that she's been deftly excluded from the conversation.

'White, no sugar, yes?'

'You got it.'

The sun lounge is cold and smells slightly damp. They enter and take what have become their normal places on the wicker furniture set. Amber nervously waits for Sally to finish reading a text.

'Sorry about that,' she says, putting the phone in her pocket.

George paces about. 'Well? What's happening? Have you found Sonya?'

'We managed to obtain her address via NHS records and made a visit to the flat last night.'

'And?'

'She wasn't there. Officers waited all night but she didn't turn up.'

'What does that mean?' says George.

'We don't know yet. She could have gone away for a few days, or moved out.'

'What did the neighbours say?'

'Nobody seems to know much about her. She lives on her own, no boyfriend as far as anyone can tell. She hasn't been seen for a while, but that doesn't necessarily mean anything. Apparently people in the block go for weeks without seeing each other.'

'If she's not at home, that could mean she's taken Mabel somewhere else,' says Amber. 'She could have gone into hiding.'

'Possibly. It's too early to draw conclusions. We're talking to her mobile provider and checking her bank records, credit cards, cashpoint use, all that. It shouldn't take too long to track her down.'

'Polly told me she'd deliberately gone off the radar,' says Amber. 'I forgot to mention it last night.'

'Yes, she told us that too,' Sally replies. 'It might mean something. Then again, it might not. It's too early to say.'

George casts a quick glance at Amber before speaking. 'We've thought of a reason why she might have taken Mabel.'

'George! We don't *know*—'

'Every little bit of information is useful,' says Sally.

'When Sonya lost her baby, Amber didn't go and see her, but the other mums did. We think maybe she was hurt and angry. Wanted to get her own back?'

'Okay. Interesting.' Sally reaches into her bag for her notebook. 'I'll feed that in.'

'She never said she was upset; we didn't actually fall out,' says Amber.

'But it makes sense, doesn't it?' George presses.

Sally writes her note then looks up. 'Try not to get ahead of yourselves. We have to find Sonya first. If she *has* got Mabel – and that's still an if – we will have to tread extremely carefully. Mabel's safety comes first.'

'Yes, of course, that goes without saying,' says George.

Vicky is hovering in the doorway, holding a mug of tea. 'Mind if I come in?' She enters anyway and sets the mug down on the glass table.

'Thanks so much.' Sally waits for her to leave, then draws a breath. 'Now, um, Amber, DI Benedict would like to have another chat with you this morning. On your own.'

'Oh.' Amber feels her cheeks instantly heating up. She has been expecting this.

'Why can't he talk to us together?' says George.

'It's normal practice to interview witnesses separately,' Sally replies smoothly. 'The boss has asked me to bring you down to the station.'

Amber gulps. 'Okay. What, right now?'

Sally nods. 'Can you be ready in ten minutes? I'll just finish my tea.'

Amber goes upstairs to brush her hair, and George follows. 'I don't like this,' he says. 'It makes me feel very uncomfortable.'

'He probably just wants to know more about Sonya.'

'Or he wants you to dish the dirt on me.'

'Why would I do that, George?' Amber turns to him. 'You've done nothing wrong. I'm the one who offended Sonya so much she decided to steal our baby.'

'I didn't say that.'

'You implied it.'

'No, I didn't. You asked for a reason and it was all I could think of,' he protests.

'If anyone should feel uncomfortable, it's me.'

His shoulders drop. 'I'm sorry, I didn't mean to … I'm just … I don't know … Everything's moving so slowly. Talking isn't going to find Mabel. We need boots on the ground; the whole country should be out there looking for her. We need action!'

Amber leaves George sitting on the bed, head in hands. She rushes downstairs and puts on her coat. Sally is already waiting for her.

'Right. Stay close to me. Keep your head down, don't respond to anything anyone says, not even with a look, okay? Neutral expression. Don't give them anything they can use.'

'If they see me getting into a police car, they'll think I'm being arrested.'

'Don't worry, we'll make it clear you're not.'

Amber hesitates. 'I'm not sure I can do this. Can't DI Benedict come here instead?'

'Not for this conversation,' Sally replies, grasping the door handle. 'Come on, let's go.'

Sally steps out and Amber falls in behind her. There are camera flashes and shouts from every corner as they walk the few metres to the waiting car. A uniformed officer has the rear passenger door already open. He guides Amber onto the back seat. Sally slides in next to her. Then the officer shuts the doors, gets in next to the driver and the car speeds off down the hill.

Not for this conversation, Amber repeats silently. The police have worked it out, she thinks. They know she's been lying. Her stomach roils with fear. She can't do this. When the car stops at a traffic light, she wants to leap out and run away.

The journey takes twenty minutes. As they reach the station, they're met with another crowd of reporters and photographers. Amber slithers down in her seat and puts her hand against the side of her face.

'Drop us off at the back entrance, please,' says Sally.

This is the beginning of the end, thinks Amber. I've lost my daughter, and by tonight, my marriage will be in tatters.

DI Benedict is waiting for her. She's hurried up the back steps and ushered into the family room, a calm, neutral space normally reserved for giving people bad news. The detective orders coffee and they sit down in tub chairs, facing each other.

'Thanks for coming in,' he says. 'I thought you'd prefer the privacy.'

'Yes,' she replies, feeling as if she's descending at speed in an elevator.

Benedict fixes her with a blue-eyed gaze. 'I'm going to come straight to it,' he says. 'We have a rapidly developing case here shooting off in a number of directions and I need to know exactly where to prioritise our investigation. It's really important, for Mabel's sake, that you don't waste my time, do you understand?'

She nods. 'Good … So, on Sunday, when you spoke to the family liaison officer, she asked you if your husband, George Walker, was Mabel's biological father.'

Amber twists her fingers together. 'Yes, she did, and I answered to the best of my knowledge.'

'To the best of your knowledge?' he repeats. 'Sally reported that you were adamant. In fact, you were very offended at any suggestion that he might not be Mabel's father.'

'Was I? I don't remember, I was very stressed …' Her cheeks burn with shame. She wants to sink into the tub chair and disappear.

'It may not come as any surprise to you, then, that our DNA results show that your husband is *not* Mabel's father – biologically speaking.'

She hangs her head. 'I didn't know for sure. I hoped …' Tears well in her throat. 'I knew you'd find out. I thought if George *was* the father, then I wouldn't need to say anything.'

'I see.'

'Things were bad enough without making it worse.'

DI Benedict pauses to breathe slowly in and out. 'Sally explained that in these cases, the abductor often turns out to be the biological father, or someone who believes they are the father. And yet you didn't mention it.' He pauses. 'I find that extraordinary.'

'I didn't say anything because I know he didn't do it.'

'I see. And what makes you so sure? Were you with this man on Saturday night?'

She squirms. 'Please, you have to trust me on this. I know he has nothing to do with it. Sonya, that's who you should be looking for; focus on Sonya.'

'Don't worry, we're exploring every possible scenario, including Sonya Garrick,' Benedict assures her. 'But I think we should check out this chap's alibi, don't you? Just to be sure.'

She shakes her head. 'There's really no need.'

'You seem very reluctant to give me his name.'

Tears roll down her cheeks. 'Please, I beg you, don't do this. You'll destroy us.'

Benedict plucks a tissue from the box on the table and hands it over. 'I do sympathise,' he says. 'You're in a very difficult situation, trying to protect yourself and everyone around you, but—'

'You can't force me to tell you.'

'No, that's true.' He sits back in his chair. 'But to be honest, I don't need you to tell me, because I already know.'

She nearly chokes. 'You know? How come?'

He pauses, almost theatrically, before delivering the killer blow. 'I'm afraid Mabel's biological father is already on the national DNA database. He has a criminal record, Amber. Did you know that?'

CHAPTER TWENTY-ONE

Day three with Mabel

I'm not sure what to do with Mabel – she's being very fractious. I'm already giving her constant attention, changing her nappy regularly so she doesn't feel uncomfortable for a moment, feeding her as soon as she's hungry, playing games, singing songs, giving her exercises to develop her motor skills. Little by little I'm discovering her likes and dislikes – the smashed avocado didn't go down at all well, but she adores porridge with banana. Yet despite all my considerable efforts, she doesn't seem satisfied. I've barely had a smile out of her since we arrived at the bungalow. She gave me such an odd stare when I went to her this morning, as if I were a complete stranger she'd never seen before. Her bottom lip wobbled and she started to whimper. It was really hurtful.

Surely she can't be missing Amber, who as far as I could tell took no interest in her at all. I know we've only been together a few days, but I'm impatient for her to switch allegiances. I love her so much and can't wait for her to love me back.

It's only 11 a.m., but I seem to have run out of steam. 'Let's see if we can spot some birdies,' I say, picking Mabel up and carrying her over to the lounge window. It's a mild February day and there's a strip of sunshine running down the left side of the lawn. The stubby tree in the centre is threatening to burst into leaf; an empty feeder hangs from one of its branches, swaying in the breeze. None of it looks very inviting.

'No birdies today,' I say. 'We must buy them some food. Then they'll come back, you'll see.'

I point out things in the garden, repeating their names several times. I know it's too early for her to talk, but it's important to get her familiar with the concept of language. Repetition is the only way to learn.

'Tree, tree, tree ... lots of trees. Lots of weeds, too. That thing over there is a shed. See? Shed. Haven't looked in there yet. Maybe Great-Aunt Dolly left some gardening tools. Or maybe there's a lawnmower. I'm going to need to cut the grass at some point, I suppose.'

Mabel wriggles in my arms, bored with the nature lesson. 'Had enough?' I say, taking her away from the window and depositing her in the baby recliner. She's momentarily distracted by the row of plastic teddies across the front, then resumes her restless kicking.

'What is it, Mabel? Are you fed up with being indoors? Do you want to go out?' She stills her feet for a few moments and gazes up at me.

I bite my lip. Dare we? A quick stroll up and down the lane, perhaps? It's extremely quiet around here. Cars hardly ever drive past and I haven't seen anyone walking their dog. The bungalow sits on the very edge of a small village. It's bound to be a close-knit community, where everyone knows everyone else. A newcomer will stand out, especially somebody with a pushchair. What if people have been asked to look out for us?

I listened to the news this morning on Great-Aunt Dolly's ancient transistor radio. Officers have expanded the search from the park to nearby canals and wetlands, presumably for Mabel's dead body, as she couldn't possibly survive in this weather. Meanwhile, locals are tying lilac ribbons to their front gates – what's the point of that? I will not succumb to the pressure of other people's sympathy for Amber and George. If the public knew about all their lies and secrets, they would realise that I'm by far the better parent for Mabel.

If only I could access social media. Twitter will be buzzing with gossip and theories, most of them wildly off the mark, but there's a chance someone has put two and two together and come up with my name. The thought of it makes me shiver. Perhaps the police have already visited the flat and realised I'm no longer living there. They could already be checking the records of my credit card and mobile phone. When they discover I haven't used either since Mabel was taken, they'll be even more suspicious and their search will intensify. But will they find out about this place? It's hard to say.

A sustained whine from Mabel cuts into my worried musings. 'All right,' I say, bending down to remove her from the chair, 'let's risk it.' I carry her into the bedroom and lay her on the spare bed. 'You can wear your new pink snowsuit. We'll take the car and drive somewhere remote, then if you're a good girl, I'll take you out in the pushchair. Maybe we'll even go as far as the sea. I don't suppose you've seen the sea yet. It'll be too cold to play on the sand, but it'll be fun to see the waves.'

I pack a bottle and some healthy snacks, then assemble her changing bag with a set of spare clothes in case she's sick or does a nasty poo. Such a lot of fuss to go out for the day! Once we're in a proper routine, we'll be fine, but at the moment I'm spending more time getting ready to do things than actually doing them.

'Come on, sweetie.' I open the front door to be greeted by a blast of cold air. 'Oh dear, let's get you into the car straight away.' I strap her into the seat, put the changing bag next to her, then get in myself. Before reversing out of the gravel driveway, I pull a silly face at her in the rear mirror, hoping for a smile, but she's staring out of the window, her young mind elsewhere.

'Oh, I do like to be beside the seaside!' I warble, driving along the twisty lanes. It's a song my grandmother used to sing when I visited her in Brighton. My parents liked to dump me with her in the school holidays so they could carry on working. 'Oh, I do like to be beside the sea!' I didn't particularly like it, as it happens. Grandma used to make me swim in the freezing grey waters of the English Channel, whatever the weather. Afterwards, I'd sit on the beach, a damp towel around my shoulders, eating gritty sandwiches with blue lips.

I glance in the mirror, hoping for a glimmer of enthusiasm from Mabel for my singing, but she's already fallen asleep. 'Come on, it wasn't *that* bad,' I laugh, shifting down a gear to navigate a sharp bend.

As we journey southwards, taking the back roads towards the coast, I start to relax a little. When all the fuss is over and everyone's given up looking for her, we'll have more freedom to go out and about. We'll head west, where there's more sand and the temperatures are milder. I'll let her toddle around on the beach, and when she's a little older, we'll dig holes to jump over and build sandcastles, decorating them with shells. We'll hunt for shrimps in the rock pools and we won't put even our toes in the water unless it's baking hot. I'll buy her ice-cream cornets with a chocolate flake and we'll stop for fish and chips on the way home. Warm Mediterranean waters and supper in a Greek taverna is more my style, but sadly, I'll never be able to take her abroad. Not without a passport.

All of which reminds me that I'm going to have to change her name. I look at her in the rear mirror again, wondering what on earth to choose. I should start using her new name now, so that she gets used to it. I've always wanted to call my daughter Miranda. Or Sophia. Or Imogen. Would any of those suit her? Difficult to decide when I'm so used to thinking of her as Mabel, even though I never would have chosen it myself. I need something more personal, more appropriate.

'What name would you like?' I ask her. 'How about Dolly, after my dear old great-aunt who gave us her home? What do you think? Would you like to be called Dolly, or would you prefer Dorothy? Or Dotty. Or even Dot?' Mabel doesn't respond. I chatter on regardless, posing the advantages and disadvantages of the various shortenings, but she remains resolutely asleep and uninterested.

We're only about five miles from our destination when I notice that we're very low on petrol. My stomach knots at the thought of stopping at a filling station. I can pay with cash, but it's the security cameras that concern me. Maybe they don't bother with them in rural locations …

I drive on, eyes peeled for possibilities. The roads are becoming narrower and narrower, twisting ever downwards towards the coast. We enter a small chocolate-box village full of immaculate thatched cottages. A sign flashes at me to slow down to the thirty-miles-an-hour speed limit. Not that there are any pedestrians to run over. We pass an ancient pub and a beautiful old stone church, but there are no shops and definitely no petrol station.

'What are we going to do if we run out?' I say to Mabel. 'I can't call out the breakdown service.' I thump my fist on the steering wheel. 'I should never have come out. I'm so stupid!' Her eyelids don't even flicker.

Pulling into a small lay-by, I programme the sat nav to direct me to the nearest filling station. It is four miles away, heading back inland. I groan loudly. 'Sorry about this, sweetie.' I reverse, almost hitting a large gate behind me, then swing the car around and off we go, back in the direction we came from.

A few minutes later, I'm pulling up at the pumps. As soon as I turn off the engine, Mabel begins to stir.

'Won't be long.' I get out, pulling my hood over my head and tucking my chin beneath my scarf. At least it's cold and windy, so it won't look too obvious that I'm trying to cover my face. Fortunately, it's not one of those petrol stations where you have to pay in advance by card. I stand very close to the car as I fill up, eyes glued to the ground. I put the nozzle back and lock the car doors, then walk quickly into the shop.

There are two people in front of me in the queue. I stand behind them, keeping my head down, glancing out of the corner of my eye towards the rack of magazines and newspapers. All the tabloids are running a story about missing Mabel, using the same photo. What are they saying? Am I mentioned anywhere?

I have this incredible urge to run out of the shop and drive away before anyone spots us and calls the police, but I know that would be the biggest giveaway of all. I have to stay here, patiently waiting for my turn to pay. Mustn't fumble with the cash, mustn't tell them to keep the change, mustn't look nervous, say too much or too little. Just have to keep calm.

The man in front of me is making a fuss because his chocolate bar has been put on his VAT receipt. I feel my knees starting to wobble and casually place my hand on the counter for support. But eventually he goes and it's my turn to be served.

'Number three,' I say, trying to keep my accent neutral.

'Cash or card?'

'Cash.'

'Anything else?' I shake my head. 'Need a receipt?' I shake it again and hand over two twenty-pound notes.

While the cashier is dithering at the till, a woman enters and stands behind me. 'Excuse me,' she says, prodding my shoulder. 'Is that your baby screaming her head off? You want to be careful, leaving her alone in the car.'

'Thanks,' I reply. 'But it's okay, she's locked in.'

'Yeah, so was that little girl … Mind you, I heard it was the babysitter that killed her and faked the abduction.'

'Really?' says the cashier, talking over my shoulder. 'I thought it was her aunt.'

'Same person. The mum's sister. Yeah, it's all over Facebook. She's not been charged yet, but it's only a matter of time.'

My ears prick up. I'm desperate to ask for more details, but daren't draw any more attention to myself. The babysitter was Amber's sister, then. I didn't realise. Didn't even know she had a sister.

'Some people,' the cashier sighs, counting out my change. 'They're just plain wicked.'

'They should bring back the death penalty for child killers.'

'Absolutely.'

I mutter a thank you as I snatch up the coins and walk quickly, but not too quickly, out of the shop. I can hear Mabel crying from several yards away. Bleeping open the car doors, I quickly climb inside and start the engine. There's no time to comfort her now; we just have to get out of here. I swoop out of the forecourt and take the road in the direction of home. There will be no 'beside the seaside' today.

She carries on bawling, her face scrunched up like a wet rag.

'Please calm down!' I shout, but it makes no difference. Either she'll fall asleep again with the motion of the car or I'm going to have to put up with this performance the whole way.

I keep looking in the mirrors to see if anyone's following me, but the coast seems to be clear. Besides, if everyone thinks Amber's sister murdered Mabel, nobody's going to be looking for me. Not yet, anyway.

'We're safe,' I tell her, but she's too busy screaming her little head off to hear me. Poor thing. It's almost as if she's crying for help.

CHAPTER TWENTY-TWO

Day three without Mabel

'Amber! What's the news?'

'What did the police say?'

'What happened to Mabel, Amber?'

Sally scythes her way through the media jungle to clear a path to the front door. Amber tucks in behind, shielding her face while reporters throw questions at her like poisoned darts.

'Do you blame your sister?'

'Are you missing Mabel, Amber?'

'Do you blame *yourself*?'

'Is your sister guilty, Amber?'

'Amber! Talk to us!'

'What's your message for Mabel's abductor?'

'Do you think your daughter is still alive?'

The women breathe out in unison as the door shuts behind them. 'You okay?' Sally asks. 'You did well there. It's hard not to respond.'

Amber slumps onto the bottom stair and hugs herself. She feels bruised, physically and emotionally. The journey back from the police station wasn't long enough for her to process the news that George is not Mabel's father, even though deep down, she's known it for months. She suspected it when she saw the positive pregnancy test and sensed it as soon as she held Mabel in her arms. When George's mother declared that Mabel had her father's little snub nose, Amber briefly swelled with hope, but later, when she studied her properly, she couldn't find a trace of her husband's genes. Fearful and ashamed, she buried the knowledge deep in her subconscious, but it refused to lie down, floating to the surface every now and then to taunt her, trying to drag her under.

'So what was all that about?' asks George, emerging from the lounge horribly on cue.

She looks up at him, bewildered. 'What?'

'Your cosy chat with DI Benedict.'

'Oh, um … just going over things again.'

'Normal procedure, nothing to worry about,' clips Sally, taking off her coat. Amber shoots her a grateful look. 'I'll see if your mum can put the kettle on.' She bustles off in the direction of the kitchen.

Nothing was mentioned on the journey back, but Amber is certain Sally knows about the DNA results. As the FLO, she's an important part of the investigation team. It's embarrassing and wrong that a bunch of detectives should know about Mabel's paternity when George doesn't. DI Benedict advised Amber to tell her husband as soon as possible, implying that he might not be able to hold the information back for much longer. But she can't bring herself to say the words – not now, not yet. Maybe not ever.

George is still prowling around the hallway. 'So? What happened? Did they ask you about Ruby?'

She removes her boots and puts them neatly under the coat rack. 'Um … a bit.'

'What did they want to know?'

She racks her brain to come up with something believable. 'Um … What was our relationship like, had we ever fallen out, did I trust her. That sort of thing.'

'And how did you answer?'

'I said we get on fine and she adores Mabel and would never hurt her.'

'Hmm …' he replies doubtfully. 'That's not what people are saying on social media. They're saying you hate each other's guts, that Ruby's always been jealous of you and wanted to get her own back.'

Amber's mouth falls open. 'Why are you looking at that rubbish? It's just evil rumour-mongering.'

'Yeah, well, maybe. But there's been a lot of activity around Batley Reservoir this morning. They've sent divers in.'

She blanches. 'Divers?'

'Yes, and they've got officers on their hands and knees searching the banks. It's the perfect place to dump a body, close by yet out of the way. Word is that someone was seen carrying a child—'

'Stop it, George, stop it!' She puts her hands over her ears.

'These people have contacts in the police; information leaks out.'

'It's fake news. Ask Sally if you want an update.'

'I would, but she's been with you all morning,' he huffs. 'Nobody tells me anything. I just have to sit here like an idiot, with all these horrible images going around in my head. I can't take it, it's killing me. I want Mabel found now, one way or another.'

'No, George, we want her alive. It doesn't matter how long it takes, as long as she's alive.'

'The police obviously think Ruby's done something to her or they wouldn't have called you in.'

She tries to lay a calming hand on his arm, but he shoves her off. 'Ruby's innocent,' she says. 'Sonya's the one they really suspect.'

'Then they'd bloody well better hurry up and find her!' he shouts. 'I'm sick of all this pussyfooting around. We need results.'

He pushes past her and storms upstairs. Amber waits to hear the bedroom door slam shut, then walks into the lounge and sits down wearily on the sofa. She understands George's frustration, but she can't allow herself to follow him into the darkness. She needs light, positive thoughts and happy pictures in her head.

Closing her eyes, she tries to picture Mabel. What is she doing now, at this very moment? She could be taking her morning nap, or nibbling a rusk, or enjoying her bottle, or having her nappy changed, or playing with her toes. Amber refuses to imagine her tiny, lifeless body lying at the bottom of Batley Reservoir. Ruby didn't kill her, either deliberately or by accident. Nor did Lewis aid and abet her, if that's what they're saying on social media. Mabel is not dead. Fact. If she were, Amber would know, she would feel it in every fibre of her being. No, she is safe with Sonya, missing Mummy and Daddy a little perhaps, but having a lovely time. Sonya is caring for her as well as she would have cared for the baby girl she so tragically lost. She's keeping her warm, feeding her delicious, nourishing food and giving her lots of cuddles.

Amber rubs her eyes. In a moment, either Sally or her mother will walk in with the ubiquitous mug of tea and try to offer some comfort. The person she really wants to talk to is Seth. but it's too risky to call him now. They haven't been in touch since Mabel was taken. She's surprised – and a little hurt – that he hasn't tried to contact her. He must know what she's going through and he'll be worried sick about Mabel. She guesses he's trying to be discreet, so as not to cause trouble between her and George, but this is an emergency. He could at least have sent a text, asking how she was and if there was anything he could do. She would have deleted it immediately afterwards, as she always did, and George would have been none the wiser. It's not like Seth to be so distant, especially not in such extreme circumstances.

Amber heaves herself off the sofa and collects her handbag from the hallway, then goes into the kitchen. Sally is sitting at the breakfast bar, making notes in her book, while her mother is pointlessly wiping surfaces over and over again.

'Thanks,' she says, taking the steaming mug. 'I'll be out the back – just need some time to myself.'

'Good idea,' replies Sally.

Mum can only manage a nod. Her eyes are rimmed red with crying and she looks older than ever.

Amber goes into the sun lounge, sitting down on a wicker chair facing the doorway to give her warning of anyone coming in. Taking her phone from her bag, she rapidly types a text.

Hi. Why haven't you been in touch? We are going through hell but we truly believe Mabel is still alive and being looked after. Have some very important news and need to talk to you. Texting is tricky. Don't call. Am at Mum's with George. No privacy here and can't leave the house because the media are camped outside the door. Will call you tonight when everyone is asleep. 3 a.m. okay? PLEASE pick up xx

She puts the phone away, feeling slightly better for having made contact. Seth won't let her down. He'll know what to do; he always does. He may advise her to wait until Mabel comes home. George will be so happy, he might not give a damn that she's not his flesh and blood. In which case, she might not even need to tell him at all.

Because if there's one thing Amber has learnt from this horrific ordeal that isn't even over yet, it's that it doesn't matter if a child is not biologically yours. Love is not a by-product of genetics; it's an attitude of mind, a belief system. Look how George is suffering, how he so obviously loves Mabel and would do anything to have her back. Will he suddenly stop loving her if he discovers there is no biological connection between them? Of course not. He'll be hurt and extremely angry with Amber for deceiving him, but that is a separate issue. Telling him the truth right now would only increase his suffering, and she's not sure he can take any more – the poor guy's already falling apart at the seams.

Amber loves George; she's always loved him and has never wanted anyone else to be the father of her children. She started planning their family when she was a teenager – practising her married signature, making lists of baby names that went well with Walker. That was long before she knew anything about sperm counts or motility or ejaculation blockages.

Ironic that for years they used contraceptives and never once risked it. It was important to Amber that they did everything in the right order. She wanted to be married and have bought her own home. George needed to have a good, stable job. She wanted to reach a point in her own career where she could take maximum maternity leave without jeopardising her promotion prospects. Ideally, all these stars would align when she turned thirty. That age felt perfect for a first baby. Factoring in a sensible age gap, she would be thirty-three when she had their second and final child, keeping her well within range of being a *senile gravida*. She stopped taking the pill three months before her thirtieth birthday, during which time they used condoms. Then as soon as she hit the big three-zero, they set to work.

Amber was disappointed and a little surprised when she didn't conceive in the first month. By the third, she was worried, even though everything she read on the internet told her she should just relax and have fun. Instead, she started taking her temperature and eating foods rich in vitamin B. After they made love, she stuck a pillow under her bottom and lay with her legs in the air for hours. Yet still her period arrived each month, with alarming regularity.

A new, frightening thought started to dawn on her. Could the problem be on George's side? A small amount of googling told her that it definitely could. She went to see her doctor, who told her to come back in a year if they hadn't conceived. But Amber didn't want to wait a year; it would put her schedule out.

She tried talking to George, but he was very resistant to any suggestion that he might have fertility issues. He told her she was treating him like a mobile sperm bank and it put him off. When she gently mentioned that she was ovulating, he made excuses for not having sex, which made her feel angry with him for wasting her precious eggs. How were they ever going to conceive if he refused even to try? His pride was coming between them, and all the while, time was ticking by. At this rate, she would be thirty-two before baby number one arrived.

Months of trying came to nothing; she was feeling desperate and incredibly lonely. She secretly started to explore other options – sperm banks, donations from friends, motorbike deliveries, turkey basters – but rejected them all. George was supposed to be her baby's father and only George would do.

Then that fateful evening happened. It wasn't planned; she didn't deliberately set out to cheat on her husband. The thought hadn't occurred to her. Yes, they'd had a bad row about his refusal to engage with the issue, and yes, she was very upset and stressed and in need of comfort. And yes, yes, yes, she got very drunk and smoked weed, which she hadn't done since uni because it made her feel out of control. It was wrong, it was a terrible betrayal on both their parts, and she should have stopped in her tracks, turned around and run away. But she didn't, and she still doesn't understand exactly why. Other forces were at work that night. For the first time in her life, she submitted to a deeper, darker side of herself and her body grabbed the opportunity. Poor George. He didn't stand a chance.

As if summoned by her shameful thoughts, he suddenly walks into the room, mobile in hand. His eyes are wide and he's looking very shaken.

'Ruby and Lewis have been arrested,' he says.

Her stomach flips. 'What?!'

'It's all over social media.'

'It's not true. It can't be true.' They rush into the kitchen, where Sally is in the middle of a phone call.

'What's going on? Have they found Mabel?' demands George.

Sally rings off as soon as she sees their anguished faces. 'No. Why? Have you been on social media?'

'So what if I have? They're saying Ruby and Lewis have been arrested.'

'Not so,' she replies. 'They've agreed to a voluntary interview under caution, which is quite different.'

George tuts. 'Different how?'

'They're helping us with our enquiries, but they're free to leave at any time.'

'But the police suspect them, right?' He gesticulates with his phone. 'A witness has come forward, is that it? That's why divers are searching the reservoir.'

Amber clutches her tummy. 'I think I'm going to be sick.'

'Please listen to me,' says Sally. 'I really want you to stay away from social media; it's full of wild speculation and misleading information. We *are* searching the area and we *are* talking to Ruby, and also to Lewis Chambers, but you mustn't jump to conclusions.'

'I don't understand. I thought you were looking for Sonya,' says Amber, weakly. Please, she thinks, please let it be Sonya.

'We've been working around the clock to locate her and I'm hoping to be able to update you on that very soon.' Sally clasps her hands together pleadingly. 'Please trust us. Sonya is a strong suspect, but that doesn't mean we stop exploring other avenues. This is a complex case and we're following a huge number of lines of enquiry all at the same time.'

'There's still got to be a reason why you're so interested in Ruby and Lewis,' grumbles George. 'We have a right to know, don't we, Amber?'

'Yes, George,' she says quietly, feeling the ground beneath her rapidly falling away. 'You have a right to know.'

CHAPTER TWENTY-THREE

Day three without Mabel

Ruby listens to Detective Inspector Benedict reciting the statement she's previously only heard on TV crime dramas: 'You do not have to say anything. But it may harm your defence if you do not mention when questioned something which you later rely on in court. Anything you do say may be given in evidence.'

She nods in acknowledgement. 'Yes, I understand.' Her calm voice belies the storm of emotions raging beneath the surface – fury, indignation, fear. It doesn't help that she knows she and Lewis are innocent. She imagines evidence being twisted around her like barbed wire, digging into her flesh.

There must be a reason for this sudden change from witness to suspect. Is it simply because she was the last person to see Mabel alive? No, a specific accusation has been made, and it can only have come from Amber and George. She feels intensely angry with them – not only because it's a personal betrayal, but because they're diverting the police from finding their daughter's real abductor.

Benedict waits to regain her attention, then says, 'As we explained earlier, you are here voluntarily and have the right to leave the interview at any time.'

It's small comfort. Judging by the frenzy of excitement when she arrived at the police station this morning, the media will no doubt have already told the world she's been arrested for murder. Benedict assured her that they'll release a press statement clarifying the situation, but as far as Ruby can see, the damage has been done. God only knows what is circulating on social media now. People will be jumping to all kinds of wicked conclusions. Even if she's proved innocent, she'll still receive death threats. Maybe she should have refused to be interviewed, but that would have made her look as if she had something to hide. They probably would have arrested her anyway.

'You have refused the right to free legal representation. If you change your mind at any stage, please say and we will suspend the interview immediately.'

'Okay.'

As Benedict finishes off the tick-list of things he is obliged to say, Ruby's mind zones in to Lewis, who is sitting in another room right now, being interviewed by other members of Benedict's team. She's worried about how he'll react to being questioned. When he feels cornered, he can be quite aggressive – he's like Amber in that respect. If there's one thing neither of them can bear, it's being treated unjustly. However, the police may take it as a sign of guilt. When DS Ali Smart asked him to come down to the station, Ruby could almost see the hairs on the back of his neck bristling, his back arching like a cat. He's not good with authority, hates anyone telling him what to do. If he's not careful, he'll accidentally incriminate himself.

She tries to send him telepathic thoughts: *Stay calm and tell the truth.*

'I've been studying the witness statement you gave,' says Benedict, turning to nod at DS Ali Smart, who is already taking notes. 'I'd like to go over it again, just in case anything else comes to mind, something you forgot first time around.'

'Okay. Yeah, I'm happy to do that.'

'But first, I'd like to hear a bit more about your relationship with your family. To fill in the background.'

'What do you mean exactly?' Ruby picks up a plastic cup of scalding tea. It sloshes and a drop splashes onto her thumb, making her flinch. It's obviously too hot to drink, so she puts it back down immediately.

'Well, how would you describe your relationship with your sister?'

She shrugs. 'Um … okay. A bit weird, if I'm honest. I mean, we were never close as kids, there's a big age gap and, um … we're very different personalities. We still don't have much in common, but we get on better these days.'

'Do you socialise together much? As a foursome, I mean.'

'Not really. We tried it a few times, but it didn't work very well.' She casts her mind back to a few awkward evenings neither side wanted to repeat. 'George and Amber wanted to go to smart, super-cool places we didn't much like and definitely couldn't afford. Amber would insist on paying and Lewis found it embarrassing. It was like we were the kids and they were the parents.'

'I see.'

'And we have different politics, which never helps.'

'But apart from that, the four of you get along?'

'Yeah, as long as you don't scratch the surface.'

Benedict seems to think about this for a few moments. 'Has Lewis ever fallen out with Amber or George?'

'No. Not that I can remember.' She tries the tea again, taking the opportunity to gather her thoughts. It's true that Lewis keeps coming up with excuses for not going around to number 74, particularly recently. She'd hoped Mabel's arrival would make things better, but if anything, it made them worse. If only he'd agreed to join her last weekend. Somehow, she's certain that if there'd been two of them on duty, the abductor wouldn't have dared enter the house.

'Would you say you've been closer or further apart since Mabel was born?' asks Benedict.

'Oh, closer, for sure. It's made a huge difference.' Tears start to clog in her throat.

'How did you feel when you heard you were going to be an aunt?'

'I was really excited. I love kids ... Sorry.' She takes a tissue from her sleeve and presses it against her damp eyes. She adores Mabel, but even if her niece is found safe and well – and she's clinging to the belief that she will be – she'll probably never be allowed anywhere near her again. That relationship is broken forever.

'You okay?' DI Benedict is studying her face closely.

'I can't bear it. I just want you to find her and bring her home.'

'That's what everyone wants,' says Ali Smart.

Ruby removes the tissue, now soaked with tears, and, not having anywhere else to put it, tucks it back up her sleeve, where it clings damply to her skin.

'Sorry.'

'Nothing to apologise for.' Benedict lets a brief silence descend on the room, then resumes. 'How do you think Amber felt about becoming pregnant?'

'She was thrilled.'

'Was it planned – as far as you know?'

'Oh yes, absolutely. Everything Amber does is planned. She's an achievement junkie.' Ruby gives them a rueful smile. 'That's the main difference between us. She's the success, I'm the failure.'

'Do you feel in competition with her?'

'Not any more, but yes, when I was a kid. Our mother used to compare us all the time and I was always way behind. I suppose I was jealous.'

DI Benedict grabs the word out of the air. 'Jealous?'

Ruby curses silently. She's thrown them a line and now they're going to wind it around her, tying her in knots. 'Yes, but I grew up and realised that it didn't matter what anyone else thought, as long as I was true to my own values.'

'And how do you feel about Amber right now?'

'I feel extremely sorry for her. She's going through hell. We all are.'

'Is there any reason why you might feel angry with her?'

Ruby takes a deep breath. 'That depends.'

'On what?'

'On whether she's accusing me.'

Benedict and Smart exchange a glance. 'What do you think she's accusing you of?' he asks slowly.

'Murder.'

'Murder?'

'Yes. She thinks I asked Lewis to help dispose of Mabel's body and then pretended she'd been abducted.'

She realises – too late – that she's just stepped into a mire of quicksand. She can feel herself sinking down, down …

'Is that what happened, Ruby?' says Benedict.

'No! Absolutely not. I would never … I was just saying …' she flounders. 'It's obviously why you've called me back, although you can't have a scrap of evidence against me. If Amber is the one accusing me, then yes, I feel extremely angry with her.'

'Fair enough.' He coughs and adjusts his position in the chair. 'You see, we have a problem here. Our scene-of-crime officers are baffled as to how Mabel was removed from the house.'

'They're not the only ones,' she snaps.

'As you were the only other person there at the time, it can't surprise you that that we need to question you further about this particular issue.'

'Yes, I understand, and I've been racking my brains to work out how it happened, but I've drawn a blank.'

'Hmm,' says Benedict. 'We couldn't find any evidence of forced entry, which means that whoever took Mabel had means of access to the flat. We have to consider the possibilities. Maybe the front door was simply left open and an opportunistic burglar got in, then saw Mabel and decided to take her.'

'I didn't leave the front door open. It's the middle of winter, I would have noticed.'

'Yes, we think so too. Which leaves us thinking that either this person had a key, or they were let in.'

'I didn't let anyone in.'

'Are you sure about that?'

'Yes!'

DI Benedict nods at his sergeant. She takes a sheet of paper from a buff folder and passes it to Ruby, describing her action for the recording. 'According to your mobile phone records, you called Lewis Chambers at sixteen minutes past one on Sunday morning.'

Ruby feels her stomach tighten. 'Okay.'

'But you didn't mention it in your witness statement,' says DS Ali Smart.

'Didn't I?' Ruby blushes. 'Sorry. I forgot. I suppose it didn't seem relevant.'

'The conversation was four minutes long.'

'Was it?'

'Can you remember what it was about?'

'Um … not really. We were just saying goodnight.'

'Do you normally go to bed so late?'

'At the weekend, yeah. Sometimes later.'

Benedict signals to his colleague and she takes a photo out of the folder, turning it around and pushing it towards Ruby. It's a grainy black-and-white shot taken on a CCTV camera of somebody walking along clutching a large object to their chest. She reels off the exhibit number for the tape. 'Do you recognise the person in this picture?'

Ruby pales. 'Oh my God. Where was that taken?'

'Please answer the question. Do you recognise them?'

'No. How could I? It's really unclear. Is that … are they … are they carrying Mabel?' She gasps, clutching her throat.

'Why did you call Lewis Chambers?' presses DS Smart.

'I already said, to say goodnight. No other reason.'

'Was Mabel awake during the phone call?'

'No. She'd woken up about an hour earlier but I'd managed to get her off again.'

'Did you ask Lewis to come over and join you?'

'No.'

'And how was Mabel?'

'Fast asleep, like I said.'

'It had been a long day. On your own, without any help.'

'I didn't need help.'

DI Benedict makes a grunting noise, signalling that he wants to take over. 'Tell us again about this call with Lewis,' he says. 'Four minutes is a long time just to say goodnight. What else were you talking about?'

'I can't remember exactly, just normal stuff about how our days had gone … What are you trying to say? That I asked him to come over?'

'You tell us, Ruby.' He folds his arms across his chest.

A feeling of dread starts to wash over her. She points at the photo. 'This isn't Lewis, if that's what you're getting at.'

'What makes you so sure?'

'Because he had nothing to do with it.'

'To do with *what*, exactly?'

'Mabel's disappearance!'

She stares at the image. The abductor is wearing a hood and a scarf around their face; it's impossible to tell whether it's Lewis or not, whether it's even a man or a woman. If it's a still taken from security footage, the forensics team should be able to analyse the person's height and even their gait. But what if there's not enough footage to make accurate calculations? What if Lewis happens to be the same height or walk in a similar way? She remembers now that he was at home when she called, vegging out on the sofa, streaming a movie. He has no alibi for the hours between two and six, when Mabel was taken.

DI Benedict cuts into the silence. 'In your statement you said you don't have your own key to number 74.'

She blinks. 'Um … yes, that's right. I always borrow the spare.'

'Have you ever taken the key away with you by mistake – to your home, or to your workplace?'

'No. Amber doesn't trust me. She always asks for it back before I leave.'

He considers. 'Has Lewis ever borrowed the spare key? When he's babysat with you, for example.'

'I always babysit on my own.'

'Oh.' He looks surprised. 'Why's that?'

She hesitates. To say he has no interest in babies will make him sound unfeeling and odd, especially in the circumstances. 'Lewis works a lot of evenings,' she replies instead. 'If he has a free night, he likes to go out.'

'He works at the escape room with you, is that right?'

'Yes. He's a games master.'

'Has he ever borrowed the spare key to number 74?'

'Not as far as I know. You'll have to ask him.'

'Don't worry,' pipes up DS Smart. 'We will.'

Unable to face the baying hordes outside the police station, Ruby calls a minicab to pick her up from the rear entrance. She shuffles down in the seat as the car drives past the group of shouting reporters. Some of them run after her, and one even manages to bang on the window.

'You all right, love?' says the cab driver.

'Yes thanks,' she replies. But she isn't all right. Not at all.

She arrives home to an empty flat. Lewis must still be at the station. She hopes he's okay.

It's late afternoon, the light already fading. The flat feels miserably cold. She goes into the bedroom and climbs under the duvet. Her head is aching and she feels weak all over. She wants to be understanding of her sister and brother-in-law, but it's incredibly hard when they're accusing her of such disgusting things. Rationally, she knows their actions are born out of desperation and frustration, also that the police wouldn't be doing their job if they didn't investigate. But this has got to stop before there's some great miscarriage of justice, and more importantly, before Mabel's real abductor does something stupid. There's still time to save her niece, but the police are looking in the wrong place.

CHAPTER TWENTY-FOUR

Day four without Mabel

Amber is worried. Seth still hasn't responded to the urgent text she sent him hours ago. They're supposed to be speaking at 3 a.m. and she doesn't know whether to try calling as planned or forget it. She's been lying in the darkness for hours, hovering on the threshold of sleep, fighting off distressing images of Mabel that make her sweat with fear.

She turns on her side to look at the clock – thirteen minutes to go. This is not like Seth. Sometimes she has to wait several hours for a reply, but he never ignores her completely. Has she done something to offend him? Or rather, has she *not* done something? Could he even be exacting some kind of petty revenge? In the past, he's accused her of turning him on and off like a tap, and there was that time when he badly needed her support and she wasn't able to give it to him – not in the way he wanted, anyhow. But it was complicated and she had George to consider. Surely Mabel's disappearance far outweighs any previous crises either of them has experienced.

Or perhaps there's a simpler explanation. He could have gone away for a few days, or there might be something wrong with his phone.

Should she call anyway, and see if he answers? She's not going to fall asleep now, so she might as well try. She turns over towards George, who is sleeping on his side, facing her. She marvels that he can sleep at all with Mabel still missing. Not that she thinks badly of him – the poor man is wrung out with exhaustion. She's jealous, that's all. He looks so innocent, curled into the foetal position with his hands clasped beneath his chin, as if in sleeping prayer. Not knowing. That's what innocent means. How will she ever tell him he's not Mabel's biological father? It will break him.

She carefully extracts herself from the bed and puts on the towelling dressing gown borrowed from her mother. Tucking her phone into the pocket, she creeps out of the room and tiptoes down the stairs. The heating went off hours ago and the house is icy cold. She goes into the living room, quietly shutting the door behind her before turning on the light. The sudden brightness stings her tired eyes, making her blink at the surroundings. She knows this room extremely well, but it doesn't feel at all welcoming. Curling into an armchair, she tucks her legs under her bottom and pulls the thin gown across her chest.

She takes out the phone, checking her text feed first to see if Seth has sent a last-minute reply. He hasn't. She sighs. Oh well … It's just gone three o'clock. If her call wakes him, then so be it. She finds his number, disguised in her contacts as 'Physio', presses the icon and waits for the line to connect. After two rings, it goes straight to voicemail. She hears Seth's smooth, calm tone as he apologises for not being available and asks her to leave a message.

'What's going on?' she says, unable to keep the irritation out of her voice. 'Why won't you speak to me? I'm sorry I couldn't call. Please don't be cross. Reply to my text at least. I need to tell you something important and—'

She breaks off at the sound of somebody coming down the stairs. Ending the call abruptly, she shoves the handset back in her pocket just as the door opens. It's George.

'What are you doing?' he says. 'I woke up and you weren't there.'

'Sorry. I couldn't sleep.'

'I thought I heard talking.'

'No.'

'I'm sure I did.'

'Oh, um … I was looking at stuff on my phone and a clip started playing by accident,' she bluffs. 'Sorry, I didn't mean to disturb you.'

He rubs the sleeves of his pyjamas. 'It's bloody freezing down here. Come back to bed.'

'Yeah, in a bit,' she says.

'Please? I need to have you next to me. It scared me when I realised you weren't there. It felt like I'd lost you too.'

'Don't be silly. I was here.'

George brushes aside his tousled hair. 'It's absolute hell, but at least we have each other. I couldn't do this on my own, I'd collapse.'

'No you wouldn't. You're much stronger than me.' She untucks her legs and lets him pull her to her feet. He folds his arms around her and she inhales the familiar sleepy smell of him. 'I love you,' she says, her voice breaking with emotion.

'Love you too,' he murmurs.

'I'm so sorry.'

'For what?'

She hesitates, then says, 'For leaving Mabel with Ruby.'

'You have to talk to her. Make her tell you the truth.'

'Yes … I'll text her, ask her to come over.'

'That's all I want – the truth, no matter how bad it is. I just have to know.'

The following morning, the same weird routine starts up again. The media gather outside the house with their insulated coffee mugs, setting up equipment and chatting easily to each other.

There is a brief flurry of excitement as Sally arrives shortly after eight o'clock, then it calms down again. Vicky makes tea and toast. Amber and George shower and dress, then go downstairs for their first update of the day. They are prisoners, scared to step outside for fear of being ambushed, reluctant to do anything normal like go for a walk or buy a pint of milk in case it's construed as uncaring or even guilty.

'There are lilac ribbons all the way down the street,' Sally says as she slips off her coat. 'I've seen them elsewhere, too.'

Amber pulls a face. 'I wish people wouldn't.'

'They want to show their support,' her mother says, bringing a laden tray into the lounge. 'And who knows? It might even jog somebody's memory.'

'But we're miles away from where she was taken,' Amber replies.

Vicky bangs the tray down on the coffee table. 'Well *I* appreciate it. At least the neighbours are on our side.'

'It's okay,' George says, laying his hand on Amber's arm. 'Let people do what they want.'

Vicky retreats, leaving Sally to distribute mugs and side plates. She offers around a plate piled high with triangles of buttered toast, some spread with marmalade, others with jam. She might as well be hosting a coffee morning, thinks Amber as she takes a piece she doesn't actually want. She's hardly eaten a thing since Sunday and her trousers are already feeling looser at the waist. Ironic that she's been wanting to lose weight but lacked the motivation. When she gets Mabel back, she's going to give up worrying about such stupid, superficial things.

'So, any news about Ruby and Lewis?' says George, finishing his toast and rubbing the crumbs off his fingers. 'I heard they were released yesterday. Does that mean they're in the clear?'

'It means we don't have enough evidence to charge them,' Sally says. 'And they weren't "released", because they weren't held in the first place. I gather they were both very cooperative, but that's all I can tell you at this stage. We're still analysing evidence and witness reports. We've had a huge response from the public, but it's going to take a while to sift through the material. Most of it won't be relevant and some will be from cranks, but that's how it is, I'm afraid.'

Amber feels a surge of hope. At least they didn't make a confession. She really, really doesn't want it to be Ruby and Lewis, because that would mean that something terrible has happened to Mabel.

'And what about Sonya?' she asks.

Sally purses her lips. 'Hmm … I'm afraid it's not looking likely. We've been examining her recent expenditure and it seems she booked a flight to India two weeks ago.' She registers the disappointment on their faces. 'I'm sorry. I know you were hoping …'

'Maybe she didn't actually catch the flight,' says George.

'Yes,' Amber agrees. 'It could have been a trick. You know, to cover her tracks, mislead the police.'

'Yes, you're right, absolutely, we're not making any assumptions either way. As soon as we've tracked her down, we'll let you know.'

'What about the CCTV footage you showed us yesterday?' asks George. 'Any more news on that? Does it look like it could be Lewis? Some other cameras must have picked the guy up; there may be a better shot of him.'

'Or her,' Sally adds.

'Exactly,' says Amber. 'It could easily be Sonya. The figure was quite slight, looked more like a woman to me.'

'The images are being analysed and another appeal has gone out for security footage. Everyone's working around the clock; there's a massive team involved.' Sally looks at her phone. 'Right. I need to make a few calls … Anything else you want to know?'

'It just feels so odd to be trapped here doing nothing,' says Amber. 'It's driving us both crazy.'

George nods. 'Perhaps we should do another press conference?'

The boss is considering it, but he'd rather have something positive to say,' Sally replies. 'We've got the still from the footage, but it's not certain it's somebody carrying a child, and anyway, it's not a clear image – we'll only get hundreds of people calling in to say they know who it is, and it'll clog up the system.'

'We need to do something, though,' he persists.

Sally stands up and puts her empty mug and plate back on the tray. 'He's also talking about staging a reconstruction.'

George's face lights up. 'Great. Let's do it today.'

'It would be better to wait until Saturday, when there'll be more people around – regular weekend park-goers in particular. We think the abductor may have been stalking Mabel, watching the house, waiting for his or her chance. Someone might remember seeing somebody hanging around.'

'Yeah, it's definitely worth doing,' says George.

'Not that we were ever aware of someone stalking us,' admits Amber, thinking of all those times she pushed Mabel listlessly around the park, eyes fixed firmly on the path because she didn't want to engage with anyone, trying to pretend that this wasn't really her boring, humdrum life. How she regrets her attitude now. Anyone could have been following her and she wouldn't have had a clue. She covers her face. 'Oh, I can't bear it, it's so creepy.'

'There's one other thing,' says George. 'I think we'd both like to go home, if that's possible. Being here is just an extra strain, and not just on us.' He nods in the direction of the kitchen, where Vicky is doing some noisy clearing-up.

'Yes, of course,' Sally replies. 'I'll find out if we can release the property. But bear in mind you'll have even more media attention if you go back. There are already crowds in the park, just hanging around. Once they know you're at home ...' She sighs. 'We'll give you protection, of course, but you still might find it very uncomfortable. There's a lot of vile stuff online. It could turn nasty.'

'We'll think about it,' says Amber.

'Fine.' Sally gathers up the other mugs and takes the tray to the kitchen. George leaves the room and goes upstairs, leaving Amber locked into her own thoughts.

She doesn't know whether she wants to go home or not.. At first, she wanted to be at number 74 in case Mabel came back but now the idea of returning without her feels wrong. The flat is heaving with signs of her existence. How will they be able to look at the empty cot, the drawers of unworn clothes, the toys that might never be played with again? They are already at breaking point – it could shatter them into a million pieces. And the thought of the media camped outside in the street, their powerful zoom lenses trained on the windows, terrifies her. Press photographers would love to get a shot of Mabel's distraught parents at the scene of the crime. And if Ruby *does* turn out to be guilty …

She remembers the promise she made to George in the small hours and, reaching for her mobile, sends a text to her sister.

Hi. We need a proper honest talk. Please can you come over?

The reaction is instant: *Happy to talk but not at Mum's.*

That decides it then, thinks Amber, typing her response. *Thanks. We are going back home tonight. Shall we meet there tomorrow morning?*

Okay.

The sound of Sally's insistent ringtone drifts into the room from the kitchen. Amber goes to the door and listens, trying to gauge the content of the conversation from her tone. 'Yup,' Sally says. 'Thanks. I'll let them know straight away.'

Amber's heart rate rises. There is news. Going into the hallway, she calls up the stairs. 'George! Come down!' She rushes into the kitchen, where Sally is busy scribbling in her notebook. 'What is it?' she asks breathlessly.

George comes thundering down. 'Have you found Mabel?'

'Hold on.' Sally lifts a restraining hand. 'There's been a development concerning Sonya Garrick.'

'And?' Amber holds hope in her breath.

'As we thought, she's in India, travelling on her own. One of our officers managed to speak to her at a hostel this morning.'

Amber feels her knees dissolving. She leans against the kitchen counter to support herself. 'It was definitely her?'

'Yes … I'm sorry. She left the country ten days before Mabel was taken and we've tracked her whereabouts during that time. Apparently she was very shocked and upset by the news about Mabel, and particularly that she'd been suspected. She, um, sends her sympathies.'

'Right …'

'She apologised for not telling anyone that she was leaving the UK or where she was going, but she said she couldn't take it any more, needed to get away and be by herself for a while.'

'Yeah … that doesn't surprise me,' admits Amber. Maybe that's what she herself will have to do, she thinks, if Mabel is never found. She won't be able to tolerate the likes of Polly and the other mums from the antenatal class circling like buzzards, feeding off the carrion of her grief. Or worse, suspecting that she killed Mabel in a fit of postnatal despair and persuaded her sister to help conceal the crime. All those friendships are over, just like everything else.

'Well at least she's been eliminated,' says George. 'Which puts Ruby and Lewis back in the frame.'

Sally frowns. 'Don't jump the gun. We still have several lines of enquiry to pursue. And now the boss definitely wants to do the reconstruction on Saturday.'

'That's good, but it's three days away,' he protests.

'Don't worry, there's masses to do, we're working non-stop.' Her eyes flicker between them, then land firmly on Amber. 'In the meantime, please go back over everything. If there's any detail you can think of, any piece of information at all, however small, don't be afraid to mention it. The media are digging for dirt on the two of you; there are all kinds of rumours flying around, so be on your guard.' Her gaze burns into Amber. 'It could get very rough. Take care of each other, eh?'

'Of course.' George squeezes Amber's hand. 'We're totally united. Nobody can break us apart.'

CHAPTER TWENTY-FIVE

Day four with Mabel

I'm afraid my little girl is unhappy. When she's not flat-out crying, she grizzles and makes ugly moaning sounds. No amount of cuddling or rocking comforts her, and I haven't seen her smile for days. I indulge her with treats, but she spits them out and throws them on the floor. She's not even that interested in her bottle. It's as if she's going on hunger strike.

I knew it wouldn't be easy, that it would take a while for her to settle into her new life, but four days on, the situation is getting worse, not better. Looking after a baby on your own 24/7 is exhausting at the best of times, but usually there are rewards to keep you going: a loving gaze, a gurgle of content-ment, a fit of giggles over a simple game. All Mabel gives me are looks of hatred.

Maybe she's sickening for something. The bungalow is damp and draughty; she could easily have picked up a germ. I keep taking her temperature, but so far, it's been normal.

'Please don't be ill,' I say, as I fasten on a clean nappy. 'I can't take you to a doctor; we're on our own here. It's me or nobody.'

She drums her feet against the changing mat. Her expression is fierce, her cheeks hot with defiance. I wrench the dungarees over her bottom and pull them up. She fights me off with her fists as I try to fasten the straps.

'Stop it! Don't be such a naughty girl!' The sound of my angry voice makes her bottom lip quiver. 'Don't you dare start crying again. I can't take any more, it's doing my head in.'

I pick her up and carry her into the living room, where I trap us into Great-Aunt Dolly's capacious armchair, sitting her on my lap and wedging her in with cushions. She wriggles in protest. Reaching for the remote control, I switch on the television for the lunchtime news. The urgent thumping beat of the theme tune fills the room, and images swirl around the screen. It seems to calm Mabel, but I feel nervous as the camera zooms in on the newsreader, who is looking suitably grave.

To my surprise and indignation, Mabel has already been bumped off the top spot. I clutch her to me as the leading item rolls out – an earthquake in South East Asia, with hundreds dead and even more missing. In the grand scheme of things, it's a tragedy more far-reaching and important than the disappearance of one little British girl. The reporter at the scene is doing her best to convey the enormity of the disaster and evoke our sympathies, but the harsh truth is that most of the public don't really care about dead, injured and missing strangers thousands of miles away. They want to tie a lilac ribbon around a tree for Mabel, because she is one of them; she could be their daughter or granddaughter. She has become a precious new member of their family.

Mabel is next up. Her image flashes across the screen – the same one they keep using. Don't Amber and George have any other photos?

'Look! That's you,' I say, pointing, but Mabel's far too young to recognise herself, and right now she's more interested in the red tassel dangling from Great-Aunt Dolly's tapestry cushion.

The newsreader informs us that despite the police question-ing two people in connection with Mabel's disappearance, both have been released without charge. This is not what I was hoping for. The babysitting aunt and her boyfriend fitted the bill nicely. Although the police would never have found a body, it wouldn't necessarily have stopped them being convicted.

It's chilling how determined I am. How I would rather see an innocent couple go down for a murder they didn't commit just so that I can keep her. I had no idea I was capable of such things; that the flame I keep for Mabel could burn with such intensity. I kiss the top of her auburn head and give her an extra squeeze, but she flinches away from me.

Now the detective leading the investigation is speaking to camera. He tells us that the police have received an enormous response from the general public. 'We strongly believe that Mabel is still alive,' he says. 'We are examining evidence and pursuing several promising lines of enquiry.'

'Hmm … What does that mean, Mabel?' I whisper. 'Are they pursuing *me*? Has Amber told them the truth yet? The police will probably have worked it out anyway. DNA is the one thing that can't lie.' I put my face close to Mabel's and sniff her, animal-like, drawing the smell of her genes into my nostrils.

What's that knocking sound? At first I think it must be coming from the television, but then I realise it's somebody at the door. Shit … Who the hell can that be? Please, please don't let it be the police. Blood rushes to my head. Another knock, louder this time. What should I do? The car's outside; it's obvious I'm in. They may even be able to hear the television. To not answer will arouse suspicion. But I can't let them see Mabel.

Another knock. I stand up and carry her into her bedroom, dumping her rather unceremoniously in her cot. She squeals in protest, like an animal forced into a cage.

'Hush now, be a good girl,' I whisper, shutting her in.

I can see a shadowy figure behind the frosted glass of the front door. My fingers tremble on the latch as I open it, and I only just about manage to contain a sigh of relief when I see that it's not a police officer; just an elderly man leaning on a stick. He's wearing a tweed jacket, brown cords and a flat cap, like he's performing 'old country codger'. I didn't think such people existed any more.

'I saw the car in the drive so I thought I'd take the opportunity,' he says. 'Been meaning to call these last few days, but you know how it is. Anyway, hello.' He holds out his hand for me to shake and I take it gingerly. 'Bob Masefield's the name – we're neighbours.'

'Oh. I didn't think we had any neighbours,' I reply stiffly.

He laughs as if I've made a joke. 'Well, I'm as near a neighbour as you've got. I live up the lane. The Nook, thatched cottage on the corner. You'll have spotted it, I expect.'

'Oh yes. Hi. Pleased to meet you.' Mabel is crying now – unless he's deaf, he must be able to hear her. My muscles tense. If I don't get rid of him soon, she's going to give me away. Her screams seem amplified. I imagine her tears seeping under the bedroom door and flooding the hallway.

'So, you've bought Dolly's place,' he says.

'Dolly?' I reply, feigning ignorance.

'Dorothy Williams. She died about a year and a half ago.'

'Yes.'

'We thought developers would buy it. Knock it down, build something new.' He waits for me to provide some information. 'We were surprised when we saw someone had moved in. I expect you're going to do it up.'

'Yes. Eventually.'

'Holiday home, is it, or are you going to live here all the time?'

'All the time,' I reply, giving him a thin smile.

He smiles. 'It'll be nice to have a young family in the village. Too many oldies like me and Barbara. That's my wife, you'll get to meet her. She was going to come with me but she does her art class today. I said to her this morning, we can't keep leaving it, it's not neighbourly.' He puts his free hand on the door frame for support, hoping, no doubt, that I'll invite him in for a cup of tea.

Mabel's cries are becoming louder, more insistent. 'Sorry,' I say. 'I'm really busy right now.'

'Somebody's got a fine pair of lungs on them.' He cranes his head to look past me, hoping to see their owner.

'My son,' I say quickly. 'He's just woken up. I really must go to him.' I start to close the door, but he edges forward, putting an invisible foot inside.

'We've got six grandchildren, one great-grandchild on the way.'

'Congratulations.' I throw a glance over my shoulder. 'Oh dear, he's sounding really unhappy. I'm very sorry, but I need to go and see to him.'

'How old is he?'

I hesitate. 'Sorry?'

'Your son.'

'Oh. Um, ten months.'

'Yes, well, nice to meet you, er ...' He grasps for the name I haven't given him, then gives up. 'Drop in the next time you're passing. The wife's out and about a lot, but I'm always in. The Nook. You can't miss it.'

'Yes, thanks,' I say, forcing a smile through my teeth. 'We will.'

As soon as he turns to go, I shut the door firmly, then lean against it for a few seconds, trying to regain my balance. Jesus, that was close. Was he just being neighbourly? You'd never get that kind of thing in London. He seemed particularly interested in the baby, although to be fair, she was making a terrible racket. It would have been strange if he hadn't commented.

She's still making a racket. I push off the door and go into her bedroom. She has rolled over and squashed herself against the rails. Her cheeks are wet with tears, and wisps of hair are plastered against her forehead.

'Shut up, Mabel!' I say, shaking the sides of the cot. 'You nearly gave the game away just then!' She continues to wail, her face turning as red as a squashed raspberry. 'I can't deal with this right now. I need to *think*!'

Covering my ears, I march back out of the room and into the kitchen, slamming the door shut. I lean against the worktop and try to breathe out my temper. If she doesn't calm down, she's going to ruin everything. Did the old duffer believe my story, or has he hobbled back to his bloody thatched cottage to call the police? I should have been more friendly, introduced myself – not with my real name, of course. I should have given him a long story about moving from the city for clean country air and a better life for our son.

But maybe he already knows who I am. Villages are full of gossip. Maybe he knows that Dolly was my great-aunt and was testing me out. If I'm already a suspect, it won't take long for even the dumbest detective to put two and two together and track me down.

I tug my hair anxiously. What I wouldn't give for a cigarette right now … I gave up for Mabel, but now I wish I'd kept a packet for emergencies. Mabel's screams are reaching a crescendo.

'For Christ's sake, stop it!' I shout, although there's no way she can hear me from the kitchen.

Opening the back door, I step outside into the cold. My muscles are taut; I'm wound up like a spring. I pull the sleeves of my jumper down over my hands and pace around the garden. The long damp grass licks at the bottom of my jeans; I curse as I almost turn an ankle in a hidden hole. I hate this fucking country life,

where everyone wants to know everyone else's business. I would
have been safer in London. Damn the nosy neighbour, damn
Mabel for screeching like a bloody smoke alarm.

I keep circling the garden, round and round, stamping out
a track through the jungle of grass. What to do? Pack our bags
and leave straight away? Find somewhere else to hide – a hotel, a
self-catering cottage? But we'd have to go somewhere hundreds of
miles away to throw the police off the scent, I daren't use my credit
card, and Mabel's photo is spread all over the media. We're trapped.

Mabel's cries are piercing my brain. Will it be police sirens I
hear next? I'm starting to hyperventilate. This isn't working. It just
isn't working. What am I going to do if she carries on fighting and
never gives in? I'll go crazy. I won't be able to cope. I'm already
not coping, that's obvious.

I go back into the kitchen and turn on the tap. Bending over
the sink, I splash icy-cold water over my face. Panic is spreading
through my body. Everything feels hopeless, just as it did when
I was lost and on my own and thought I'd never be happy again.
Having Mabel was supposed to put things right. I was sure she
would take to me instinctively, that all I had to do was show how
much I loved her and she would love me back. But she doesn't
want me. She's sobbing her little heart out and I don't know how
to help her.

Yes, you do, says a voice in my head. *Give her back.*

I shake my head. No, no, that's out of the question. I'm in too
deep, have made too many sacrifices, committed crimes I never
thought I was capable of, and all for one purpose: so that the three
of us can be together. And we *will* be together, one day in the
future, when the story of *Missing Mabel* has vanished from the
headlines and the world has given up thinking she could still be
alive. This is the only thing that keeps me going and makes the
hard work worthwhile. In the meantime, I have to be strong, have

to find a way through. Be more patient with Mabel. Deal with Mr Masefield – do whatever it takes to keep us safe.

I breathe out until all the air is expelled from my lungs. Then in again, filling myself to the brim. We'll get through this, I tell myself. It's going to be okay. Mabel is *ours*. She belongs to us.

CHAPTER TWENTY-SIX

Day five without Mabel

Amber feels herself tensing as George pulls the car up outside number 74. It's just gone midnight. The street is quiet and empty of onlookers; the crime-scene tape has been removed and there's no police officer guarding the front door. Only the lilac ribbons betray the appearance of normality. They are tied around the trees that line the edge of the park, all the lamp posts and most of their neighbours' front gates. Amber knows they are meant to be a symbol of hope, but to her they look morbid. How long will they remain there, she wonders – until the rain has washed away their colour or they've grown tatty in the wind? Until some other child is taken and needs ribbons of their own, perhaps.

'Are you sure you're okay about this?' says George. 'If you want to go back to your mum's …'

She looks up at the dark upper windows of their flat. 'No. It's going to be tough but we need to be here – for when she comes back.'

'Yeah, that's what I think. It's the right thing to do.'

They get out of the car and shut the doors as quietly as possible to avoid alerting the neighbours. George lets them in and they hurry up the stairs.

'It's bloody freezing,' he says. He takes their bags up to their bedroom, leaving Amber hovering on the landing. She's suddenly seized with a crazy idea that this has all been a huge mistake. Mabel is in the nursery, fast asleep in her cot. If not there, she'll be in the kitchen, sitting in her high chair, or in the bathroom having her nappy changed. Or maybe she's asleep in the buggy at the bottom of the stairs and they stupidly walked straight past her. Yes, that's what's happened. For the last four days, naughty little Mabel has been playing hide-and-seek, but the fun's over now – she needs to reveal herself.

She walks into the nursery, turning on the overhead light, willing her eyes to make the fantasy real. But of course the cot is horribly empty, as is the changing unit and the play mat. The surfaces are covered with fine grey fingerprint dust, and the laminate floor looks as if it's been sprayed with something and badly wiped clean. The SOCOs were looking for traces of blood, she guesses. A vision of Mabel explodes in her brain, bile rises into her throat and she rushes out, gagging.

She goes into the kitchen next, where Mabel is not in the high chair, although there are a few indistinguishable crumbs lurking on the tray. Nor does she find her in the sitting room, playing with her Sea World Activity Gym; or in the bathroom, lying on her changing mat, legs kicking the air. There's not even the merest trace of a baby smell, unpleasant or pleasant.

Amber feels sick with guilt. She used to resent somebody so small and powerless having so large and dominating a presence. Mabel descended on them like baby royalty, accompanied by a huge train of equipment, soaking up as many people as there were available to attend to her every need. She took over the flat, squeezing Amber into the corners, making her feel like a low-grade servant with no right to a life of her own. But now there's too much freedom, too much space, too much air to breathe. Mabel's absence is more overwhelming than her presence ever was.

She wonders what they will do with all this stuff if Mabel never comes back. How long is 'never' – five, ten, twenty years?

She suspects it's a state of mind rather than a measure of time. The Mabel who remains alive in their hopes will grow like any other child. One day she'll be too big for the high chair and baby bouncer, even for the cot that converts into a toddler bed. The toys and books will no longer amuse her and none of her clothes will fit. What then? Her belongings will serve as nothing more than an emotional obstacle course, tripping Amber up whenever and wherever she tries to move.

Unable to bear being in any of the rooms, Amber retreats to the landing and sits on the bottom step of the upper staircase, folding herself into a ball. She doesn't know why she's allowing such dark, negative thoughts to torment her. Coming back here was supposed to be a positive step forward, a sign that they weren't skulking away guiltily but actively joining the campaign to find Mabel – although for Amber it was more about getting away from her mother. George is all for leading new search parties and raising funds for advertising campaigns; he's even considering an appearance on breakfast TV. Amber doesn't want him to do any of it. The more public his appeals, the more stupid he's going to look when it's revealed that he's not Mabel's biological father. She suspects the news will leak eventually, like slime from a stinking bin bag. The media will smear it all over them. She ought to tell him before that happens – and she *will* tell him. But not tonight, not when they've only just returned home.

He's still upstairs. She can't hear him moving about above her – maybe he's already gone to bed. She takes out her mobile and checks the time. Half twelve. Too late now to try Seth again, not that she feels inclined to leave yet another message. His lack of response is completely baffling, not to say hurtful. Why have you deserted me? she thinks. Now, when I need you the most.

*

It doesn't take long for the media camp to realise that Amber and George have left her mother's house and returned to the scene of the crime. It ups sticks and descends on William Morris Terrace, where the various news agencies stake out their territory on the pavement opposite number 74. There are no houses there, just the edge of the park, and the railings form a useful crowd barrier, separating journalists and rubberneckers. The park was closed while police made a meticulous search of the undergrowth, but now the gates have reopened.

Amber is up early, although she never actually went to bed in the first place, preferring to lie on the sofa under the TV blanket rather than in the bed with George. She peers through the gap between the blind and the window frame, watching the hungry crowd gather. Even from inside, she can sense the febrile atmosphere out there, the anticipation, even bloodlust. The more appalling the truth, the more disgusting the crime, the better they will like it. She shivers inwardly. God, how she loathes every single one of them.

She goes up to the top-floor bathroom and takes a shower, then enters the bedroom in search of clean clothes. George is already awake, sitting up in bed, scrolling through his phone.

'I missed you last night,' he says.

'Sorry. I knew I wouldn't sleep. Didn't want to disturb you.' She takes a long-sleeved top out of the wardrobe and pulls it over her head. 'Ruby's coming round this morning, remember.'

'Okay. I'll go to the gym.'

'The gym?' she echoes. 'What? Back to work?'

'No. I need to train. My muscles are really stiff.'

'Is that a good idea? What will that lot outside think?'

'I don't give a toss what they think. I've got to expend some energy or I'll go mad.'

'Won't it be misconstrued as …' she feels for the word, 'uncaring? Our daughter's missing but life goes on, that sort of thing. Sally said we needed to be careful.'

'I'm going out of my mind, Amber. I can't stop thinking about her, wondering what happened to her, where she is now, if she's still alive. All these questions are constantly charging around my head.' He gets out of bed. 'You know me. I have to do something physical.'

'Okay, fair enough.' She's relieved, in a way, that he won't be there to see Ruby. 'Just be careful. And don't say anything to anyone, not even people you think are your friends.'

'Yeah, I'm not an idiot,' he replies tersely.

Amber finishes dressing, then goes back downstairs and into the sitting room. She looks out of the window again. Even more people have turned up. Some are drinking takeaway coffee while others are munching on what look like bacon sandwiches, probably from the greasy-spoon café at the top of the road. There's almost a party atmosphere. It's like they're waiting for a celebrity to come out and pose for photos. She pities George trying to leave the house. Rather him than her.

Sally texts to say she's been called to a team briefing and won't be around until the afternoon. Amber feels relieved. She doesn't want the woman in the flat; it's too small, they'll be falling over each other. Nor does she want her eavesdropping on the conversation with Ruby.

Dragging herself away from the window, she goes into the kitchen at the back of the flat. George is eating cereal at the table. He's wearing his gym clothes and trainers, still flicking through his bloody phone. The scene is so normal that for a nano second she forgets Mabel is missing, but then he lifts his head, and the look of desolation in his eyes jolts her back to reality.

He leaves the flat at a quarter to ten and, as predicted, is attacked by a barrage of questions and camera flashes. Amber watches him push through the crowd, then sprint defiantly up the street. A couple of the younger reporters try to follow, but soon give up. She hears someone shout, 'What are you running away from, George?'

Twenty minutes later, there are several loud knocks on the door and the bell rings urgently. Amber can only just hear it above the hubbub outside, which has reached a crescendo. She rushes downstairs and positions herself behind the front door, opening it just wide enough for Ruby to dive through the gap. She lands in the hallway and Amber shuts the door with a slam.

'Are you okay?' she asks. 'It's a bear pit out there. George had the same trouble earlier on.'

'I bet they weren't calling him a murderer.' Her sister is visibly shaking. She leans against the wall to steady herself. 'Did you know there's stuff online about me and Lewis running a paedo sex ring?'

'Oh God. I'm so sorry.'

Ruby huffs. 'Why are you apologising? Did you start the rumour?'

'Don't be stupid.' Amber starts to climb the stairs. 'That's a horrible thing to say.'

'I don't know why I agreed to come.' Ruby follows her up. 'Lewis told me not to. He's so angry with you and George. The police gave him a really hard time yesterday. He thought they were actually going to charge him.'

Amber doesn't react. 'Shall we go in the lounge, or would you rather sit in the kitchen – it's quieter at the back of the house.'

'Wherever, I don't care. I'm not staying long.'

'Are you taking part in the reconstruction on Saturday?'

'Sort of. They're using a police officer to be me, but I've got to be there in case there are any questions.'

They go into the kitchen. Amber's gaze passes over the empty high chair as she takes the kettle to the sink, and her hand starts to tremble. 'Do you want some tea?'

'No.'

'Actually, nor do I.' She plonks the kettle back on its stand. 'I've been drowning in the stuff. Poor Mum, she doesn't know what else to do.'

'We're all feeling powerless,' says Ruby, adding pointedly, 'It's why we lash out, looking for someone to blame.'

Amber sits down at the table. 'We're not blaming you – we're just trying to get to the truth.'

Ruby leans against the bookcase and folds her arms across her chest. 'You already know the truth. I didn't kill her.'

Amber nods. 'Yes, I really want to believe that, but …' She hesitates. 'Did the police show you the CCTV photo?'

'Yes, and it's not Lewis.'

'How do you know – for sure?'

'Because I love him and I know he's a good person.'

'But what if—'

'Lewis had no reason to harm Mabel, okay?'

'I know, I know,' agrees Amber. 'But whoever took her has to be somebody we know, someone who had a key or who was let in.'

Ruby groans. 'I didn't let anyone in, you've got to believe me.'

'I don't want it to be you or Lewis, but there doesn't seem to be any other expla—'

'Listen!' Ruby leans across and shakes her sister by the shoulders. 'Lewis and I are totally innocent. You know that. You're just creating a diversion.'

Amber removes her hands. 'What on earth do you mean?'

Ruby sighs audibly. 'Look, I know you weren't at Gaia Hall.'

'Well you're wrong there, because I was. The police have already checked my alibi.'

'Okay, then you were meeting someone there. You must have been, otherwise you would have told George.'

Amber's face tightens.

'I think you're having an affair,' Ruby continues.

'That's ridiculous. How on earth would I have time for an affair?'

'Well, it's obvious that something's wrong between you and George. You've been acting weird for months.'

'I've had a few problems adjusting to motherhood, that's all. That's normal.'

'No, it's more than that. You've been carrying a secret around. A big secret. And I've a pretty good idea what it is.'

'You clearly don't. Just leave it, okay?'

There's a dangerous pause as Ruby sharpens her stare. 'Is George Mabel's father?'

Amber recoils. 'That's really none of your business.'

'I guess the police know. DNA results must have revealed it.'

'I'm not talking to you about this. It's got nothing to do with you.'

'Does George know?'

Amber sets her mouth. 'I'd like you to go now.'

'Ah … so he doesn't.' Ruby's eyebrows flash up and down. 'God, no wonder you're stressed.'

'I'm stressed because my daughter is missing!' Amber's voice rises. 'This is a private matter, Ruby, just butt out.'

'But we're sisters. Aren't we supposed to confide in each other?'

Amber scoffs. 'Get real.'

'Yup, you're right.' Ruby starts to walk around the room. 'I know you've always resented me, ever since the day I was born. You disapprove of everything I do, the people I mix with, how I live my life. You've never been a proper sister – somebody I could rely on. For years you didn't give a shit about me. You only allowed me to look after Mabel so you could meet your lover.'

'I don't have a lover.'

'You've hated every minute of being a mum.'

'That's not true.'

'Mum thinks you're Little Miss Perfect and I'm the fuck-up, but actually it's—'

Something inside Amber snaps. 'Oh, shut up, for God's sake. This isn't about your jealousy or your relationship with Mum. It isn't about *us,* Ruby. It's about Mabel.'

Ruby swings round. 'Yes, absolutely. You asked me over for an honest conversation, Amber, but you're the one who's lying, not me.'

CHAPTER TWENTY-SEVEN

Day seven without Mabel

Ruby squeezes Lewis's arm as they stand in the front garden of number 74. 'Thanks for being here,' she says. 'Means a lot to me.'

'It's important to be seen together,' he replies. 'A show of solidarity.'

'Yes. I guess.'

It's Saturday morning, the day of the reconstruction. Ruby has loaned her jacket and bobble hat to the police officer picked to play her role – a woman of her height with a similar hairstyle, although facially completely unalike. Ruby offered to do it herself, but DI Benedict was worried that she might get attacked by a member of the public on route. Feelings against her and Lewis are still running high on social media, and although they were both released without charge, the police haven't yet publicly exonerated them. She is still being treated as a witness, but she feels increasingly like a suspect, Lewis even more so. That's why they have to be here today. To tough it out; be as cooperative as possible and behave as if they've nothing to hide. It's the truth anyway.

The front garden looks like a location shoot, littered with open metal boxes full of camera equipment, and hefty bearded guys muttering into their phones. Ruby and Lewis huddle in the downstairs neighbour's porch, trying to keep out of the way. The garden offers a safe haven; neither public nor press can touch them here. Two uniformed officers are guarding the gate, and sections of the street and park have been cordoned off with fresh plastic tape. The media have been forced back and are pushing against the tape like paparazzi waiting for a celebrity to emerge from the house. Their distasteful excitement stings the back of Ruby's throat, making her want to throw up.

She stamps her boots in the cold. She would rather be inside the flat, cradling a mug of coffee, but neither she nor Lewis is welcome there. Amber and George are holed up indoors, protected by bricks and mortar and the family liaison officer, who keeps popping in and out in order to talk to her colleagues, never missing the chance to throw them a furtive, almost hostile look. DI Benedict, the boss, is walking up and down the pavement, speaking earnestly into his phone with his hand cupped over the receiver. DS Ali Smart, to whom Ruby has taken a dislike for no rational reason, is sitting on the neighbour's wall, making notes. In the park opposite, the rubberneckers are out in force, lining the route as if they're about to watch a fun run or a cycle race. Several of them are clutching cups of takeaway coffee – the park café must be doing a roaring trade, Ruby thinks, curling her lip in disgust. Everyone seems to be busy but nothing is actually happening. It's been like this for the past hour.

'What's going on?' whispers Lewis, digging his hands into his pockets.

She shrugs. 'Not sure.'

'Nervous?'

'Very. I hope I've remembered everything properly.'

When DS Smart asked her to detail the route she took last Saturday morning, Ruby struggled to disentangle the memory from the previous week. At first she told them that she'd gone to the farmers' market stalls at the top end of the park, where she'd bought a wrap and a chocolate brownie. Then she sat on a bench and ate them, feeding a mouthful of brownie to Mabel. But when the police contacted the stallholder, he insisted he hadn't been there last week. Suspicions were raised immediately and Ruby had to apologise for getting muddled. Even now, as she stands here replaying her actions in her head, she's not sure about exactly what she did, or in what order.

They went to the play area, she's pretty sure of that. She took Mabel out of the buggy and sat on the swing with her on her lap, kicking off with her heel and gently swaying back and forth. Another mum was hovering impatiently with her three-year-old, expecting Ruby to get off immediately. If somebody *was* following them at the time, maybe the woman noticed. Ruby certainly didn't, but she'd had no reason to be suspicious.

Her thoughts are interrupted by the sound of the front door opening. There's a kerfuffle in the hallway, and a guy with a headset rushes up to them.

'Excuse me. Can you stand somewhere else – like over there?' He points to the privet hedge on the other side of the safe area. 'We need a clean shot of the babysitter leaving the house.'

Don't make me stand there, she thinks. *They'll eat me alive.*

'Yeah, sure,' says Lewis, pulling at her to move. 'But that's too close to the crowds. Ruby needs protecting. She's the significant witness,' he adds importantly.

'Yeah, I know … Okay, you can stand behind the van as long as you keep well back.'

They go through the front gate and take up their new hiding place. Another five minutes pass, then the camera operator takes up position in front of the door. It opens and a young man backs the buggy out, turns it around, then backs it in again. The door closes. A few moments later, he comes out again, pushing the buggy forward this time, which according to Ruby is correct. The camera operator declares herself happy and he's sent back inside. The rehearsal is over. It looks like they're about to start for real.

'Okay, here we go,' whispers Ruby as action is called and the door opens yet again.

This time, a distorted vision of herself emerges with Mabel's buggy, which now has a large doll strapped into it.

Ruby's mouth dries. It's like she's starring in her own dream, watching herself from a distance while being simultaneously aware that this figure isn't her at all. She realises that the woolly hat with its bright orange bobble looks stupid on a grown-up, and that the jacket has definitely seen better days. It came from a charity shop in the first place and has been abused ever since – worn in all weathers, stained with carelessly eaten meals, laid on muddy grass, squashed under bar stools, crumpled into makeshift pillows and cushions and never once washed. As she watches herself trundle the bright red buggy across the road, she thinks what an incongruous sight she makes – the pusher so worn and scruffy and the buggy so new and smart. That childish hat and that tatty jacket have become the costume for the worst moment in her life. She will never wear either again. After the reconstruction, she's going to throw them both away.

'Do you want to follow?' Lewis asks as 'Ruby' and the buggy pass through the park gates and head off in the direction of the play area.

'No way.' She shudders. 'I'll stay here. If they've got any questions, they can send someone running back.'

'Fair enough.' He puts his hands in his pockets again and kicks the ground. 'Still want me to hang around?'

'Why? Do you need to be somewhere?'

'No.' He gestures with his head in the direction of the upstairs flat. 'Just uncomfortable being here. I can feel waves of hate coming through the walls.'

'Me too,' she says. 'I'm sorry.'

'Not your fault.'

'Yeah, but you're in this mess because of me.'

'Not completely,' he replies. She wonders what on earth he means.

The film crew has charged ahead, followed by the media scrum. Apart from the officers guarding the garden, and a runner, they're alone now. They lean against the back doors of the van in silence, each plagued by their own thoughts.

Ruby is thinking about Mabel. She's always there, a thick layer of worry spread over her life. In fact, Mabel *is* her life now. Nothing will ever be the same again. She can already tell that her relationship with Lewis is altered forever and may not survive this onslaught. He was very shaken by the police interview, even though he was willing to be questioned. She doesn't know what went on, because so far he's refused to confide in her about it. As soon as he came home, he took a beer from the fridge and went onto the patio. It was early evening and freezing cold, but he stood there for about twenty minutes, drinking by himself, staring into the darkness. At one point she stepped outside and asked if he was okay, but he waved her away with his can and said, 'Just need some time to myself.'

He's still in that mood, locked into the room of himself, refusing to let her poke her head around the door, let alone walk in. There's a strange atmosphere between them, a sense of distrust, even though on the surface they are vowing allegiance to each other. It will be like this for as long as Mabel is missing. If she's never found – dead or alive – they will always be smeared with guilt. The stain may fade with time, but it will never come out completely, no matter how much they try to wash it away. Lewis has already had to take two weeks' holiday from work – his inbox was jammed with hate mail, even death threats, and the escape room has had several bookings cancelled on account of him being 'a paedophile'. He will probably have to resign.

'They're coming back now,' he says. Ruby looks up to see her impersonator pass through the gates, pause briefly at the pavement edge as if checking for traffic, and then calmly cross the road. It doesn't look quite right. Then she remembers. She was hurrying. Mabel had done a stinky nappy and she was rushing home to change her. A memory stutters into life.

'Lewis? Do you remember? You called me,' she says, nudging him. 'You called me just as I was opening the front door.'

He looks at her doubtfully. 'Don't think so. It was between eleven and twelve, right? I was in the middle of running a game; the bookings were back-to-back, I had no time for a break.'

'But I remember it really clearly; it's just come back to me. I unlocked the door and my phone started ringing, so I pushed the buggy inside and—'

'That was the week before,' he says. 'When George and Amber were on their night away. I was at home, off sick.'

'Oh yes …' Her expression dulls. 'I'm getting muddled up again.' She watches herself take a key out of her trouser pocket and unlock the door. The bright red buggy is pushed inside and the door closes with its characteristic judder. Somebody shouts out, 'Cut!' but Ruby's memory keeps playing. Yes, it's coming back to her now. She kicked the door shut behind her while she spoke to Lewis. Then she took Mabel out of the buggy and went straight upstairs to the nursery to relieve her of the dirty nappy.

'Oh my God,' she says under her breath.

Lewis turns to her. 'What is it?'

'I left the key in the door.'

'What? Last Saturday?'

'No, no, the week before.'

'Well it wouldn't be the first time,' he says unhelpfully. 'You've done it at least twice at the flat when you've come home pissed. So how come you've only just realised?'

'When Amber came home the next day, she asked me for the key but I couldn't find it.'

'That doesn't necessarily mean—'

'Oh God! Now I understand!' Her hand leaps to her mouth. The memory is churning at full speed now, sending her head into a spin. 'In the morning, when I got up, I had this really weird experience. There was a feeding bottle on the draining board in the kitchen; it had been washed and left to dry. I couldn't remember giving it to Mabel or cleaning it or anything. And she slept in late, as if she'd been up in the night and needed a lie-in.'

Lewis scratches his head. 'Okay ... so you think someone took the key from the door, then came back at night and let themselves in? Like for a snoop about?'

'Yes! Exactly. They found Mabel, took her out of her cot and gave her a bottle.' Ruby feels a cold chill spreading through her veins. 'Urgh ... it's disgusting.'

'Really creepy,' he agrees. 'If that's what happened.'

'It did. I'm sure of it.'

'Hmm ...' He looks sceptical. 'And you didn't hear anything?'

'No, you know how deeply I sleep.' The memory sparks again. 'But I remember that in the morning, the baby monitor was switched off and I thought at the time it was really odd because I was sure I'd turned it on when she went down. I was really cross with myself for forgetting to do it.'

'Excuse me,' says the bearded crew guy, trolleying a large metal box towards them. 'We're packing up now.' They move away from the van and stand by the privet hedge.

'This is really bad, Rubes,' Lewis says. 'You're in deep shit.'

'I know. But I'm going to have to tell the police. It's an important piece of evidence.'

'I'm not sure they'll believe you, that's the trouble.' His forehead creases with concern. 'It sounds like you've made it up to get us off the hook.'

'But it's the truth! Everyone's concentrating on last Saturday, but it's the week before that matters. That's when it all started.

They'll have to do the reconstruction again. I need to tell them now.' She turns on her heel and makes for the front door.

'Just hold on!' He pulls at her sleeve. 'Think it through first, get your facts organised. When did you realise that you'd lost the key?'

She hesitates. 'I didn't, that's the thing. When I couldn't find it, I assumed I'd just mislaid it. Then it turned up in the flat a few days later, so I stopped worrying about it.'

'What?' He wrinkles his nose. 'Well surely, that means you *didn't* leave it in the door.'

'But I did. I know I did,' she insists. 'The memory was buried deep in my subconscious. The abductor must have left the key in the flat so we wouldn't get suspicious.'

'In which case they couldn't have got back in! Ruby, none of this makes any sense.'

'I need to talk to Amber, ask her exactly when and how she found the key.'

'She doesn't want to talk to you.'

'I know … I feel so bad. I've been so angry with her for blaming me – blaming *us* – and it turns out it was my fault all along.' She feels the tears marshalling. 'God, I even accused her of having an affair – of Mabel not being George's baby. How mean was that?'

'Ruby—'

'I've got to talk to her!'

'Before you wade in, I think we should—'

But she doesn't care what Lewis thinks. She knows she's on to something, that this is important, that the answer is there, ready to be teased out. She barges her way through the film crew and the police guard and bangs loudly on Amber's door.

CHAPTER TWENTY-EIGHT

Day seven without Mabel

Amber turns anxiously to Sally. 'Who's that? I thought there was a guard outside.'

'There is. Don't worry, I'll get it.' Sally rises and goes downstairs.

'This is crazy,' says George. 'We can't even answer our own front door any more.' He leaps impatiently from the sofa and starts pacing around the room.

'Shh!'

Amber listens. Somebody is trying to persuade Sally to let them in. She knows from those persistent tones that it's Ruby. Her sister has been shivering outside all morning, observing the reconstruction. Even though they parted on very bad terms two days ago, Amber still feels bad about not letting her wait indoors. But George wouldn't hear of it, and anyway, Lewis is with her. She doesn't want to see him if she can help it. He makes her feel scared.

Her thoughts twist into a knot. The idea of him wanting to harm a little baby is monstrous, but seeing that photo taken from CCTV unnerved her. It's been blown up and analysed to the nth degree, but the results are inconclusive. The police can't say for sure that it's Lewis carrying Mabel, but as he's of a similar height and build, he can't be ruled out either.

'Amber! I have to speak to you,' says Ruby, bursting into the lounge.

Sally is close behind. 'Are you okay with this?' she asks. 'I'm sorry, but she barged past me. She says it's to do with the investigation.'

'I can speak for myself, thanks ... Amber, please? This is really important.'

'Going to finally tell the truth, is that it?' snarls George.

'I've always told the truth – *always*.' Ruby shoots Amber an appealing look.

'Go on then.' Amber gestures at her sister to sit down.

Ruby takes the small upright chair by the desk. She leans forward, hands gripped over her knees. 'I think I know what happened,' she says. 'Not last Saturday, but the one before. I think I know how the abductor got hold of the key.'

'And you've only just remembered?' George says incredulously. 'That sounds a bit convenient.'

'Please, listen!' Ruby draws in her breath. 'That weekend, when you had your night away, remember when you came home and asked me for the key, I couldn't find it?'

'Yes ...' replies Amber slowly. 'But it wasn't lost, I found it later, it was in the flat—'

'Yeah, I know, but ...' Ruby swallows hard. 'The thing is, I think I left it in the front door when I came back from the park. The next morning, when I got up, I noticed a few odd things. The baby monitor wasn't on, and a clean, empty bottle was sitting on the draining board, which I was certain I hadn't given to Mabel ...' She pauses. 'I know it sounds absurd, but I think the abductor let themselves in that night and spent time with her.'

'Oh my God,' gasps Amber.

Sally can't contain herself a second longer. She reaches for her notebook. 'This is completely game-changing. Why didn't you mention it before, Ruby?'

'Because she's only just made it up,' growls George, banging the mantelpiece. 'It's bullshit. She knows you lot are closing in on her and this is a last-ditch attempt to throw you off the scent.'

'Shh, let her talk.' Amber intervenes, recognising the ring of truth in her sister's voice. The tone is urgent, but steady. And she's not blinking rapidly like she used to when she was a teenager and trying to lie to Mum.

Ruby deliberately turns away from George and focuses on Amber. 'I didn't say anything at the time because I was embarrassed and I didn't want you to think I wasn't capable of looking after Mabel.'

'Which you obviously weren't,' barks George. 'There was an accident. Admit it!'

'Please can we listen to what Ruby's saying here,' says Sally. 'It could be important.' George makes a loud huff of disgust and strides out of the room. 'Go on, Ruby.'

Ruby pauses for a few seconds, then continues. 'When exactly did you find the key? And where was it?'

Amber thinks, letting the memories come forward. They arrive hesitantly at first, but then there's a rush of remembering as the pieces suddenly slot into place. Yes, Ruby's story makes sense. She can corroborate it, even enlarge upon it.

'Well?' prompts Sally.

'George found it on Thursday evening,' Amber says, feeling her throat constrict as she forces the words out. 'It was in the saucer of a flowerpot in the kitchen. I couldn't believe it had been there all the time and I'd missed it. I wasn't suspicious or anything; just blamed myself for not looking properly.'

'Did you go out any time on Thursday during the day?' Sally says, writing everything down.

'Yes, I went to the mums' meet-up, got back soon after lunch, and …' She hesitates, replaying the moment in her head. Why hadn't she put two and two together? Why had she blamed her own shortcomings instead, just as Ruby had?

'And what?' presses Ruby.

'I put a load of washing on before I went out. When I got back, there was this clean, wet sock on the floor, just beneath the washing machine, like somebody had opened the door and it had fallen out. Only the programme was still going when I left so I couldn't understand it. I know it sounds really stupid now, but I thought it was me, that I was going mad.'

'So the abductor let themselves in with the key while you were out, snooped around a bit …'

'A very risky thing to do,' muses Sally. 'They must have had some guts.'

Ruby's speech gathers pace. 'It was a rehearsal! They were getting ready for the abduction. Staking it out.'

'But why leave the key?' says Amber. 'That doesn't make sense.'

'They must have made a copy. They left the original to lull you into a false sense of security. Otherwise you might have changed the locks.'

'Clever,' says Sally, rising. 'Right now, it's just a theory, but given that you both had strange experiences – and that the timing works out – it's definitely worth pursuing. I'm going to talk to the boss right now. We'll need you both to add to your witness statements.'

Ruby nods. 'No problem.'

'I told George about the sock,' adds Amber. 'He dismissed it – said I'd just got muddled up. I was really worried. I thought my depression must be getting worse. That's why I went to the yoga retreat. I was trying to sort my head out.'

'Then we'll need George to make a statement too,' Sally says as she leaves the room and bounds down the stairs.

The sisters remain seated, staring at each other. Amber feels excited because something has shifted, and she feels closer to finding Mabel. But the thought of the abductor letting themselves into the flat twice without them realising is also creeping her out.

'If only we'd talked about it to each other,' she says. 'We could have gone to the police immediately, or at least had the locks changed.'

'Yes, you're right. I'm really sorry, it's all my fault,' says Ruby. Her eyes fill with tears. 'If I hadn't left the key in the lock …'

Amber gets up and goes over to her, crouching down and taking her hands.

'I know what it's like when you're looking after a baby. It's hard, you make silly mistakes. The thing is, Rubes, we know what happened now. It's a breakthrough.'

'But it means some paedophile has got her,' Ruby croaks. 'I can't bear it. What if—'

'Stop it!' says Amber, shaking her. 'We mustn't think like that. The police have got a lead now, and there's been the reconstruction today. Somebody will have seen something suspicious, they'll come forward, there'll be more CCTV images …'

'I hope so, I really hope so.' Ruby sniffs up her tears.

'Try to remember if you saw someone lurking about that day, following you around the park.'

'Yeah, I will.' Ruby stares into Amber's eyes. 'I'm so sorry for the things I said, Amber; you know, about you lying, and about George not being Mabel's father.'

Amber gasps. 'Shh! For God's sake, Rubes!' She looks anxiously towards the door. Did George hear that?

'Why? What's wrong?' Ruby gives her a strange look. 'Amber?'

'It's nothing, nothing,' she replies quickly, feeling her cheeks heat up. She stands and moves away from Ruby. 'Things are bad enough without George thinking …'

'Yeah, of course. Sorry, I didn't mean to … Are you okay?'

'He's really suffering right now. I mean, we all are,' Amber rattles on, 'but it's even harder for him because he wants to do something and he feels powerless.' She puts her hand on her chest to steady her breathing. 'But this is good news in a way, because now the police know what they're looking for.'

'Yeah, that is good. It's really good.'

'Because it didn't make sense before and now it does, even though it's horrible and unthinkable and makes me feel sick. It means it was a random person, some stranger, nobody connected to us.'

'Well that's how it looks, but we mustn't jump to conclusions,' warns Ruby. 'You know what the police say about keeping an open mind.'

Amber feels her sister's gaze boring into her, mining for secrets. She braces herself. Now is not the time to confess. It would only cause more pain, send everyone spinning back into the abyss. DI Benedict wants her to tell George the truth, but her instincts have been telling her to hold off until absolutely necessary, and now she's been proved right. She *will* tell him, but only once they have Mabel back safely and there's a chance, however slim, that he might forgive her.

'What is it, Amber?' asks Ruby. 'You've gone all weird. I can almost see the cogs whirring in your brain. You seem ... well, pleased. Why? Were you thinking it was somebody in particular?'

'No! If I thought that, I'd have told the police immediately,' Amber snaps. 'I was just trying to process it, that's all. To work out what this means for Mabel.'

'Of course, sorry. She's all that matters.' Ruby gets up. 'I'd better go. Lewis is waiting outside.' She offers a small smile. 'He said you wouldn't believe me. I'm so relieved you did.'

'It's George who's got a problem,' Amber says. 'He sees things very simply. You were the last person to see Mabel alive, therefore you—'

'She's *still* alive,' Ruby insists. 'We have to keep believing that.'

'Yes, I know, and I try, but it's hard sometimes …' Now it's Amber's turn to take the baton of tears and run with it. Ruby hesitates for a second, then rushes forward to embrace her.

'We'll find her, I know we will.'

George comes back into the room. He looks disgusted by the sight of the sisters hugging.

'How can you believe her?' he says. 'Can't you see it's just a story?'

Amber pulls away and turns to him, throwing an apologetic look at Ruby. 'But what about the wet sock I found?' she says. 'That was the same day the key turned up. It proves the abductor was in the flat.'

He huffs. 'Now you're really clutching at straws.'

Ruby stands her ground. 'The police believe me.'

'Hah! You think? Sally made all the right noises, acted like it was an important moment in the investigation, but she wasn't fooled for a second.'

'I'm going,' says Ruby, not rising to the bait. 'Let me know if you hear anything.'

Amber nods. As soon as her sister leaves the room, George snarls.

'This is exactly what murderers do,' he says. 'They hang around pretending to be helpful, leading search parties, making cups of tea. And all the time they're hiding in plain sight. Don't you see, this makes it even more likely that she and Lewis are guilty?'

'No … I don't believe it. She was telling the truth, I could see.'

'Get real, Amber,' he scoffs. 'People lie all the time and get away with it.' She feels her blood run cold. 'That's the problem with human beings. They want to believe.'

'But she's my sister, I *know* her.'

'And I know you, but that doesn't mean you couldn't fool me. For a while, at least.'

'That's ridiculous,' she retorts. 'Why would I want to fool you?'

His gaze hardens, making her stomach quiver with anxiety. Maybe the police have already told him and he's waiting for her to confess. Or maybe he's known for ages and is playing games.

CHAPTER TWENTY-NINE

Day seven without Mabel

Ruby feels strangely exhilarated as she exits the flat. For the last few days she's been like a fish wrenched out of the water and left flapping on the bank with a hook in her mouth. Now she's been released and thrown back in. She can breathe again. Even though it's her fault for leaving the key in the door – and she'll never, ever forgive herself for that – they finally have an explanation for how the abductor got in. The police can stop hassling her and Lewis and concentrate on finding the real criminal. They're one step closer to finding Mabel.

'Well?' says Lewis, who has been waiting for her outside. 'How did it go?'

'Good mostly,' she replies, hugging him. 'Amber believed me – she had a weird experience too. It all fits.'

'How did George react?'

She shakes her head. 'He still thinks we did it. He's in a bad way, out of control.'

'Poor guy.' He sighs thoughtfully. 'Can we go? I've had enough. They must have taken hundreds of photos of me by now.' He points to the crowd of photographers jostling behind the police tape. 'And people have been shouting out, calling me a murderer.'

She winces. 'They're despicable. Yeah, come on.'

They go over to their bikes. She picks up her helmet and puts it on.

'Ruby? Can I have a quick word?' DI Benedict walks briskly up to her. 'I gather you want to add something to your witness statement. Something about leaving the key in the door?'

'Yes. I think it could be really significant, don't you?' She looks at him hopefully, but he doesn't respond.

'Would you rather do it at the station or shall I send DS Smart round to your flat?'

'At the flat, please,' she replies, fastening the chin strap. 'Every time I go to the station, the media think I've been arrested.'

'Will an hour give you enough time to get home?'

'Yes, should do.' She wheels the bike down the path. 'The family liaison officer seemed to think it was a game changer.'

'Possibly,' he replies, but his expression remains inscrutable.

'You need to concentrate on the *previous* Saturday. Witnesses may have seen someone hanging around the front door. They came in during the night, so you need to check CCTV – oh, and there's last Thursday morning. Amber reckons they let themselves in then too.'

He gives her a 'don't tell me how to do my job' look.

'Make sure you're in when DS Smart calls,' he says before pushing open the front door and entering the house. 'And please don't say anything to that lot.' He cocks his head in the direction of the media.

'As if!' Ruby glares after him, then turns to Lewis. 'Why was he so off with me?'

'Because he thinks you're wasting his time.' He wheels his bike onto the pavement.

She huffs in exasperation. The officer lifts the tape for them to pass under and they set off down the street in the opposite direction from the media.

They cycle home the back way, avoiding most of the Saturday traffic, safe in the relative anonymity of their helmets and high-vis waistcoats. But the media manage to get ahead of them, and by the time they arrive, there's a small welcome party crowding at the entrance gate.

'How was the reconstruction, Ruby?'

'Any news on Mabel?'

'Do the police still think you did it?'

'What happened to her, Ruby?'

'Talk to us, Ruby! We can tell your story!'

'Just leave us alone, okay?' she shouts, unable to hold on to her temper a second longer.

Lewis punches in the entrance code. 'Don't respond,' he mutters under his breath. 'You'll make it worse.'

The heavy gate clicks open and they wheel the bikes in. Ruby makes sure the gate is firmly shut behind them. The high metal railings that surround their block are supposed to keep burglars out. She used to find them a little oppressive, but she's grateful for them today.

Lewis unlocks the padlock of the cycle store and puts the bikes away while Ruby enters the flat. She takes off her jacket and helmet, unlaces her boots and kicks them off, then flicks on the central heating. It's a relief to be home.

She surveys the mess, which is even worse than usual. These last few days neither of them has had the slightest interest in tidying. It's as if getting on with their normal lives is somehow disrespectful to Mabel. She goes into the kitchen and stares at the dirty crockery building up next to the kitchen sink, the scattering of breadcrumbs on the counter, the pint of milk she forgot to put back in the fridge before they left this morning, the takeaway boxes waiting to be recycled …

How will this chaos be interpreted by DS Smart when she arrives in a few minutes' time? Are innocent people more likely to be clean and tidy, or do they tend to live in a tip? Do murderers ever wash up?

Is an unmade bed a sign of a guilty conscience? It's absurd to have such thoughts popping into her head, but DI Benedict's reaction has made her nervous about the slightest thing. She's told the truth from the beginning, but somehow it doesn't seem to be enough.

Lewis comes in and divests himself of his gear, throwing his helmet and high-vis onto the chair in the hallway. He joins her in the kitchen. 'I'm hungry,' he says. 'Is there anything for lunch?'

'We should wait until the detective's been and gone, don't you think?' she says. 'I feel uncomfortable about munching a sandwich while talking about Mabel.'

'Well I need to eat something,' he grunts, opening the fridge. He crouches down and peers inside. 'Not that we've got much. We'll have to order a supermarket delivery. Daren't go shopping, not with those bastards following us around.'

Ruby presses her palms against her face. 'It's like being in prison. I can't bear it, Lew. I just want it to stop.'

'It won't – not until they find out who took her.'

'But it could go on for years. Suspicions will hang over us, we'll never shake them off. And they could still charge us. You don't have to have a body – if the police think they have enough evidence …'

He pulls out a half-eaten packet of vegan cheese and a wrinkled tomato. 'Any bread left?' He opens the cupboard and finds the hard remains of a sourdough loaf.

'You're not listening to me,' she wails. 'This is serious!'

'I know how serious it is, Ruby,' he says sharply, holding his thumb to his forefinger. 'I'm *this* close to being charged with murder. And this key story has probably made it worse.'

'It's not a story! It's what happened.'

'It's what you *think* happened – you don't know for sure.'

'I do. It's the only explanation that makes sense.'

'Listen, Rubes. I appreciate what you're doing. I know you're trying to protect me, but you mustn't lie—'

'I'm not lying.' She feels stung. If *he* doesn't believe her, she's got no chance. 'And I'm not trying to protect you. I don't need to – you're innocent. We both are.'

He pauses, bread knife in hand. 'Yes, *we* know that, but the police think otherwise. Can't you see? They're waiting for one of us to crack. You coming up with a last-minute bullshit story about—'

The entryphone rings. Ruby hurries into the hallway and picks up the receiver. 'Yes?'

'DS Smart,' says a familiar voice. Ruby presses the button to buzz her in.

'And how many more times, it's *not* a story,' she continues.

'Okay, leave it now. Don't let her see we've been arguing,' Lewis warns.

It's the first time Ali Smart has been to their flat. From the moment Ruby lets her in, she senses the detective scrutinising the scene, making judgements, perhaps even looking for clues. Smart keeps her coat on and rejects the offer of tea or coffee without so much as a thank you. She walks into the lounge and sits on the sofa uninvited. These small gestures of unfriendliness make Ruby feel jittery. The woman has clearly been told to be on her guard.

'Right. Let's get started,' she says briskly, reaching into her briefcase for a statement form. 'Tell me what you told the FLO and we'll take it from there.'

'Okay.' Ruby shifts some jumpers off a chair and sits down. 'Sorry about the mess. We've both been so upset …'

Lewis pops his head around the door, a plate of sandwiches in hand. 'Hi … I'll be in the bedroom if you need me,' he says.

DS Smart narrows her eyes at him and he scurries away. 'Okay. So, this incident took place on the previous Saturday, when you were also babysitting Mabel …'

Ruby gives her account again, starting with the walk around the park, buying lunch from the food stall, sitting on the bench, then stopping to look at the ducks – another detail she's only just remembered – before returning to the flat.

'Lewis rang me,' she says. 'If you check his phone, you'll get the precise time.'

'And you didn't realise at any point in the day that you'd left the key in the front door?'

'No. I was busy looking after Mabel and I didn't go out after that, so why would I?'

'It just seems strange, that's all, that you forgot so completely, even when you were interviewed, and then suddenly remembered this morning.'

'It was the reconstruction that triggered it,' Ruby replies, feeling increasingly defensive. 'I don't see why that surprises you. That's the whole point of them, isn't it?'

'Indeed,' DS Smart murmurs.

'I'll never forgive myself for leaving the key in the door – never! It was totally my fault, but if I hadn't mentioned it, nobody would know. I'd be off the hook, to some extent. I truly didn't realise until today. I'm owning up because I want to find Mabel, that's all I care about.'

Smart scribbles something down. 'Let's see if any witnesses come forward,' she clips.

'Amber believes me; she experienced weird stuff too. She can corroborate—'

'Can we stick to what *you* saw or heard? Or didn't hear?'

Ruby stares at her indignantly. 'Why are you being like this?'

'I'm not being like anything,' DS Smart replies coolly. 'I'm just taking your witness statement.'

'Yes, but you clearly don't believe me.' She can feel flames of anger licking her insides. 'And you were really hostile to Lewis just now.'

'I'd like to continue with the statement, please.'

'There's no reason he should be a suspect – it's not fair, it's intimidation.' Ruby stands up. 'He's being trolled, you know. It's causing real problems at work. He could lose his job over this—'

'Ruby, please calm down.'

'No, I won't calm down. Mabel is missing and you're blaming the wrong people. I can see why you might suspect me, but not Lewis.'

'We *do* have reason to include Lewis in our investigations, as it happens. And not just because he's your boyfriend.'

Ruby puts her hands on her hips. 'Oh. I see. It's because he's got a criminal record. That's discrimination. The situation was completely different and he only got a suspended sentence. It was self-defence anyway.'

'I suggest you talk to Lewis, ask him to explain.' DS Smart draws herself in. 'Right. Is there anything more you'd like to include in your statement, or shall I start writing it up?'

'Write it up,' Ruby barks. 'Shout when you want me to sign.' She marches out of the sitting room and into the bedroom, where Lewis is perched on the edge of the bed, his sandwiches lying uneaten on the plate. His face is etched with anxiety.

'I thought you were hungry,' she says, plonking herself down next to him.

'Lost my appetite.'

Ruby lowers her voice to the quietest whisper. 'She's vile. Can't stand her. She's been aggressive right from the beginning. I'm going to complain.'

He takes her hand. 'Don't. You'll make it worse.'

'She's got it in for you. Said I needed to ask you to explain why you were a suspect. What's that supposed to mean?'

'Ruby ... Ruby ... please, be quiet.'

'She obviously thought you hadn't told me about the assault conviction. Like we don't have an honest relationship.'

He releases his grasp and leaps up, moving away from her. 'Stop! Go back to the lounge and finish the bloody statement. Get rid of her, then we'll talk.'

Ruby jolts. 'Talk about what? Lew?'

He goes to the window, leaning heavily on the sill and taking short, rapid breaths.

'What? Come on. You're scaring me. What is it? Lewis! You have to tell me now.'

'I'm Mabel's father,' he says.

CHAPTER THIRTY

Day seven with Mabel

I turn to Mabel. 'Gosh, look, it's time for the evening news,' I say, reaching for the remote control. 'Would you like to watch it?'

She gives me one of her filthy looks in reply. That's all I get now. No smiles, no gurgles, just dumb insolence. Had Mabel been a purchase on Amazon, I'd probably have sent her back by now, accompanied by a scathing one-star review. The trouble is, when you steal someone, there's no method for returning them if you're not satisfied. I could leave Mabel on the neighbours' doorstep, I suppose. She'd be safe at the Nook with Bob and Barbara Masefield and they'd become instant national heroes – they'd probably love that. But then the police would know who'd taken her and I'd be easily hunted down. Game over.

No, I can't take her back, no matter how badly she behaves. We're bound together forever. I just have to be patient with her – unfortunately not one of my virtues. It's not her fault; she just needs more time to get used to me and the new environment, to adapt to the new routines. She's very young. Her memories of Amber will quickly fade and soon it will be as if her biological mother never existed. And once the three of us are together – please God – we'll be like any other family. We'll choose a new name for her and she'll have no reason to suspect that she was ever the notorious Missing Mabel.

I sit down in the armchair, close enough that I can bounce the edge of her chair with my foot. 'I wonder what's been happening in the world today,' I say. 'Is everyone still frantically looking for you, or have they moved on to more important things?'

She makes a grumbling noise and I turn up the volume. The Saturday news is often disappointingly thin, feeding off the leftovers of the previous few days. We are the third item tonight, sliding down the charts towards oblivion. It's likely that we're still top of the bill in the local news, but nationally, interest is clearly waning. Today's angle is the police reconstruction, which was filmed this morning.

'This should be interesting,' I say, leaning forward as they show a clip.

There's Lilac Park in all its glory, and there's the babysitting sister – or somebody pretending to be her – wearing that ridiculous bobble hat. She wheels Mabel's buggy past the duck pond and out of the gates, crossing the road and entering the front garden of the house. She unlocks the door then pushes the buggy inside.

Oh yes, I remember it well.

We cut to the detective leading the investigation. 'We're asking the public to think back not only to last Saturday, but just as importantly to the Saturday before. If you were in Lilac Park or William Morris Terrace and saw anyone, male or female, acting suspiciously on either or both dates, in fact at any time in recent weeks, please call Crimestoppers immediately. You could hold vital information that leads us to Mabel.'

'Ha! They're clueless,' I laugh. 'They don't even know if I'm a man or a woman.' I remove my foot. 'Although one thing worries me a little.' Mabel stops bouncing and immediately starts to complain. 'Oh, stop making such a fuss. I'm thinking … Why did the detective mention the Saturday *before*? That's new … Well, sweetie, what do you reckon? Has the dozy sister finally remembered that she left the key in the front door?'

I close my eyes and perform my own reconstruction in my head. I was very careful; nobody saw me wriggle it out of the lock, I'm almost sure of that. And I didn't hang around afterwards, but went straight home, walking quickly but without hurrying, keeping my head down all the way.

But what if people come forward to say they used to see me hanging around in the park and that I disappeared after Mabel was taken? Would there be enough information to put an e-fit together? I always made sure to hide my features as much as possible, without going so far as to attract undue attention. Luckily, in winter you can get away with a large hood and a scarf over your face. And the other park users were always on their phones or chatting to friends or looking after their kids. Nobody ever talked to me or even met my eye. I might as well have been wearing a cloak of invisibility.

Even Amber, who would have recognised me in an instant, never noticed me. *If only*, she'll be thinking as she watches the reconstruction. *If only I'd paid more attention to the people around me. If only I hadn't been so wrapped up in myself.*

To be fair to her – and I detest being fair to Amber – I was a very good spy. I always kept my distance, turning the other way whenever she started walking in my direction, nipping behind a tree or the café building, diving into the toilets, or even just crouching down to do up my laces. And if she *had* spotted me, my excuse was already prepared. *Oh! You've caught me out. I was about to surprise you with a visit.*

I'm confident she won't have given my name as a possible suspect. It won't even have occurred to her. No doubt when the police asked, as they always do, whether there was anyone who might want to do her harm, she wasn't able to think of a single person. Such a joke. Insensitive, entitled people like Amber never realise how many people hate them. They trample through the jungle of life without a thought for creatures like me who live in the undergrowth. Either they don't notice us at all, or they pick us up, use us and then have the cheek to call it friendship. Like we're supposed to be grateful they've spent any time with us at all.

'Mummy thought she could have everything she wanted,' I say to Mabel, bouncing her chair vigorously. 'Career, marriage, family, friends, baby, happy-ever-after. But it's all based on secrets and lies. She uses and abuses people for her own gain, doesn't care who gets hurt as long as she gets what she wants. Oh yes, Mabel, Mummy's been very bad. She wrecked my life, robbed me of my future, made my whole world fall apart. That's why she had to be punished.'

Mabel's bottom lip trembles and she starts to cry. Again.

'Sorry, did I upset you? I'm only telling the truth, you know. Your mummy's a complete bitch. You're far better off without her.' I twist her out of the seat without bothering to undo the strap. 'Anyway, enough of her. Let's give you your bottle.'

I carry her into the kitchen, propping her on my hip as I flick on the kettle and take a pre-prepared bottle of formula from the fridge. I put the bottle in a jug and then pour in hot water. It doesn't take long for the milk to warm through, then I remove the bottle, drying it on a tea towel before returning to the living room. I sit back down in the armchair and put the teat into Mabel's mouth. She sucks gratefully.

The news has moved on to other trivial items of no interest, so I switch off the television.

A noise rises from the silence. It sounds like a car outside. I hold my breath, screw up my face with listening. Yes, that's the dull throb of an engine …

'Did you hear that, Mabel?' I ask, removing the half-drunk bottle to give her a break. I sit her upright on my lap and lean her forward to encourage a burp. She isn't interested, just wants the rest of her feed. 'Oh, okay then, greedy guts.' I push the teat back into her mouth.

A car is definitely idling outside the house. I'm not imagining it this time. It must be the neighbour. What's he doing snooping around? Maybe he wants to introduce his wife to me, or invite me over for a cup of tea so he can drone on about their wonderful grandchildren. Really, this is too annoying. I am so not interested in being their friend. I stand up and carry Mabel into the hallway, peering through the frosted glass of the front door. Can't see anything. It's too dark.

Why is he sitting there watching? Why not get out of the car and ring the doorbell? Fear starts to creep over my skin. What if he suspects me? The stupid old codger could ruin everything. I don't want to leave Midsummer Cottage, even though the place is a dump. I *can't* leave. This is my safe house, and more importantly, it's where I have to wait. Wait and hope.

The police won't connect me to this address. Great-Aunt Dolly's estate is still going through probate, so it doesn't officially belong to me yet and nothing is in my name. I was frustrated by the time it was taking before, but now it's a blessing. Even if the police were looking for me, they wouldn't be able to trace me here.

No, the only threat is from the Nosy Neighbour from the Nook. I feel like walking out and confronting him, telling him to mind his own f***ing business. But I know that would be a mistake. If he does suspect that I've got Missing Mabel, my aggression might prompt him to go straight to the police.

Got to play it cool, mustn't let him see I'm rattled. In fact, I should go to the other extreme. Reach out the hand of friendship. Invent some story about my partner being away on business but coming to join us next week. Be brazen. Stop hiding Mabel like she's a guilty secret. Cut off her curls and dress her up as a baby boy.

Except all the clothes I bought for her are pink …

I hear the gentle slam of a car door and gasp, startling Mabel. 'You mustn't cry,' I tell her. 'Keep quiet, okay?'

Silence.

I listen for footsteps crunching up the gravel driveway, but can't hear a sound. Turning off all the lights, I cross the hallway and go into my bedroom, which is at the front of the house. The curtains are still open. With my back against Aunt Dolly's wardrobe, I edge my way to the window. Mabel wriggles in my arms, as if trying to escape.

'Shh,' I say. 'Keep still. Don't make a sound.'

I peer around the side of the curtain. A tree is obscuring my view of the road, but I can just make out the edge of a dark-coloured vehicle parked outside the house. My breath catches in my throat. So I wasn't imagining it. Somebody is watching me. It *has* to be the neighbour. There's nobody else it could be.

'This could be trouble, Mabel,' I whisper. 'What are we going to do?'

At least there are no flashing blue lights. Not that the police would advertise their presence. They definitely wouldn't hang around outside; they'd storm the bungalow, kicking the door down and bursting in, screaming at me to put down my weapon.

'But *you're* my weapon, aren't you, my darling?' I say, walking away from the window and out of the room. 'And I'm not giving you up. I'd rather we both died in the process.'

CHAPTER THIRTY-ONE

Day eight without Mabel

Amber wakes at 5 a.m. after a couple of hours of fretful sleep. She slides out of bed, careful not to wake George. He's lying still now, but for most of the night he was tossing and turning, crying out in his dreams. She tried rubbing his back and whispering calming words in his ear, but he shoved her away. Sleeping in the same bed is so difficult at the moment. It shouldn't be the case. This should be a time to cleave to each other, to lie locked in a needy embrace, but their bodies don't seem to fit together any more. When Amber rested her head on his chest, his flesh felt hard and unyielding; she didn't know where to put her arms. Her secrets lie between them like a fidgety child.

Ruby sent the text last night. Amber doesn't need to read it again; every word is etched on her brain. *You lying, cheating bitch. This is all your fault. I hate you. I will never forgive you. You have 24 hours to tell George. If you don't, I will.*

She dresses quietly in the darkness, feeling in the drawers for clean underwear, putting on yesterday's jumper and jeans. The heating doesn't kick in until six and the flat feels cold. She goes down to the first floor, holding in the emotion as she walks past the nursery. The sight of Mabel's empty cot is unbearable and they've had to shut the door. Amber has made a private vow not to open it again until her daughter returns. But when will that be? How long does it take for spiders to weave their cobwebs? How many layers of dust will have settled on the surfaces? Time has become distorted. Hours seem like days, then suddenly a whole week has slipped by. This is Day Eight without Mabel.

It's strange how she's only been part of their lives for a few months and yet a future without her is impossible to contemplate – even though her very existence has always been problematic. She is the product of a terrible but miraculous mistake; a tiny time bomb that started ticking from the moment of her conception. Deep down, Amber always knew she wouldn't get away with it, that some day the truth would explode, potentially destroying the happiness she'd fought so hard to achieve. She also knew that one day she would have to pay for Mabel. She just never imagined the price would be the child herself.

She puts on her winter coat and boots, then grabs her keys and leaves the flat. Thankfully, it's too early for the media, and apart from the ribbons tied around every front gate and tree trunk, the street looks its normal, quiet self.

Walking along the icy pavement in the footsteps of the abductor, Amber imagines holding Mabel just as they did, tucked inside their coat. She can sense the weight and warmth of her daughter now, pressed against her chest. Mabel snuggles down against the cold, her little heart beating furiously.

Who carried her away that night? George still thinks it was Lewis. He hasn't bought the key-in-the-door story, even though Amber can corroborate it, and when he finds out that Lewis is Mabel's biological father, he'll have no doubt at all. The police still seem to think Lewis and Ruby are guilty, although they can't prove it yet. Amber has to admit, it does make a grim, logical sense, but she refuses to believe it because it would mean that Mabel is dead.

Besides, Lewis didn't know he was definitely the father until the police confirmed it a couple of days ago. Amber didn't know either, not for sure. Of course, she had a suspicion – a strong suspicion – but she didn't share it with Lewis. They've avoided each other since that night and not spoken at all privately. When Mabel was born, Amber was grateful to him for showing no interest, for making excuses not to babysit, for standing as far away from Mabel as possible for the family photo. When the picture arrived as her mother's Christmas card, Amber instantly spotted that father and daughter had the same heart-shaped face. She tore the card up, telling George the photo made her look fat. But if Mabel is returned, who knows what new similarities will reveal themselves as she grows up?

Ruby is right. George needs to know, although Amber doesn't appreciate the threats. Did Lewis confess, or did the police tell her?

Amber walks past the rows of Edwardian terraces, which look identical in the darkness, turning left, then right, then back the way she came, lost in a maze of her own thoughts. She cannot keep the fantasy that she's carrying Mabel alive. Her arms are empty; it's only her own heart that she can feel beating. As she meanders through the ghostly grid of streets, the memories of that night with Lewis walk by her side, pulling at her coat for attention.

It all started with Amber and George having a bust-up – they happened very rarely but when they did, they were huge. This time it was about making a baby, or trying to. They still hadn't conceived and Amber dared to suggest, very gently, that they see a doctor together. George took huge offence, claiming it was Amber's anxiety that was preventing her getting pregnant, not any lack of virility on his part.

'All I'm saying is we get some tests,' she said. 'Then at least we'll know if there's a medical reason.'

'I don't need a test,' he retorted. 'I know there's nothing wrong with me.'

'How?' she pressed. 'How do you know?'

His face darkened. 'I just do, that's all.'

'Oh! So how many babies have you fathered to date then?' she said sarcastically. 'Please tell me, I'd be very interested to know.'

He rounded on her then. 'What about that time you got pregnant when we were seventeen, remember?'

Of course she remembered; it had been a scary time for both of them. 'We never knew for sure I was pregnant,' she reminded him. 'I think it was probably just a late period.'

'That's not how you reacted at the time. You told me you'd had a miscarriage. You made a great song-and-dance about it.'

'I panicked. I didn't want a baby back then – we were too young.'

'But you want one now and don't care what you have to do get it,' he riposted, the tone of his voice venomous. The conversation developed into a bitter shouting match. She packed an overnight bag, flounced out of the flat and caught a cab to Ruby's place. It was the first time she'd done such a thing, and she was so angry and upset she didn't think to call ahead. Usually she preferred not to reveal any vulnerability to her little sister, and she wasn't in the habit of confiding in her, especially not about problems with George. But that night, she couldn't think of anywhere else to go.

'She's not here,' said Lewis when he answered the entryphone. 'She's having a night away with the girls.'

'Oh …' Her heart sank. 'I didn't realise. Sorry to bother you.'

He heard the desperation in her voice and invited her in, took her coat and bag and told her to sit down. When he offered her a glass of wine, she almost snatched it out of his hands.

'Sorry to barge in on you like this,' she said, holding out the glass for a top-up.

'It's okay.' He passed her the bottle. 'Help yourself.' When they finished the wine, they started on the gin. Then he rolled a spliff.

Amber didn't really know Lewis. He was Ruby's boyfriend, that was about it. She didn't even know Ruby that well, their relationship still in the early stages of rehabilitation. They'd met up socially as a foursome a few times, but it hadn't been successful and they'd tacitly agreed not to continue. But now, as she lolled on the sofa getting pissed and high, Amber decided she really liked Lewis. He was very laid-back, unlike George. And he was a good listener, unlike George. He wasn't quite up to George's level of attractiveness, but he had a kind, open face. And when she broke down in tears, he held her in his arms and told her it was okay to cry. He wiped her tears away and kissed her gently on the forehead, then on both cheeks. An electrical surge went through her body as their lips brushed. She opened her mouth for him, and from there it was a short walk to the bedroom.

They tore off each other's clothes like they were in a movie and had sex on top of the bed covers. Later, when Amber replayed the scene in her head, she redirected it with Lewis leading the action, but in truth she was the one who pulled him into her, clamping her legs around his thighs so he couldn't get away. They didn't speak a word until it was all over and they were lying on their backs, naked and sweaty, panting for breath.

'Oh my God,' she murmured eventually.

He sighed. 'That was amazing.'

'Hmm … amazing and very, very wrong.'

'That's why,' he said. 'Forbidden fruit …' He ran his finger over her stomach and her insides rippled in response.

'We mustn't tell them. And we mustn't do it again. Ever.'

'A one-off,' he replied, kissing her neck and breasts. 'Our secret.'

'I love my husband.'

'I love your sister.'

'This doesn't change anything.'

'No. Not at all.'

But it changed everything. Forever. At the time she'd felt like a sex goddess, but three weeks later, when she discovered she was pregnant, her true motivation became clear.

Had Lewis known it too? Had her confession that George was shooting blanks inspired him to show what a real man could do? Lewis despised George – he felt belittled and patronised by him. Had fathering 'his' child been an act of spite, or even revenge? Or had they both just drunk and smoked too much that night? Amber didn't dare to unpack it. She felt frightened and yet triumphant. The long wait for a baby was over. She was thrilled, George was thrilled. Ruby was over the moon at the prospect of becoming an aunt, and her mother broke out in a rash of knitting.

And what about Lewis? He played it very cool, never asked Amber if the baby was his, and once she was born, never looked at her longingly or asked to hold her. He behaved as if he'd done her a small favour and didn't need recognition or thanks. His attitude allowed her to feel safe, to pretend – even to believe – that George was the biological father after all. The identity of the sperm giver didn't matter; it was *being* a dad that counted, and George would be the best father in the world.

Now the balloon has gone up. Ruby is beyond angry with Amber, and no doubt with Lewis too. That's three out of four of them who know, plus the entire bloody investigation team. George can't be the only one left in ignorance. She won't let him find out from Ruby; she'll tell him this morning, before the FLO turns up. It'll be the hardest thing she's ever had to do in her life.

Amber walks slowly back to the house. Her fingers are as cold as crab sticks and the tip of her nose is frozen. As she puts the key in the front door, another shiver runs through her. It's as if Mabel's abductor is standing there now, watching her from the shadows of the trees. She hears a sound like fabric rustling, and turns around quickly, peering into the gloom.

'Who are you?' she says. But it's only the lilac ribbons, flapping in the breeze.

CHAPTER THIRTY-TWO

Day eight without Mabel

Ruby stops at the red lights on the brow of the hill, panting for breath. She's been cycling around for hours in an attempt to burn off her anger, but it hasn't worked. Her insides are still bubbling like a witch's cauldron – eye of jealousy, toe of humiliation … The intensity of her emotion is disturbing; she's never experienced anything like it before.

The lights change to green and she sets off again, finding it hard to concentrate on the road. Her head is crowded with sickening images: Lewis and Amber's naked bodies entwined in a mocking embrace; having hot, steamy sex in her bed, up against the wardrobe, on the sitting room rug, under the shower, sprawled over the kitchen table …

Her vision blurs with tears. This is no good. She needs to slow down and pay attention to the traffic before she has an accident.

Just as the images repeat, so do the internal arguments. It makes no difference to her that the pair of them were wasted, or that Amber allegedly threw herself at Lewis. She doesn't buy the excuse that his sexual hardwiring entangled him and he was too weak to break free. The man's a grown-up, in his thirties. It wasn't as if he was drugged and raped; he was a willing participant.

She cycles on. Her leg muscles ache with effort, yet she can't stop. He must have been attracted to her, she thinks – surprising because she and Amber are physically so unalike – although knowing Lewis, it was probably the violation of a taboo that really got him fired up. And he would have seen it as a way of getting one over on George, whom he despises. It's true, her brother-in-law is a bit of a tosser, but he didn't deserve that kind of treatment.

As for what was going on in Amber's head ... Ruby just doesn't understand. It's so out of character. Her sister is conventional to the point of dull, and a dedicated law-abider with high moral values. She's usually the first to throw the stone of disapproval at people who cheat on their partners. What's more, she's been besotted with George since she was a teenager and has never shown the slightest interest in anyone else. She couldn't wait to get married and be Mrs Walker. Ruby always assumed that George was Amber's one and only love, but clearly that's not true. Maybe she's been putting it about for years. Ruby would be the first to say that she and Amber aren't close, but now she realises she doesn't know her sister at all. She might as well be a stranger. That discovery in itself makes her feel very alone.

The lack of care and love that's been shown to her – by both of them – is shocking. And the fact that sweet, beautiful Mabel is the product of such a disgustingly selfish act twists the knife in deep.

As Ruby weaves in and out of the light Sunday-morning traffic, she starts to feel panicky. No wonder the police suspect her – casting her in the role of betrayed lover and vengeful sister. Now it makes sense. What if Mabel was killed? If they find her body, Ruby's DNA will be all over it. She had the opportunity *and* the motive – she could be convicted of murder. She starts to shake and the bike wobbles, almost sending her into a parked car. She pulls up sharply and stands for a few moments with one foot on the kerb, breathless and furious and scared.

To her surprise, her surroundings look familiar. She thought she was cycling with no sense of a destination, taking random turns, even going round in circles. But now she sees – like a homing pigeon – that she's been gradually heading towards Mum's place, the house where she grew up. Has she ridden here by instinct, looking for refuge and comfort, a shoulder to cry on? It seems unlikely. Normally Ruby would never go to her mother in times of trouble, fearing that any heart-to-heart would end in that well-worn phrase, 'Well, dear, you've only yourself to blame.' But this time, there's no blame that can be attached. She's entirely the victim.

Taking out her phone, she sees that it's just gone eight o'clock. Early, but not too early to call. She doubts Mum has been sleeping anyway. None of them have had any sleep since Mabel's disappearance. She pushes off and makes a U-turn, then hangs left.

But as she pedals with a revived sense of purpose, a new emotion starts to course through her veins: an ugly triumphalism. The instinct that drove her to her childhood home was born not out of a need for sympathy, but a desire to redress an ancient imbalance. She's going to tell her mother just how appallingly her favourite daughter has behaved.

She turns into Faversham Road and starts climbing the hill. Lactic acid burns through her muscles, but she presses on until she reaches the top. The street is Sunday-morning sleepy – curtains drawn, cars resting in the driveways. Now that Amber and George have gone back to number 74, the media circus has left town and her path to the front door is clear. Ruby dismounts, removes her helmet and tucks the bike behind the wheelie bins. She doesn't bother to lock up – it should be safe here, for a while at least.

Ringing the doorbell, she steps back and waits. After a few seconds, the front-room curtains twitch and her mother's wan face peers out. She frowns when she sees her daughter and immediately withdraws. Ruby taps her foot impatiently. Is she going to be allowed in or what?

Just as she's about to give up, the door opens. Her mother is still in her dressing gown, her naked face lined and drawn, her short hair poking up at odd angles from a restless night. Ruby's never seen her look so old or vulnerable.

'What do you want?' she says, standing sentry with her hand firmly around the door frame.

'I need to talk to you. It's important.'

Her mother casts her a withering look. 'I think we've said all there is to say.' She starts to close the door, but Ruby rushes up the steps and puts her boot in the way.

'George isn't Mabel's father,' she blurts out.

Her mother gasps. 'What? How dare you?'

'It's true, Mum. And there's more. Do you want me to shout it out to the neighbours, or are you going to let me in?'

'I can't believe Amber would do such a terrible thing,' her mother says for what must be the fifth time. They are sitting in the lounge, keeping a physical and emotional distance. Ruby draws up her knees and wedges herself into the armchair, while Vicky pulls her dressing gown tightly across her chest and folds her arms.

'Yeah, I agree it's not like her, but it's true. She can't deny it, the DNA evidence is there.' Ruby gestures towards the landline phone sitting on its base. 'Ask her yourself.'

Vicky waves the idea away. 'Poor George … Does he know?'

'I've told Amber to tell him today, otherwise I will.'

Mum shakes her head. 'No, that's not a good idea, Ruby. It's their business. Keep out of it, don't get involved.'

'But I *am* involved! Amber cheated with *my* boyfriend, remember!'

'Hmm, I expect he instigated it.' Mum pulls a face as if an unpleasant taste has just popped into her mouth. 'I never liked him much, if I'm honest. Always seemed rather a dodgy character, untrustworthy. Not Amber's type at all.'

'But *my* type, obviously,' Ruby retorts. 'Charming. And don't let Amber off the hook. She wasn't some blushing virgin; they're equally to blame.'

Her mother pauses for a few moments, deep in thought. She frowns and pushes out her bottom lip. 'Ruby …' she says at last. 'Do you think it's all connected?'

'To Mabel's disappearance?'

'Yes. I mean, if Lewis is Mabel's father …'

'He didn't kill her, if that's what you're thinking.'

'How do you know for sure?'

Ruby hesitates. Yes, how *does* she know? Less than twenty-four hours ago she would have bet her life on his innocence, but now she realises she doesn't know him any better than she knows Amber. He cheated on her with her own sister; what else might he be capable of? But it doesn't make sense. The chronology's all wrong. Lewis didn't know he definitely *was* Mabel's biological father until after she was taken. Unless he's lying about that too …

'You're right, Mum, I don't know anything any more.' A surge of fatigue suddenly overwhelms her and she screws her fists into her eye sockets. 'The world's turned upside down. Mabel is still missing and the police don't seem to have a clue about who took her or what they did with her. It seems it was some random person who stole the door key, but we don't know for sure.'

'It wasn't random,' Vicky says firmly. 'It's connected, it's got to be.'

'That's what the police think,' says Ruby. 'They think it was me, but it wasn't, Mum, honestly it wasn't. I would never—'

'I know, love,' her mother replies in a rare moment of tenderness. 'You love Mabel, that's obvious to anyone.'

'I do. I love her like she's my own. If she doesn't come back, I'll never forgive myself, you know that. If she turns out to be dead, I don't want to be alive.'

'Hush now, let's not talk like that. We have to be positive. I'm not saying Lewis harmed her, but I know the two things are connected. They have to be.' She clasps her fingers together and lets out a long, anxious breath. 'Even before this, I was worried about Amber. I thought it was just postnatal depression, but I can see now it was more than that. She's been racked with guilt, terrified of George finding out. And I have a feeling she's not telling the whole truth either.'

Ruby shrugs. 'I'm so tired. I just want Mabel back, that's all I really care about. Lewis and I are dead in the water, and right now I'd like to kill Amber. I don't want to see either of them ever again. But if we get Mabel back safely, none of it will matter, we'll all be so happy nobody will give a shit about whose child she is. Maybe not even George.'

'Hmm … I wouldn't be so sure about that.' Vicky looks uneasily towards the window, as if somebody might be spying on them. 'He's a very proud man. He won't take this lying down.'

'I still don't get why Amber cheated on him. Unless it was to get at me. Does she hate me or something?'

'It was Lewis, he seduced her. She found she was pregnant and didn't know what to do, but decided to keep the baby. It must have been agonising …'

'That's bollocks, Mum.' Ruby uncurls herself and gets up. 'You're always the same. Nothing is ever Amber's fault. It makes me sick.'

Vicky's eyes flare with anger. 'Oh stop it, for God's sake. The poor girl has lost her child!'

'I know, I know, it's awful.' Ruby feels the tears welling up. 'But can't you have some sympathy for me too?'

'Mabel was taken on your watch,' she replies tersely. 'She was an innocent child and you let her down. I won't forgive you for that, and I'm sure you'll never forgive yourself.'

'Okay, fine. Pile on the guilt and blame like you always do.' Ruby grabs her jacket. 'I just wanted you to know that instead of one shit daughter, you have two. Hmm … I wonder whose fault that is?'

'Oh Ruby, you've always been so jealous. You have such a nasty streak.'

'I've had enough of the character assassination, Mum. I'm going home.'

Her eyebrows rise. 'To Lewis?'

'He won't be there. I told him he had three hours to get out.'

'Ruby—'

She storms out, slamming the front door behind her. She picks up her cycle helmet and is fastening the strap under her chin when her phone bleeps, announcing a new text. Whipping the handset out, she sees the message is from Amber.

Told George. He took it extremely badly. My daughter is missing and my marriage is over. Thanks a lot. Hope you're happy now.

Despite being exhausted, Ruby pedals furiously back across London, carelessly navigating the increasingly heavy traffic. The cauldron is still bubbling and frothing, spitting out bile. She curses herself for going to see her mother; she should have known she would take Amber's side. It was supposed to be payback time, but it misfired. As ever. And now she has nobody to turn to, except George perhaps – they could form a victims' support group. The thought of the two of them bonding almost makes her laugh.

Mum didn't even offer her a cup of tea, her water bottle's empty, and after burning hundreds of calories on the bike, she's hungry for a big breakfast. The vegan café a hundred yards from the flat beckons. But the real motivation for going there is to delay going back to the flat. The deadline she gave Lewis elapsed hours ago; he should be long gone, but what if he's still there, waiting for her? Her nerve endings feel raw and exposed; she can't take another bout of emotional outpourings.

The café is busy with people having Sunday brunch. The rough wooden tables are full and there's a queue of hopefuls crowding at the counter. As she surveys the scene, a memory stabs her in the gut – this is where she came with Lewis after the first night he stayed over at her flat. They were in that embarrassing loved-up phase, constantly stroking and pecking lips, unable to leave each other alone. She remembers holding hands across the table while they waited for their veggie sausages, beans and hash browns. With a sudden loss of appetite, she turns on her heel and leaves.

Fortunately, the media are no longer camped outside her block. Since the reconstruction yesterday, attention has been refocused on Lilac Park. Or maybe the journalists are bored with Missing Mabel and have moved on to new stories. Either way, she's thankful to be able to get through the metal gates unmolested. She wheels the bike down the path, feeling more and more apprehensive as she approaches the flat. *Please don't let him still be there.*

Heart in mouth, she pushes open the front door and walks into the hallway. Silence greets her and she lets out a sigh of relief, only for the breath to catch immediately as she sees two large rucksacks stacked outside the bedroom door.

'Lewis?' she calls. 'Lewis! Why haven't you left?' Bubbles of anger immediately rise to the surface and she goes into the kitchen, then back across the hallway towards the sitting room. 'I thought we agreed you'd be gone by—'

She stops in her tracks and gasps. Lewis is lying motionless on the floor, his clothes dishevelled, limbs askew. His face is covered in purple bruises and dark, sticky blood is pooling around his head.

Ruby recoils in horror, then a sense of urgency kicks in. She rushes forward and crouches down at his side. He doesn't seem to be breathing. Hands trembling, she reaches for her phone.

'Who did this to you?' she whispers as she dials 999. But Lewis can't answer. And besides, she already knows.

CHAPTER THIRTY-THREE

Day eight without Mabel

Amber opens the fridge and takes out a half-drunk bottle of white wine. It's been sitting there for over a week and will probably taste like vinegar, but she doesn't care. She needs alcohol to dull the pain that's emanating from every nerve. Pouring herself a full glass, she knocks it back in one go, coughing as it whooshes down. As she guessed, it tastes disgusting.

How the media would love to get this shot of her, she thinks bitterly as she refills. *Mabel's Mummy Hits the Bottle.* They are gathered outside again, fewer of them today, but still enough to be a nuisance. A small number of rubberneckers are there too, almost constantly pointing their phone cameras at the house. And at last they were rewarded for their patience. When George stormed out – three hours ago now – there was a great frenzy of excitement. Reporters and photographers clustered around him, firing questions as he tried to get into his car. She was watching from the bathroom window, fingers parting the slatted blinds, praying that he wouldn't rise to their bait. But he was already way out of control. He swore violently at the throng and deliberately bashed the driver's door into one of the photographers. Then he screeched off at high speed. All caught on camera, of course. It's probably already been posted on social media, accompanied by wild speculation.

After George drove away, journalists crowded at the door and rang the bell several times. Somebody even shouted through the letter box, asking for Amber's side of the story. As if … She ignored them and eventually they retreated to the pavement, but now she daren't step outside the door.

A searing pain stabs her between the eyes. Oh, this is all too much. If the press finds out, they will make mincemeat of all four of them; the headlines will be lurid and vile. Worst of all, it will take attention away from the search for Mabel. That's the only thing that really matters. Her baby is with a stranger – who knows what they're doing to her? She may not even be alive. Violent images start to invade her mind, fuelled by the alcohol, which is now on a helter-skelter ride through her body. She feels dizzy and grips the edge of the granite worktop to steady herself.

'Damn you, Ruby,' she mutters. 'You should have let me tell him in my own time.'

She pours a third glassful, then throws the empty bottle into the sink. Staggering across the room, she collapses in the armchair in the corner, where she so often sat to breastfeed – or rather, *try* to. The cushions smell vaguely of stale milk and sicky infant dribble, conjuring up the feel of Mabel wriggling in her arms. Curling herself into a hedgehog-like ball, Amber buries her head and cries.

Where has George gone? she wonders. He shouldn't be driving in that state. When she told him the truth, he went all rigid, as if he'd been tasered, and his mouth gaped, but no sound came out. Then suddenly he exploded like a bomb. He thumped the walls with his fists and even his forehead. His anger was uncontrollable; at one point she thought he was going to strike her and had to lock herself in the bathroom. The neighbours must have heard it. The whole street was probably listening in. The shame of it … the shame. She was terrified for herself, but now she's terrified for George. He could easily have an accident or knock over a pedestrian. She needs to find him before he does something that he'll later regret. Not that he'll listen to her. Their marriage is wrecked. Over. Irreparable. She feels utterly alone.

George is her life partner. Amber can't remember what it was like to be single and can't imagine being without him. He is part of her, an extra limb. She could no more cut him off than she could her own hand. If that's a definition of love, then she loves him with all her heart. But as time has gone on, she's realised they have little in common. The uncomfortable truth is that if she met him now, she would find him sexually attractive but not be that interested in his personality. It's a horrible thing to admit, even to herself. She hasn't even said that to Seth, and he knows *everything*: how much she misses her dead father, how problematic she finds her mother, how ambivalent she feels towards Ruby, how much she longed to have a baby, how frustrated she was with George for refusing to get tested …

When she and Seth decided – after several vodkas in the Ice Bar in Mayfair – that he would donate his sperm, their friendship moved to a whole new level. They were having one of their secret get-togethers – usually a pizza in Soho followed by either a film or cocktails, occasionally both. George didn't know about their meetings, because as far as he was concerned, Seth was banned. It was absurd. Amber and Seth were best friends, that was all; there wasn't a glimmer of attraction there. They were on the same course at university and went through three significant years of growing up together, supporting each other through some rough times. George didn't have the imagination to believe that a man and woman could be friends without wanting to jump into bed. He decided for no good reason that he hated Seth, and after they graduated, he refused to meet up socially or invite him over to their house. At first Amber continued to see Seth on the quiet because she was embarrassed; then she told him about George's reaction and they began what they laughingly called their 'sordid affair'. It was a bit of fun really, pretending to be lovers, making secret phone calls and sending saucy texts almost every day. They even had a running joke about deleting messages. Beneath it all, however, there was something deep and genuine. Quite simply, Seth was the dearest friend she'd ever had.

He'd always insisted that he didn't want children: 'Population is the world's biggest problem and I'm not going to add to it.' But for Amber he would make an exception. He swore he would never tell a soul or stake a claim to the child if she conceived. 'Your secret will be safe with me, darling,' he said. 'I'll take it to my grave.'

But a decision made in drunkenness can be hard to carry out in the sober light of day. They didn't know how to do it. There was no question of actually having sex. That would have felt totally wrong, not to mention embarrassing. Besides, Seth had a girlfriend at that point and hadn't yet resolved whether he was bisexual or totally gay. Amber knew he was gay, one hundred per cent. Everyone at university had known it; even the girlfriend knew she was fighting a losing battle, although she didn't want to admit it. Only George persisted in the theory that he was straight and pretending to be gay so he could get closer to Amber.

Seth researched DIY artificial insemination online and ordered a turkey baster. Amber calculated when she should be ovulating and took the day off work. He came round to number 74 and went into the bathroom for what turned out to be a considerable length of time. Amber remembers how nervous and excited she felt waiting for him to come out with his plastic bottle. Then it was her turn to go into the bedroom and do the business with the giant syringe. It didn't seem to work very well; what little sperm Seth had managed to produce dribbled out. Nevertheless, she lay on her back with her legs in the air for an hour while Seth made tea and brought it to the bedside. It was all a bit of a laugh, she remembers, like they were a couple of kids playing doctors and nurses. Considering the immensity of what they were trying to do, and the implications of them succeeding, neither of them took it seriously enough.

Amber didn't have to wait for her period to know it hadn't worked. Turkey basters weren't the answer; she needed proper professional help. That was why she broached the subject with George again, and why they had such a bad row. And that was how she ended up having sex with Lewis. It was a game of consequences, only instead of a funny picture at the bottom of the page, she created a real-life human being.

Her heart heaves with love for Mabel and dark thoughts loom, but she bats them away.

She needs to talk to Seth urgently, before the story breaks in the media. He still doesn't know that he's indisputably *not* Mabel's father. Despite his assertions that he had no interest in parenthood, she worries that he's still holding a flickering torch of hope that Mabel is his. Why else back away the moment she was taken? Amber can only guess that he was thinking of her, as always, not wanting to complicate the situation and put her under more pressure from George. But they're well beyond that now. Picking up her mobile, she dials his number. As before, it goes straight to voicemail without giving her an opportunity to leave a message. Sniffing back the tears, she sends him what she promises herself will be a final plea.

Darling, please call me. I've lost everyone – you're the only one left. Why are you ignoring me? Have I done something wrong? Please, please get in touch. Love you. A xx

And as a reminder of all that they've been to each other, she adds a PS: *Don't forget to delete.*

Eyes bleary, she lifts her head. Somebody is knocking and ringing at the front door. Wretched journos. 'Piss off!' she shouts, covering her ears. She won't speak to any of them. They are hyenas, picking over the dead scraps of her life. 'Leave me alone!'

But the knocking and ringing continue. What is going on? She gets up and walks onto the landing, where she stands at the top of the stairs hugging herself protectively. The flap of the letter box opens and she half expects to see a flaming rag thrown through, but instead she hears a familiar voice.

'Amber? It's Sally. I know you're there. Please open the door.'

The FLO was supposed to turn up this morning, but in the trauma, Amber forgot all about it. She runs down the stairs, her brain already tripping over itself. Sally's tone sounded urgent. Something has happened. Has Mabel been found?

She opens up and quickly lets Sally in. The dark expression on the officer's face immediately tells Amber that she's not bearing good news.

'What is it?' she gasps.

'Let's go upstairs. Away from this mob.' Sally nods at her to lead the way. Amber's legs feel like jelly as she climbs back to the first floor. Can Sally smell the alcohol on her breath? She covers her face with her hand and surreptitiously sniffs. The results are inconclusive.

They go into the front room. Amber glances out of the window and sees two patrol cars parked outside the door, blue lights flashing.

'What's going on?'

'We're looking for George,' says Sally. 'When did you last see him?'

'Um … about three hours ago. He left the house and drove off.'

'Do you know where he went?'

'No. Why? What's happened? Is he okay?'

'Lewis Chambers was attacked in his flat this morning,' Sally replies, keeping her tone even. 'He was severely beaten and is fighting for his life.'

The words punch Amber in the stomach, winding her. She reaches out for support and lowers herself onto a chair. 'Oh my God …'

'Your sister thinks it was George that attacked him.'

'No … no … he wouldn't …' She stops. Inside, she knows it's true. His parting words were along the lines of 'The next time I see Lewis, I'll kill him.' Stupid, stupid man. As if that's going to make things any better. As if it's going to help find Mabel …

Sally clears her throat. 'Do you know where George is? We've tried reaching him by phone …'

'He took the car, that's all I know.'

'Did he say anything about going to see Lewis?'

'No, but …' She hesitates. 'It's possible. He was very upset. And angry.'

'With Lewis?'

She nods. 'And me.' She chews her lip. 'We had a bad row.'

'Hmm … You told him, I presume? That Lewis is Mabel's biological father.'

'Yes.' Heat rises to her cheeks. 'He took it very badly. But I didn't think—'

'Have you any idea where he might be now?'

'No.' Sally shoots her a disbelieving look. 'Honestly, I've no idea. If I knew, I'd tell you.'

'Okay.' The FLO puffs out. 'We're monitoring his phone, but if he gets in touch with you, let us know straight away.'

'I'll tell him to hand himself in,' Amber mumbles.

'You do that.' Sally walks over to the window and looks down into the street below. 'You should know that pictures of Lewis being loaded into an ambulance are already flying around social media. Some people are saying he tried to kill himself, others are pointing the finger at George. There are all kinds of theories circulating; it's getting extremely nasty. You're going to be besieged, I'm afraid.'

'Don't worry, I'm not going anywhere.'

'The patrol cars will stay outside. The officers will make sure nobody gets too close.'

'Thanks.'

There's a long pause. Sally turns to her. 'This must be very tough. How are you? You look … worn to a frazzle.'

'It's just going from bad to worse,' Amber says. 'Everything's falling apart. And all this time, Mabel is still missing. Everyone's forgotten about her.'

'No they haven't. We've got a huge team working around the clock, processing all the intelligence that's come through since yesterday. We've had an amazing response from the public, we feel very positive that—'

'Don't bullshit me,' she snaps. 'I know you all think she's dead.'

'That's not true. This is a missing person case, not a murder. Finding Mabel alive remains our overwhelming priority.'

'For once, can you stop talking like you're at a press conference?'

Sally stiffens. 'I was just trying to reassure you that we're doing …' She stops, takes a deep breath and starts again. 'I'm sorry. You're right. I can see you're under tremendous pressure. The last thing you need is some trite—'

'Please, don't say any more,' Amber sighs. 'Just find my daughter, that's all I want.'

CHAPTER THIRTY-FOUR

Day eight with Mabel

I can't get the Nosy Neighbour out of my head. Yesterday evening, I went into the garden, convinced that he was snooping around, lurking in the shadows. I couldn't see him, but I sensed his presence, creeping towards me in a game of grandmother's footsteps. When I had my back to him, he inched forward, little by little, but the moment I turned around, he froze, invisible in his country camouflage of tweed and corduroy. I knew he was there, though. I could hear his threatening voice in my head. *I'm coming to get you ...*

Later, as I lay in bed, I kept listening for twigs cracking underfoot and rustling in the undergrowth. The hinges on the side gate were creaking and at one point I thought I heard him trying to get in through the back door. As soon as I got up this morning, I went outside again to check for footprints and patches of flattened grass, but he'd covered his tracks well. If he comes back tonight, I'll be ready for him. There must be weapons in Dolly's shed that I can use. Spades, pitchforks, a hammer ...

I pull myself up short. No, no, that won't work. I must put all thoughts of violence aside. There is too much at stake, too much to lose. I have to pretend to make friends with the ghastly Bob and Barbara and banish all suspicions from their minds. A cake will do it. Muffins, perhaps. Blueberry or chocolate chip. I've never made a cake in my life, but I'm sure I can whip up something edible. Besides, it's the gesture that counts rather than the quality of the baking. Sunday is the perfect day for acts of kindness. Nobody will suspect me if I come bearing gifts.

Resolved, I drag Mabel's bouncy chair into the kitchen, parking her by the back door while I search for suitable equipment. She watches me curiously as I rummage through Great-Aunt Dolly's cupboards, pulling out a large biscuit-coloured mixing bowl, a plastic sieve and a metal patty tin with spaces for twelve little fairy cakes.

'Pity I can't look up a recipe online,' I moan, reaching for the most battered-looking cookery book on the shelf. Motes of ancient dust are stuck to its greasy cover, the spine is in tatters, and several pages fall out as I open it up. I turn to the baking section. 'Here we go … Hmm … butter, caster sugar, eggs, self-raising flour … none of which we've got.' I sigh loudly. 'What a nuisance. We'll have to make a trip to the shops.'

Taking Mabel out is a risk, but it'll be worth it. Anything to get Bob and Barbara off my back. I make a quick list and put some cash in my pocket, then dress my darling in her pink snowsuit. She's not very impressed by the idea of an outing and fights me as I buckle her into the car seat.

The weather is miserable – leaden skies and a biting wind. Deciding to avoid the nearest village, where I might bump into the locals, I drive northwards. Ideally I need to find a large out-of-town supermarket where everyone is busy doing their own shopping and won't give us a second look. I won't be able to leave Mabel in the car; I'll have to push her around in the buggy. I'll drape a little blanket over the hood so that nobody can see her face. Parents do that all the time when a baby's sleeping. Nobody will think it out of the ordinary. We'll be fine. Just a quick nip in and out, pick up the stuff, pay in cash …

I drive along the twisty lanes, negotiating a series of bends, hugging the hedgerows where the road narrows, shifting gear to climb the hills, swerving to avoid ruts and puddles. Mabel falls asleep and thoughts of the past skitter through my mind.

This was the route we took when we first visited Midsummer Cottage, although we were travelling in the opposite direction. It was a Friday evening; we'd both left work early, hoping to miss the weekend exodus from London. The car was packed with food and booze and there was love in the air. After some rocky times, we were going through a settled phase and I was feeling more confident. We hadn't had an argument for weeks.

I insisted on being at the wheel for the last bit of the journey. It made me feel more in control of the situation. This was *my* cottage, *my* inheritance. I was more than happy to share my good fortune but I needed it to be understood that for once, I was in charge. Stupid, really. I never was in the driving seat of that relationship. Not that I care any more. When we're back together, I'll be content to play second fiddle.

I glance across at the empty seat next to me and make a silent plea to the ghost sitting there. *Please come and find us. You know where we are. Don't make me wait much longer. Mabel needs you. I need you. It's time to be a family.*

After a few miles, the road widens and straightens, and we reach a roundabout. Following a promising sign, I eventually reach a small retail park on the outskirts of the next town. The place is heaving with Sunday shoppers. Perfect, I think, pulling into a space.

As soon as the engine stops, Mabel annoyingly starts to stir. I get out of the car and open the boot, removing the buggy I bought in anticipation of many happy outings. I haven't had the chance to use it yet. I give it a shake, expecting it to open and fall effortlessly into position, but nothing happens. Perhaps it's fastened, I think, examining the handles and legs. Strangely, there doesn't seem to be anything to press or twist or undo.

Mabel is properly awake now and making grumpy noises from the car seat. 'Won't be a minute!' I call, turning the contraption this way and that with an increasingly puzzled look on my face. How the hell does the damn thing unfold?

'Having problems?' says a voice. Looking up, I see a young woman standing over me wearing leggings and a large waterproof coat with a fur-rimmed hood. She has a toddler in a pushchair – a far cheaper model than Mabel's – who's sitting quietly, stuffing his face with crisps. Bags of shopping swing from hooks on the handlebar.

'No, it's just I ... er ...' I falter.

'Need help?'

'No thanks.'

'New, is it?'

'Hmm?'

'The buggy.'

'Yes,' I mutter, turning my face away from her, trying to avoid eye contact. I'm getting hot, my fingers are sweating, fumbling at the mechanism. Mabel starts to cry.

'Oh dear,' says the girl. 'Somebody's not happy.' She walks around to the other side of the car, bending down to peer into the side window.

My heart almost stops. She's looking right at Mabel, her face pressed close to the glass.

'Oh bless! She's all upset because she can't see you. It's okay, darling, you haven't been abandoned,' she soothes.

I want the nosy bitch to move away from the car. Mabel's face is in everybody's news feed; it's probably on the front of all the Sunday newspapers today. She could so easily recognise her. And here I am behaving like an idiot, unable to perform the simplest parental task. I might as well have 'abductor' tattooed across my forehead. I hurl the buggy to the ground, swearing under my breath.

She straightens up. 'Sure you don't want help?'

'Yes! Just leave me alone!'

'All right, keep your hair on.' She shoots me a hostile look. 'What's your problem?'

I pick up the buggy and fling it back into the boot, then get into the driver's seat, slamming the door shut. She puts her face up to the window, and tells me to get a life. I turn the ignition and hurriedly reverse out of the space without looking properly. There's a horrible moment when I can't see her toddler and slam on the brakes. But he's safe, stowed at her side.

So much for the low-profile in-and-out approach, I think bitterly as I zoom out of the car park. I made a complete spectacle of myself back there – how stupid was that? I don't think she recognised Mabel. At least, I hope not. But maybe she memorised the number on the licence plate. Maybe she's calling the police right now.

I drive back towards the roundabout, constantly checking the rear mirror, listening for the sound of sirens. Mabel is still crying, her sobs building towards a crescendo. I imagine her tears filling up the car, our chins bobbing above the waterline as we gasp for air.

'You're driving me nuts!' I shout. 'Shut up! For God's sake, just shut up!'

My hands are sweating, sliding off the steering wheel. The engine surges as I put my foot down, and jolts when I release the clutch. I'm driving like a learner; my timing gone to pot. Got to concentrate. Make sure we get home in one piece. Forget the shopping, forget the baking. It was a stupid idea anyway. Fuck the Nosy Neighbours, they can go to hell.

Mabel's screams are drilling a hole in the back of my head. As I swivel around to shout at her again, I catch sight of something in my peripheral vision: a large solid shape coming around the bend towards us. I whip back, but it's too late; I've drifted too far into the middle of the road and now the large solid shape – a truck – is bearing down on us. As I pull sharply to my left, it clips me on the front wing, only slightly, but enough to send the car shooting across the tarmac like a silver ball in a game of bagatelle. We bounce off the hedge, then lurch back, heading for the opposite bank. I slam on the brakes and everything goes into slow motion. The wheels screech and rubber burns. We spin around, missing a tree by centimetres, skimming a fence and finally stopping just short of a hefty farm gate.

My heart is thumping out of my chest. I rest my forehead on the steering wheel and try to steady my panting breaths.

Gradually I become aware of the stillness around me. Everything has gone deathly quiet. The engine has stalled. Mabel is no longer crying. Oh God, what if she's hurt? I don't dare look round.

Suddenly the passenger door opens and the red face of the truck driver looms in. 'What the hell do you think you were doing?' he barks. "You were on the wrong side of the bloody road. We could have both been killed.'

'It wasn't me!' I protest. 'You came around the bend way too fast.'

'Bloody didn't. It was you that—' He spots Mabel and immediately softens his tone. 'Christ, I didn't realise you had a kiddie in the back. Is she okay?'

I turn to look at her. She's staring at me stony-faced, bottom lip pushed out, eyes narrowed in judgement. 'Yes, by the look of it.'

'And yourself?'

'Fine. Just a bit shocked. I thought I was going to end up in the ditch.'

There's a pause. I think he's expecting me to get out and inspect the damage to the car, but I really don't want to. There's been far too much face-to-face contact already.

'Right, well I guess we'd better call the police,' he says, taking his mobile out of his pocket.

'No, no, don't do that,' I reply hastily. 'There's no need. We're not hurt, the damage is minimal. I'm sure neither of us wants the fuss.'

He frowns. 'You have to report it or you can't claim on the insurance.'

'Oh, I won't be claiming. Can't be bothered.' He looks at me doubtfully. 'I'm sure the damage is minimal, and you're right, it was my fault. My excess is horrendous, it's not worth it.'

He looks back at his vehicle, parked on the verge. 'Hmm, the truck's okay. Maybe a slight scratch where we made contact … nothing much, not worth fixing. I must admit, I could do without the paperwork.'

'Exactly. And it's Sunday. We could be ages waiting for the police to turn up.'

Our eyes lock. I sense him weighing up the situation, deciding whether to agree to break the law. If he calls the police, I'll have no choice but to drive off at speed. He's thinking I don't have a driving licence, or proper insurance. Will he take pity on me?

'There's no real damage to your vehicle,' I say, giving him a pleading look. 'Does either of us really want the bother?'

'Hmm …' His eyes flick back to Mabel, who rewards him with a half-smile.

'I can't see the point in involving the police,' I add. 'It'll be such a hassle.'

'No, you're right. I'm behind with my deliveries as it is. If you're happy, I'm happy.' We exchange a few more pleasantries, then he returns to his truck and pulls away.

I drive back to the bungalow at a snail's pace, trembling as I think of the narrow escape I've just had. That was close. *Too* close. I can't let all my plans fail for the sake of a stupid road accident. We're going to have to stay at home from now on, and only go out when it's absolutely necessary.

Pulling onto the driveway, I park up and turn off the engine. It's a relief to be home, but I'm still breathing too fast and my nerves are on edge. Oddly, there hasn't been a peep out of Mabel since we crashed. Nor has she fallen asleep again. I get out of the car and open the rear passenger door.

She glares at me as I undo her straps. 'No need to sulk, madam,' I say. 'It was your fault we had the accident. I've had enough of your screaming. Do that again and I'll dump you in the ditch and drive away.'

CHAPTER THIRTY-FIVE

Day eight without Mabel

Amber takes the casserole and puts it down on the granite worktop.

'I was going to bring flowers,' says Polly. 'Then I thought, no, make her one of your lamb tagines. I don't suppose you feel like cooking at the moment.' She moves towards the table and parks herself on one of the dining chairs.

Amber tries to suppress a frown. Why ever did she agree to Polly 'popping by'? She could easily have told the officer guarding the door to send away all visitors, even so-called friends bearing gifts.

'Have you lost weight?' Polly says, scrutinising her.

'Not deliberately.'

'I didn't mean … I just …' She falters. 'I can't imagine … The stress must be unbearable.'

'Yes, it is. Do you want a tea?'

'Please. Do you want me to make it?'

'It's okay, I can still boil a kettle.'

'Of course.' Polly shrugs apologetically. 'It's the little everyday actions that keep you going, I expect.' Amber plonks a tea bag in a mug and pours over hot water. 'The other mums send their love, by the way. We've given out hundreds – I mean literally hundreds – of lengths of lilac ribbon. The response has been fantastic, they are *everywhere*. People are mad keen to help. We want to launch a Find Mabel campaign on social media. We've already had offers of sponsorship for T-shirts, posters, leaflets, Facebook ads, but it needs you and George to front it.' She stops and draws breath. 'You may not realise it, but the negative press your family's getting is terrible, Amber. There are all sorts of disgusting rumours flying around. The police can't protect you forever.' She trails off, stalled by Amber's hostile expression.

'I know you all mean well, but I'm not interested in being the new Kate McCann.' Amber walks across the room and bangs the mug on the table.

'Well, who would? But that's not what I meant.' Polly picks up the mug and sniffs its contents curiously. 'We're really worried for you, Amber. You're already getting death threats; if you don't start being more proactive—'

'Shut up, Polly!' Amber shouts. 'I don't need you or your opinions, or your T-shirts or posters or fucking lilac ribbons.' She shoves the casserole across the counter. 'And you can take back your Le Creuset while you're about it too. I can't eat, can't sleep, can barely manage to wash and dress myself. You have no idea of the hell I'm going through. I don't give a shit what people are saying about me. All I want is Mabel back.'

'That's all we want too,' replies Polly stiffly. She puts down the mug without taking a sip. 'Sorry, I shouldn't have come. I was trying to show my support, trying to help. But if I'm not wanted …'

Amber sighs. 'Look, things are really difficult right now. I need some time to myself.'

'By the way,' Polly says, rising, 'Sonya rang me from India. She was very upset that she'd been a suspect, but I managed to calm her down. We had a long chat about George …' She walks towards the door, the words trailing behind her like a toxic cloud.

'Why?'

'Well, obviously you know …'

Amber feels the blood draining from her extremities. 'Know what?'

'Sonya feels really guilty about what happened,' Polly carries on. 'But as I said to her, it takes two. And it wasn't as if she was the only one. Anyway, she wanted me to tell you that George definitely wasn't the father of the baby she lost.'

Amber's head starts to swim. This can't be true. It *can't* be true. Yes, George can be a flirt. He's gorgeous and fit; women queue up to have him as their personal trainer, especially the older ones, but surely … surely he'd never …

'Sonya's lying,' she says firmly.

Polly lingers at the threshold, observing her reaction. 'Oh God, you *didn't* know … Sonya told the police, so she assumed it had all come out. I'm so sorry. Oh dear, now I feel awful. I came here to help—'

'No you didn't, you came to gloat,' Amber spits. 'Get out, Polly.'

Polly holds up her hands. 'Hey, don't blame the messenger. We're on your side. All we want to do is find Mabel.'

Amber picks up the casserole, its weight tempting her to throw it at Polly's head. 'Take this and fuck off out of my life.'

Polly snatches the pot back. 'Charming,' she says. 'That's the thanks I get. Don't worry. I'll see myself out.' She swings around and exits. Amber only just manages to stop herself pushing the woman down the stairs.

It's early evening when Sally rings, rousing Amber from a strange delirious sleep. After Polly dropped her bombshell, a migraine came on. She threw up and collapsed on the bed, feeling as if she'd drunk two *crates* of wine rather than only two glasses.

'Yes? What is it?' she rasps. Her teeth feel slimy, while her tongue is as rough as sandpaper.

'We've located George,' says Sally. 'But it's tricky. We need your help to bring him in.'

'Why? Where is he?'

'At Batley Reservoir. He's in a bad way, won't come out of the water. Will you talk to him?'

Never again, Amber thinks, if what Polly told her is true.

'Amber? Can you be ready in five minutes?'

'Um …'

'I'm on my way. Oh, and wrap up warm. It's freezing out there.'

Sally ends the call, leaving Amber in a daze. She doesn't want to see George. She doesn't care about him. He's a violent monster. A sexual predator. A hypocrite. But the police are coming. They're expecting her to help. And they already know about his reputation anyway. Oh, the shame of it …

She puts on her thickest jumper and double-layered socks, then washes her face and combs her hair, tucking it under a woollen beanie. Going downstairs, she takes her winter coat off the peg and stuffs her arms into the sleeves. The jumper is so bulky she can only just do up the buttons, and she struggles to bend down as she pulls on her boots. Next, she slips on the knitted gloves George put in her stocking last Christmas. They're soft and beautiful, the perfect match for the emerald-green coat. What a bastard …

Sonya wasn't the only one, that was what Polly said. If that's true, how long has he been cheating on her? Was it going on at sports college? Is this a new thing, or has he behaved like this at every gym he's worked at? Have they all been one-night stands, or have there been more serious relationships? Who are these women – has she met them? She wants names, addresses, full details.

Sally's five minutes become ten. Amber sweats as she waits. She feels faint, partly due to the fact that she hasn't eaten all day. Her thoughts turn to Lewis. How is he doing? She hopes to God he doesn't die.

The doorbell rings. She takes a deep breath and waddles downstairs. Sally is wearing a large padded anorak and a hat with ear flaps.

'Ready?' she asks.

Amber nods automatically and follows her to the waiting patrol car. She heaves herself onto the back seat. Sally gets in next to her and the driver speeds off.

'Okay, here's the situation,' says Sally. 'George was spotted over an hour ago. When an officer approached, he waded into the water and refused to come out. He's threatening to drown himself.'

Amber flinches. 'Jesus ...' she murmurs.

'Obviously we're not going to put you in any physical danger. But if you could talk to him ...'

'Why would he listen to me?'

'Because you're his wife, and although he's very angry and hurting, he loves you. That's why he attacked Lewis.'

A week ago, she would have agreed, but now George's love for her holds no meaning. She turns her thoughts away from him and towards the man lying in hospital. 'How is he? Lewis, I mean.'

Sally pulls a face. 'He's been put into an induced coma,' she says. 'I gather it's touch and go.'

'And my sister?'

'She's at his side.'

Amber raises her brows. Yet why is she surprised? Ruby is the most generous-spirited person she knows. Of course she would set aside her anger with Lewis and support him in his darkest hour.

Amber really wants to see her sister – to explain, to apologise, to beg forgiveness. Maybe when Mabel comes back – *if* she does come back ... She sinks back in the seat, feeling defeated.

'All this, this shit,' she says. 'It gets in the way, doesn't it? Stops you finding her.'

'Not at all. Mabel is still our primary focus.'

'Has anyone interviewed George's colleagues at the gym?'

'Um, yes, I believe so. Why do you ask?'

Amber stares out of the window at the flitting scenery. 'A sort of friend came round today. She told me George had ...' the words catch in her throat, 'a fling with Sonya. Do you already know that?'

There's a short pause, then Sally takes a breath and speaks. 'A couple of female colleagues mentioned it, yes. It's been a line of enquiry. At one stage we thought he might have been the father of Sonya's child, but she said not. Said the timing didn't tally.'

'You knew but you didn't tell me.'

'George begged us not to. Just as you begged us not to tell him.'

'You must think we're both utterly appalling.'

'Everyone has complicated lives,' Sally replies. 'I don't judge.'

They've reached the reservoir. The car slows and turns down a service road, reserved for maintenance workers. It's a narrow, bumpy track swathed in darkness. From her side, all Amber can see is a tall, thick hedge. Beyond that, she knows there is a large expanse of murky, swirling water – an angler's paradise during the day, but treacherous at night.

The driver pulls up behind three other vehicles – two police cars and an ambulance. DI Benedict is there, blowing on his fingers and stamping his feet. He's not dressed for being outside in this weather. As soon as Amber gets out of the car, he walks over to her.

'Thank you for coming,' he says quietly. 'George is still in the water. We're getting very concerned about hypothermia.'

Amber gulps. 'What do you want me to do?'

'Just stand on the bank, where he can see you. That may be enough. If you want to say anything, keep it simple. My guess is that he's scared.'

'Okay.' She follows Benedict down a narrow path and through a gap in the hedge. It opens out onto a small gravel beach.

There's no moon visible tonight; it's hidden behind a cloud of orangey-brown pollution that hovers over the reservoir like an alien presence. George's silhouette rises from the water, making him look as if he's been cut off at the knees. Even in the dark, from a distance, she can tell that he's shivering.

The anger she felt so strongly in the car evaporates, and she's overcome with pity for him. For both of them. They've both behaved abominably towards each other, but what does it matter? They are just a grimy subplot of the main tragedy. Lewis is lying in a coma. Mabel is missing. Gone. Vanished. Spirited away. The last sighting of her no more than a bulge in a jacket creeping through the shadows.

'George?' she calls, moving towards the line of inky water. 'It's me. Amber.'

'She's here somewhere!' he shouts. 'This is where he dumped her.'

Her heart flutters like a bird trapped in her ribcage. 'How do you know? Did he tell you?'

'No … couldn't make him confess, the little shit … But I know she's here.' He brushes the water with his hands. 'This is where he dumped her. It's the obvious place, virtually within walking distance. I've looked everywhere else. I'm going to find her, bring her home.'

She inches forward. Icy rivulets lap around her fine leather boots. 'You can't see properly in the dark,' she says. 'Wait until it's light and I'll help you. We can search for her together.' It's a lie, but then what's one more after so many that have passed between them?

He shakes his head. 'No, I need to find her now.'

'It's too cold, too dark. Please come out, George.' She takes a step. Then another. The water is up to her ankles now. Next it will find the hem of her coat. 'You'll freeze to death. Come out and we'll try again tomorrow.'

He tugs at his hair and lets out a long, anguished moan. 'I'm sorry,' he cries. 'I fucked it all up.'

'We both did. I'm sorry too. For everything.' She extends her arm. 'Please come out. It's dangerous. You'll die of cold. Please? I can't lose you. I need your help to find Mabel.'

He doesn't respond. It feels as if it's just the two of them out here in the dark and wet, even though there are a dozen people behind the hedge – still as statues, collectively holding their breath. The seconds are ticking by and the temperature is plummeting. DI Benedict won't let this go on forever.

The water creeps up her coat, making the woollen fabric cling to her thighs. Her bones ache with cold and the heels of her boots are sinking into the mud, trapping her. 'George!' she tries again. 'I can't go any further. You have to come to me.'

Suddenly there's a thunderous roar as officers rush out of the bushes as if fired from a starting gun. They charge into the water, almost knocking Amber over as they lunge at George. He topples backwards and goes under for a few terrifying moments before he's wrenched out, dripping wet, spitting and spluttering for breath. He's dragged out of the water and onto the gravel beach. Officers surround him, shouting out his rights and applying handcuffs. A paramedic hovers, clutching a foil blanket.

Amber feels strong arms around her. 'Well done,' a voice says. Her heels squelch as she twists them free and allows herself to be led back to the bank.

CHAPTER THIRTY-SIX

Day nine without Mabel

Amber watches sadly as George is taken away in an ambulance, escorted by two patrol cars, blue lights flashing, sirens blaring.

A paramedic puts a blanket around her shoulders. 'You need to get out of those wet clothes,' he says. 'I'd like to take you to A&E, get you checked out.'

She shakes her head. 'No, I'm fine, really. I just want to go home.'

By the time she arrives back at William Morris Terrace, it's late. Now that George is in custody, the police vehicles have left, along with the media. Thank God. An old guy is walking his dog and a few teenagers on bikes are hanging around the park entrance. If it weren't for the lilac ribbons festooning every gate and tree, the scene would appear normal. She could be simply returning home after a night out.

She lets herself in and wearily climbs all the way to the top floor. Her trousers are still soaking and the sensation of standing in the freezing water won't leave her. Her bones are like icicles, and the pungent smell of the reservoir has penetrated her skin. She takes a long, hot shower and washes her hair, then puts on clean pyjamas and her thick dressing gown.

Pangs of hunger are gnawing at her stomach. Realising she hasn't eaten all day, she goes down to the kitchen, thinking she might manage a sandwich. But the bread's stale and the sliced ham smells dodgy. Cheese on toast, then, she decides. Simply turning on the grill makes her feel utterly exhausted.

It's only as she's cutting open a fresh packet of cheese that the idea comes to her. Once she thinks of it, she can't let it go. She can't stay locked in the flat forever, afraid to go out; a sad, demented creature, the object of some people's pity and others' speculation. But neither can she bear to court the media or ask for help from celebrities and billionaires. She will not give her side of the story to the tabloids, or appear on breakfast television, or write a book to raise money for the Find Mabel campaign.

With the scissors still in her hand, she takes an empty bin liner and goes out into the street. She's barefoot and clad only in her nightwear, but she doesn't care. Starting at the end of the terrace, she goes from gate to gate and tree to tree, cutting off the lilac ribbons. They fall gracefully to the ground like discarded items of lingerie. She scoops them into the bag, popping it in the wheelie bin before going back inside the flat.

Early the next morning, Amber squeezes her fingers around the bunch of flowers as the lift takes her up to the intensive care unit. She's not sure why she bought them, considering Lewis is in a coma, but visiting hospital empty-handed doesn't feel right. In this case, they are symbolic. A sign to Ruby that she wants to make peace.

The lift doors open and she steps out. Following the signs, she walks down the corridor, pulse rate increasing with every pace. She didn't sleep last night and feels light-headed, detached from herself. After several hours of imagining coming to the hospital, it seems strange that she's actually here now – so strange that she might be dreaming it.

She wonders whether George is still here, in a private room guarded by a police officer, or whether by now he's at the station, being questioned. She pauses outside the double doors of the intensive care unit and tries to summon up the courage she felt last night on the banks of Batley Reservoir. Stuffing the bouquet under one arm, she applies hand sanitiser, then presses the entry button.

The nurse who answers takes a little persuading to allow her in, but when he realises who Amber is, and that she only wants to talk to her sister, he finally relents.

'I'm very sorry to hear about your daughter,' he says, meeting her at the door. 'It must be agony for you. Everyone here is rooting for Mabel. We all want her to be found alive and well.'

The ward is quiet, bathed in calm. Private rooms, their doors closed and blinds pulled down, surround a small waiting area by the reception desk. Ruby is sitting there, hunched over, elbows on her knees, head in her hands. She hasn't seen Amber walking towards her.

'Hi, Ruby,' Amber says softly.

Ruby starts and looks up, her eyes immediately narrowing. 'What the hell are you doing here?' she says. 'Have you no shame?'

Amber absorbs the blow, then sits down on the chair next to her sister, shoving the bunch of flowers out of sight. 'I had to come.'

'Well I'm afraid your lover isn't receiving visitors at the moment.'

Amber swallows hard. 'How is he?'

'In a bad way. Might never wake up.'

'Oh I'm so sorry, Ruby.'

'So you fucking well should be. Lewis behaved appallingly, I'm absolutely furious with him – with both of you – but he doesn't deserve to die for it.' Her eyes flash angrily. 'Why did George think he had the right to attack him? God help anyone who defiles his property, was that it?'

'No, he was just … Oh, I don't know. He was trying to make Lewis confess to killing Mabel, I think. He felt I'd humiliated him; he couldn't cope with not being Mabel's father ... But Lewis isn't my lover – he never was. It was a stupid one-off thing we both instantly regretted. And yet ...' She pauses, fighting to get the words out. 'Yet Mabel came out of it and I can't regret her.' The tears roll down her cheeks. 'I wanted her too much, you see. Losing her is my punishment.'

'Look, I'm not really interested in your angst.' Ruby's tone is icy. 'I've got enough of my own to worry about. If you need a shoulder to cry on, go and see Mum.'

'But I need *you*! You're my sister.'

Ruby shrugs. 'My birth sister, that's all. It doesn't count for much.'

'I know, I know, I don't deserve you. I've never treated you well,' Amber sniffs through her tears. 'But I've always loved you, Rubes.'

'Don't "Rubes" me.'

'I'm so, so sorry. Please forgive me. I'm begging you.'

'Go away, Amber, I can't be doing with this. Lewis could die!'

The nurse standing at the computer shoots a reproving look towards them. Ruby holds up a hand in apology, and when she speaks again, her voice is quieter, the tone calmer. 'Forget about us, we're not important. Concentrate on finding Mabel, that's all you need to do right now. And get the police off my back. Every minute they spend investigating me is time wasted.'

'Yes, I know ...' Amber hangs her head. 'I'm sorry,' she mumbles. 'Sorry for everything.'

'Just go away and leave me be. Find Mabel.'

She nods. She rummages in her pocket for a tissue and blows her nose, then stands up, eyes full of liquid, tears choking her throat.

'Ah, Amber, you're here too,' says a surprised voice. 'Bit early for visiting.' Both of them look up to see DI Benedict, carrying a large brown envelope. He stops in his tracks as he takes in the scene, eyes flicking between them, looking for signs and clues. 'What is it? Lewis? Is he …?'

'No change,' replies Ruby stiffly.

'Right … Okay.' DI Benedict breathes in. 'Amber, I didn't realise you'd be here. Sally is on her way to your place.'

'Why? Is there news?' Amber asks.

'We've been processing all the data and interviewing new witnesses. I think, at long last, we might be getting somewhere.'

'What do you mean?'

'We put together various descriptions and have an e-fit. Our witnesses think it's pretty good.' He casts around. 'I'd rather do this somewhere else. Would you mind? There's a café downstairs; it's not open yet, but we can sit at a table. It's very quiet.'

Amber and Ruby follow him out of the ward. Nobody says anything as they wait for the lift. Its arrival is signalled by a loud ping that makes Ruby jump. They step in together, still unable or unwilling to speak. Amber gulps back her tears and tries to surreptitiously dry her cheeks with the back of her hand. The tension between her and Ruby is thick and suffocating – you don't have to be a detective to be aware of it. But Benedict doesn't say anything; just bangs the brown envelope absent-mindedly against his thigh as the lift descends.

He leads them to the corner of the deserted café and they sit down at a white plastic table.

'Pity it's not open yet,' he says, breaking the silence. 'Don't know about you two, but I could really do with a coffee.' He opens the envelope and takes out a sheet of paper. 'Okay. So, here is the e-fit for a woman who's been seen hanging around Lilac Park for the last few weeks – general consensus is that it *is* a woman, although a few witnesses say it's a man, so keep your mind open.' He puts the paper in front of them and sits back. 'Take your time …'

Amber and Ruby zoom in on the image. A face stares back at them, passive and robotic. The expression is neutral and yet looks sinister. She or he is white, with short brown hair and small, nondescript features. Either a woman or a feminine-looking man, it's hard to know.

'Do you recognise them, Amber?' asks Benedict.

Amber's brain is scrambling at high speed, sifting through millions of stored images, putting them into piles, assessing and mainly discarding. 'Hmm … sort of … I'm not sure … Trouble is, there's nothing distinctive about this person. They could be anyone. And yet …' She studies the face again. 'They look familiar.' She shakes her head. 'Sorry, but I don't think I ever saw them in the park.'

DI Benedict looks briefly disappointed, then rallies. 'According to our witnesses, she – or he – usually wore their hood up, or put a scarf over their face. One of them said they looked like they were trying to hide. Importantly, they haven't been seen since Mabel was taken.'

'Really?' Amber feels a surge of hope. 'And what about on the day Ruby left the key in the door?'

Benedict's eyes twinkle. 'One of the witnesses – who thinks this is a man, incidentally – saw them hanging around the front garden of your flat, though she didn't see them actually take the key. She says she thought they'd rung the bell and were waiting for someone to answer, but nobody did so they gave up. About five minutes after they left, the witness saw the window in the bathroom being opened, meaning somebody was in the house. She thought it was a bit odd, but as it was the week before Mabel was taken, she didn't think it was relevant.'

'That was me,' says Ruby. 'I opened the window after I changed Mabel's nappy.'

Benedict nods. 'Okay, that's helpful. Do you remember seeing this person – or somebody similar – on either Saturday?'

'No, not at all … Sorry.'

Amber stares and stares at the e-fit. This could be the man or woman who took Mabel, who is with her now. Judging by the fine cut of the jaw and the slender neck, she thinks it's a woman. There's something slightly familiar about her, the shape of her eyes perhaps, or the length of the gap between mouth and nose … The face flies around her head like a butterfly, landing every so often on a memory, only to fly off again just as she reaches out to pin it down.

She has seen millions of faces in her life, but only stored a fraction of them in her brain. Even so, she must have many thousands filed away, grouped in categories for easy reference. Work, home, university, family, journeys, experiences, childhood, past and present, immediate surroundings … She definitely doesn't recognise this face from the park. Or the shops, or the gym, or the medical centre, or anywhere else locally. No, it comes from another part of her life. But which part, and when? Maybe she's imagining it, wanting to recognise it too much and playing tricks on herself. But no, she's seen this woman before – or at least somebody who looks a bit like her … Then it hits her.

'Oh my God!' she cries out, slapping her hand across her mouth. 'It's Terri.'

CHAPTER THIRTY-SEVEN

Day nine with Mabel

I wake this morning to joyful news. There has been a significant development in the Missing Mabel case. George has been charged with the attempted murder of the sister's boyfriend. The BBC is being boringly circumspect, but the implications are obvious. George attacked Lewis because he believed he killed his daughter. If Lewis dies, he'll take the secrets of Mabel's whereabouts to his grave. How tragic, how delicious. Social media will be on fire.

I switch the television off and skip into the kitchen to make breakfast. My mood is euphoric, despite the close shaves yesterday and another terrible night with Mabel. I can't have had more than a few hours' sleep. But not to worry, I'll catch up when she goes down for her morning nap. I can relax now, give myself some much-needed rest. My shoulders have already dropped and the knot of tension at the back of my neck is loosening.

Mabel is sitting in her bouncy chair with a face like a smacked bottom. Every toy I've given her to play with has been thrown grumpily to the floor. 'Have some toast,' I say, returning to the lounge and tearing off a piece. She curls her little hands into fists and refuses to take it from me. 'Oh, hunger strike now, is it?' I quip. 'That's fine. All the more for me.'

I plonk myself down on the sofa and chew my toast thought-fully. How is Amber feeling right now? I wonder. She must be distraught. First she loses her baby, now her husband faces several years in prison. If Lewis dies, it'll be a life sentence. A smirk spreads across my face. Poor Amber, what a shame ...

The stupid bitch never realised I was stalking her in the park, even though sometimes we were only a few metres from each other. I wasn't surprised. Amber only notices people if she thinks she might have something to gain from them, otherwise her brain filters them out. The first time we met, she looked straight through me, as if I were invisible.

It was so insulting it made me sizzle with indignation, but I didn't say anything. I was new then, a fringe member of a well-established group. Amber didn't think I should even have been there, although she never said as much. She didn't have to – it was clear from the way she behaved: talking over me with an abrupt change of subject, standing between the two of us and then turning her back so that I was left out on a limb. I wasn't the only plus one at the party. Several other guests had brought their partners, although everyone else seemed to know each other.

We made a mistake, thinking it was more of a social get-together rather than an official university reunion. But there was no need to blank me like that, to make me feel like I was an intruder trying to muscle in. The event was full of obscure in-jokes and photo-sharing and unfunny anecdotes about people I'd never heard of. Nobody had any desire to get to know me; they were too busy rummaging around in the past.

I stood quietly on the outside, looking in. Observing in my usual way. As the evening wore on, I could see the threads running between the men and women, broken in some places, tangled in others. Who was enjoying themselves and who was wishing they hadn't come? Who had once been in love with whom? Who was *still* in love? Who were the truest friends and who were secret enemies?

Amber was at the centre of the action. The party was held upstairs in a pub, but as she'd organised it, she behaved as if she were entertaining at home. She was the queen and George her handsome consort. Everyone else was a mere attendant whose job it was to follow the golden couple around and laugh in all the right places. To make matters worse, I seemed to be attached to the Court Jester. I was the sidekick's sidekick, and by that I mean Amber's sidekick, not George's. Oh no. He did not like my boyfriend. There was bad blood there, for sure. I found him smug and overconfident, although who wouldn't be, with a nickname like Gorgeous George?

I have to admit he was incredibly attractive …

I spent the evening studying Amber over the rim of my wine glass. She wasn't as stunning as her husband, but her looks were striking in their own way – healthy Pre-Raphaelite, I dubbed it privately. Wavy auburn hair, skin so pale it was almost transparent, and an aquiline nose artistically dotted with freckles. Her laugh was rich and deep and she had this habit of raising her eyebrows in mild disbelief when anyone spoke. She was so entitled, so sure-footed, like she knew exactly what she wanted and where she was going in life. I immediately wanted to trip her up.

Admittedly, I was jealous. I'd heard a lot about her in advance and resented being required to be impressed. The way she exchanged glances with my boyfriend across the crowded room that evening made me realise that the bond between them would be hard to break. I guessed they'd had sex in the past and now kept each other's secrets. I'd probably already been discussed in great gossipy detail. No wonder she gave me that supercilious smile when we were introduced. We'd only just met and she already had power over me. I couldn't stand it.

I wanted to destroy her. Don't ask me why, because I can't explain it. It was an instinctive dislike, a deep-seated knowledge that she was my enemy. Which, as it turned out, she was. Of course, my reaction was deemed unreasonable, even pathological. When I made negative comments about her, I was told that Amber was a beautiful person, soft and vulnerable beneath that hard, shiny exterior. Yeah, right. When I refused to invite her over, I was made to feel mean. So I changed tactics, kept my mouth shut and my bad thoughts to myself. I'd find a way to get at her, I decided. But Amber, being Amber, found a way to get to me first.

There's a loud knock at the door, jolting me out of my musings. I start to panic, then remember that I'm safe. Brushing a few crumbs from my lap, I put on my game face and open the front door.

'Yes?' I say to the elderly woman standing before me.

'Hello, I'm Barbara,' she says. 'Bob's wife. You met him the other day, we live at the Nook.'

'Oh yes.' I smile, seething inside. 'How can I help you?'

'It's more a case of how we can help *you*.' She takes a small photocopied booklet out of her bag. 'We thought you might like a copy of the parish magazine. There's lots of useful information inside about the local area, services and activities, adverts for tradesmen. And we have a mother-and-baby group you might be interested in. They meet every Wednesday morning in the community hall in the next village.' She plants the booklet in my hand.

'Thanks,' I say. 'Very kind of you.'

'Well, I thought, seeing as how you're on your own, you might like to get to know a few people your own age.'

I put on a confused expression. 'But I'm *not* on my own. Where did you get that idea from?'

'Um ... I don't know ... I thought ...' She squirms uncomfortably, cheeks pinking beneath her powdery make-up.

'My husband's been working abroad. He's due home next weekend.'

'Oh. I see.'

'Our little boy has been missing him so much; he can't wait to see him,' I add for extra authenticity.

She tries to peer around me. 'Where is he? I'd love to meet him.'

'He's having a nap at the moment,' I reply, mentally crossing my fingers that Mabel doesn't choose this moment to bawl. 'Anyway, I must get on. Thanks for the mag, very helpful.' I wave it dismissively at her and start to close the door.

'You haven't told me your—' she says as I shut it firmly in her face.

No, dear, I haven't told you my name and I've no intention of doing so either. Not my real name, anyway …

I stop off in the kitchen to hurl the parish magazine into the bin, then go back to the sitting room to check on Mabel. She glares up at me from the bouncy chair, kicking her chubby little legs in defiance.

'That was Busybody Barbara,' I say. 'We don't want to go to a silly mother-and-baby group, do we?' I extract her from the seat and parade her around the room. 'Old MacDonald had a farm …' I sing. 'Did Mummy used to sing that to you? Your old mummy, I mean. I'm your mummy now.' I pause in front of the gilt-framed mirror above the fireplace and lift her up so that our faces are close together. Hmm, I think, nobody's going to believe for a second that we're mother and daughter. I'm going to have to dye my hair auburn for a start.

The idea of turning myself into a version of Amber makes me feel slightly nauseous. I squint at my reflection, remodelling my features – lengthening my nose, arching my brows, grinning through even white teeth. No thank you, I'd rather stay as I am. The hair colour, however, is a concession I'm prepared to make.

I take Mabel into the bedroom, spread a towel over the bed and lay her down on it. As I remove her sleepsuit to change her nappy, I go back over the recent encounter with Barbara. Was it a genuine call, or did she come to check me out? If so, the parish magazine was a clever prop, allowing her to bring up the mother-and-baby group and find out whether I was indeed a single parent. *And* she asked to meet my 'son'. Was that neighbourly friendliness or smart detective work?

As I pluck a baby wipe from its packet, my earlier optimism fades, darkening my mood. The neighbours are a problem.

'Is it all worth it?' I ask Mabel, forcing her into her nappy and sticking down the flaps. 'You're a bloody nightmare.' She puts up a fight as I re-dress her in pink floral leggings and a white woolly jumper. 'I guess it would be different if you were *really* mine.' I lift her up and set her on my hip. 'I assumed that because I love your father, I'd love you too. But it hasn't worked out that way. I actually find you quite objectionable.'

She scowls back at me. If she could speak, she'd deliver quite a mouthful, I think. I cross the room to the window and draw the curtains across, blocking out the winter sun. 'Right, I say, enough chat. Time for your nap.'

It takes nearly an hour to get her off to sleep, by which time my edges are frayed and I could kill a cigarette. I toy with the idea of leaving her in her cot and driving to the petrol station to buy a packet, then decide it's too much effort.

Instead, I lie down on the spare bed next to the cot and close my eyes. The darkness cocoons me, and fresh thoughts of Amber and George rumble through my consciousness. I imagine George sitting in a cell in some remand prison, waiting nervously to know his fate. Murder or attempted murder? What an idiot. Typical of him, though, to make some macho gesture.

We were briefly introduced at that university reunion, but I was aware that he hadn't registered me – he was too busy swanking around, flirting with all the other women. I was pretty confident that if he saw me again in another setting, he would behave as if we'd never met. And I was right. I knew he was a personal trainer, and a quick internet search located him at a gym in Waltham

Green – part of an exclusive national chain. The subscription was way beyond my budget, instantly dashing my plans. But I signed up to their mailing list and after a couple of months received an email announcing an open day with free taster sessions, a meet-and-greet with the staff, complimentary healthy snacks and home-made smoothies. *Perfect*, I thought.

I treated myself to some sexy new kit and turned up on the day, panting with eagerness. George was running a spinning session, so I made sure I got a bike in the front row and spent the twenty minutes fluttering my eyelashes in his direction as sweat poured down my cleavage. He clocked me immediately and rewarded me with a few winks of encouragement. After it was over, I made a point of going up to him and asking some inane questions. 'You were so inspirational,' I said. He gave me his card, saying that if I decided to join and wanted a personal trainer, to get in touch.

I didn't join, but I got in touch anyway. We met in a bar near the gym one evening after his shift ended. It was obvious from the get-go that, if I was up for sex, he'd happily oblige. I asked him if he was married or had a girlfriend, and he told me was single. He said he had no desire to settle down yet and enjoyed casual, fun relationships with no strings attached.

'I'm exactly the same,' I lied. We got quite drunk together, and when the bar closed, he tried to come home with me. I made an excuse, saying I had a friend staying over and it would cramp our style. Funnily enough, he didn't invite me back to his fictional bachelor pad and we ended the evening with a gropy snog.

I never intended to sleep with him, as gorgeous as he was. I just wanted ammunition against Amber. I was already in a relation-ship – it wasn't the smoothest of rides, but I was determined to stay on the horse. We were living together, talking vaguely about marriage, and even more vaguely about the possibility of having children one day in the future.

Children. Ah yes, that explosive word …

A noise drags me back to the present. I open my eyes and wrench myself free from the memory. It's the front door. Again. Somebody ringing the bell this time.

I swing my feet over the side of the bed and stand up. Pushing my feet into my mules, I march out of the room and into the hallway, swearing under my breath. What's the excuse going to be this time? Am I interested in joining the WI? Would I like a jar of home-made jam? With an irritable sigh, I open the door.

CHAPTER THIRTY-EIGHT

Day nine without Mabel

Amber twists her fingers in her lap, as DI Benedict makes notes. They are at the police station, in the family room, seated around a low coffee table. The detective asks his questions calmly and methodically, but she can sense the frantic atmosphere in the rest of the building, as everyone tries to trace the woman who may – and it is still only a 'may' – have taken her child.

'Okay, so you think her full name is Theresa.'

'Yes, but I don't know for sure. What else is Terri short for?'

'Don't know, we're looking into that now … And you've no idea of her surname.'

She shakes her head. 'Sorry. I only met her a couple of times. She wasn't very interested in getting to know me. I think she was jealous that Seth and I were so close. Like George. Neither of them understood that we were just friends.'

'Is there anyone else apart from' – he looks down at his notes – 'Seth Williams who would know her surname? Or where she lives or works?' He puts down his pencil. 'At the moment, we've nothing to go on. Please think.'

'Seth will be able to tell you all about her. I've given you his details.'

Benedict nods. 'I'm just trying to get ahead of the game. He hasn't responded to our messages yet. I've sent officers to his address and workplace.' He heaves a frustrated sigh. 'When did you last see him?'

Amber looks into her lap. Some very uncomfortable thoughts are circulating in her head, spinning faster and faster. She feels dizzy and sick, as if she's on a fairground ride and can't get off.

'I was with him the night Mabel was taken,' she says finally. 'At Gaia Hall, on the yoga retreat. I'm not really into that kind of thing, but Seth thought it might help with my depression.'

'You didn't mention that before.'

'I didn't want George to know, that's why.'

'It was Seth's idea?'

'Yes. I was in a bit of a state and he suggested I join him.'

'So he knew you'd be away that night.'

'Yes, but …' She screws her face up.

'Did you share a room?'

'No. I told you, we're not lovers, just best friends.'

DI Benedict makes a considering noise in his throat. 'What time did you last see him?'

Amber has a moment of total recall. She hears her sister's strangulated voice uttering words she recognises but whose meaning she can't grasp. Weakness spreads through her limbs. Her fingers start to tingle as the blood rushes away.

'You okay, Amber?' DI Benedict leans in. 'Take your time.'

She coughs, trying to clear the emotion that's welling in her throat. 'After Ruby rang to tell me Mabel had been taken, I immediately went to Seth's room and woke him up. He was really upset and offered to come back to London with me, but I said no. We agreed it would only complicate things if George found out we'd been together.'

'Did Seth stay on at Gaia Hall after you left?' She shrugs. 'Don't worry if you don't know, we can check.' He makes a note.

'We didn't text or speak that day – there was so much going on. I tried contacting him the day after, I think … I'm not sure, I can't remember. It'll be on my phone. I texted, called, left messages on his voicemail, but he didn't reply.'

Benedict frowns. 'Did that seem strange to you?'

'Yes, very. It's not like him. I mean, we're besties, usually we're in touch most days. I thought maybe he'd backed off because he didn't want to make trouble for me with George. I was hurt, but so much has happened, I haven't … you know … dwelt on it too much. I've been focused on Mabel.' She draws in her bottom lip and bites down. 'But it *is* strange to ignore me, as if he doesn't care. After all we've done for each other …'

'What do you mean?'

She feels herself flushing bright pink. 'He, um … oh God, it's all so embarrassing … He … um … offered to help me conceive by donating sperm. It was a DIY job – didn't work. We only tried it once; it was a mistake.'

'I see.' Benedict looks thoughtful. 'Did Terri know about that?'

'Jesus, no! It was a massive secret between the two of us.'

'Hmm … So, he tried to help you have a baby. And what did you do for him?'

She puffs out. 'Oh, loads of things over the years. Seth's quite fragile. He's one of four sons; the other three are rugger buggers, full of testosterone. His father's openly homophobic and his mother's a drip. She knew about Seth but wouldn't stand up for him. It's been hell for him trying to come to terms with his sexual identity. For years he pretended he was straight, then bisexual. I encouraged him to finally come out as gay.'

Benedict writes it down. 'And was he still with Terri when all this happened?'

She nods. 'Sort of … It was a very on-off relationship, quite stormy. Seth found her high maintenance – to be honest, I don't know what he saw in her. When he finished the relationship, she took it pretty badly, although I don't understand why it was such a shock.'

'Did she blame you?'

'Why would she?' she huffs. 'It was Seth's decision.'

'And you're sure she didn't know about the sperm donation.'

'Absolutely. There's no way he would have told her.' Seth's words float out and write themselves on the wall above the detective's head.

Your secret will be safe with me, darling. I'll take it to my grave.

Benedict thinks for a few seconds. 'Is there any way she could have found out?'

'No. Not that I can think of.'

'Okay, but let's say for now that she *did* find out. Might she believe Seth is Mabel's father?'

Amber's stomach turns over. 'Um … I don't know … I can't see how. He wouldn't have said anything. I remember him telling me Terri wanted them to have a baby and he'd said no and she'd got all upset …' She catches her breath. 'Oh God. What if …?'

Benedict rises, a fresh look of determination on his face. 'I think we might have a motive. Excuse me, I'll be back in a minute.' He leaves the room.

Amber puts her head in her hands as the uncomfortable thoughts turn fearful. She didn't take to Terri from the beginning. Their first meeting is etched on her memory, even though they only exchanged a few words. Seth brought his new girlfriend along to their university reunion, probably in an attempt to prove his heterosexual credentials. Not that anyone was convinced. It was the wrong kind of occasion to choose, anyway. Unsurprisingly, Amber and her mates wanted to catch up and reminisce about old times. Terri felt ignored and hit the bottle big-time. She spent the evening scowling at everyone and making loud off-colour remarks. Poor Seth had to pour her into the taxi home.

Amber never understood why Terri was keen on someone who was so obviously not interested in women sexually. Perhaps she hadn't noticed. The relationship with Seth was all about *her*, not the two of them. She wanted things from him that he couldn't or didn't want to give her, but instead of accepting defeat and retreating gracefully, it made her even more angry and demanding. Poor Seth felt guilty about rejecting her, so he battled on. When he finally came out and ended the relationship, Amber felt pleased for him and relieved that Terri was no longer around. In truth, she didn't give the woman's feelings a second's thought.

Until now …

She remembers one of her secret encounters with Seth in a cocktail bar, shortly after the sperm donation fiasco. Their conversations usually lurched back and forth between their individual problems, but that night it was Seth's turn to have the most airtime.

'She keeps going on about making things more permanent,' he said. 'Her mother wants to know when I'm going to propose – apparently she's already seen a hat she likes. It's ridiculous. *And* she's been hinting about having a baby, even though I made it clear from the start that I don't want kids.'

Amber rolled her eyes. 'You need to be careful. I mean, what if she gets pregnant?' She put an imaginary shotgun to his head.

'Don't worry, there's no chance of that,' he replied. 'She's on the pill.'

'Are you sure about that? Do you see her take it every day? I wouldn't put it past her to—'

'Darling, stop being so suspicious,' he said, patting her hand. 'She's all right, you know, she has a good heart. But she lacks confidence and that makes her needy. It's my fault, I'm messing her around, giving her mixed signals.' His eyes filled with tears. 'I'm the problem, not her.'

'You're not a problem. You're gay – simple as. You know it, I know it, your friends know it – none of us care either way, we still love you to bits. Apart from George,' she giggled, 'but he doesn't count. Even your family knows you're gay, although they pretend otherwise. Get it all out in the open. Honestly, Seth, you'll be so much happier if you stop apologising for yourself. You've a right to be who you are and have some bloody fun!' She raised her glass in triumph and knocked back her mojito. It made her cough and they both burst into hysterical laughter.

'Oh darling,' he said, thumping her on the back as she sputtered. 'You are so right. What would I do without you?'

A few weeks later, he ended the relationship with Terri and came out to the world in an emotional Facebook post, receiving hundreds of likes and uplifting comments. But his timing wasn't great. Amber was in the middle of her own trauma by then – having just discovered she was pregnant by Lewis – and wasn't able to give him the level of support she'd promised. He was a little off with her about it at first, but soon threw himself into his new gay life. Their 'secret affair' carried on as before and she assumed she'd been forgiven. He was incredibly sweet to her over the whole Lewis debacle and had been a real rock these past months. She couldn't have got through it without him.

The door opens and DI Benedict comes back into the room. 'Okay, here's what we've got so far,' he says, sitting down. 'Seth Williams isn't at home or at his office. According to his boss, he booked a week's holiday at the last minute and nobody's heard from him since. We've asked for a location trace on his phone and his recent call history – I'm still waiting on that.'

'Maybe he's gone abroad,' Amber says, trying to fill her voice with hope. There has to be an innocent explanation, there *has* to be. 'He likes European cities. Berlin, Paris … Recently he's been going there on his own, getting into the gay scene, letting his hair down, you know …' She drifts off, embarrassed by how it sounds.

'Hmm,' says Benedict sceptically. 'I want to know why he hasn't been in touch with you or answered your messages. I'm thinking he doesn't want you – or anyone else – to know where he is. We're looking at his credit card transactions, that should help locate him, but it all takes time, which we haven't got.' He runs his fingers anxiously through his hair. 'I don't like it – don't like it one bit.'

'And Terri?'

'Nothing yet. A neighbour remembers her being at the flat – apparently there were some noisy rows. She moved out months ago and he hasn't seen her since. Doesn't know her full name or anything. We're asking Seth's work colleagues, but so far nobody's come forward with any concrete information. It's annoying … Do you remember how they met?'

'Online, I think.'

'Of course,' he sighs. 'Gone are the days when you dated the girl who lived on the next street.'

'You think Seth is involved in this?' she asks, although her instinct is telling her it's impossible. He loves her and would never do anything so evil. He split up with Terri last year and has had nothing to do with her since, and besides, he can't really believe he's Mabel's biological father. There's no logic to them abducting her.

'I think it's a possibility, yes,' replies DI Benedict flatly. 'We certainly can't rule it out. But don't worry, we'll find them – they can't stay off the grid forever. They've probably ditched their smartphones for pay-as-you-go, but at some point they'll run out of cash or food or petrol or nappies and use their bank cards.'

'Or somebody might spot them,' adds Amber. 'I've got loads of photos of Seth. Put one out on the media along with the e-fit of Terri. Ask the public if anyone can identify her.'

Benedict twists his mouth. 'There is that option, yes, but I'd rather have them lulled into a false sense of security. If they think they're safe, they'll relax and make a mistake. But if they realise that we're closing in on them, there's a danger they'll panic and—' He stops himself, not wanting to elaborate. 'Rescuing Mabel alive and well has to be our number one priority. Right.' He stands up again. 'I've a lot to do, it's all action stations out there. Thanks, Amber, you've been an enormous help.' His gaze zooms in on her face – the liquid eyes, the quivering lip. 'Are you okay?'

'Yes … I mean, no … not really. It's a shock.'

'Of course. But you're doing really well, considering.' He gives her a tentative smile. 'We're a lot closer than we were even two hours ago, remember that. This is a massive breakthrough. We're going to find them. Have faith, eh?'

He gathers up his papers, picks up his jacket and leaves the room. The door swings shut and Amber gulps in air, as if she's been holding her breath under water. Seth and Terri working together – could it be possible? Did they take Mabel because they wanted a baby, or was it to get revenge on her? She can't imagine Seth doing either, but the last week has proved that anything is possible: Mabel abducted, Lewis in hospital at death's door, George in prison on remand for attempted murder. Once he finds out that Seth is behind this – *if* he is – he'll be even more enraged. He never liked Seth, never trusted him. She used to think it was jealousy and narrow-mindedness, but now she wonders … Was there something she missed?

Amber folds in on herself. How did she get everything so horribly wrong?

CHAPTER THIRTY-NINE

Day nine with Mabel

I raise my glass of champagne and we clink. 'Here's to the three of us,' I say.

Seth's eyes twinkle at me as he echoes the toast. He parades around the room, glass in hand, sipping as he surveys the scene. 'Yes, it's just as I remembered it,' he says. 'Very chintzy.'

'Good old Dolly, she loved her braids and fringes,' I agree, fingering the tassel on one of her tapestry cushions. 'I'll rip it all out eventually, open it up, bring some light into the space.'

'I thought you were going to sell and put the money towards a place in London?'

'Probate hasn't gone through yet, there's some delay over Dolly's tax liabilities. But I've got the keys, so …'

'Possession is nine tenths of the law,' he finishes, crouching down at Mabel's side. 'Isn't that right, lovely?'

She's sitting in her bouncy chair, behaving herself for once. Ever since he arrived, she's smiled and cooed, her eyes following him around the room, enchanted. Strange how human beings can detect genetic connections. It's as if she knows him on an instinctive level. I can't explain their mutual attraction, but I don't care. It's a relief that she's not whining and pulling grumpy faces at me. Daddy can take over for a bit and give me a much-needed rest.

He sits on the floor and rests his glass on the patterned carpet. 'How are you doing, little one?' He takes her chubby hand, opening her fist and tracing a circle on her palm with his forefinger. 'Walkie round the garden, like a teddy bear ...' Mabel stares solemnly as the finger crawls up her arm. 'One step, two step – tickle you under there!' She bursts into delighted giggles.

Huh, I think, trying not to feel jealous. She never laughs for me.

I take a seat on the sofa and watch them entertaining each other as the bubbles of champagne fizz through my body. Seth is looking good: trimmer, fitter, sexier. The new beard – close-cut, not too shaggy – adds warmth to his sharp, chiselled features. 'I can't believe you're actually here,' I say yet again.

He looks up. 'Well I am! Believe it.'

'I know it sounds melodramatic, but it's like a dream come true.'

He blows me a kiss. 'Sorry it took so long. I really wanted to get in touch, to check that my hunch was right and you were here waiting for me. It was so hard being patient. But I had to make sure neither of us was a suspect. The last thing I wanted was to lead the police here by mistake.'

'No, I understand ... I wanted to get in touch with you too, but I didn't dare take the risk. It was agonising, not knowing whether you'd come. I hoped that one day in the future you'd turn up and we'd all be together, but it was a fantasy really. I even told the neighbours that my husband was due home next weekend – how weird is that? I must be a witch!' I laugh. 'Come and sit,' I say, patting the cushion next to me. 'I want to know how you worked it all out.'

He stands up and stretches his legs, then lopes over and joins me on the sofa. My body shudders with pleasure as he puts his arm around my shoulders. I lay my head on his chest and sigh. 'I've missed you so much.'

'Me too,' he murmurs, kissing the top of my head. 'It's been a long time, Terri.'

'I always believed you'd come back to me,' I say. 'Even when you didn't get in touch after we split up to ask how I was, I still kept the faith.'

He grimaces. 'I'm so sorry for how I treated you. I was an idiot.'

'Shh, that's in the past now. We're together again, that's all that matters.'

'And with a ready-made addition to the family,' he says, waving at Mabel, who is still gazing at him adoringly. 'Gosh, she's beautiful. And she looks so well. You've done a great job of looking after her.'

'Hmm. She doesn't make it easy sometimes ... Come on, tell me the story. How did you know it was me who took her?'

Seth contemplates for a few moments, his hand idly kneading my shoulder. 'I remembered how much you wanted us to have a baby, and how upset and angry you were when you found out that I'd donated sperm to Amber.'

I don't deny it. The pain I felt that day has never completely gone away. It lurks deep inside my system, stabbing me at moments when I least expect it. Anything can trigger the memory: opening my laptop, searching the internet for something completely unconnected. I shouldn't have been snooping on Seth's computer, but I felt I had no choice. There was something going on, something he was hiding from me; I had to find out what it was. When he went out for a run, I took my chance. It didn't take long to browse his search history – 'DIY sperm donation', 'sperm donors on Facebook', 'techniques for home insemination'.

My mind was spinning. Why on earth was he so interested in the subject? I knew he didn't want children of his own – we'd had a few heavy discussions about it. He'd said he was worried about global overpopulation, but secretly I thought it was because he was still confused by his sexuality. By that stage, our sex life had become problematic. Sometimes it worked well; at other times it felt awkward. Seth confessed he'd had a few encounters with men in the past, but I assured him that didn't necessarily mean he was gay; he'd just got lost while looking for the right woman. *I* was that woman – I had no doubt about it. Once we were married with a little family, all our problems would vanish. I firmly believed I could win him over.

I stared at his computer screen, utterly baffled. Then I remembered that he had mentioned that Amber and George were having trouble conceiving. Usually I only half listened when Seth talked about his best friend. I couldn't care less about where she was going on holiday, or what exciting new job she'd been head-hunted for. But hearing that her life wasn't going according to plan had secretly delighted me.

It was obvious. Amber had asked Seth to help her get pregnant. It was so typical of her to use him in that way, especially when she must have known that he'd refused to make a baby with me. That was the killer blow. I slammed the laptop lid shut and kicked back the chair. Anger raged through me like a forest fire, consuming everything in its path. I stormed around the flat, swearing and screaming my head off – throwing ornaments at the wall, pulling books off shelves, smashing cups and plates. I was burning up, out of control. But my fury wasn't with Seth, it was with her. That she was part of Seth's life was bad enough, but now she was destroying mine.

She was the person I wanted to harm, but instead I ran into the bathroom and raided the cabinet for pills to take myself. I couldn't stand the intense emotional pain, couldn't breathe. I found a packet of paracetamol and was trying to force them down my throat when Seth came back from his run and found me. There was a terrible scene. We never recovered from it.

Now he takes my hand, pulling me back to the present. His eyes are glistening. 'I hurt you so much, Terri,' he says. 'It was unforgivable.'

'It was Amber's fault; she virtually forced you to give her a baby.'

'That's true, but I should have been stronger, should have said no. At the very least I should have discussed it with you first. I separated myself from the idea of actually being a father and saw it as a medical thing, like giving blood. Now I realise how stupid that was.' He threads my hair between his fingers, sending ripples of lust through me. 'When Mabel was born, I instantly felt a connection, like she was part of me.' He glances over at her, happily bouncing away. 'Isn't that right, precious?'

'She *is* lovely,' I admit, 'but she's also a tyrant.'

He chuckles. 'She knows her own mind, that's for sure. But she'll settle down. It's early days yet. She'll be fine – we'll all be fine. I know it.'

We sit in easy silence for a few moments, absorbing the atmosphere. He finishes his glass of champagne and pours another. I feel my limbs tingle and loosen.

I get up and cross the room to the window, drawing a large heart in the condensation on the glass, an arrow through the middle and our initials on either side.

'What are you, a teenager?' he teases.

'That's how it feels,' I reply. 'Like falling in love all over again.' I rub a clear patch with the edge of my sleeve and look into the garden. The skies are leaden and there's a strong wind blowing across the lawn, bending the trees and making the long grass shiver with rain. I could stay here indefinitely in our romantic bubble, but I know it can't last.

'What are we going to do, Seth?' I say eventually. 'We can't hide forever.'

He frowns at me, surprised by my sudden pessimism. 'I don't see why not. Nobody knows we're here; we've both covered our tracks really well. The police think Mabel's dead, and the sister and her boyfriend are very strong suspects.'

'But what about as she grows? We can't keep her locked up. What if she gets ill and needs a doctor? What about school?'

'You can buy fake ID,' he replies. 'It's expensive, but perfectly possible – if you know the right people to ask.'

I turn to him. 'And do you know the right people?'

He looks abashed. 'Well, um, no, but I could find out. I've got savings, Terri. I can afford new ID for all of us, if necessary. I'll move out of my flat, come down, find a new job. We can make it work.'

'Yeah, but not here, unfortunately. The bloody neighbours are already poking their noses in. I told them Mabel was a little boy. I've managed to keep them away from her so far, but as soon as they see her face, they'll know. Her photo is all over the media.'

'We'll sort it out, I promise,' he says, beckoning me to come back to the sofa. I pad over and sit down again, curling my legs under my bottom. 'Let's just enjoy ourselves this evening, eh? Make the most of it.'

'Yes, you're right.' I inhale and take a deep breath of him. 'It's so good to see you.'

Mabel gurgles happily in agreement.

Later, I cook pasta and we eat with the bowls on our laps, passing the parmesan and grater back and forth, drinking the second bottle of champagne Seth brought to celebrate our reunion. Mabel has gone down – if not for the night, at least for several hours. She was worn out after all the attention Seth gave her this afternoon. I can already tell he's going to make a wonderful dad.

'I hope I'm not bringing up a sensitive subject,' I venture, chasing a piece of fusilli around my plate. 'But what made you decide you weren't gay after all?'

He chews thoughtfully, then puts down his fork. 'I just didn't enjoy the scene. I thought I'd feel that I belonged somewhere at last, but I just felt lonely and isolated. I looked at everything I'd given up – you, my relationship with my family – and I realised I'd made a terrible mistake.'

I grip his hand and squeeze it tightly. 'My poor love. It was Amber who pushed you into it.' I remember him nervously delivering a speech about needing to discover who he really was and putting himself first. The words were Amber's, not his – she was the ventriloquist and he her dummy.

'Yes,' he admits. 'It suited her for me to be gay because she could keep me as her plaything. But when I came out, she wasn't there for me.'

'That's disgusting.'

'She'd got what she wanted by then.' He cocks his head in the direction of Mabel's bedroom. 'I'll never forget the look in your eyes when I told you Amber was pregnant,' he says. 'It was like I'd sucked all the life out of you. I knew you didn't like her, but until that moment, I had no idea how deep your hatred was.'

'I loathed her,' I reply. 'She treated you like a pet, a little lapdog she could carry around in her handbag and show off to people, throwing you a few titbits from time to time to keep you keen. It was sickening to witness.'

'Was it that obvious?'

'Yes! I'd never met anyone who was more entitled. She was jealous of our relationship so she destroyed it.'

'You're right.' He nods slowly. 'But I allowed her to do it.'

'You should have told George you were Mabel's father,' I say, wiping up sauce with a hunk of bread. 'That would have served her right.'

He sighs. 'I know, I should have done, but I've always been so weak when it comes to Amber. She has this hold over me – I can't explain it. It's a love–hate thing.'

'No, sweetie, it's fear, pure and simple,' I say. 'But she has no hold over us now. It's the other way around. Mabel belongs to us and Amber's life is in ruins.' I sit back, observing his beautiful features in the candlelight. 'Did you hear about George being charged with attempted murder? His sister-in-law's boyfriend. I mean, what the hell is that about?'

'I've no idea,' he replies, gathering up the plates. 'They're all falling apart.'

He goes into the kitchen and I listen to him clattering around. It's so nice to have somebody else in the house, breathing the same air, moving around the space, making their own noises. Although I was trying not to admit it, I was feeling lonely before he came, even wondering whether I could carry on. I was frightened of the neighbours calling the police and had all sorts of unsettling thoughts about how I'd escape and what I might have to do with Mabel. Thankfully, all that has been swept aside now. From the moment Seth knocked at the door, my world changed dramatically. He's come back to me. I've finally won him round.

There's no doubt that we'll make love tonight. It'll be a healing. My insides skip as I imagine him undressing me and carrying me to bed. It's been so long since I had sex, months and months. I've almost forgotten how to do it.

He comes back into the room carrying two plates of tiramisu. He sets them down on the table. 'Your favourite,' he says. 'See? I remembered.'

'You'll make me fat.'

'Nonsense.'

'Mm, kiss me.' I lift my face, and he bends down, brushing my lips softly with his. A shiver runs through me.

'You're such a clever girl,' he murmurs. 'I knew you'd manage to take her somehow.'

'The stupid sister made it easy for me,' I say. 'She left the key in the door. All I had to do was steal it and make a copy.' I point in the direction of the fireplace. There it is, hanging on its string necklace, glinting in the candlelight among Dolly's horse brasses.

Seth nods approvingly. 'It must have taken some guts to let yourself in.'

'Yes,' I admit. 'And it was touch and go getting her out without waking her. I like having the key hanging up. It's my trophy.'

'Surely Mabel's your trophy,' he grins. 'God, you look sexy tonight, Terri.'

I put down my spoon. 'Sod the tiramisu. Let's go to bed.'

CHAPTER FORTY

Day nine without Mabel

Ruby emerges from the lift and follows the red line on the floor leading to the hospital exit. Her eyes prickle with fatigue and the harsh overhead lighting. Her mouth is dry. She needs fresh air – at least as fresh as one can ever find in this crowded, polluted city. Pushing her way through the revolving door, she steps onto the pavement, and is greeted by a whoosh of cold air.

She arrived in the ambulance with Lewis yesterday afternoon – or was it the day before? It's dark now, evening. She didn't notice the sun rising or setting. Time has been passing without her knowledge or permission, and she feels cheated.

'Get some rest,' the nurse said. 'There's nothing you can do. We're looking after him. If anything changes, we'll call you immediately.'

Ruby gazes about her as ambulance sirens fade in and out of the soundscape. She only vaguely knows her location and has no idea where the nearest Tube station or bus stop is. She walks a few paces in one direction, then stops and changes her mind. Her phone is running out of juice and there's nobody to ask for help. The entrance door is constantly turning, even at this late hour, gobbling people up and spewing others out. Everyone is caught up in their own story; they don't even notice her.

Where to now? Home is the obvious choice. The police have finished their forensic examinations and the place is hers again, if she wants it. A few journalists may be hanging around outside the block, but with a bit of luck they'll have given up by now. There's no fresh news as far as Lewis is concerned; he is still alive but it could go either way. She couldn't stay there any longer listening to those bloody machines bleeping incessantly, sitting at the bedside staring at him unconscious, full of tubes, covered in wires, looking like a robot or an alien, not the man she used to love. Or still loves, perhaps. Does being at death's door trump everything else, automatically entitling you to forgiveness? Ruby hasn't worked that one out yet.

She needs to do something, go somewhere. Get some rest before another gruelling bedside ritual. Her brain isn't functioning properly. She hasn't eaten for many hours and the hospital coffee was disgusting. All she really wants to do is sleep, but the thought of going home to bloodstains on the carpet makes her feel nauseous. But where else can she go? Not to some hotel – it's too late, and anyway, she couldn't afford it. Not to her mother's either. There's only one other place she can think of, and although most people would consider it an odd choice, she knows it's where she wants to spend the night.

She takes out her phone – just one bar of battery left. It should be enough. Opening up the taxi app, she punches in Amber's postcode. There are several cabs lurking in the vicinity, the nearest only a minute away. She walks down the ramp and stands at the drop-off point by the entrance to A&E.

Checking the licence plate against what's on her screen, she waves at the car coming towards her. The driver draws up, winds the window down and leans over. 'Ruby?' he says. She nods and gets into the back seat. The cab sets off and she leans back against the leather upholstery. Should she phone ahead to ask if she can stay? Probably. She clicks on Amber's name, but before it has a chance to connect, the phone dies. Oh well, she thinks, I'll just have to chance it.

*

'Ruby!' cries Amber, opening the door. Her face looks deathly pale, her vibrant hair tousled around her face. 'What is it? Has something happened? How's Lewis?'

'No change,' Ruby replies. 'Um … is it okay if I come in?'

'Of course. Please.' Amber looks grateful. She steps back to allow Ruby inside, and they hug. 'Thank God the reporters didn't see us,' she says, glancing out at the empty street before closing the door. 'Or that photo would have been all over the tabloids tomorrow.'

'*Sisters Back Together*,' says Ruby grimly.

'Hmm … probably not as kind. Come up.'

Ruby follows Amber upstairs. 'Sorry I didn't call ahead,' she says. 'My phone died.'

'I'm really glad to see you. I was going out of my mind here.' They go into the sitting room and Amber gestures at her to take the sofa.

She takes off her coat and sits down. 'Any news about Mabel?'

'Yes and no.' Amber sits in the armchair. 'The police contacted Seth's family and they knew Terri, rather liked her apparently. His mum remembered her full name and where she worked. To cut a long story short, she went on sick leave with stress months ago and never came back. Luckily, the company still had an address for her – only a mile or so from here.'

'And? Did they go round? Any sign of Mabel?'

'No. The flat was deserted. However, the police accessed her financial records, and in the week before Mabel was taken, she bought loads of baby equipment.'

Ruby gasps. 'Oh my God. Then it's true, she *has* got her.'

'So it would seem …'

She digests the news for a few seconds. 'But that's amazing, it's a really good sign. If she bought baby equipment, it means she's taking care of her – that she's still alive.'

'That's what DI Benedict said, but I'm still so worried. What if something goes wrong? If she finds out the police are looking for her, she might—'

'No, they'll be careful. They won't just barge in all guns blazing.'

'I guess … They've got to find her first. They're searching hotels, holiday lets, caravan sites, Airbnbs and stuff, but so far, nothing.'

'And what about Seth?'

Amber shakes her head. 'He's completely disappeared.' She chokes back a tear. 'I'm still hoping it's a coincidence that he's gone AWOL without telling anyone. But the police are convinced he and Terri are a couple again and planned it together.'

'Yeah, well, it's looking like it at the moment,' admits Ruby. 'Sorry. I don't mean to make it worse, but you have to face up to it, Amber. It doesn't look good.'

'No, I know it doesn't. But he was my best friend. I completely trusted him; we used to say we'd walk through fire for each other. I can't understand … I mean, *why*? Am I the bitch from hell? Did I deserve this?'

'Of course not,' Ruby says. 'I don't know Seth very well, but I do know how much you mean to each other. You once told me that if you hadn't been with George and Seth hadn't been gay, you'd have married him like a shot.'

'Yes, that's true, I would have.' Amber puts her head in her hands, speaking through her fingers. 'I just have to hold onto the fact that he really loves Mabel. He's so good with her. He might hate *me*, but I don't think he would harm her or let Terri do anything bad.' The tears start to flood out of her. 'But I'm so scared! It's almost worse knowing they've got her but not where they are. We're so near and yet so far.'

Ruby gets up and crouches down in front of her sister. 'Hey, come here, it's okay.' She holds her firmly but gently, like she's trying to save a cracked egg from breaking. 'Just let it out … feel it …'

'I hope Lewis is going to be all right,' Amber sobs. 'I don't want him to die. I know George attacked him, but I feel like it was my fault.'

'Lewis is in good hands,' Ruby soothes. 'The doctor thinks there's been a very slight improvement, though it's too early to know if that means anything.' She strokes Amber's back. 'There's nothing we can do now apart from wait. As for Seth and Terri, the police will track them down. It's good news, hon, really it is. Mabel's alive and well; she's going to be back with us very soon. You've got to hold onto that.'

Ruby raids the drinks cupboard in the kitchen and finds a bottle of Armagnac. She pours two glasses and takes them to the sitting room. Amber drinks hers, spluttering through her tears, and then downs another one.

'Will you stay tonight, Rubes?' she asks. 'Please? We can share my bed, like we used to when we were kids. I don't want to be on my own.'

'Of course I'll stay,' Ruby replies, although she can't remember a time when she and Amber ever shared a bed. On holiday perhaps, when there was only a double available, or when staying with relatives? But no, not even then. They always had separate bedrooms at home, and Ruby wasn't allowed to enter Amber's room without knocking first. She was never invited to cosy up in bed, giggling and whispering secrets, or eating popcorn while watching videos of *Friends*. That was what other big sisters did with their younger siblings, but never Amber. She didn't teach Ruby how to put make-up on, or help her with homework, or give her advice about boyfriends. But it doesn't matter. Let her rewrite history if that's what she needs.

It's gone midnight and both of them are shattered. They go upstairs to the loft room, taking it in turns to use the bathroom. Ruby undresses and puts on a pair of borrowed silky pyjamas.

'We probably won't sleep,' says Amber, getting into her side of the bed. 'I've almost given up trying.'

'No, I think we will.' Ruby pulls the duvet over them and lies down. Amber turns out the light. The sheets are cold and the bed is so large that she has to shuffle across to reach Amber, who is lying on her side, facing away from her. Ruby snuggles in, curled against her sister's back. If only they had been as close as this when they were children. It shouldn't have taken this tragedy to bring them together.

Amber, for all her doubts, is already drifting off, her breathing gradually slowing. Ruby closes her eyes and fills the darkness of her mind with a vision of Mabel, smiling and laughing as they play peekaboo. She feels herself sinking, sinking. The sisters are utterly exhausted, more tired than they have ever been in their lives, but a long night of deep slumber beckons for them at last.

Ruby's head is thick with muddled dreams. At first she is back at the hospital, sitting at Lewis's side, then suddenly she's running through the park, searching for Mabel. Her heart is beating loudly in her chest and her legs are aching. She tries to shout Mabel's name, but her throat cracks and only a strangulated squeak comes out. The action cuts to somewhere else, a street she doesn't recognise – maybe it's near the hospital, she can't remember. She's on her bike, racing down a hill, trying to escape or chasing after something, she doesn't know, can't work it out. Now she can hear a baby crying in the distance, a high-pitched whine. Or maybe it's an ambulance siren, or the machines in the hospital, bleeping to a crescendo.

'Ruby? Ruby, wake up!' Amber shakes her. 'Wake up!'

'Whaaa?' She unsticks one eye.

'Can you hear that noise?' Amber flings off the duvet. 'That noise! Coming from downstairs. It sounds like … like …' She turns to Ruby. 'Can you hear it? Or am I going mad?'

'No, I can hear. I thought I was dreaming—' But Amber is already out of the room.

Ruby gets out of bed, wobbling as she tries to make her legs hurry. The noise – it's clearly crying – is getting louder. She clambers down the stairs as if they're a rock face, almost slipping as she rounds the corner and crashes into the nursery. Her heart stops.

Amber is standing by the cot, shaking and weeping. She is holding Mabel in her arms.

CHAPTER FORTY-ONE

With Mabel

Amber backs away as the SOCO advances towards her and Mabel. 'I'm sorry, but we need to take her clothes and a few swabs,' the woman says. 'We'll be as quick as we can.'

'I don't think I can let her go,' Amber replies. From the moment she picked Mabel up, they've been fused together with maternal superglue.

Downstairs, detectives, uniforms and forensic investigators are swarming all over the flat, buzzing like insects, brushing and dusting and dropping items into plastic bags. Outside, the road has been blocked off again and there is a lot of activity by the front door and garden. The media guys who have harangued and bullied them for the past week are jockeying for position at the police tape like excited children. Onlookers are assembling by the park railings in eager anticipation, as if waiting for a carnival procession to pass by.

'Just for a few seconds. Come on, it's important,' whispers Ruby. 'They need evidence.' She gently peels Mabel off her mother and helps lay her down on the plastic sheet.

'You can undress her, Amber,' the SOCO says kindly. 'Just take it very slowly and carefully.'

They've been banished to the loft bedroom, where's there's less chance of forensic contamination. Amber and Ruby have been put in the same protective clothing that everyone else is wearing –

paper suits, masks, gloves and shoe coverings. On no account are they allowed to move until DI Benedict says it's okay. He is trying to organise the best way for them to leave the building. Although there are no obvious signs of injury and Mabel is smiling from ear to ear, an ambulance is on its way to take her to hospital, where she can be properly checked out.

Amber starts to undo the poppers on the hideous pink sleep-suit. She eases Mabel's arms and legs free, then removes her vest, gasping with relief as she reveals her daughter's soft, milky skin. It's clean and unblemished, not a scratch or bruise in sight. She bends over and, despite being told to keep physical contact to a minimum, lifts her mask and kisses Mabel's cheek. She's already done it a hundred times anyway. A faint floral scent fills her nostrils – some kind of synthetic fabric conditioner, she suspects.

The SOCO snatches up the clothes and deposits them in evidence bags, then takes countless photos of Mabel from every angle. That done, she clicks open a case and places various packets of sterile swabs and test tubes on the plastic sheet.

'Be as quick as you can,' urges Amber. 'I don't want her to get cold.'

They watch the investigator work quickly and efficiently. Amber is reminded of the morning after Mabel was taken, only this time everything is in reverse. *What is the opposite of a crime scene?* she wonders. First the police wanted to find out who'd taken Mabel; now they want to know who brought her back. At this moment, she doesn't care who did it or why or how, although she thinks she probably knows who's responsible. All she wants to do is cuddle her precious baby and never, ever let her go again.

The atmosphere outside is feverish. Amber can feel it rising like heat to the top floor. Press and public know something big has happened inside number 74 but not exactly what. The police have yet to release a statement and everyone is being kept on tenterhooks.

It won't stop them making up stories, though: one of the sisters has killed the other; Mabel's corpse has been discovered under the floorboards; Lewis has woken from his coma and confessed to burying her in their non-existent garden. They probably have their hopes pinned and cameras poised for a shot of a body bag being wheeled out of the front door. The journalists are already composing their headlines, mulling over alliterative possibilities – *Mabel, missing, murder, mummy, monster*. Amber smiles inwardly. Those are not the words they need today. How about *miracle, marvel, magic*?

She hears muffled footsteps on the stairs and Detective Inspector Benedict enters in full protective gear, panting heavily. 'Everything okay?' he says to the SOCO. 'Have you finished?'

'For now. We'll take some more swabs at the hospital, with a doctor present,' the woman says. They exchange a knowing glance and Amber shudders involuntarily. She cannot even allow such thoughts to enter her head.

'Okay. The ambulance is waiting outside – the media don't know what to make of it; they're whipping themselves into a right old frenzy.' He grimaces. 'God knows how I'm going to get the three of you out of the house without causing a riot.'

'Nice problem to have, though,' says the SOCO, putting the swabs away and labelling the containers. 'Makes a change to have a happy ending, don't you think?'

'Makes no bloody sense,' DI Benedict mutters under his breath.

Amber can tell he's not convinced by the account she gave him at six o'clock this morning. 'She was just there, sitting in her cot,' she said, her voice liquid with tears of joy. 'Like she'd never been away. It's a miracle!'

'No. Somebody put her there. She didn't let herself in and climb up the stairs.' There was an unpleasant tone to his voice; he didn't sound at all pleased or even relieved. 'You must have heard something,' he added. But they hadn't, neither of them. They'd been fast asleep at the top of the house.

Maybe DI Benedict thinks it's all a big con: Amber faked the abduction, hid Mabel in some mystery location and then pretended to find her again so that she could sell her story to the media and make loads of money. It's an absurd idea, but seeds of worry are scattering themselves through her mind. If nobody believes her, if she ends up being prosecuted … George is already in prison; what will happen to Mabel?

'She's getting cold; she needs fresh clothes,' she says. 'They're downstairs in the nursery. Can I go and get them, please?'

The detective shakes his head. 'You'll compromise the scene. Tell us what you need and I'll get someone to bring it up.'

'I'll do it,' says the SOCO, snapping her samples case shut. 'I've got a little one, I know what to choose.'

'Thanks,' Amber replies gratefully. 'Everything's in the drawers under the changing unit.'

'Okay. Be back in a tick.' The SOCO leaves the room and goes downstairs.

'How long do we have to wait?' asks Ruby. 'I need to get back to the hospital.'

Benedict sighs. 'You can't just appear at the door with her. The media will go crazy and you won't know what to say.'

'Yes I will,' Amber replies. 'I'll say my best friend Seth brought her back and I'm the happiest mum in the world.'

'No, no, you won't. You can't mention Seth. You don't know it was him.'

'I do!' Her eyes shine with happiness. 'It has to be.'

'That's pure supposition.'

'He's right, Amber,' interjects Ruby. 'We don't even know if Seth and Terri took her in the first place.'

The SOCO comes back. 'Here you go.' She hands over a small pile of tiny clothes. 'And congratulations, it's amazing news. I'm really happy for you.'

'I'm glad somebody is.' Amber shoots a rueful glance at DI Benedict.

'I need to speak to the communications team,' he says. 'Work out a strategy. I'll be back. In the meantime, stay here, please. Sally's just arrived. I'll send her up with some tea.'

DI Benedict and the SOCO go back downstairs, leaving the three of them alone. Amber dresses Mabel, then picks her up and sits on the bed, hugging and rocking and kissing her. Ruby sits next to them, playing with Mabel's fingers and pulling silly faces.

'Pass me my phone, Rubes,' says Amber after a while. 'I should call Mum and let her know. Don't want her to find out from the television.'

Ruby leans back and picks the handset up from the bedside table. 'We should get a message to George, too. As soon as we're allowed out, I'm going to see Lewis. I don't know if he can hear me, but I'll tell him anyway. Who knows? It might even help.'

Amber takes the phone and clicks it into life. 'Oh my God!' she gasps. 'It's Seth! He's sent me a text!' She reads it out.

I'm in the park, by the play area. Meet me there and I will explain all. Love you always, S xxx

PS Don't forget to delete.

She puts Mabel back on the bed and starts tearing off the paper jumpsuit. 'I knew it was him, I just knew! I've got to go to him now, got to see him before—'

'No, no, you can't,' says Ruby. 'You've got to tell DI Benedict …'

But Amber isn't listening. She rips off the gloves and shoe coverings, picks Mabel up again and sprints down the stairs. Ruby chases after her, calling out to her to stop. A uniformed officer tries to intercept her on the landing, but she shoves him to one side and, with Mabel glued to her hip, thunders down to the ground floor, flinging open the front door.

There is a split second's pause as the media reacts to the extraordinary sight before their eyes, followed by an electrical storm of flash photography. People shout out, even scream at her, but she can't hear a word they're saying. Lowering her head, she makes a run for it, sprinting across the road and into the park. Mabel jiggles about on her hip, as if riding horseback.

Amber rushes towards the play area, quickly glancing behind her at the police who are trying to hold back the press. DI Benedict, sweaty and alarmed, is heading towards her, accompanied by the FLO and two uniformed officers.

'Amber! Where are you going? Stop! Wait for us!' Sally cries.

Ruby is a few paces behind her. 'Amber! Be careful!' She shouts at DI Benedict. 'She's gone to meet Seth! He's waiting for her.'

And there he is, sitting on the low wall of the sandpit, playing with a small object in his hands. It's a key on a piece of string. He puts it down as he sees Amber hurtling towards him and stands up, opening his arms wide, waiting for her to fall into them.

'Darling,' he cries. 'You came. I knew you would.'

'Thank you, thank you,' she says breathlessly. 'Thank you for bringing her back to me.'

But before they can embrace, the officers arrive. Seth doesn't resist as they bear down on him, even offers his hands for cuffs. DI Benedict brings up the rear and breathlessly tells him his rights.

'There's an address in my pocket, on a piece of paper. That's where Terri is,' Seth says calmly. 'I understand why you're arresting me, but I didn't abduct Mabel. I rescued her.'

'Oh yeah? Why didn't you call the police if you knew where she was?' Benedict says, directing an officer to search Seth's pockets. 'Leave the job to the professionals.'

'Here it is, sir.' The officer holds up a scrap of paper.

DI Benedict whips it out of his hands. 'Get a SOCO over here right now,' he orders. 'I want that key bagged.'

The two policemen grip Seth on either side as they wait for backup. Mabel leans forward and reaches out with her chubby little hand, trying to touch him.

'Stand back,' DI Benedict barks, putting himself between them and almost pushing Amber away. A patrol vehicle enters the park and drives slowly up the path towards them.

Amber can't bear to see her friend cuffed and cowed. He's a hero, not a criminal. 'Tell me quickly,' she says. 'What happened?'

Seth spurts it out rapidly. 'I had an idea it was Terri, but I wasn't sure. I went to the cottage and snooped around, saw her with Mabel. I wanted to call the police but I was frightened of how she'd react. I know what's she like. She's mad … dangerous. I didn't want Mabel to get hurt.'

'That's enough,' says DI Benedict. 'You can tell the rest of your story at the station.' The car draws up.

But Amber has heard all she needs to make up her mind. 'I believe you, Seth,' she says as her dearest friend is bundled roughly onto the back seat. 'I believe every word you say.'

EPILOGUE

Five months later

Ruby crosses the junction just ahead of the first car. It's a warm day in July and she feels hot and sticky under the high-vis plastic vest. Strands of hair poke out from beneath her helmet, sticking to her sweaty forehead. The sky is hazy with pollution and there's no breeze at all, not even as she coasts down the hill.

She feels happy because it's Mabel's first birthday and she's on her way to celebrate. Whenever she's having a difficult day – and to be honest, there are a lot of them – she tries to focus on her niece and remember how lucky they all are to have her back, seemingly unharmed by her ordeal. Ruby doesn't see her very often, but Amber regularly sends photos and short amusing videos – Mabel feeding herself with a spoon, Mabel standing up rattling the bars of her cot, Mabel trying to eat the bubbles in her bath.

They are having a picnic this afternoon in Lilac Park – just a small gathering in the far corner of the playing field that hopefully won't attract attention. The media don't bother them any more, having migrated to the fertile ground of other people's tragedies, but Mabel has become something of a local celebrity. Whenever Amber takes her out, she's approached by total strangers, who behave as if they know her. Most of the time they wish her well or ask for a selfie with Mabel, but occasionally she's told that she's an unfit mother and that her daughter would be better off in care. Ruby thinks it's brave of Amber to set foot in the park at all, after everything that's happened. Amber is being extremely brave these days. Ruby is seeing her sister in a whole new light.

The park is heaving, just as you'd expect in this hot weather. Ruby cuts across, snipping a corner off the route to William Morris Terrace. She slows down, weaving carefully through the strolling families, loved-up teenagers, toddlers on scooters, elderly people concentrating more on their melting ice creams than on the human traffic. The memory of running frantically around these same paths on the fateful morning when Mabel was taken suddenly ambushes her. Her stomach sickens and the bike wobbles, forcing her to put a foot down. It's okay, she tells herself. Just breathe.

She's been having cognitive behavioural therapy for her PTSD, but the memories still return unbidden, in this case literally throwing her off balance. Maybe the shortcut was a bad idea, she thinks. Maybe the picnic is a bad idea too. But it's what Amber wants. She's reclaiming the park for her and Mabel – path by path, tree by tree, blade by blade of grass.

Ruby pushes the bike the rest of the way, passing through the open gates where an ice-cream van is humming, and she crosses the road to the house. A large orange balloon is defiantly attached to the knocker of number 74. Brave, she thinks again, as she padlocks her bike to the railings and removes her helmet. Her black hair is pressed damply against her skull. She ruffles it up, tucking the wayward strands behind her ears. Then she pulls a thin leather necklace over her head and approaches the front door.

The key glints in the sunlight. She holds it in her palm and stares at it, unsure whether to proceed. Her plan was to ring the bell, then let herself in and wait at the bottom of the stairs. But now she's here, it feels presumptuous.

The gift was symbolic rather than practical – it meant that not only had Amber forgiven her for her terrible mistake, but she was placing new trust in her. Ruby felt humbled by her sister's generosity. She wears the necklace all the time as a reminder of how lucky she is not to have a child's murder on her conscience, although her conscience still weighs heavily enough.

Amber hasn't said that she's *not* to use the key, but so far, Ruby hasn't dared. Nor has she needed to let herself in. She hasn't babysat once since Mabel was returned, although nobody has been allowed to babysit – not her mother, not even Seth. In that respect, Amber, who is trying her best to be the world's number one survivor, still has a way to go.

Ruby doesn't want to cause trouble by doing the wrong thing, not today of all days, so she replaces the key around her neck and rings the bell.

'Gosh, you're early,' says Amber, pulling the door open thirty seconds later. 'Wonders will never cease.'

'I'm a changed woman.' Ruby grins as she steps inside. 'How's it going?'

'Fine.' Amber lowers her voice. 'Mum arrived at the crack of dawn with a load of extra food. I told her there were only going to be seven of us plus a few babies but she won't take any notice.'

Ruby swings her rucksack off her back. 'I've brought a few beers, is that okay?'

'Great, but there's no room left in the fridge.' Amber turns around and walks up the stairs, Ruby following close behind. 'You should see the size of the cake Mum's made. It'll feed the entire park.'

'Where's the birthday girl?'

'Watching Nana make the sandwiches.' Amber unlocks the stair gate – a new safety measure – and shuts it behind Ruby. 'Please make sure you never leave this open. Not even for a moment. She's so fast now that she's crawling, I daren't take my eyes off her.'

'No problem.' Ruby removes the high-vis vest, revealing a voluminous sleeveless jumpsuit – black with a sort of stained-glass-window pattern. 'Did my present arrive?'

'Yeah, yesterday. I didn't open the box. It's in my bedroom if you want to have a look.'

'I need to wrap it.' Ruby opens her rucksack. 'I've brought some paper …' She takes out a four-pack of beers and rummages. 'At least I thought I did … Shit, it's not here. Must have left it at home.'

'It doesn't matter. Mabel won't care, she hasn't a clue it's her birthday. She'll just be pleased to have all her people around her, making a fuss.'

'The celebration is for us, really,' admits Ruby, annoyed with herself for forgetting the gift wrap. She wanted to impress Amber with her new efficiency – ordering the present well in advance, paying extra for named-day delivery when she could ill afford it. Since escaping from the escape room, she's been scratching a living from temporary bar work while she gives her life a makeover. Last week she heard she'd been accepted onto a degree course in fashion design, starting in the autumn. It's a big step forward. She's excited, but also nervous about seeing it through.

They go into the kitchen-diner. 'Hi, Mum,' Ruby says. 'How's it going?'

'I could do with some help.' Vicky puts down the butter knife and looks her younger daughter up and down. 'Is that what you're wearing?'

Ruby prickles. 'Er … obviously.'

'You know what I mean.'

'Yes, Mum,' she groans. 'This is my party outfit.'

Vicky screws up her eyes. 'What is it? Some kind of bag?'

'Look who's here, Mabel!' says Amber, quickly intervening. 'Auntie Ruby!'

Mabel is sitting in her high chair, playing with a piece of bread, the tips of her fingers shiny with grease. She looks up at Ruby and smiles a toothy grin. 'Da!' she says.

'Happy birthday to you!' Ruby sings, bending down to kiss her niece's cheek. 'Oh no! Who's done a smelly poo?'

'Typical!' Amber laughs. 'I knew she'd do that as soon as I put her new dress on.' She unstraps Mabel and lifts her out of the chair, then carries her out of the room, leaving Ruby stranded.

'The salad needs washing,' Vicky says after a pause. 'Or you could grate some cheese. Apparently, there are vegetarians coming.'

Ruby hesitates. She came to help Amber, not Mum, and feels resistant to being ordered about. The difficulties in their relationship were briefly swept aside by Mabel's return, but there is still an undercurrent there – disapproval at the very least, maybe even dislike. She knows she will never be forgiven for leaving the key in the door. As if Amber was a completely innocent party. She sighs inwardly. Not everyone has been transformed by their recent experience, it seems.

'Better wash my hands first,' she says, fleeing down the corridor, followed by her mother's irritable sigh.

Amber is in the bathroom, cajoling Mabel, who is refusing to lie still and be undressed. 'You okay?' she asks as Ruby sneaks in and sits on the edge of the bath. 'I love the bag, by the way. Where did you get it?'

'I made it.'

'Wow. Your own design?'

'Well, I draped the fabric over me and scrunched it up here and there, if that counts.'

'I'm so pleased for you about the course,' Amber says, grimacing as she removes Mabel's dirty nappy.

Ruby watches as her sister gently cleans Mabel's bottom with a cotton pad soaked in warm water. There is a tenderness in her actions that was missing before. The postnatal depression seems to have gone and Amber seems happier than ever, even though she's a single mum now with nobody to share the everyday care.

'Is George coming?' Ruby asks as he drifts into her thoughts.

'No.' Amber sits back on her heels. 'I invited him but he said he'd feel awkward with family there. And he was worried about the media turning up in the park. I don't think they will, but … you know … He's very fragile.'

Ruby nods while Mabel kicks her legs in the air, enjoying the freedom. 'How often does he see her?'

'Once a week. Sometimes he misses. I don't think he'll keep it up. He still loves her, but …' She sighs. 'He's confused. He's her father and yet not her father – doesn't know what his role is any more. I feel really sorry for him, but I can't help.'

'No chance you'll get back together?'

'No,' she replies quickly. 'There's too much to fix. I think we'd been pulling apart for years, we just hadn't realised it. We're putting the flat on the market in September. It's the best thing. We all need a fresh start.' She turns to Mabel. 'Right, you, time to get a lovely clean nappy on.'

'I can't believe how brave you're being,' Ruby says. 'You amaze me.'

Amber gives her a grateful look. 'Mum's been an absolute rock, and so have you. And there's Seth, of course. He comes over all the time – cooks meals, cleans the bathroom, hangs the washing up. He keeps offering to babysit, but I'm not ready yet. Hopefully, in time …' She pauses for a moment to gather herself, then resumes dressing Mabel.

'Seth's coming to the picnic, I presume.'

'Oh yes. Mum's not very happy. She regards Seth as a rival in the contest to be Mabel's favourite.'

'Hey, I win that hands down.' Ruby grins. 'But seriously, Mum should adore Seth; he saved her granddaughter's life. God knows what would have happened if she'd stayed with Terri.'

A hole opens up in the conversation and the two sisters pour their thoughts into it. By the time the police raided Midsummer

Cottage, Terri was already dead – both wrists slashed, Seth's note crumpled in her bloody hand. He'd been right to trick her, to steal Mabel from under her nose. It would have been too risky to call the police. If Terri had realised that she was about to be caught, she would have killed Mabel before taking her own life. Even DI Benedict declared Seth a hero in the end.

'Well, I'm really pleased he's coming,' says Ruby. 'Mum will just have to put up with it.'

Amber sits Mabel up so that she can fasten the button at the back of her neck. Her dress, having its first outing for the party, is exquisite – grass-green cotton with tiny yellow flowers, perfectly complementing her peachy skin and auburn hair. Rows of smocking across the front, puffy sleeves and a white Peter Pan collar complete the classic look. She could be a baby from almost any era since the 1950s.

'She's gorgeous,' Ruby exclaims, instantly regretting the choice of adjective, forever to be associated with George. Before she can stop it, her mind instantly flits to Lewis. How come she'd never noticed the similarity between father and daughter before? A flame of anger ignites deep inside and she looks away from Amber, biting hard on her lip to beat back the tears. She loved Lewis, really loved him. He hurt her very badly, but he didn't deserve his punishment. He's out of hospital now, being looked after by his parents. His mother occasionally sends Ruby updates by email. The last she heard he was predicted to make a full recovery, but it's been a long haul. He says he can't remember being attacked, let alone by whom. Ruby's not sure she believes that, but if he's lying, she's impressed by his ability to forgive. The police debated for ages whether to proceed with the prosecution, but eventually the case was dropped for lack of evidence. George was released and, strangely mirroring his victim, went to stay with his parents. It's as if the men have become children again, leaving the women to carry on with the adult work.

Amber lifts Mabel up. 'Shall we give her your present now?' she asks.

'If you like.'

'Are you all right, Ruby? You've got your troubled look back.'

'Yes, I'm fine. Just a bit … you know … sad. Thinking about everything.'

'I know, it's tough, but we're doing really well, don't you think? In the circumstances.' Amber smiles at her hopefully. 'I feel closer to you than ever before. It's like we're proper sisters at last.' Ruby doesn't reply, just squeezes out a thin smile. Disappointed, Amber leaves the bathroom.

Ruby exhales loudly. Oh, it's all so complicated and challenging, trying to be grown-up and forgiving, remodelling primitive emotions like sexual jealousy into sophisticated, reasonable attitudes. She was so looking forward to the picnic, but now it feels like an ordeal they all have to get through. It's okay, she'll manage it. Amber, Mabel, Mum, Ruby, Seth and a couple of Amber's mum friends – they'll put on their bravest faces and have a jolly time, sticking to safe subjects, eating cake and sandwiches, chasing balloons across the park …

Only the child matters, only the child. And she is safe and well.

A LETTER FROM JESS

Thank you so much for reading *The Night Away*. If you enjoyed it, and want to keep up to date with all my latest releases, just sign up at the following link. Your email address will never be shared and you can unsubscribe at any time.

www.bookouture.com/jess-ryder

This book started in a back-to-front way, after my editor Lydia told me she had a good title up her sleeve and wondered whether I was interested in using it as the springboard for a story. I was keen to accept the challenge and started jotting down some ideas.

I remembered something our eldest son Renny had told us. Renny lives in Spain with his partner Maria and young son Leo. One evening he went out to play a gig, and when he arrived home late that night, he absent-mindedly left his key in the front door of their apartment. This wasn't discovered until the next morning. Luckily the key was still there and nobody came to any harm, but with my writer's imagination I speculated about all the awful things that *could* have happened. Starting with that small real-life incident, I added some extra ingredients and complications and eventually the story of *The Night Away* was born. I guess I should be grateful to Renny for being so forgetful, although I doubt Maria would agree!

I hope you enjoyed reading *The Night Away*. If you'd like to write a brief constructive review and post it online in the appropriate places, I'm sure other readers would find it useful.

If this is your first Jess Ryder book, you might want to try my other psychological thrillers – *Lie to Me, The Good Sister, The Ex-Wife, The Dream House* and *The Girl You Gave Away*. It's easy to get in touch via my Facebook page, Goodreads or Twitter.

With best wishes and thanks,
Jess Ryder

jessryderauthor

@jessryderauthor

www.jessryder.co.uk

ACKNOWLEDGMENTS

I would like to thank the following people who have helped me in the writing of this novel:

Brenda Page, for her help with research and proofreading and for her unfailing support, both moral and literary. Her feedback on early drafts of the story is always really helpful. Her willingness to read the book several times over is also much appreciated!

The detective who gave me time out of a very busy schedule to explain how the police would respond to the abduction of a child, and how social media can affect an investigation – for better and worse.

My literary agent, Rowan Lawton at The Soho Agency, who is always there for me with her support, insights and understanding. I can hardly believe we have already published six books, and I'm looking forward to the next exciting phase of our working together. Also, Christine Glover, my media agent at Casarotto Ramsay & Associates, who handles the film and TV side of my writing career and who has enthusiastically embraced my psychological thrillers. More news on that soon!

Very importantly, my wonderful editor Lydia Vassar-Smith. We have a great working relationship and I'm looking forward to more brainstorming over coffee for the next two books!

Everyone on the Bookouture team. They work incredibly hard for their authors and I really appreciate it.

And finally, as ever, my husband David. Life would be a damn sight harder and less fun without him.

CPSIA information can be obtained
at www.ICGtesting.com
Printed in the USA
LVHW030914271120
672640LV00004B/125

9 781838 889364